Down
the
Long Table

Down
the
Long Table

Earle Birney

Introduction by Bruce Nesbitt
General Editor: Malcolm Ross

McClelland and Stewart Limited

The Canadian Publishers
McClelland and Stewart Limited
25 Hollinger Road, Toronto

Printed and bound in Canada

For
Leonard and Reva
Brooks

Introduction

"Revolution is revolution," Leon Trotsky noted in his autobiography, "only because it reduces all contradictions to the alternative of life or death." And so Gordon Saunders, the haunted "summer-time rebel" of *Down the Long Table,* emerges as a failed revolutionary, unable to accept the ultimate implications of his evolving commitments during the early years of the Depression in Utah, Toronto and Vancouver. As one of his political friends, Ole Hansen, observes, "ravvalution iss making someting get born, yaw. Iss killing too. Ay tink you run avay from dat part." Yet a deeper question posed by Earle Birney is not answered by the simple rule proposed by Trotsky for all revolutionaries: *fais ce que dois, advienne que pourra.* Rather the novel forces each reader to challenge his or her own abilities to understand – and withstand – the social forces wrenching us away from our own places and lovers, dissociating both from our individual minds and wills.

Written in the 1950s, *Down the Long Table* is one of very few novels concerned with the political milieu of the 1930s in Canada; only now are increasing numbers of younger Canadians coming to realise that the optimism of the apparently revolutionary 1960s and 1970s has some of its authentic roots in the desperation of the Depression. Birney himself has suggested that

> I think the book can stand and will have something to say to those born after the Thirties who did not experience what it was like to live and move about Canada in the Depression, poor and jobless and virtually without govern-

ment aid. There is a good deal also in it about what it was like to risk jail and physical assault for the ideals of Marxist-Leninism and at the same time to be denounced as a fascist, and attacked and isolated from the working masses by those who were themselves the equals of the Nazis, the Stalinist supporters of a new Russian autocracy as murderous in the long run as Hitler's.[1]

The physical stakes of survival were higher for those who lived through the "ten lost years," but for those who didn't, the emotional stakes of the last decade and its subsequent disillusionments may have seemed more devastating. Birney's novel brings together forty years by posing two related questions: what is the cost of emotional integrity, and what is the price of intellectual honesty? In the answers lies one of the particular strengths of *Down the Long Table*.

Gordon Saunders, the questing, questioning, naïve and anguished academic is the centre of it all: a success at the opening and closing of the novel, but essentially a man tortured by his idiosyncratic past. In one of his more pretentious (albeit realistic) moments, he thinks of himself as a man "who was already many people; who was a grown child drawn to willful children; a solitary man stung by the flesh and gnawed by the spirit; a pedant who was also an adventurer, swimming out to the most adventurous of all the world's pedantic utopias; a being of grandiose thoughts and microscopic cares, a blocked teacher, a reluctant martyr, and a self-betrayed poet." In 1933, at the age of 28, he was indeed most of these: in short, a thorough-going bore. What sustains him, and our interest, is Birney's dextrous manipulation of Saunders' interior dialogue, the real working out of the novel. As a Canadian at the end of his second year of lecturing in English at Wasatch College, Utah, Saunders and his tortured thoughts and conversation are constantly balanced by the observations of his sanely materialistic other half, Gordy. A few weeks later in Toronto, now an aging graduate student, Saunders hears his voice as that of the dégagé cynic, commenting acerbicly on his initiation into Stalinist and then Trotskyist politics. With his

[1] "Epilogue" to Bruce Nesbitt, ed., *Earle Birney* (Toronto: McGraw-Hill Ryerson, 1974), p. 217. By permission of Earle Birney.

move to Vancouver and his assumption of a pseudonym ("Paul Green") as a political organizer, the voice of his alter ego becomes more darkly modulated: less the schizophrenic chirpings of a Jiminy Cricket than the plaints of a personal Job. However unlikeable Gordon Saunders/Paul Green may be, his progress is true to the development of his own internal perceptions, the growth of his own self-honesty.

Part of that development centres in his guilty consciousness of himself as what he ironically at first calls a "Man of Sin." He was given the tag by his earliest inquisitor, Dr. J. Caesar Crump, the Mormon head of the English Department at Wasatch College. Throughout the novel it constantly rises in Saunders' mind as a term for the tragic consequences of his own moral cowardice. Unwilling to accept Anne Barton's children if he broke up her home, he then flagellates himself with the possibility that it might be his foetus-child which will be destroyed when Anne decides on an abortion, his "little sea-horse, raked dying out. . . . This has been love." Later he learns that Anne has died as a result of the bungled abortion, a trauma linked in his mind with the murder of a friend who turns out to be a police informer. It is left to his academic mentor, a professor *ex machina*, to lecture him on "what a great bloody melodramatic fool you are. You're determined to martyr yourself out of an oldfashioned sense of sin." With this diagnosis, Saunders' irresponsible philandering and political dilettantism are brought into joint perspective; as he says, "I kidded myself I wanted to do great deeds, be a prophet and pioneer, a destroyer of sin. I thought it would be easy, just like my father who thought he would pick up nuggets on the next river bank."

But Saunders' willingness to become a martyr has its origins in forces more convoluted than simple guilt, for he is clearly intended to be a product of his times. His emotional life is just as much an expression of his search for self-knowledge in a world spinning apart as his political activities represent an attempt to change that same world. The implications of both are examined in a series of six trials, each an extension of earlier ones, and all leading to Saunders' final investigation by an American Senatorial Committee whose hearing forms the novel's prologue and epilogue. His interview with Crump in Utah is important only because it is a rigged trial, but eventually it triggers the others.

With his position about to disappear, nominally because of the Depression, Saunders weakly asserts his academic freedom to teach "sexy poems"; and more important, he reveals his academic ambition to gain a PhD as being of far more consequence to him than his deadly job. In his last meeting with Anne, again the trial is rigged because she recognizes that another kind of ambition is at the root of his fear of marrying her: that he would lose control over his own egocentricity, his ability to work his own way within the system he accepted. The accident of receiving a fellowship at the University of Toronto allows him to escape, only to undergo two more interrogations, one almost inadvertently by the brittle Stalinists of the Social Problems Club, and the other more deliberately within the warmth of the Barstow home, a cell of the Trotskyist Communist League of North America. His acceptance by the cell coincides with his falling in love with Thelma Barstow, and he undertakes to prove himself by facing his most violent trial, organizing unemployed workers in Vancouver. He fails, but the knowledge that all the various "silenced colleagues and poised informers and frightened friends" of his past have each asserted their irreducible individualities allows him to face his final accusors twenty years later.

That Gordon Saunders appears to act throughout the novel in response to the confusing mélange of minor characters is not fortuitous. As he is a man of his times, so his acquaintances collectively embody the conglomerate spirit which was determined by both the urgency and lethargy of the Depression. From this perspective the Utah chapters are necessary, for they outline many of the forces and influences from which he must free himself: Joan Krautmann, the unlovely but available daughter of capitalism; Oscar, the level-headed opportunist misplaced in college teaching; the underlay of sanctimoniousness which Saunders senses among religious fanatics; and the glib Communist rhetoric of Charlie. In Toronto, the cold-blooded Stalinism almost parodied by Roberts and Kay dogmatically drives him from their group, where he is denounced as a "supporter of the social-fascists, a hater of the workingclass, and an agent of counter-revolutionary Trotskyism." Curiously enough, given Saunders' nascent political consciousness, they were right by their lights: Saunders did instinctively oppose the Soviet bureaucratic dictatorship and its privileged managerial class as well as the leadership cult of Stalin.

Birney's skill in explicating the ideological distinctions between Stalinism and Trotskyism in Canada is obvious once Saunders finds himself among the Barstows, but even here his satiric irony constantly provides alternating counterpoints: Mr. Barstow's drunken espousal of Social Credit and Leo Sather's realism, tempered by his experience as a founder of the original Communist Workers' Party in a Guelph barn in 1921; Thelma's absurdly luscious romanticism and MacCraddock's dedicated Marxist trade-unionism. Riding the rails between Toronto and Vancouver provides Saunders with the base point which his adventurism was barely ready to touch: thievery, prostitution, violence, even Sammy Archibald's cheerful humanity, all united against the railway police. Vancouver is more complex. Trust and friendship turn into deception, and Bill Smith is murdered as a police informer. Fred Hughes, the skilled political agitator struck down by a mounted policeman, denounces Trotskyism and is eventually found floating in the harbour. Saunders' most notable convert, Mike Halloran, eventually deserts him as Halloran watches his variegated South Vancouver Workers' Educational Army disintegrate because of Trotskyist machinations in Toronto; the premature proclamation of the Fourth International by an ultra-leftist rump group drives Halloran's executive back to organisations as disparate as the newly formed C.C.F. and the Young Communist League. Finally Saunders is abandoned by Ole Hansen, plodding on as the last lonely revolutionary, determined that his right ideas will eventually triumph. The aptly named Hotel Universe returns to normal, a flophouse for prostitutes. Only his principal enemy is left, McNamee, the Stalinist organizer who will resurrect himself as a sleek witness at Saunders' last trial. Professor Channing's charity may have saved Saunders, but the reality of Vancouver is humiliation, chaos, deception and death.

For Canadians no longer familiar with that reality, or critics unwilling to accept it, *Down the Long Table* raised some unexpected problems when it was first published in 1955. The *ad hominem* proclivities of Canadian reviewers were unleashed in ignorance, and Birney himself stood trial as a self-indulgent autobiographer or confused apostle of American realism. One politically motivated critic, for example, assuming that the novel was "highly autobiographical," chose to comment on the "vicious, malicious, scurrilous picture he draws of the radical movement of the thirties and its most farseeing section, the Trotskyists." And elsewhere, when the novel was published in London four years later, another felt moved to note that Birney was "suspiciously well informed on some details of these dubious activities of so long ago." That Birney was politically active in both Canada and England during the 1930s is a matter of public record. Interviewer of Trotsky, part-time political organizer in England and full-time in Canada, visitor to Nazi Germany (where he was assaulted when he failed to show sufficient enthusiasm for saluting): only Birney's autobiography could reveal the full influence of much of this period immediately before he began some of his more important creative work as a poet. When his first novel, *Turvey*, appeared in 1949, many critics could write with some personal assurance of the realism or otherwise of the events faced by Private Thomas Turvey during the Second World War. Few understood the atmosphere in Canada engendered by political infighting and criminal syndicalist laws, as Birney experienced them during the Depression. Writing to a friend in 1934 he described some of his summer activities:

> I have renewed contacts with my Vancouver comrades and at last seem to be constructing a solid unit here. Bad luck dogged my efforts here both last summer and at Christmas. A year ago . . . I got a branch going here but after we left the key comrade got sick, two others had to leave town for relief camps, and another proved to have been a Stalinite borer. Then at Christmas I got things going again, but again one of the key men had to go to camp and another got hit by a mountie's quirt and is now in the asylum. I managed to ensure regular distribution of the *Militant*, and other periodicals, however, and to get a university nucleus going. . . . Moreover the Socialist Party of Canada is much more respectful of my position now and actually made me guest speaker at their open forum last week. I spoke, of course, under a new name – the Stalinites would have got wise if I had used my old pseudonym and would have organized hoodlums to break up a "Trotskyite" speech. . . . Another ubiquitous problem is the *agent provocateur*. He's getting smarter, has stopped hanging around doorways like a private detective, and is

joining workers' organizations and penetrating into all revolutionary circles.[2]

In more strictly literary terms, other reviewers objected to Birney's including fifteen chapters of newspaper clippings – some actual, others fictitious – as a late imitation of John Dos Passos' *U.S.A.* While Birney's purpose is similar to that of the American novelist, the sections are, in fact, adaptations of the technique: less the "Newsreel" of Dos Passos than his far different "Camera Eye." The documentary chapters are an integral part of the plot of the novel, commenting on the necessary trivia and the larger horrors of the Depression, occasionally revealing the fate of the characters, and always expanding the irony which is the dominant mood of the novel. Nevertheless *Down the Long Table* (or *Down the Losing Trail*, as one typesetter inadvertently called it in galley proof) still presents some awkwardnesses. The device of framing the novel with the Senatorial committee hearing, for instance, may strike some readers as stilted, given the activities of more recent Congressional investigations which have helped remove an American president from office. Yet the witch-hunting McCarthy hearings did occur; the climate of persecution endemic in the early 1950s extended far into Canada, and demonstrated our vulnerability to the political policy of the United States. That the dossiers of the R.C.M.P.'s Security Service Branch can be up-dated now through computer links with the FBI in Washington could redound just as devastatingly in the future to contemporary Canadian radicals. The romantic tone of parts of the novel, finally, has attracted some comment, although much of this criticism probably stems from a misunderstanding of the function of Gordon Saunders. It is not the romanticism of Kay, for instance, "Fragonard face in Lenin's jacket" who sang for the Loyalists during the Spanish Civil War (perhaps the Mac-Paps?), and who ordered Ronnie Mandell shot as a Trotskyist: the ambiguously sexual romanticism of *cojones* and Hemingway. Rather it is the romanticism of *temps perdu*, time restructured and re-ordered.

The patterns of the novel are easily discernible: the trials

[2] University of Toronto Library, Manuscript Collection 49, Birney Collection, Earle Birney to S. Angleman, 20 July 1934. By permission of Earle Birney.

and debates; the recurring presence of an amoral natural world; frequent literary allusions and quotations, especially from Early and Middle English; and the newspaper reports and headlines. (Saunders' position as a Canadian academic *vendu* might even be considered as a pattern, or at least a symptom of a time before the 1960s.) And all are evident in his poetry, for through them, among others, Birney has explored one of his most consistent preoccupations as a literary artist. Central to his poetry, poetic drama and *Down the Long Table* itself is his definition of man's place in a world blind to the ironic consequences of the simultaneity of time. Variations on the nature of that time, then, provide a structural principle; the interplay between time lost and imaginatively recovered, between exorcised ghosts and inescapable memory, is the source of the philosophical irony and Birney's irony of manner. Both, in turn, suggest a further strength of the novel, its verbal irony through Birney's experimentation with varieties of Canadian dialect and speech rhythm, both oral and written. The letters, dramatic dialogues, conversations, internal monologues – these *are* in a sense the atmosphere of the times. Smith sums up one aspect of the psychology of the Depression in response to Saunders' question "What did you do?"

> "O the usual buggerin around – protest marches, siddowns on the main drag, letters to the papers, beef p'rades to the Council. The public was kinda on our side an the Unions give us a pat or two. One thing and another we made the bastards fork out a dole for a while. But when we yelled for relief jobs the TUs got the wind up we was tryin to cut in on what little work there was, an they shied off. Then the Black Monks – they'd come hornin in once we got a going concern, naturally – they started beatin their breasts for us and so a course the boss press howled we was Reds. And with the Unions scared, the cops knew we was orphans and they broke us up, run every mother's son of us out a town."

That struggle and many others would be lost before the Second World War, which virtually swallowed the revolutionary socialist movement. The roll-call at the end of the novel is intensely pessimistic; one after the other the "in-between generation of little Davids" has been picked off by Goliath, whether in the form of capitalism, self-interest, sweet ease or death. Indeed (Isaac Deutscher notes), a few months before Trotsky was interned in Canada – he spent most of April 1917 in a prisoner of war camp near Amherst, Nova Scotia – he described Canada to a thief in Spain: "you know, there are many farmers there, and a young bourgeoisie, who, like the Swiss, should have a strongly developed sense of property!" But this is not Birney's point. While *Down the Long Table* records the failure of a revolutionary, it is also a manifesto for humanism, the "tranced dancing of men," a muted celebration for a cause.

Bruce Nesbitt
Simon Fraser University

1

"THE SENATOR IS READY FOR YOU NOW."

Like a dentist. The new specialist, Extractor of Political Heresies. Gordon got up. Guaranteed painful, fillings probed, old rot exposed. He followed the blank-faced clerk into a larger room. Heads swiveling; this place holds a hundred perhaps, and who are they all? There was little time to see but going down the one dividing aisle he recognized the shaggy terrier's neck of the Dean of Arts, and near the front, the President's pink scalp, which would be pinker soon. They do not swivel, the heads of gentlemen and scholars.

The clerk led him around the professional stares from the littered reporters' table under the rostrum. Two of them are scribbling already—describing the twist in my arm? He felt his tie as they went up the steps, and straightened his shoulders. Four men sat, easily spaced, along a table. Three on the wall side, at the far end the Grand Inquisitor, less than *Life* size. Folksy thatch of hair, nondescript face; he is a bit like a pine-marten.

The clerk motioned him to the empty chair at the table's nearer end and he sat. A damned hard seat but armrests at least. He looked over two squat microphones, past the three profiles, to his enemy, who, behind another mike, was writing something on a wide pad and had not looked at him. He seems more comfortably chaired. Nearest me? A shorthand clerk, and the other two must be lawyers, federal whatyoucallems, whispering. Postmortem on Professor Hill, or antemortem on me? I wonder if—Flash! From the reporters' table a youth had risen, silent and sudden, aiming a cyclopean camera. Gordon's thoughts exploded with the bulb.

His eyes, still blinking, now traced a sleek black cord from one of his microphones over the rostrum carpet; against the wall, under the crossed American flags, a white-bloused blonde, perched at a desk, was delicately inserting a new roll into a tape-recorder.

Calm nurse, collector of my intellectual blood. At least the President held out against television. Victory for academic decorum. But only perhaps because we are small fry, so small the rest of the good Senator's committee are off netting other fish.

There were the usual preliminaries; he agreed to testify under oath, gave the clerk his name, facts of birth, education, professional career, declared he was not and did not wish to be represented by counsel. They did not ask for his war service.

The Senator bent sideways and whispered meanwhile with the cherubic lawyer next to him, and then went back to—was it only an elaborate doodle? When the clerk had finished, the Senator laid his pencil down, gave Gordon a slow confident stare, and spoke.

"Doctor Saunders, what is your idea of the function of a university teacher?"

We start on a high level, a question straight out of something by the American Association of University Professors. The voice does not belong to his face; crisp and crackling. Marten chewing a nut.

"To help students to think."

He could not resist glancing at the President below. The round face was nodding almost imperceptibly.

"And to give them something to think about." The President stopped nodding.

"You mean—tell them what to think?"

Smiling. He is no fool. *The smyler with the knyfe.* "No, that would be doing their thinking for them." I would leave that to —don't say it—to congressmen.

"Do you think a teacher should have no other loyalties?"

Loyalties? What is a *non sequitur* to a Senator! I will say what I believe. "Yes. To his own thinking. To a freedom which allows others their own thinking. And to—to institutions which preserve it." Preserve what? An ambiguous pronoun, I am nervous.

"And what about the moral code, doctor?"

The—? "What moral code?" The listeners are buzzing. Let them. He became aware that a strange face far over in the first row of spectators had been watching him with peculiar fixity. Still was.

The Senator leaned back, a man astounded. "You are a teacher of young Americans and you dont know what is meant by 'the moral code'?"

"By *a* moral code, yes. There are perhaps as many as there are morally concerned people. I try to be loyal to my own." A spectacled reporter, hand hopping like a fly over his notebook, shot him an enigmatic glance. Approving, or pitying the arena Christian?

The legislator fished from his lapel pocket a pair of spectacles, metal-rimmed, put them on, becoming at once humbler, a little endearing and folksy, the unpretentious servant of the state. He bent his head solicitously to the papers beside him, shuffled them, read while the silence thickened.

"In the spring and summer of 1932, professor, you were, according to the testimony you have just given, employed as a teacher by Wasatch College in the State of Utah. Right?"

"Right." Despite himself, his eyes turned again to the stranger in the front row on the room's farther side. I have seen him before. Unpleasant. Where? Not on this campus.

"Wasatch College is, and was at that time, a state institution?"

"True." Where did I know that flat little face? Bald, tweedy, prosperous.

"And is it not also true, professor, that you were dismissed from that college because of your immoral conduct?"

"No, that is false!" False! But not all false. Who has been sending him tales? Crump is dead. "I was granted a year's leave of absence because I had won a fellowship to pursue graduate work."

The Senator took off his spectacles, balanced them in a steady hand. "I must remind you, Doctor Saunders, that you are under oath. Is it not true that the Dean of your Faculty in Wasatch College refused to hire you back because he considered both your classroom teachings *and* your private life to be immoral?"

Immoral! What does the word—? O God, where to begin? This must be Wollonby's work; someone's been reviving the old fool's malice. "It is only half-true. I *was* re-hired, even before my year's absence was ended. I taught at Wasatch another year after that. But—"

"Answer my committee yes or no. Did the Dean of your Faculty and the Head of your Department accuse you of immoral teachings and immoral conduct?"

Yes or no, yes and no, yes and. . . . "They accused me, or that is the Head spoke to me once, but it was on false and—and on stupid evidence."

"You wish to tell us that a Dean and a Department Head accused you of these grave charges on completely false evidence?"

"I—I would say so. But it was also a question, I suppose, of their moral code being different from mine."

"Ahhhh." The Senator slid his glasses back in his lapel pocket, looked around. Then he inclined forward, sliding the words out softly. "And what *is* your moral code, Professor Saunders?"

Pinned already. "I—if I could fit it coherently into, into expression, it would be a work of philosophy, I suppose, a book, or a"—not a bible, be careful—"religion. I—I dont have the ability." I sweat the truth out of me, but all they see is that I'm wilted. That bald watcher in the front row is deliberately keeping his stare on me. As if gloating! Who is he? Too far to see his eyes.

The Senator leant back again, histrionically puzzled. "You cannot tell my committee your own moral code, and you have been for eight years a senior professor in a great American university?"

"I teach medieval English literature."

Someone in the audience laughed, but the Senator came in quickly over, resonant now and righteous. "Does your code include loyalty to the Government of the United States?"

"Certainly." No, for godsake be honest today, if ever in your life. "That is—in so far as I have a na-national loyalty." Why must I stumble over it? I am not afraid. Damn that squashed-faced starer! He knows me, hates me.

The Senator took his time, regarding the room impassively. "And how far is that, Dr. Saunders? Just how much of our form of government do you believe in?"

He has the kind of long-suffering politeness that angers, all the tricks.

"Three years ago you became, at last, an American citizen,

4

at which time you swore loyalty to our government, and yet when I ask you if you are loyal to it you begin to qualify."

His tone convinces. Perhaps he's no hypocrite at all? "I believe that it is good for humanity, myself included, to"—don't get pompous—"to keep hoping for, and keep thinking toward a peaceful federation of all countries, whose citizens will owe their first loyalty to the—well, to the world." (The Senator is bouncing his pencil on the pad.) "In so far as the United States Government is working toward that goal, I am loyal to it. And," he rushed on, seeing the Senator put the pencil down to level a rhetorical finger, "I sincerely believe that—" that what?—"the present American Government was elected by a people not—not opposed to those ends."

The Senator arranged another pause, which embraced them all. When will he ask—?

"But," the word seemed to smack the table, "your first loyalty is to internationalism?"

Gordon shifted in his chair. "To a peaceful, freely achieved internationalism, a world state, yes." Yes, I have my beliefs and it is a pleasure, after all, to say them.

"And the days you decide Congress isnt being loyal to you, you are disloyal to Congress."

Why argue! "In a way, yes."

"In what way? How do you express your disloyalty? Are you a member of any international organizations?"

Silence. I can hear the clerk's pencil.

"Yes."

"Which?"

"The United Nations Society."

A little sound went through the audience, like a small wave breaking on pebbles. An anti-climax they appreciated. But the starer did not relax his confident watching.

"And?" The word rose above the sound.

"No others." His pious face would never register my score.

"Do you preach internationalism, as you call it, to your students?"

"I teach them medieval English literature. A foreign import, perhaps." No one laughed this time. Bad taste? I was Canadian.

5

"The committee would appreciate a straight answer, Dr. Saunders." He says it wearily, as if I were merely the latest of a thousand twisters who have tried to dodge his righteous eye. "Do you preach internationalism to your students, yes or no?"

"In the classroom, no, not consciously. There wouldnt be time, if I wanted, since I have to cover a course."

"And outside the classroom?"

"Outside? I doubt that's within the scope of this committee. However, I—well, I'm not a preacher anywhere. No doubt students, among others, are influenced by my ideas, particularly if they become my friends. And my ideas are sometimes influenced by theirs." I will not look toward that bald evil starer again. It is what he wants me to do. But who—who? A witness for the Senator?

The Senator's mouth widened. More like a badger's now, a small but not anonymous badger. "Very well. You have admitted that you, an *English* teacher"—he makes the subject sound unimportant —"try to influence *and* succeed in influencing the thinking of your students in matters of politics and economics." Carefully not a question, said for the record. Let it stand. "But you dont believe in telling them what to think!" The Senator gave him the bewildered smile of a father to a capricious girl-child and there was a buzz in the room. "The voters of this country pay you to teach their children literature, but you teach them to vote against their parents."

Quietly then, tenderly, "Are you, Doctor Saunders, a member of the Communist Party?"

At last. "No."

Sharper now. "Do you believe in communism?"

"No." The truth, but I am blushing.

The Senator glanced wearily at the lawyer next to him, the long-nosed one, who at once shoved an open file of papers over to the base of the Senator's microphone. In the silence the file made an odd sighing sound on the polished table. The Senator slowly took out his spectacles from his lapel pocket again and looped them awkwardly over his ears. Man of the peepul. He looked carefully at the top page, took them off, asked now almost musingly and as if indifferent to the answer:

"Were you ever at any time a member of the so-called Social Problems Club of the University of Toronto?"

He has a dossier, for certain. Who told him? Roberts, perhaps? Roberts' cold face, that shabby inconsequential hawk. Is this his latest racket, to be in their pay? The Senator makes it sound like a ring of master-spies.

"I was a—a kind of probationary member for—I've forgotten—about a month, I think. It was a long time ago."

"And you knew when you joined it that it was a communist organization?"

"I understood it was, well, Marxist. But I left it, by mutual consent, because I disagreed with some of its communist dogma." Is this all he knows? Is it enough?

"Some? Only with some?"

Gordon was silent. The Senator watched him ironically and then looked down again at the papers beside him. The bastard didn't really need the glasses.

"Have you ever corresponded with a man by the name of—let me see, Leo . . . yes, Leo Sather?"

Christ, had those foolish forgotten letters survived? Did the committee *have* them, even one of them? The Senator indeed was in the act of picking up a cluster of what looked like vaguely familiar scribbling paper clipped together—though it could be anything, it was too far away for his eyes—surely to God not Leo? —picking it up with disdainful triumph between blunt thumb and forefinger. But then he dropped it on the table as if changing his mind.

"Do you know, or have you ever known John Langdale, *alias* Sam Long, *alias*—" and in the half-second that the Senator paused, Gordon caught out of the corner of his eye a sudden forward thrusting of the bald man's ugly little face and knew in that instant who he was and knew what name the Senator would fire now like a bullet up the table to him—"*alias* Stephen McNamee, onetime District Organizer for the Communist Party of Canada in the Pacific Coast Region?"

McNamee! McNamee, of course! The tailored suit, the gleaming skull, had helped to block his frightened memory. McNamee, here, brought here, *he* is their Informer. How much does he know,

7

how much? Worse, how much can he invent that I can't disprove? Anger shot through him, making him taut in his seat. McNamee's spouting gargoyle face. *Fascist scum! . . . In the Workers State of North America, you'll be one of the first to be shot. And I hope to Christ I live to have the personal pleasure . . .* The faded melodrama of twenty years ago, but my flatnosed Fury still. He has changed his gods, but not his character, the Petty Inquisitor to this, the Parody-Grand.

"You have become suddenly silent, professor." Smooth oil of hate. I have not escaped.

"I wont answer any more of such questions."

"Because you know the answers will incriminate you?"

"Because the questions have nothing to do with me, with me today, or with my work, or—or with this University. What I think, what I believe now, yes, ask me. That is relevant." A crumpled figure in a black lane. Smith is dead, Hughes is dead, even Channing; there's no one to care or to tell. Unless. . . .?

"Actually, Dr. Saunders," the Senator gave him a sideways scowl, "you have betrayed what your reply is, but as chairman of a sub-committee appointed by Congress, I, not you, must be the judge of what is relevant to ask. You can answer, or you can try to escape into the Fifth Amendment. But if you remain silent, you run the risk of being cited for contempt; and if you answer falsely, of perjury. You are aware of these penalties?"

"Yes." Power. It gives even him polish, the pseudo-grand style. Penalties. But I have paid long ago, with coins of my own minting.

"Very well, Doctor Saunders. And with all this in mind, may I be so bold as to ask you a slightly different question?" Dramatically his tone changed to the rage of denunciation, and he pounded both fists upon the table, shouting "Have you *at any time* been, *under the name of Paul Green,* or any other *alias,* a member of a communist organization?"

Flash! A moment's intolerable light leapt at him unawares. The photographer pulled down his camera but stayed crouched, ready to spring again.

Gordon blinked, knuckling his hands, and stared down the long table.

8

2

STARED, NOT INTO THE IRRELEVANT BLUR OF THE SENATOR'S FACE,
but down through the varnish and the circling veins of the veneered
table-top, on which papers and mouthpieces floated like flotsam on
a pool, into the darkening depths. Stared from the harsh light and
the windy air of the implacable present into the shapeless waters
of his past, down through the already liquid undersurface of yesterday into the greening, darkening years. From the wide present,
free still even under the toadstool sky of the Fifties, from the Now
of professional ripeness, the graduate seminar, the full professorship,
and the general editorship of the new Oxford & Yale collection of
the *Scottish Writers of the Fifteenth Century,* looked down through
last year, in Rome with the family on his Fulbright, to the year
before, when Anne won the High School Poetry Prize and he
published his Langland monograph; and the year before that
again—or was it still deeper in the flecked past?—when young
John—yes, it was five years ago, the boy was only twelve—saved
a small girl from drowning and was awarded a Humane Society
Medal. And before that, he had gone back to England as a guest
lecturer; and before that again were the veteran-crowded class-
rooms, the exciting work-burdened months of teaching at last
(and it would never happen again in his time) to a mass of
students who wanted to know, who had come to learn out of
their own deeds and desires, themselves the involuntary and ad-
mirable products of the war they had not begun but had willy-nilly
embraced and outlasted. Down still through the swirl of such
faces he stared, into the last months of the war itself, seeing again
in the half-strange loving eyes of Diane and in his children's wholly
new and yet familiar gaze his personal resurgence of hope in a
world frightening itself to hopelessness. Down then through floating
images of pain, white corridors, the leaning masks of nurses, the
sundering patterns of murder and maiming, to his own blood-letting

9

on the trembling sands under the shell-split air of Iwo Jima. And before that, before Pearl Harbour and his transfer to the American forces, the long score of lonely months in English barracks and Canadian training camps, meaningless now and unrecallable.

The flecked waters gave no resting here, descended darker, into the hungry thirties, down, down into the deeps, no longer truly decipherable, of that second year in Utah, where there was perhaps something one could pretend was a bottom to these still troubled waters of his living, this abyss of time which a new generation, sailing on the surface of the dimensionless present, required him to plumb and chart and somehow fit into the map of the future. As if the bottom were there or anywhere that the lonely diving of his brain could reach, for the past of a man shifts and shades with all the past of his age, and of those ages before him that were not his but that formed him, within the eternally formless and invisible wells of the sea.

3

12 Million U.S. Workless

―――――

**MATCHBOX LABELS
LATEST HOBBY FAD**

―――――

U.S. Steel Hits New Low
Now 21¼; was 261¾ in 1929

**Mollison Makes First
Westward Solo Air
Crossing of Atlantic**

―――――

Social Insurance Schemes
Would Destroy Initiative
says L.D.S. Apostle

WITH THE POETS

Eternal Things

. . . . And though this life seems full of change,
The prosperous days all gone,
There still are dear old Mums and Dads
And Grandpaps on the lawn,
And skipping children full of glee
And Music's magic sound!
The old eternal, real things—
Will always be around.

Edna McSprogg Backhus

**Sir Josiah Stamp Sees Dawn
Breaking After Dark Night
Of World Depression**

Leg O'Mutton Sleeves
Trend on Town Frocks

―――――

FIVE CENT COTTON

Labor Warned Against Hysteria

NUDE PORTRAIT ROCKS UTAH ART WORLD

NAZI CHOSEN REICH SPEAKER

Berlin, Aug. 30 — Hermann Goering, a prominent Nazi, was elected Speaker of the new Reichstag today. He assumed the chair dressed in high riding boots and full Hitlerian regalia . . .

DARWIN DISPROVED: MAN SPRANG FROM FISH NOT APE

HITLER ON WAY OUT, PREDICTS SAVANT—PAPEN MAN OF FUTURE

DANCE
By the Shores of
THE GREAT SALT LAKE

IOWA FARM STRIKE SMASHED

FIVE-YEAR PLAN FAILS IN RUSSIA
Stalin said Losing Influence

GERMANS DEMAND ARMS TO STAY IN LEAGUE

TODAY'S BIBLE MESSAGE

And the Lord God said Behold the man is become as one of us, to know good and evil; and now, lest he put forth his hand, and take also of the tree of life, and eat, and live forever: therefore the Lord God sent him forth from the garden of Eden, to till the ground from whence he was taken. So he drove out the man.

THREATENED WITH EVICTION
JOBLESS THROTTLES OFFICIAL

HARVARD PROFESSOR ATTACKS 'INTERESTS'
Economics Savant charges all Profit-Taking is at Expense of People

HOME EC TEACHER
CHARTS WAY FOR FAMILY
TO LIVE ON $5 WEEK

4

AT NINE IT WAS ALREADY HOT WHEN HE WALKED UP THE EMPTY
slope of the campus, one of those sage-spiced mornings at the
far end of summer. From the high glittering breaker of the Wasatch
Mountains, however, clouds rose like spume; there might be a
thunderstorm. But of what consequence was weather when there
were bluebooks to read? Summer Session results were due in
the Dean's office tomorrow noon. *The red-eyed scavengers are
creeping. . . .*

There was a note on his desk in the elongated cell he shared
with Van Bome. Doctor Crump wondered if he'd mind dropping
in for a moment this morning. *A Polonius for my Laertes? Or is
it trouble?*

"How very kind of you to come so promptly, Mr. Saunders." *It
was trouble.* The organ tones rolled to the booklined walls and he
was drawn in by a spongy grip. "Especially when you must have
so many things to do."

Ah? Something he hadn't done? "Not at all, sir." *Perhaps he
counted how many were still to mark on my desk?* He looked into
the crockery-blue eyes of the Head of the English Department
but, as usual, found in them no flicker of a clue. The manner,
however, was more than usually avuncular. *More likely something
he had done.*

"Do take a seat." *The* seat, for apart from the swivel into which
Dr. Crump had already got with the smooth dignity of a cougar,
there was only the bulky armchair, placed to ensure that the
window's light fell flat on the face of its occupant. Gordon sat
stiffly on its edge. Outside, the lawns stretched dry and tattered
toward a silent road, lonely now, the football captains and the
queens departed.

"And when do you plan deserting us for the University of
Toronto?" *Eyes innocent as cloisonné.*

"Well, I don't know about desertion, sir." Better keep the record straight. "My year's leave of absence starts next Monday, so I plan to be off Sunday. I want to find cheap digs and get settled before the graduate school opens. I dont know Toronto." *Alone, withouten other compagnye.*

"I am sure you are not worrying about adjusting there." *Vox celeste,* but there was the tiniest tremolo on 'there'. "It *is* your native heath, so to say." Now the stress was unmistakable. Just what the hell are you getting at, you long saintly soft-soaper?

"I've come to feel very much at home in the U.S., sir." It was getting more difficult to maintain a casual tone. If only I could pull out my cigarettes.

"Of course." There was an indulgent wagging of the great eyebrows under the big head, on the noble face, the face like Lincoln's, a professional asset I'll never—"You have been with us two years now."

"And two at the University of California." As Crump knew perfectly. "I'm only a year from my final citizenship papers."

Over the desk Dr. Crump made a fleshy tent of his hands. A bee sizzled recklessly past the open window. Citizen born.

"Then you do want to become an American, Mr. Saunders?" The benevolent tone, come on, spring it, whatever it is. Gordon shifted as the sun reached his eyes.

"Certainly. This is the country that gives me the opportunity to teach. Besides"—he managed a smile—"I *like* Utah. Most of my friends are here." And Anne, who is more than. . . .

"But your relatives?" Leaning back, as if all he wanted was to spend the whole blessed morning in chat.

"Well, as you know, sir"—yes, you damn well do know—"my parents are dead and I'm an only child. My relatives are strangers living in Scotland."

"We can be fairly confident, however, that Toronto will want to retain you." Presented as a compliment, with a gallant inclination of the splendid head. What's he getting at? Gordon felt his lips tightening.

"No, sir. You will recall the underlined sentence in the letter I showed you, offering me the fellowship. It made it clear that

14

under no circumstances would the fellowship be extended beyond next May."

A manly pout. "Let us trust that they will, nevertheless, find ways to assist you until you have obtained your doctorate."

Let us trust! Keep your temper. "Sir, the University of Toronto requires two years' residence for the Ph.D. And my fellowship's only five hundred dollars. It'll take all my savings, as well, to get me through this one full year. I thought it was understood I'd be returning to my job here, at least until I'd saved enough to go back and finish the degree."

"It was hoped, rather than understood," said Dr. Crump suavely. "Unfortunately the President is not able to extend to you a definite promise. We are," he joined the sentences quickly, "reducing staff in every department as you know and unless there is a decided lifting of the Depression very soon, we can expect further economies, particularly in the Faculty of Arts. The budget. . . ."

The blood sounded in his ears, blotting out Crump's soft rumblings. California, two years ago, I thought I had escaped. And the first time, how long, my God nineteen-twenty, what did they call that—the Post-War Slump? Temporary and local only, of course. Adjustment to peace. And the papers coming out at last with the dirt about the war-profiteers. Sitting cramped on the snow, twisting the icy drill, watching the hammers, one-two, one-two, of the big Swedes hitting the drilltop inches from my nose, praying the flaking iron would miss my eyes, and the hammers my hands. How an ex-con feels, going straight under a new name, when the record catches up.

You are dramatizing again.

". . . wish it otherwise, we do feel you should be free to make other plans."

"Plans!" This was why they'd never given him his leave in writing. "Plans for what? There's a Depression in Canada too." Crump was nodding sadly. In Berkeley, in Timbuctoo. We regret. . . not possible to renew your fellowship in. . . .

"These are indeed difficult days."

The sigh is genuine, he has his troubles. But Crump was never in the long line in the rain outside the Vancouver Loggers Agency. Dangling my old calk boots, unwanted.

"Nothing personally would gratify me more than to be able to guarantee your return."

Yet the chintzy eyes are expressionless. I might as well try a bluff. "Well, sir, if you now say you cant, I'll wire Toronto I'm not coming at all, rather than risk losing my job here." Useless; I can guess what the voice of Judgement Day will say: The budget for the academic year is already determined, Mr. Saunders, and no provision—

Dr. Crump opened massive jaws and said it, with polite flourishes, then went on, with a wave of a leathery hand: "It is a great pity that you are the most junior member of our department —in point of service only, I mean." Playful pout again. "Of course, if you had already obtained your doctorate it might have been less difficult, but as I informed you when you joined us, instructors without The Degree, Mr. Saunders, are on a temporary basis only."

"But Wasatch doesnt give Ph.D.s." Gordon heard his voice rising. "You fire me if I havent one, I cant get one here, and you fire me if I go off to get one. Do you think that makes sense?"

"Now, my dear Mr. Saunders, you know it isnt really like that. You must realize that since the stock market, ah, débâcle three years ago the investment losses of this country have reached, I have been informed, something like fifty billion dollars. My university, like everyone else, must suffer in these unprecedented events. We are *poor*, Mr. Saunders. It is not your fault, of course, nor ours, it's"—his hands opened benignly over the desk as if he were about to receive a rather large volley ball—"the unfortunate times."

Gordon looked desperately out the window, at the dry bright grass, and the unfortunate times. I never had a stock to lose. Ivar Kreuger, a hundred and seventy-nine million dollars in debt. Falling. . . . But the College Stadium is not in debt. Along the far driveway a lank yellow car slid by, a girl at the wheel. There's gold yet in them thar hills. All is not lost, the unconquerable. . . . What if I said—?

"But a young bachelor like you"—damn you, I am twenty-seven—"with the academic and, indeed, literary ambitions which I am happy to know you entertain"—ah, a shift of attack—"you dont want to bury yourself in our little Wasatch College and all its, hmm, oddities."

Archness in that word, he's reminding me I'm not a Mormon. But I *am* a bachelor. "For that matter—" Gordon turned back to Crump, clutching now the little fantasy he had seen dancing toward him from the long convertible—"I'm hoping to get married here, as soon as I get back from Toronto." Very well, it could happen if Anne—"It's another reason why I'm counting on my job being held for me."

"You must not count on it at all, Mr. Saunders." That took the mask off, bully's voice, china-hard to match the eyes. "And if you can bear with an old man's admonitions, I think you should consider carefully before adding to your economic burdens until you can see more clearly how to—unless. . . ."

Why is he fumbling suddenly, as if he had made a slip? He has! He's taken it for granted she would be poor. What if I nerved myself to Joan? O ho! "I didnt say I was marrying an economic burden, Dr. Crump. As a matter of fact she belongs to a rather, uh, influential Utah family." Anne, forgive me. "It's just that a man likes to feel independent of his wife's income." I do believe the reverend face is sagging. Both plain and double-dealer I can be.

"Do I know the fortunate lady, Mr. Saunders?"

Yes, very much on guard now. You could know her all right, Dr. J. Caesar Crump, and how worried you'd be. But watch it. "Perhaps, sir, but, well, the engagement hasnt been announced yet." Waiting for me to say more. I don't really know how to lie.

"I see." Crump had slipped on his winning look again, and the patriarchal tone. He wasn't bluffed. "Well," he rose and thrust a puffy paw at Gordon, "I am happy we have had this little chat, in any case, Mr. Saunders, and I do want you to understand that there is nothing personal, and that I shall be doing whatever lies within my power to bring you back to us; but I know you agree with me that you must plan apart from us and in whatever way seems best for your own career."

Peroration. To thine own self be true. Crump dropped his soft grip, slid quietly across the carpet toward the door.

17

I won't be shoved out. His cheeks went hot. A showdown. "Look here." He stayed by the chair. "If you've got anything against me or my teaching, I want to know what it is. If you think you can fire me without—"

"Mr. Saunders!" Crump turned and came back, eyebrows at full tilt, angry innocence in his voice. "I really do not think I deserve to be addressed in this way. I have not yet 'fired' you, as you put it; in fact I have more than once interposed myself between you and those who have wished to—let you go." The Head of his Department towered over him like a wronged archangel. "But I am not, Mr. Saunders, I am not responsible for the economic ills of this world."

Gordon did not move. "Nor am I. And this is the first I've heard anybody wanted to 'let me go', as you put it. May I be told what it's all about?"

Crump stared coldly, then walked with deliberation to his desk and sat down. "Very well. I shall furnish you with an instance." He did not ask Gordon to sit. "Dean Wollonby complained to me last month that you had been reading rather, well, what he called sexy poems in one of your classes, poems not on the assigned reading lists, and—"

"Sexy! What's that?"

"And—"

"What class?"

"The literature survey for pre-medicals. If you—"

"Dean Wollonby never attended it."

"You are not helping matters by being flippant. As it happened, Dean Wollonby's son audited your section one day."

"That sneaking puppy, that—that half-witted bird-dog! I suppose he's keeping in well with his old man by fetching home tales on the professors. The non-Mormon professors." Trivial provincial mangy Puritans! Bushed Philistines! I will shake their ugly little temple down.

"If you want to discuss this any further, you will leave my Church out of it, Mr. Saunders."

Whoa, whoa, riding at windmills again. "I'm sorry, Dr. Crump. But all this prissy pussyfooting makes me sore. It was an all-male class, and whatever I read was literature, not pornography. That class enjoys poetry now, for the first time in their twelve years of getting an American education. And why wasnt I given a chance to defend myself when I was informed on?"

Crump leaned back. "Because, my dear young sir, if I had given you the chance you would have spoken to the Dean the way you have been speaking to me, and he undoubtedly would have demanded your resignation on the spot."

True? Obscurely, along some dim tunnel of himself, there was another Gordon waving down the train—Crump isn't so bad, he's been shielding you, and what else could a department head—but the Gordon in the cab had the throttle open. "Did you trouble to find out what poems I *had* been reading?"

Crump swallowed, remained pointedly calm. "I understood there were some of the earlier Herrick, and the drinking song, 'Back and side go bare'. I suggested to the Dean that they were quite harmless. But unfortunately he felt that some of your interpretative remarks had been, well, a trifle coarse."

"Wollonby would. He has a coarse mind. But what was his evidence? Were the pre-meds objecting?"

Crump rose, tall and noble, except for his ears, which had pinkened. "I do not like the tone in which you are speaking to me, Mr. Saun—"

"I dont like the way you've condemned me without a hearing," Gordon shouted, "you and that doddering fugitive from a Speech Department and his stool-pigeon son." The little Gordon in the tunnel dropped his flag and jumped.

Crump stood silent and straight, a reproachful pillar of self-control. "Perhaps you have a point," he said at last. (Ooh, what a nasty, hard, stiletto-icicle tone. An enemy now.) "You were also reported to have remarked that"—(What? What? Lord, he *had* said some pretty raw things!)—"what this country needs is more gin and less virginity."

Gordon laughed, feeling virtuous and delightful anger run through him; a lie; this is luck! That little twerp has overreached himself. "Who said I said it? Young Wollonby?"

Dr. Crump nodded sorrowfully.

"Well, Dr. Crump, you can tell dear Latter-Day-Saintly Dean Wollonby from me that his son is a goddamned little liar, as well as a sneak. And if you'd had any decency you'd have given me a chance to prove it long ago. I never said it"—Crump was around the desk and striding to the door, paw already crooked for the knob—"and what's more I dont agree with it." As Crump heaved the door open, Gordon's voice rose, hysterical with battle. "Because I hate your lousy bathtub prohibition gin, and I havent found a decent-looking virgin here yet and—"

"Get out," Crump roared purple-eared, shoving him, "you—you Man of Sin!" Slam!

Gordon found himself alone in the hall.

He walked, dazed and feeling already a little foolish, down the corridor and into his office. Van Bome was in now, humped over a pile of bluebooks as big as his own. His shirt was on the chairback and he sat naked to the waist, hairy and sweating in the draughtless air, humming tunelessly something that might be *Minnie the Moocher.*

"Looks like I'm fired."

The big Dutchman glanced up, saw he was serious and, dropping his pencil, swung corduroyed legs lazily up on the desk. "Congratulations, chum." You couldn't surprise Oscar.

Gordon sat down and pulled out his cigarettes. "Have one?" He was annoyed to find his hands were trembling.

Oscar grinned, shook his head. "On Mohonri's campus? You want me fired too. What's the story?"

Gordon told it, beginning to relax, and under the stimulus of Oscar's whole-minded if ironic interest, building the scene a little already in spite of himself.

"Hell then," Oscar interrupted, hearing Crump's reaction to the marriage threat, "you've still got him by the short hairs. Somebody already must have told him the daughter of the chairman of the Board of Regents has a crush on you. Everybody knows it. You did really jolt him. Now all you have to do is phone up Miss Joan Krautmann and marry her before you leave."

Half-serious; he would do it, yes, even if he were in love with Anne. "But wait." Gordon finished the scene.

"Man of Sin!" Oscar leant forward, the folds of his brown midriff quivering. "You'll have to invite Crump to the wedding dinner . . . Forgive me," he straightened, "for I shall miss my old flatmate. But why all the heat? You don't really want to come back to Cloud-Cuckooland, do you? Fourteen hundred bucks a year teaching goon-English to a flock of desert hillbillies who couldnt even make the grade at the State University?" He chuckled. "But I forgot. On account of you have your M.A. you get fifteen."

"You dont know what it's like to be out of a job. I've had my bellyful of it more than once."

"Come Christmas maybe we'll have the Democrats back and we'll all live on unemployment insurance. Or you could hole out in Canada in an igloo or something. Your fair Dominion didnt let you starve before. Anyway," Van Bome sent him a mildly puzzled look, "why worry about it till next summer?"

"It's"—Gordon got up and went to the window. Two years of living on a campus that banned smoking made it impossible for him to enjoy a cigarette in the office even as a gesture of revolt. He ground it out on the window ledge. Above the campus acacias hung the hot naked mountains, elephant-grey, seamed with green where the canyon lay hidden. Anne. "You think I'm a worrywort, but dammit, Oscar, I'm twenty-seven and I'm still trying to hop onto the back of the truck. I want an income secure enough to marry on, I want professional advancement, I want—"

What? You're too sniveling sorry for yourself.

Oscar gave a sardonic grunt. "I hear the Ph.D.s digging ditches aren't making much less, and they're working shorter hours. Which reminds me," he looked up, smoke-brown eyes anxious, as Gordon turned from the window, "you *are* going to finish those bluebooks before you check out of town?"

"You selfish bugger, all you're worried about is you might have to do them. Sure, I'm grading them, I want my last cheque." He went back to his desk and glowered at the fat unmarked stack. "I never looked to see if Eli Swansen did well; he fainted when he came out of the exam." Gordon sat down and began thumbing through the S's.

Oscar slowly brought his feet to the floor. "You really like teaching, don't you?" He sounded almost mystified.

"Well sure—dont you? For God's sake, why else would we be doing it?"

Van Bome pondered, scratched a bushy armpit. For him no question was rhetorical. "I'm not sure about you. As for me, my old man was a teacher and I couldnt dodge college. I took English because it was easy. It is, you know." He gave Gordon a half-serious scowl. "At California anyway, if you salute the more obvious posteriors. And when they threw a graduate fellowship at me I grabbed it because I thought I was going to be able to loaf every summer." He paused. "Jesus, it couldnt have been all that logical. Maybe I was just too dumb to duck. Dazzled by a Father-Image." He took up his purple pencil.

Gordon pulled out Swansen's paper. "O.K. But you're still at it."

Oscar belched morosely. "Inertia of the underprivileged. If I'd had your chance, if I'd been born into an honest workingclass home and apprenticed to—what did you say your father was, a paperhanger?—I'd be a respectable trade-union bureaucrat now, and in the dough."

"Nuts." But he means it, as I could not. He envies the senior men their salaries and I their seminars.

Prig, you want their money too, and their prestige.

I want more, much more—creation? "What you and I really want to do, Oscar, is write novels as good as Faulkner's."

"As good as *The Sound and the Fury*. I have already banged out three which are better than *Sanctuary*."

"At least you try, while I'm still a stack-worm, eating my way through the Early English Text Society, series one and series two."

Van Bome grunted, rubbed a chubby cheek with the butt of his pencil. *"Wind from Sausalito* blew back from Doubleday this morning." He opened a bluebook.

"Sorry, Oscar." It will always come back, like the first two, yet he's started a fourth. Whilst I, a dull and muddy-mettled rascal. . . .

Van Bome shrugged indolently, not looking up from his marking "There wasnt any mail for you."

He will not receive sympathy, nor give it. Gordon got up

suddenly hot and restless. Anne. "I think I'll. . . ." but Van
Bome gave a choked whistle and slapped his pencil down.

"Man of Sin! I must remember! It's like a Hawthorne tale
twice-told by Aldous Huxley. Do you mind, sir, if I work it into
a short story?"

"You know where you can damn well work it. I'm going for a
walk."

"Oke."

"Lunch in the caf?"

"Eh?" Van Bome's snub pertinacious nose was already pointed
at his bluebook. "Sure. But wait, what do you suppose Miss Young
means, my Miss Delphine J. Young, when she tells me the friars
of the Middle Ages were led by Asses? Capital A-s-s-e-s. St.
Francis? Or do I have to credit her with a thought?"

But Gordon was already in the corridor.

He telephoned from the drugstore, keeping his finger tensed
to click down the hook if someone else answered. But it was her
drawl, mellow, unsuspecting; a little rush of excitement jabbed in
his spine. She was alone.

"Anne, I've got to see you."

"O, no! . . . My dear, I cant say good-bye again." She sounded
almost frightened.

"Something's happened. I cant tell you over the phone. Have
you the car?"

"Yes, but—the children are just over in the park. I must get
their lunch. The maid's still away sick."

"It's only ten. I'm walking up to the usual place. Pick me up
in fifteen minutes."

She gave a little sigh. "Alright." He hung up.

Rapidly, filled with a confused boyish energy, he strode up the
long sidewalks, knobbly with the shadows of chestnut leaves, his
thoughts refusing to be focused on the meeting ahead. He should
be deciding what he would say to her, but instead he found himself
composing a letter to Crump, who perhaps deserved after all
some apology for whatever he had said that was pointlessly insult-
ing; the letter grew into a defense before an extraordinarily atten-
tive Board of Regents, and then it was a chapter in an autobiography which the world would read. . . .

23

It was now the year nineteen twenty-four, the year of—(of what?)—of Tutankhamen (probably), and messages from Mars that no one got and—yes, wasn't it?—the year that fellow in England, Wood (or Wall or something), was hawking a death ray he claimed could set fire to anything and even perhaps split the atom (did he ever?) *and I first read Aldous Huxley and T. S. Eliot and heard of Freud and Marie Stopes. For I was twenty, too young for Gertrude Stein's lost generation, too old to have found another, and far too old and too young to be blundering, after four years of body-scoring vacuous work, into the esoteric world of a university. . . .*

Clichés. But I would write it better. . . . *At last I could, and did, study with unconscionable zest, winning a Christmas bursary which, with the few dollars I got for sweeping out an infallibly dirty Vancouver chain-store six nights a week* (It was only five) *. . . But in no time it was summer again, and fickle science, I discovered, was now to use airplanes for spraying mosquito swamps. I was technologically outdated. Yet this was all part of the new Prosperity of the century which was to belong to Canada, had been officially announced in every address of welcome to Edward, visiting prince, imperial canvasser, a prosperity now declared visible indeed in the vast flotillas of logs streaming down the west coast to the smoking mills . . .* (the whirling mills?) *. . . of Vancouver. I dug out my calked boots and went off to a lumber camp to increase Prosperity. What with all this* (he was addressing perhaps the Board of Regents again), *and my mother's pension, and the sewing she did with her arthritic fingers, I was able, gentlemen, to return for another winter to the university and even occasionally, though it was a shameful extravagance, to take my mother to Buster Keaton at the neighborhood movie. Always my mother, gentlemen, for I was a loan-and-scholarship student and a sophomore, as far away from a wife as . . . as I am now, gentlemen, eight years and an M.A. later . . .* Ham, pure ham.

He came beyond the last houses into full brightness and crossed the shimmering highway that rimmed the valley's bowl. A great cliff of cloud was darkening the southern mountains now, but over the city, and on the mounting sage slopes, the sun fell like a blow. He walked along the road, turned quickly into the shadow of the quarry, stilling the clatter of invisible crickets, and climbed to his customary niche from where he could watch the highway.

In a few moments the black Chev rounded a curve toward him. There was a car behind, but, as she slowed, it passed and disappeared, grey and enigmatic, beyond the next hill-spur. She turned into the quarry mouth, stopping with the motor running.

When he jumped in, he was startled to find her almost in panic, her lips dry and unresponsive. "O, Gordon, I think they knew me in that car." She backed the Chev, pointing it the way she had come. "We've got to get out of sight. I'll turn up the first canyon-road." She drove fast, eyes on the highway, mouth pinched. But he was suddenly gay, feeling the excitement of risk, conscious of her whorled ear, of the scent from her dark fine-spun hair, and savoring his power and luck, for he had summoned her once more after all, and she was beside him, warm-shouldered, quick-breathing.

"Stuff", he said, happily. "Nobody's bothering about us. And supposing we were found. It'd be a good thing!" She had a new yellow frock.

Anne threw him a surprised glance. "What are you saying?"

"I mean we've got to have a showdown." It wasn't at all what he meant, he needed phrases as elemental and passionate as—as D. H. Lawrence, but words, any words, were tumbling out of him. "I've had a row with Crump. He was letting me get away, letting me think I was on leave, and then he was going to fire me at long distance. He will now, for sure. I can never come back here. Anne"—O damn I can't get hold of the woman when she's driving —"you've got to come to me. Or better come *with* me, now—" I am mad—"I've got enough for both our tickets to Toronto. Let him divorce you, what do you care, you dont want to live with him; we'll manage—"

"My poor dear," she had been murmuring, her face held to the road. "Tell me what happened. I cant talk till we're out of the car."

He went over the scene again, leaning away from her to concentrate, but it was no good. The great things, the shining realities of his spirit, he had not spoken them to Crump, he had not flashed them like a sword round that fraudulent head. And now when he could think of words for them, they were only in the way, bewildering his memory and perverting the truth, the honesty that she expected—or did she?—and that he longed to honor her with.

She turned off the highway and they sang into second, bouncing up the dirt road of a canyon bottom. The city and the darkened saltplain beyond it swung out of sight and they were in a light-dusted world of birch and aspen. At a gap in the flanking trees she edged the car off, parking so that the license plate was concealed. Automatically he pulled the tartaned blanket from the back seat and stumbled up ahead of her, scattering grasshoppers from the dry weeds, into a natural clearing in the woods. Beyond sight of the road, he spread the rug between sumac on the shaded grass.

She came toward him slowly over the little glade, then in a soft rush, her long brown arms half-raised. O Anne, this is our happiness, the one creature of which I am half. But on the rug she struggled from him.

"Darling, no. We must talk, it's our last chance."

He sat up, hearing his foolish heart beating. A tree-toad clacked below, and suddenly a magpie flashed black-and-white over their glade, scolding. "Last? No, you're coming with me." Oscar is right, you have been a coward. He pictured her sitting beside him in the train. Starting a new life, alone no longer. The long curve of her stockinged leg under the seat.

"Alone?" But it was she who had said it, her eyes, deep, almost lavender out of the sun, searching him. What am I doing to my life? I cannot—

"G'way-quaak," said the bird, swaying awkwardly on a choke-cherry bush. Nest robber.

"Leonard's a full professor with a private income. And he wouldnt get fired if his Gentile wife ran out on him. They'd even let him divorce you and marry a good Mormon."

"And the—?" She stared at him blankly, making him say it.

"The children?" She wants a promise. A definite . . . unfortunately the President—"I—suppose he would have them,"

She turned her head at once, her shoulders drooping, the dark hollow deepening between her breasts. I can't lose her, I—

"Anne, you know I want them too, but"—he could hear the flatness of his own voice—"we'd have to live on almost nothing, till I got my degree." If they weren't such brats, if even they didn't look like Leonard.

She turned back, her red mouth quizzical. "Yes, I might even have to support you." She reached out quickly and took his hands. "My dear, forgive me. I wanted you to see for yourself it's impossible. Jimmie's only five, Harry's seven, and if they were twice that old I wouldnt leave them. Not to him, Gordon. And if I took them and went off with you he'd get them back through the Courts. They'd take them *from* me, darling." She was emphasizing her words as if he, too, were a small boy.

He drew his hands away. "Then you've never intended to leave him. This has all just been—" Her steady eyes stopped him.

"This has been love, my dear." She made an attempt at a smile.

"But—" he was genuinely bewildered now, there was something remote and untouchable about her, as if she had already put him out of her mind when they said good-bye in another canyon, when was it? only three days ago—"all this talk about your getting a divorce and marrying me—"

"My dear, it was you who always said you must get your degree first."

"That was then but now—"

"Now the degree looks farther off than ever, and you've lost your job, and you want me to run away with you!"

"All right, I'm inconsistent," he shouted, reddening, and heard his words echoing blatantly up the hushed slope. "But so are you," he added, low and miserable.

"Darling, we've both been living off the romantic moment, that's all. So long as I thought you were coming back to Salt Lake, I didnt face what—what I knew. That is, I didnt until I said good-bye to you this week."

"What do you mean? Face what?"

She plucked a piece of grass. "O, a lot of things." She studied the little green sword. The wedding band glinting on her finger moved him suddenly to anger that it was not his and that his one heirloom, his mother's engagement ring, lay useless among the buttons on his bureau. "The main thing is that for you nothing, nothing, matters so much as your career, using your brains—even though your glands sometimes persuade you otherwise."

There was a dry motherly tartness in her tone which stung him. "Career in 1932! That's a pre-Depression word. It's not me, it's you who cant think beyond a cosy home and a professor's salary. That's what you love, not me, you wont risk losing them, you've never really loved me, you've just—just wanted to come out in the woods with me, that's all."

She paled. "You talk like a child!" She faced him, still on her knees, nostrils quivering. "I'm the one who's taken all the risks. Every time I see you I've risked everything. O, not my 'cosy home'," she gave a dreary little laugh, "you couldnt understand how much I want to be rescued from—what I pay for that. And not just my reputation and my friends—dont sneer, Gordon, these things mean something—no, let me finish—what we come back to, my dear, always, is the children."

"Geg-geg-get-get," said the pye suddenly from a nearer aspen. "Awaaag!" Its gaudy tail shone iridescent in the shadows. Eater of eggs. From the south came the first low reverberations of thunder.

He sat baffled by a world of feeling he could not share, did not even want to experience, not now, not yet. She is conventional, after all. Adjusted. Why is everyone afraid to break through to a life of honesty, of emotional integrity? "I see," he said, beginning to make a cold little speech, but her slim fingers, twisting now the tassel of the blanket, and the unconscious plea of her mouth, brought a rush of desire over him. "O Anne," he took her quickly in his arms, "I'll marry you yet."

She clung to him. "You must want us all."

He tilted her head, felt her sinking beneath him, her lips opening.

Up through the alder came the purr of a motor, growing quickly. The magpie squawked away as they scrambled to their feet. The car was below them already—pausing? They stood motionless, separate, peering at the screen of trees, a bright incongruous tableau in the glade. Had it stopped? Leonard? Hunting them out? The car by the quarry. Christ, after a year, to be caught in the last meeting! Then it whined into second, rumbled up the canyon. Whew!

Anne swayed, eyes shut. She put out a hand and he steadied her. Oddly, at that moment the light changed as suddenly as if the sun were a lamp being dimmed.

"I must get back at once. The children will be home!" She began stumbling toward the road. "It's going to storm."

He was deflated. "Always the children." He picked up the rug. Noisy square little Leonards, shrieking into the house from Sunday school, rattling helpless frogs in a tin can, little frogs themselves, growing up in the chorus of the Faithful, like their father, hopping into the best jobs, *brek-ke-kek-kex,* mating with women too good for them, and begetting more squat tadpole Leonards. *Ko-ax, ko-ax.*

Near the car he came up with her and she stopped, turning. The tops of the aspens swayed and hissed above them, caught in a sudden wind as in flame. "Yes, always the children!" She had heard him. "Tell me, Gordon, if Leonard—died, would you marry me?" She held him with her great dark eyes.

She would murder him! No, you melodramatic bloody fool, she is simply asking you if you want her children supposing she were left with them, now, his children, and what kind of a monster are you to be silent even for a split-second, can't you say yes? You can, why not, she would have his insurance money, if that's what you're worrying about, you could go and get your precious degree, stop standing there like a half-wit, it isn't as if you didn't love her, you do and you'll lose her, too, as you lose everything—see, she's turning away, she's crying—

"Yes, yes I would, Anne, you know I would. I want them too. They're part of you, dont—" but she was already in the seat fumbling for the switch.

She would not let him take the wheel and they drove in silence back down the canyon road, eerily shadowed now under the tormented sky. She was quickly tearless again and calm. It was as if he had never shouted his 'yes'. Or rather that she had heard a voice he himself had shut his ears to, a voice saying—what?

That you are still mamma's boy, wanting love without marriage, afraid to grow up—

Untrue, I am more adult than fat spawning Leonard. I know how to love a woman.

Ah, but can you love children? Can you suffer the little children?

Yes, my own I could but first—

First? The years slip by you.

Let them, I am more than child-maker, earner; I have power for mankind, I am a teacher born, a good one, students turn to me, and I could be writer, prophet even.

You! Where is your cause?

I will find it. I will not be trapped here.

But you have lost her.

They drove, still in their spell of silence, out of the woods into the rim highway, seeing the city now grey-green, unreal and metallic, under the poised storm. A hot little wind came running up through the sage like an animal toward them. Anne spoke quietly, slowing the car but not turning:

"There is something I was going to write you, Gordon, but now I will tell you before you go." The long dusky curve of her cheek betrayed nothing. "I'm two months pregnant."

What! His mouth went dry. He couldn't think. "Anne!"

"Don't worry, I know a doctor."

A truck roared by them. Was all this happening?

"But my dear, why didnt you tell me?" Himself, curled within her.

"Why should I worry you just when you were leaving? What could you do? Besides," she took a slow breath, "it might not be yours."

"What do you mean?" He seized her shoulder, roughly, making the wheel swerve, trying to force her to look at him.

"Mind," she murmured almost matter-of-factly, "you'll put us in the ditch. I only mean it may be Leonard's."

O shame! He drew away, and a gross image of her husband, hunched naked and hairy over her, leaped before he could close it out. "But you told me—"

"It was just about that time he last—insisted."

Insisted! How could she sit there, efficiently driving, calmly saying these things? She was hard, all women were strangely hard.

My God, man, they have to be. You ought to feel sorry for her.

"My darling." He put his hand on her cold arm.

"It's all right. But I would like to have kept it."

Anger caught him again. "God damn him for a drunken rapist—" but she stopped him sharply.

"Dont be melodramatic. He's not that; and anyway, it's not because the child might be his that I'm having an abortion."

He was utterly astounded. "You want another—by him?"

"I'd like another child," she said, "why shouldn't I? It might even be a girl this time. But there's no nice curly yellow hair and brown deer-eyes in his family, nor in mine. If the child were yours he might guess. You dont look the least bit like him."

"So you'll kill it only because it might be mine."

She stopped the car off the pavement, let the engine idle, and caught his cheeks between her hands, almost harshly. "Dont you see! It's because *you* don't want it. You must see that. That's why I am telling you—to make you see that." She let her arms fall. "How can you think that I—" she was genuinely hurt, bent away from him, slim blue-veined hands to her own face—"O my dear, I want nothing in the world more than I want your child." She was crying again, silently.

He stroked her hair, fumbling to comfort her, but he did not argue. The storm growled on each side, clawing the range-tops. The city lay parched, waiting. Quickly she sat straight again, drying her eyes, talking, almost whimsically now. "O, you dont know what dreams I had. I even began a plan to save it, when I first knew I was pregnant. I wrote my sister Ellen, the one in Los Angeles. I was going to her with the boys. I'd have pretended to Leonard it was just for the summer holidays. But I'd have left them with her and gone to Reno. I've evidence enough on him now, and it takes only six weeks. He wouldnt have contested, as long as he didnt know about us, and then I'd have had alimony, and custody of the children, including this one, whoever's baby it was."

"And you've kept all this from me!" These—these secret schemes and murderous decisions, elaborate, hard-headed, unguessed—he did not know her at all. Dumbly he watched the dead leaves scurrying now like mice across the road.

She gave a dry laugh. "It was a silly plan, anyway, moonshine. Something I dreamt before I admitted to myself that you didnt want children, any children, and therefore wouldnt ever marry me. But I faced that, even before I said good-bye to you this week."

She would have lived off Leonard's money, even if the new child were mine. She would do anything for—for her children. Was it only this that women really loved! Well, and why not? What else is there for her, living her life with that cold and croaking hypocrite, that secret drunk and haunter of brothels? What about yourself?—and you know he's not really that bad. He is, the pot-belly. Then why are you leaving him to her, making her kill the child that may be yours? Yours is the sin. It's no more a killing than contraception, I won't be caught in theological verbiage, there is no sin, only—only what? Release from repression the cultivated *mores*? . . . Man of Sin . . . Man of Gin. A gust of wind shook the cartop.

He clutched her knees. "Anne, you're wrong, I do want children, my children. And I want you. It's not too late—"

She shook her head almost with pity. "My dear, if I went through with this, you would have to take me with three kids—perhaps none of them yours."

Say it, say you will anyway.

But how, when? I would never—

Suddenly she put her soft lips to his and he held her, thinking wildly she can't resist, she's giving in, she'll run away with me alone after all; but she slid from him and set her feet on the pedals.

"Good-bye, my love. Dont make it difficult." She released the brake. "Please. You must walk from here. We cant be seen coming into town together." When he did not stir, she reached over and sprang his door open. It was as if she had shoved him.

He got out, stung, wordless, looking at her.

She put the car in gear. "Someday, my darling, you'll love me for this. Meantime, perhaps, you will do great things. Perhaps?" She looked at him almost jauntily and then turned her head. Staring he watched the car slide away, gather speed down the hill, vanish behind the first boulevard of trees. Beyond them a slant curtain of rain was being pulled across the flat suburbs. All the mountains had gone.

He continued to stand, conscious of no direction in which he wanted to move, till another car emerged from the boulevard, whining rapidly toward him. Gordon pivoted automatically, rain spitting in his face, and went down under the whirling sky to the campus. As he set his foot on the top marble step of the Arts building a great bull-whip of lightning lashed the hill's back, over the canyon, and the air above him seemed to split with the instant crack of its thunder. Looking back, he saw a wall of rain moving over the roofs toward him. *I have escaped.*

There was another note propped on his office desk, but this time in Van Bome's thick purple pencil. "Hell with lunch. Gone home." Oscar's desk was bare; he would be sunk in the one armchair in their flat, morose and smoky-eyed within a horseshoe of beer-quarts and bluebooks arranged on the floor; he would not eat till nightfall. *But belly, God send thee good ale enough . . .* With some self-contempt Gordon admitted that he, on the contrary, was very hungry.

He went down the familiar brass-edged stairway and had lunch in the staff cafeteria, managing to avoid company. Rain drenched and darkened the basement windows and the air was cool at last. When he had eaten he ascended at once to the office, locked the door, and read steadily through the heap of papers, a solitary firefly of concentration. He worked while the storm crashed and rolled away, and the late reborn sun brightened his cubicle and swung and sank unnoticed. He wrote the last grade, Zaporsky, on the Dean's form, put the envelope in the mailslot, and came out with aching eyes into the deserted campus under the silent mountains, knowing that he was about to get drunk.

He opened two more cokes, splashing them into the watery alcohol at the bottoms of the tumblers Pedro had just set on the sticky table. *I have not spilled.* Pouring the maroon crude-oil into the spray pump while the mosquitoes stabbed my neck. *I am not drunk.* He peered through smoke whirls at Oscar, but

33

Van Bome was still arguing with the jumpy little feather-haired youth—who was he?—who had sat down, restless-eyed, at their table some vague time ago.

"How can you, how, my dear sir," Oscar was saying in half-serious rhetoric, "can you say there is or there should be a class struggle when by definition each human being is incapable of becoming a larger unit than himself and—"

"No, no, boorj—" the little man jogged in his chair, trying to break in.

"Therefore is unable to unite for any effective length of time but must always struggle against every other human being who, in turn, is strugg—"

"Boorj-waw individjulism," the other shouted, eyes darting everywhere, "pessimism, Shopenhoor, that's wy we have depressions, y' get me?" He kept tucking the bottom of his tie into his shirt and pulling it out again, bright, bright yellow tie.

Way-away, lost forever. The romantic moment. "And howja explain Russia, the workin class are in power there, wy?"

Power. I struggled alone. Splashing the dirty bucket of paste in haste over the new-papered wall, roses-in-bowers, that last morning when Becket came in, already tipsy, and wouldn't pay me my back wages. In haste and hate—

"Because—" Oscar reached a burly hand for his drink.

"I'll tell you," the little man moved in on the second's advantage, with a rapid glance at Gordon, "because they fought as a class, get me?" All I had saved went to buy those boots for the lumber camp. "W'en the western proletarian learns—"

"Are you a proletarian?" asked Gordon suddenly, leaning forward in the rickety cane chair.

"Call me Charlie," said the youth quickly and flashed a smile—or was it only a tic? "Sure, I work in a cement plant, see, time-keeper's office, I get to know what goes on, lemme tell—"

"That's not working," Gordon said loudly. O.K., if he wants to stay here let him listen to me. Shooting bird-looks at my hands. All right, they were hard once. "I became a proletarian at the age of ten, a butcher's boy. I—" but now Oscar was cocking a quizzical eye—"school holidays, of course, and I sold papers in the street, and—wait!" Gordon rushed on, seeing both of them with their mouths half open like rising trout, "That was work, and when I was fourteen I had to quit school and slap paste for a paperhanger at two bits an hour, nine hours a day."

Oscar got up. He is bored, he has heard all this and I am exaggerating, I was nearly sixteen. You always exaggerate. But Van Borne was only going, gleaming-haired and stately, to Pedro's toilet.

"Well, but look, fellah, if you'd had a union," Charlie dropped his voice and leant toward him with a knowing air, "that's just exac'ly—"

"Union, my dear man," Gordon interrupted grandly, feeling the gift of tongues beginning at last to descend upon him, "I am talking about a small town, a piddling tourist resort, where there were only two paperhangers. One was my father, who was a sign-painter too and an excellent honest craftsman, till he volunteered to kill Huns. Ah yes; then with the last month of the war, my mother received an apologetic telegram from an unknown gentleman in Ottawa" (someday I will write all this) "to the effect that my father had unexpectedly been eliminated by one of the very Huns he had gone off to eliminate and that in consequence a bereaved and ever-grateful government would pay her sixty dollars a month for life, and"—but what did I start to say?—"and so there was now only one paperhanger, and he was an amiable feckless drunk who was known to have hung whole rooms with the pattern sideways. So I worked for him, because, my young friend, there wasnt anybody else to work for, union or class struggle or what have you." My career.

Charlie, who had been taking the opportunity to gulp from a beer bottle, set it down. "You're a Canadian then?"

For God's sake, I deserve a better audience; am I one of the backward races, a Tibetan? I have first papers. Ah, but if you're out of the States a year they'll cancel them. You *do* want to become an American, Mr. Saunders? A compatriot of Senator Smoot. Gordon drained his own glass. "You say that as if it explained me." His tie is too bright.

"Not at all, Canadians, Americans, the same—you'll be part of us in ten years," Charlie said hurriedly, grinning—it *is* a tic—"you hangin paper here?"

Quick little sparrow! He knows I'm not. He was looking at

the ink stains on my fingers. "My friend and I—" but at that moment Van Bome loomed over them, sat impassively down. Be careful, he has a job yet. He doesn't want to be identified in Pedro's blind pig. "I've just been fired. I'm unemployed." A silly remark; he sees me drinking alcohol at four bits a shot, and he has only beer. All right, I was unemployed when he was in rompers.

"That so," said Charlie, "w'ere were you workin?"

"Sir," Oscar cut in with his best Johnsonian manner, "there is only one category of work which is of importance to the human race. And do you know, sir, what that is?"

Saving me, or himself. If I had Oscar's bass, even his two hundred pounds. No Johnson I, no Lincoln either.

Charlie blinked, alertly turned his head. "I'd say wage-labor, socially-useful, that is." He fumbled at his tie.

The pick bouncing from the frozen gravel, aching palm-bones.

Oscar belched. "Pardon me, no offence. I refer to the labor of creation, which—" he rolled sombre eyes at them—"has two media: Art and—"

"Copulation," Gordon interjected.

"Child-bearing," Oscar corrected him gently, "to which, I think you will agree, only a small portion of contemporary copulation contributes."

He knows? No, a coincidence. My little sea-horse, raked dying out. . . . This has been love.

"Fine," Charlie was saying, jogging in his chair like a jockey, "that's fine, fine, I kin take a joke, but you wear shoes?" His small black glance darted slyly under the table and Gordon repressed an impulse to draw in his feet. Hipboots leaking, the rubber coating eaten by crude-oil, squish-squashing down the trail. "You both wear shoes, doncha? O.K., a shoemaker's important, socially important, creative, Stalin was one, so was his father. Get me?" A silly bloody conversation. Swinging a fourteen-pound sledge on that windswept mountain highway, widening the curves so that even the most neurotic tourist would feel safe to drive too fast around them.

"But have you ever—?" pounded a hand-drill, Gordon was going to ask, but Oscar was ahead of him.

"I am not sure, sir, if I follow your logic but I would say that

the point is whether Stalin made the best shoes, and I mean—"
Oscar frownd pedagogically—" the aesthetically best possible shoes
in the given circumstances. I take it that he did not, or he would
not have abandoned his cobbler's shop for the uncreative role
which he now plays."

"Uncreative!" Charlie clutched his fluffy hair dramatically.
"Joseph Stalin plays the greatest, the—the most creative role in
the world today. If you had said Hitler now, who was a paperhanger—" he shot a surprisingly malicious look at Gordon—"I
would agree with you, but—"

Hitler? That's the German fascist, I think. Is Charlie a Bolshy?
What's it all to do with us? With this continent? Intellectuals,
both of them.

"Look," he broke in, "I've had all sorts of jobs. You ever muck
in a frozen sewer trench?" I have caught their fancy. "Let
me tell you the last day I did that." All right, I want to talk
about myself; privilege of the condemned, eve of Siberia, Tibet.
"I'd quit paperhanging,"—he bowed to Charlie—"and gone tie-
cutting for a haywire lumbercamp, but it closed down in September
with the first flake of snow. It was what they called the Post-War
Slump, relief work. Back in town they'd thrown a sheet over the
government ditch-digger and wheeled it into the back of a garage
and stored the new air-drills, and given all the unemployed picks
and shovels."

"Sure, an old story," Charlie broke in. "It's what Roosevelt
wants to do if he gets in. Patching up the system."

"Hell, at least that's better than letting the system walk around
with its ass hanging out," Oscar said jovially, "but let us not
interrupt." He settled back.

Damn, he's anticipated my climax and I can't stop now. "By
coincidence my story makes reality of Oscar's metaphor. As you'll
see. They shoved as many as possible into any sewer that froze.
Well, that day, it was twenty-five below"—it could have been—
"and a wind howling, and there was a dreamy kid behind me with
a sharp new pick, he'd just been let out of the local bank"—but
no dreamier than I—"and I bent down to shift a boulder when—
whoosh—I felt a queer tug and a rush of air up my back and I
looked around and there was my one good pair of overalls and

my long winter undies flapping like a mucking big bird around my bare backside." Laughing; I can talk their language.

"Jeeze," Charlie said, with a high snicker, squirming in his chair, "that reminds me—"

"Wait! So I hightailed it back to the tool-hut, and there was the bloody strawboss on a bench up against the heater reading *Culture and Anarchy* that I'd lent him, and damned if he didnt think it was my fault. 'Trouble with you is,' he said, 'you got your head in the clouds.' 'Head hell,' I said, 'it's my ass and it's damned well frozen just running here.' And it was too, I couldnt feel it was there even. 'So shove off,' I said, 'and find me some safety pins while I thaw it out. Lucky it's not as fat as yours, or that stamp-licker you gave a pick to would be up for manslaughter. And you too.' "

They were laughing at the next table too, overhearing. Students? I'm in good form. "But there wernt any pins and he had to use wire and pliers to clamp my pants together. 'You gotta have eyes in the back of your head in this job,' he says. 'You're what they call an intella-jent-see, you are, and you oughta go to college. Plenty room at the top.' 'That's what my ma says,' I told him, 'but how the bloody hell do you save on twenty-seven-and-a-half cents an hour?' 'Well, as a matter of fact,' he says, 'I've had my eye on you, you know how to swing an axe, and I'm sticking you down on the foreman's bug-list, forty cents an hour swampin trails for the Mosquito Control. There's a big bug-man here from Ottawa and he wants college types. But until then you'll go on the barrows and keep your arse between shafts.' And by God he worked it for me, he wasnt a bad sod really. Though that job was no picture either." Have I gone on too long? "Because—"

"A good story," Charlie came in quickly with a flash of teeth, "but supposin that pick had bust your back, there's a serious side—"

"Backside," said Oscar.

"No, no." Charlie made a perfunctory giggle and hurried on, bobbing and frowning. (The bloody little bore, determined to make politics out of it. I want to describe that mosquito job.) "Let's get to the point; your friend here," he nodded brightly at Gordon as if he were an exhibit, "has given us an example of why workers got to have Compensation Laws, which have never been achieved in any country without—" he made a little bony fist in front of his face—"struggle; when—"

"But what," Oscar rumbled over him, "is your definition—if you insist on gravity, and I do not say the subject does not merit it—what is your definition of the term 'struggle'?"

"Struggle? Well, take the Bonus Army March, when—"

"Hell," Gordon said, "I'm going to find Pedro and get another drink." He got up. I am still struggling to escape from the fate that bookkeeper glorifies. They can't understand. Utopians. New Atlantis. Island mirages. Do they think I'm running away from them? He glanced back but they were absorbed in their technique of mutual interruptions. They've forgotten me already, each believing in something—yet I too have beliefs. But you can't organize them, beliefs without belief, you got on the wrong tack somewhere. For where are you now? I am in Pedro's bootleg joint in Salt Lake City, September the second, nineteen hundred and thirty-two. And so is Bookkeeper Charlie. You are alone, alone and dying, *we who were living are now dying with a little patience*. He bumped into a chairback. "Pardon." That naked bulb in the ceiling dazzled me, I am not drunk really, only alone, six blocks south and two blocks east of where she is lying asleep with—*One ticket to Toronto, please*. I can't afford another drink.

He walked through an archway into the babble of the next room. Less stuffy; a door open into the back garden, moonlit: when the moon comes over . . . ; mountain air, new-washed, sliding down through the canyon, over the sumac in the glade. Where's Pedro? *More gin and less*— Once this was an ordinary home and this the diningroom; fruit pattern on the ceiling border. Ugly, but the paper was good quality, five years ago perhaps. The other room a nursery, Jacob Grimm's dwarfs, where the children played who had escaped the long lancet. But now all the rooms are for what the preachers call scoff-laws, people like me, to get plastered in, around secondhand garden tables. All but the kitchen, where Pedro and his ox-eyed wife live and stay sober and make money. I made it once. *The East Vancouver Daily Echo,* four years ago, the far-off lovely Twenties, before Adam fell. Thirty percent commission on advertising. Bonhomie, hypnotic zeal.

'Try it for a month.' Shove a smile and your pen at them. Gordy, my other half. Right, after all? Gordon was fumbling at the kitchen door when a voice from a corner table stopped him.

"Well, look who's here. Hunting for a drink, professor?"

He flushed with alarm before he remembered it no longer mattered who saw him, and turned. It was Joan all right, peering forward at him from a flimsy rocker, and incongruously clean in this dive, some white outfit. I see her again, the fortunate lady. Good luck or bad or nothing? There was a sleek youth in a blazer and flannels, and another girl, pretty, with a peppermint-striped scarf, at her table. Students too. The young dumb rich, in town to write off supplementals—or else they'd be loafing in a lake resort, not here on Labor Day week-end.

"Come and sit down." She pulled out the empty chair and patted it. He felt an absurd rush of pleasure; somebody wants me; but what am I getting into? A crush on you, everybody knows it. Not wearing her horn-rims.

Sweet and lovely, Morton Downey murmured from a neglected radio on a blue-painted buffet in the corner. She introduced him, took his empty glass from his hand, and filled it from a bottle on the table. Flashing rings. Pedro's real Scotch, fifteen dollars a quart, money. Will I be sick?

"Dont tell me you're alone." There was a spiky bit of hair, like a ruffled cat's fur, over one of her ears. At least she doesn't bleach it. Red-faced, she's a little tight, or is it that old skin-complaint? They clinked glasses. *Sweeter than the roses in—*

"Just—another chap," he waved vaguely toward the other room. If they hadn't spotted Van Bome, so much the better.

"Well, Mister Saunders," she gave her odd gap-toothed grin, "what would the Board of Regents do if they saw you now?"

"Is that a threat, Miss Krautmann?" he asked unsmiling over another voice whispering within him 'stop it, you want to be friendly'.

"Why Gordon," she laughed, a little startled, "you dont really think we'd tell my old man on you?" She poked at her hair aimlessly. Gopher-colored.

"Why not?" He was enjoying this. Daughter of the Chairman, it's not I who am being led on. "He wouldnt do anything you didnt want him to, would he?" But he hadn't meant to sound brash. The room, beyond the laconic eyes of the other two, was beginning to recede.

She made a little canting gesture with her heavy chin. "As a matter of fact he wouldnt."

She means that. Power again, she walks in power like—like the night, no, that's beauty. Gliding over the leaves. Darling, we must . . . He took a deliberate drink. I am free! Free as a bee. "Well, as a matter of another fact, I wouldnt give a good goddam if you told the lot of them." Free! "Tell Wollonby, the sanctimonius old kangaroo; tell his stool-pigeon son. Tell all the undergraduates." He waved his glass at her companions, watching their faces tighten. All right, I am not a gentleman, my mother was a waitress. "Tell the—" look out, not that word—"fuddy-duddy President."

Joan's moon face shone with puzzled admiration. "My dear teacher! I think I like you even better this way."

"And I like you, I like—" he looked quickly at the others—"almost everybody. Even myself, my other self, Gordy. Shall I tell you all about Gordy?" What does it matter what I talk about?

"By all means," said the blazered youth a little too politely, and his girl giggled. All right, my supercilious last year's fashion-plates, you think I am drunker than I am. Play up to them, tonight's my gabby saturnalia; drunk I am thinker. He has a moustache like a thin brown swallow. (Go away.)

"I only got to know him when I graduated from the University of Vancouver, in—" he made a pedantic bow to Joan's friends—"Canada, a-a territory in the far, far north, the continent's root-house. They have there certain academic skirmishes of a sort which Wasatch College would consider quaint, quaint as bows and arrows. Honors Courses. There's one in the English language and its literature, for students hoping to fight their way into that indispensable, quasi-noble but may I say somewhat undernourished profession of university teaching." Prickly snob, you're embarrassing her.

"Hear, hear." The youth—Gordon had already forgotten his name—bounced his glass on the table in mock assent.

Merited, get on with it. "After four years, then, I emerged

reasonably victorious from this, alas, only preliminary campaign and received for booty a teaching fellowship in that greatest of all graduate schools—greatest, that is, west of the Great Salt Lake, and east of Peiping—the University of California." Heavy, I need a cigarette.

"O, were you in California? My brother started there this year; he's taking Commerce." It was the little blonde, trying to be friendly, perhaps a little impressed. Decent, a decent-looking virgin—

Someday I'll find you, Morton Downey whispered now.

"Dont interrupt," said the Blazer, with ironic anxiety, "the professor is talking."

"Can it, you brats," Joan said. Her little blue eyes lit dangerously. She is loyal to me. The bastard knows quite well I'm only an instructor; instructor without The Degree, Mr. Saunders. "And what about Gordy?"

"Gordy? Ah yes, Gordy. Well, the only catch was the fellowship paid me five hundred bucks." Blank. It means nothing to them, the unreachable rich. Goddamn you, that's all I'll get paid next year now, too. He took out his cigarettes. "Sorry, let's talk of something else; Mr. Hoover's emergency loans to big business, or the Sino-Japanese conflict? I am boring you." I am boring myself.

"Not at all, professor; have one of mine?"

Condescending pup. Glancing at his elegant little watch. "Thanks, I like my own. Look, the point is I didnt have any dough, kale, cash; I even owed money to my old Alma Mater, and I had to buy a ticket and study, live a year, twelve months, on five hundred dollars." Christ, why did I ever start talking about this? But Joan is listening. "And that's where Gordy came in. There were three months before I had to be in California. I stumbled on a job hawking advertising for a suburban weekly, and I discovered him. He's the me that wants to own a house, a car about the same size, a streamlined wife, four kids and a yacht— or maybe the yacht first—and by God Gordy knows how to get them. He's a man of business who can bully half-bankrupt store-keepers, clap them on their crooked backs and flatter them, feed their stinking prejudices, and sign them up for quarter-page ads they dont need. He corraled all the pavement and sewer contractors and stampeded them into thinking, if they didnt advertise in his cheesy little rag, its owner, who was also Chairman of Works on the Municipal Council, would chuck their next bids in the public ashcan. And my old pal Gordy cleared fifteen hundred bucks for me that summer."

He paused for breath. Silence. The blonde has been fishing something from her handbag—snapshots! What the hell is fifteen hundred bucks to them? All you've done is make a talking jackass of yourself. It was only a thousand too. We are poor, Mr. Saunders.

"And so then you went to California," Joan said helpfully. Definitely, her pimples were back. The other two were now in a sly tête-à-tête, the girl palming snapshots along for Blazer to see. So then my mother—but that wasn't the point. He took another drink. I'll make them listen.

"What I started to say was that I, Gordon, always hated that slick go-getting twerp, Gordy, me, and I gave him the gate. From then on I've been a nice boy who did all his lessons and tried to keep his academic nose clean in the hope to be a Great Harvard Professor someday. But, dear children," the tone of his voice had caught them, the blonde had shoved the snaps away, "I couldnt keep my big Gentile nose clean enough for your sanctimonious little Alma Mater. And so today I was fired and—and now my little pal Gordy is laughing his long pointed head off at me."

"Fired!" Joan sat up. "Gordon, no!" The other two glanced sideways at each other.

"Booted. I've given my last lousy lecture and marked my last fat illiterate Morm-moronic bluebook in good old screwball Washed-up Wasatch." Leave my Church out, Mr. Saunders.

Blazer whispered something quickly to his girl and got up. "I think we ought to push on, Joan." Mormons too. And I've hurt their jeezly campus pride. Or maybe they're even frightened to be seen with a leper. "May feels tired." Yes, he's mad, but too much the little Lord Fauntleroy to have a brawl. You eternal pinhead, a hundred of you's not worth an Eli Swansen, but Eli failed his exam, Eli lives on what you spend for gasoline, Eli is undernourished. And you—shall I start one, throw the drink in his face? Movie stuff.

"Do you mind?" The blonde smiled artificially, and clutched her purse, rising, embarrassed. "Sorry, Joan."

Sorry? Maybe she is; and she wants to stay, mere curiosity.

"O, dont be sorry," Gordon said loudly, "it's time you were both in bed—"

"Look," Joan interrupted quickly, "you kids leave me." She leaned urgently toward Gordon. "I want to hear all about it, Gordon—unless—" She made a fat *moue*.

Manners. He scrambled up belatedly. "I shall be happy to escort Miss Krautmann home." He bowed elaborately, but they turned off without looking at him. Get out! . . . At least they've left us the Scotch. *Night and dey-ee, ny-height and . . .*

"Lissen Gordon honey, t'isn' too late." Yes, too late, I have been telling it all over again, a third time, no not all, never all, never the truth, always less, or more. He was staring across at her pudgy arms on the table. "Li'l Joaney'll fix it. Crump's nobody." She tried to snap her fingers.

Am I drunk too? I'm fine. Don't want to talk about Crump any more. How long have we been sitting here? Somebody's turned the radio off.

"Wyncha come and tell me right away?" She frowned. Mothering me, a good girl, intelligent even, a C-student but only because she didn't work, why should she? "Honey, you know—" Her face went blank.

He felt a great hand on each shoulder. Crump? Leonard? He was suddenly rigid with unnameable dread.

"Well," said Joan, "the great Mister Van Bome." O Lord, it's Oscar, I forgot him. I forgot Oscar, my friend.

"I'm hitting the hay. I'll leave the key under the mat." Van Bome, discreetly ignoring Joan, was gone before Gordon could assemble his words.

Is he angry? I am abandoned. Was that other fellow with him, the one with the yellow tie? He started to rise. "What time's it?"

"Siddown, honey, you're a'right, on'y midnight maybe; here, still some." She poured out the rest of the bottle, watching the glasses with myopic care, pursing lusty lips, grave and earth-homely, an unaccommodated Ceres.

He subsided, drinking, feeling suddenly tender, and caught in a banal flow of his own words. "You're a good girl, Joanie, you're such a good, good girl you're too good for me, you know that's why I stopped seeing you, dont you?" Liar, you simply couldn't face going to bed with her. No, not just that . . . Someday you'll love me for this. "You dont know me; I wouldnt be any good for you. You dont really know—" Somebody's loud laugh penetrated through the humming in his ears. The next table—listening? Joan did not turn, she doesn't care, why should I? My only priestess now. But there are spies—

"What don' I know, honey?"

"What?"

What? A doctor, a certain doctor. I do not know him either, who will know my fetus face. You do not know that Crump is right, I am a man of—"I am a failure, born of failure." Don't shout. Spies behind every altar, in every back seat, in passing cars—He dropped his voice. "Shall I tell you about my father? My father, ran way from 'prenticeship to a paperhanger in Liverpool, ran away to British Columbia to pick up nuggets from the river banks. My father, walked up all the rivers, up one side, down the other side. No nuggets. Then one day—" sit straight, you are getting soused—"one day, I think maybe was the day Queen Victoria died, good day for it anyway, my father married a waitress from—Scotland somewhere. A waitress who'd run away from waiting, way-away, ran away to pick up a man, pick up a man picking up nuggets." I'm still O.K. He blinked his eyes, a little dizzy; is she listening? "So they settled down in li'l mountain town and hung paper and she—she waited on him. So—" He peered at her. *Gat-toothéd was she, soothly for to seye.*

"Tell me more."

"So they were failures. She was beautiful woman, but she was failure." The dizziness passed. "And so they wanted me to be a success, belong to the bour-bourgeoisie. O yes. So they were all for education. 'You let somebody else find the gold,' my father'd say. 'You let them find it; and when you get through a university you'll take it away from'm.'" Joanie shaking her head, laughing; pities me—why? Because I think this important. "And you know what my mother always said then? 'I only wish I had

45

a chance and I wouldnt be here now,' she'd say. And then the fight would start." He tried to laugh. Dead. She took in boarders to help you, and you can't even talk about her without clowning it up.

"But Gordon dear," her voice was liquor-husky, "les talk bout *us* now. We gotta decide; you musn go way, not t'all, not ever, not from Joanie." Way-away from sweet pine where tourists ride on glistening horses, way from little Frieda next door, fat flashing legs always way-away. When do you plan deserting, deserting the deserts of Deseret . . . ?

"Why you want this old degree old Phoo-Dee for anyway?"

Dr. Saunders. Is my great privilege to introduce . . . our celebrated professor medieval literature . . . "Trade-Union card, my innocent. Meal-ticket." What am I now? Swimming instructor in Great Salt Lake, where water's denser than flesh, even stupidest floats.

"But you don' need—" She was stopped by a burst of singing from the next table. *There was once a learned phys-eek-i-an.* "O hell, le's go home to my place where we can really talk an'—"

She left it unfinished. To sleep, perchance to—? "Your father'd jus' love it, jus' adore it."

"He's not there. Family's still up at the lake lodge." Lucky, lucky family, and I'd be there, catching Dolly Vardens in nice cool morning off a raft. Free, free as the bee—how free is he? "Jus' the servants and they're gone to bed. Come on, honey, I'll get Pedro call us a taxi."

"No." He was feeling dizzy again.

"Well then we'll walk, s'not far, walk's what we need, walk in nice moonlight. And 'en Joanie'll make some coffee, eh?"

Stumbling in snow over the frozen swamps. Awaaag! A magpie, I. Willows. Slash, cut them down, cut down all staffs. I will heap a brushpile high enough to make the awakening beaver envious. Where is my axe? But this is no alder, this ribbed dinosaur hide, loose round the knot. It has an evil face, frog-face, obscene, insisting—Slash! I need no axe, Ajax, I call the lightning down—

"Gordon!"

Snow turned to gravel; moonlight. Where—?

"Professor honey,"—somebody laughing at me—"what's daddy's

old hickory done to you?" Joan. We have been walking. "Come **on in,** you dont want that bark. Jus' a lil step now and we'll be **home."** Home? What is home without children, three children, always three, and none of them—? "Feeling better?" Twenty-four Second Avenue East, Vancouver, B.C., 'cross from the Rat Portage Sawmill, third floor, number four. Have to walk up. Or dance up the stair, like Fred Astaire. Two rooms and kitchenette our home; I live with my mother, Madam, and no other, a humble slum with mum. She pays the rent, the meter, the gas, the heat, all these are her mite, but is it mete, for—"Gordon!" I? I, madam, haunt a store by night and sweep the university by day.

"Here we are."

I know these granite steps, parados of the Regents' Regent. They lead to soft rugs, soft beds, soft—No, I am coming awake. Tomorrow I must—"Look, hon, we'll go straight through to the kitchen and brew us some coffee, eh?" Good old Joanie, wants to marry me, good old dumpy unhappy Joanie, unpregnant of her cause, two months and more, she will brew me a cup to banish care, black cup to sup, Socratic cup, hemlock for talk, to poison Crump, *sic semper tyrannis,* but never, no not ever, never, not— If Leonard died . . . ?

"What you care? Two o'clock maybe. 'Nother cup? No?" She set her cigarette on a tray, as if reaching a decision, came over and kissed him. Wet lips, vaguely remembered, wide slack breasts. He was unquickened, bleakly sober. I have been sick.

"I got to go home." My head aches.

She huddled beside him on the chesterfield. "There's a guest room all ready. Dont tell me Mister Van Bome will be waiting up."

Jealous of Oscar? Does she think we're pansies because we don't go steady with women? Those two sorority girls did, when I was undergraduate, didn't know I heard them; and the campus pansies put me down for a swot—or merely afraid to try? Only Nadine's house understood; three dollars, once a month, cheaper than taking nice girls to supper dances, less frustrating. Only the poor understand. In Ireland you wait till father dies, get your piece of peat bog, then a colleen. But mine died long ago, he left no bog.

She was rubbing his ear. "Or you frightened somebody'd find

out, dear puritan professor? Are all Canadians tall and curly and scared of women? Dr. Crump doesnt know you like I do."

Man of Sin. "Tomorrow's Saturday—today I mean. Got to get cheque, cash it, buy my ticket for Sunday. Got to get up early."

She reached for her cigarette and sat back facing him. Red round legs below a wine dressing-gown. Must have gone to her room and changed while the coffee was brewing, sometime—was I asleep? "Gordon, why go to Toronto at all?"

Eh? because, my dear dumb little rich-bitch—he shrugged. "Have to live, or do I? Something on called a Depression. Mr. Hoover's reducing income taxes to cure it. Meanwhile, however—but maybe you havent heard—"

"Now dont be like that. It's not my fault daddy owns a copper-mine or grandma left me a cement company." Cement? Perhaps Charlie works there. The Struggler. I was unkind to him. Cement, my God, I didn't know, she even has her own cement. "What I'm trying to say, Gordon, if you force me, is—O hell." She stubbed out her cigarette, her face suddenly pitiful. "Why Toronto?"

Sober up. "I told you, only place that offers me a chance to get started on the doctorate."

"Would Harvard be better?"

"Harvard thinks so."

She took his hands. Squawk went the magpie. "If you had a chance to get a good job in—in business, be a tough daytime Gordy for a while, could you still be nice soft-eyed Gordon too?"

And give up teaching. "What business?" But I know.

"My father kind of likes you. I could see to it."

Son-in-law to the local copper king, copper-faced son-in-law to the kingly sonofa— My Lord, you've earned it, reward for loss. No, I have escaped. Sober. "Look, Joan, maybe I'm just a bloody little idealist, I dont know, but I hate making dough out of people. What I want to do is—" to make something else out of them, to make them into—? He sighed. What do I want? The world at your own terms. "I want to be of some use in this stinky world." *Sin I from love escapéd am so fat ...*

She watched him with her bizarre toothy smile. Like a Hallowe'en pumpkin's. "Teaching?"

"All right, so teaching's pretty silly, but at least I can change a few minds, or make them grow, the best that come my way. It's not that I hate money, God knows; I'd like to have leisure, time for—" He stopped. I'm tired.

"To write?"

She is smart. "O.K."

She got up, lit another cigarette, inhaled, put it down. "Will you let me give you what you want?" She stood over him, plump hands clenched.

She is ludicrous, my God is this how I looked to Anne? You are a coldhearted coward. She is honest and good and lonely, lonely like you. No, not like me; she is bored, not desperate, and rich, while I—You are a fool, she is simply a healthy-minded modern woman who knows what she wants and, what is more, has what you really want, what you gave up Anne for—almost anybody would marry her, all right, so she's plain, and who are you? But I won't be bought. Not by money, not by love, not—I have escaped.

"What do you mean, Joan?"

"O"—she suddenly sagged, thrusting her head into his lap, seizing his arms almost savagely—"you know, you know." She raised her face, blowsy with tears, sobbing out words. "Marry me. Now. You know I love you. Ever since we met that time—O Gordon, promise me. Wire Toronto you're not coming." He was seized with an impulse to put his hands over her mouth, but she would not free his arms. "No, no, dont go. I know I look like nothing on earth, but cant—"

"Shh, my dear, it's not—"

"I'll let you study, I promise. You wont need to take a job with Dad. We'll go to Harvard till you get your degree and—and we'll never come back here if you dont want. Gordon, darling, we—"

"Joan, stop, stop—"

"—spend our summers in Europe, anywhere you want. I'll buy you any—"

In a frenzy of shame he shook her off, struggling to his feet, and she went sprawling on her back on the carpet, the wine-silk dressing-gown flaring open. She did not attempt to move but lay with eyes tightly shut, while from her puffed lips came a continuous moan, soft and utterly abased. He turned, stumbling over her splayed and brawny thighs, and rushed through the half-darkened rooms, down cement steps, and into the waning moonlight.

5

PRICE RISE BRINGING
BACK PROSPERITY SAYS
RAMSAY MACDONALD

Jobless Fail to
Break into Jail
"This is no boarding house,"
Chief tells crowd

Marconi Sends Typed
Messages by "Television"

CANADIAN UNIONS REFUSE
TO FORM A LABOR PARTY
Favor Legal Sweepstakes

Montreal, Sep. 16—Many jobless would not work even if they
were offered jobs, said the Minister of Labor last night in an
address to the World Service
Club Executives. Initiative and
. . .

GANDHI FASTING AGAIN

DOOLITTLE SMASHES
RECORD
Hurtles Through Air
At 296 MPH

POLICE ORDERED TO
STOP RAIL HOBOES
   Ottawa, Sep. 6 (DP)—Canada declared war today on all
"knights of the road." Speaking from . . .

Governor-General Says
Depression Peak Passed

LEGION DEMANDS BEER
AND BONUS

   Special to the Victoria Herald,
Sep. 17—. . . Where are the unemployed going to live now,
demanded the Mayor indignantly
at last night's meeting of the
City Council after a letter had
been read from the Provincial
government outlining a new cut
in relief grants. Married jobless will now get fifteen dollars
a month and an extra $2.50 for
each child. The Mayor pointed
out that many of the families
affected could scarcely find shelter for fifteen dollars a month,
let alone food and clothing.
Councillor Chalmers, however,
remarked that there was already a thirty million dollar relief deficit across the country
and . . .

VANCOUVER WIDOW WINS
$30,000 ON IRISH SWEEP

New Wage Cut on
British Railways

STRAUS CO. INTO RECEIVERSHIP

WOODSWORTH DEMANDS LOWER INTEREST

Leader of new "CCF" Party Hits at Banks

PRINCE OF WALES IS EMPIRE'S BEST SALESMAN

Wheat Prices Stir French Farm Revolt

BRITISH JOBLESS TRY TO STORM PARLIAMENT

Scores Hurt, 30 Arrested

Home Secretary Blames Soviets

$8000 A MONTH NOT ENOUGH FOR CARROLL HEIR, MOTHER SAYS

WHEAT CHEAPER THAN SAWDUST ON PRAIRIES— 20c IN KANSAS

Washington, D.C., Nov. 7 (AP) —Declaring that he felt quite certain of victory despite recent prediction in favor of a Democratic majority, President Herbert Hoover today . . .

National Wealth of Canada 30 Billion

Belfast, Ireland, Oct. 11 (BP)— Eleven were killed and twenty-two wounded when police fired on thousands of rioting unemployed here today. Looting has broken out and tanks are being rushed from England to . . .

HATS HAVE SAUCY TILT

REDS LEAD PENITENTIARY RIOT

Tim Buck Incited Kingston Prisoners

BANK OF ENGLAND GOVERNOR SAYS ROAD BACK TO PROSPERITY UNCLEAR

Ottawa Plans Camps for Single Unemployed: Promises Food, Shelter to All

---

MOSLEY'S FASCISTI CLASH WITH REDS

Hundreds Injured as Bareheaded Millionaire Socialist Leads Shock Troops Into London Streets Today

Sir Oswald declares War on Communists

CAPONE GANG NABBED BUT POLICE UNCERTAIN WHAT TO DO WITH THEM

6

MUDDY CLOUDS BRIMMED THE SKY, STREAMING VAGUELY FROM THE wind, a devious wind that unhooked the stubborn grey leaves of November from the oaks and hurried them over the old grass to be crunched under the feet of the listeners. Sunday autos, like dark sharks, cruised the encircling highway, a noisy reef between the park's atoll and the silent stony waves of the city. At one end of the bandstand, in the park's centre, the cluster of people stood like survivors cast up from a shipwreck.

Framed by the dim interior of the stand a man leaned hatless, straw hair coxcombed by the wind, shouting ". . . work . . . name of the single unemployed of this Province . . . fullscale program . . . union wages . . ." The wind, and the honk and squeal of traffic, shredded his sentences, which in any case came jerkily, slowly, from the swaying figure. "Twenty cents a day . . . starvation . . . Bennett government . . . slave camps . . . winter . . ." In a ragged topcoat buttoned to the neck he rocked, beat on the railings with bare fists. "Organize . . . bosses . . . mass action . . ." Above him a canvas banner bellied: WORKLESS UNITE—JOIN PROTEST MARCH TO CITY HALL MONDAY.

Most of the listeners stood close under the speaker, male, docile, interrupting only with little rumbles of approval, a few claps. From their dark anonymous shoulders an occasional cardboard placard projected: RELEASE TIM BUCK and JOIN NOOWOO. Where the crowd fanned out and thinned, its greyness was broken by feminine hats. One small round woman in a black raincoat stood guarding a faded blue baby-carriage. "Starving in Toronto . . . Canada's richest city . . ." A tall girl in a leather-jacket moved with a boyish swagger on the edge, passing out leaflets. "Leadership . . . National Unemployed Workers Union . . ." Under nearby oaks the Sunday strollers loitered, carefully remote but held by curiosity; beyond them a solitary policeman sat blankfaced, his idling motorcycle pointing at the crowd. "Workers of the world . . ." In a little star-burst of slogans the speaker ended and backed himself into the obscurity of the pavilion.

He was replaced by an anxious clapping chairman. "An now comrades . . . surprise . . . one a the leadin fighters . . . Canadyin workin-class . . ." A vague stirring took hold of the gathering. Who? Some looked sideways at the unmoving figure on the motor-cycle. The next speaker carefully not named, wanted by the police? Daring to appear? The chairman ducked away and a nondescript man in a grey gabardine materialized, raising a dark fedora to the sudden cheer of the crowd. He began to speak rapidly, proficiently.

The policeman gunned his engine, wheeled and burred down one of the cinder paths that radiated to the highway. There were shouts from the listeners and the chairman bobbed up nervously, but the speaker went on. The motorcyclist joined the circling traffic, turned abruptly, and disappeared into the driveway of the rococo Parliament buildings that rose, Sunday-blank, beyond the park's southern boundary.

"Look out, he's gone for a squad," a woman yelled.

"Naw, he just hadta go," a man said sourly, and there were uneasy laughs. Some of those under the trees and on the fringes of the crowd began drifting north, self-consciously casual. "In Germany, under the fighting leadership of the Communist Party, the working class is marching to power. In the Soviet Union . . ." The speaker sped on, resonant, unperturbed; the audience, smaller and tighter, lapsed into quiet.

"Here they come!" Quickly, one after the other, a dozen dark figures shot from the driveway down which the policeman had disappeared. "What did I say!"

"Kozzacks," the dumpy woman with the baby-carriage shouted. "Wid sidecars."

The crowd writhed with activity; some stumbled, half-running, toward the open parkland, others crowded closer to the stand, and a few young men scrambled up over its rails to face the scene, a ragged bodyguard around the chairman. The speaker had vanished. With surprising quickness the motorcyclists, stringing out, made a loose cordon around the park, turned and came roaring down the various paths, as down the spokes of a wheel, to its little hub of humanity. By the manoeuvre, fifty or more people were backed against the speaker's side of the grandstand, and the nearest half-dozen onlookers found themselves penned, still under their oak, in a tightening ring of authority. The motorcycles halted within a dozen yards of the crowd and a policeman leapt from each sidecar, baton drawn, closing the circle, except for one path. Near it a large officer with stripes on his sleeves sat in his streamlined throne, adjusting a loudspeaker.

"Here come the goddam cops," one or two had been chanting under the bandstand, but the chant was lost in the bedlam of motors, lost with the shouts of the chairman, waving his arms for attention, and the jeers of his bodyguard.

The sergeant in the sidecar raised his hand, the police cut their engines, the loudspeaker imposed attention.

"All right, break it up. All of you. Walk quietly down this path, leave the park and go home, and there wont be any trouble."

"Yaaah, Mussolini," someone shouted, " 's a public park."

The cracked voice of the loudspeaker rose. "This meeting is illegal. Permission to hold it was refused by the Chief of Police. You got two minutes to get out."

"All right, comrades," the chairman's voice came over, high and anxious, "they're too many for us today, let's march out orderly." There were a few boos but the crowd began shuffling along the pathway and the platform group came down the pavilion steps, a silent rearguard.

"Look out! They're after the speakers!"

The back of the long line was suddenly convulsed with struggling figures; the police had converged, batons flashing. The farther motorcycles snarled into movement, cutting the rearguard off. Great billows of surprisingly black smoke poured from their exhausts, sending a wave of coughs and curses down the file. Quickly the chairman and the early straw-haired orator were isolated, pinioned by uniformed arms.

A thin little man charged back toward them, brandishing a spindly placard, but the nearest policeman brought a baton down with a long swing; the thin man clutched his head, staggered, sagged to the grass. From the neglected bystanders under the nearby oak a high boo sounded; it was taken up, distorted almost into a cry of anguish, by the crowd, herding far down the trail now, dogged by the machines. In the rear of the retreaters went the black-coated woman with the baby-carriage; suddenly she stopped, turned and made a feint at the nearest motorcycle with the buggy, handling it like a lawn-mower. "Gangsters!" she screamed. "Son-wabitches." The policeman-driver — intentionally, or caught off guard?—swerved too late, nicked a wheel of the baby-carriage, toppled it.

Instantly the high voice renewed its boo from under the trees, a boo prolonged and passionate, triumphing over the motorcycles, the lesser jeers, and even the little screaming woman struggling to right her baby-carriage. He had put all his strength into it.

Almost at once two big hands pressed down on his shoulders. Oscar! Who? The hands powerfully pivoted him, slid the same instant down to pinion his wrists. He found himself staring into a square smooth face inches away. Blue-green eyes, squinting, coldly measuring, like a great Siamese cat. He has been standing here all along!

"You looking for trouble?" Slow, contemptuous voice. Knees pressed against his. Caught by teacher. Hell, why did I—? He backed as far as his held hands would let him. He is strong; working clothes, not a policeman?

Coward, you're trembling. No, it's just the surprise. He felt stubborn resistance flow into him, a need to be loyal to this impulsive act, as if the emergence of a greater self depended on it. He glared back, said nothing, tensed to wring his hands free.

But they were flung, given back to him by his antagonist who, still calmly staring, flicked from his pocket a card, held it in his palms. "Police." He slid it back, brought out a notebook and pencil. "What's your name?"

Plainclothesman, sneak! I have rights. "Why?"

Pencil poised, the man looked at him with unwavering distaste. "You want to go to jail?"

He had an impulse to say yes; the temptation to yell out into the smug face, lash at it. But he checked himself.

"Gordon Saunders. Look here, I have a right to—" He glanced around; the other strollers had somehow melted away with the crowd streaming over the highway; no one but police. Alone.

"I heard you yelling. Inciting to riot. How do you spell Saunders?"

Fool, you're getting into trouble anyway, you should have made up a name, this is serious, what will the university—? Sullenly he spelled it, trying to regain coolness.

"Address?"

Must he answer? "Knox College." All right, I don't care, let him arrest me, they knocked over a baby, the cowards, and smashed a man down, perhaps killed him.

"You a theological student?" Incredulous.

He was tempted to say yes. "No. Graduate School. It's a cheap place to live." Cold macaroni and lukewarm coffee. "Are you arresting me?" They'll take away your fellowship. Your last job. Let them.

The sea-green eyes, the set face, said nothing. "What are you doing here?"

"What business is that of yours? It's a public park. I was having a Sunday afternoon walk, that's all. I saw the crowd and came over to—"

"You saw it was communist."

"When I got here, yes—no, I dont even know that. It's some unemployed organization." Fight resurged in him. "And what if it is? I'm a Canadian citizen and I have a right to be here if I want to be."

"This was a bunch of reds holding a meeting without permission."

"I didnt know that until the police came. Anyway, why shouldnt they hold meetings? This is a democracy. What's going on in Toronto anyway that you police come and club people down for talking?"

"The man you saw hit wasnt talking. He was swinging a board with a spike in it. He's a well-known trouble-maker, and he was obstructing the officers. So were you."

"I wish I *had* obstructed them." His wrath grew, till he had to struggle for coherence. "They were shameful. It was like—like Mussolini's fascists. All that black smoke from the exhausts was on purpose. You put something in the gas-tanks. I've read about it. And what about that baby?"

"Baby?" For the first time the man looked puzzled.

"Your cops ran over a baby-carriage. I saw them. It was deliberate."

Something that was almost a grin flickered over the straight lips. "How long you lived in Toronto?"

"Look, I dont have to answer all this. I'm talking to you just because I've got nothing to hide. Two months."

"I see. Where did you come from?"

"The United States."

"I thought you said you were a Canadian citizen."

"I am. I've simply been teaching down there for several years."

The detective regarded him as if appraising a new species of life. "A lot of things have been happening since you went away, mister. Perhaps you didnt know the Communist Party was supposed to be underground in Canada?"

"No." Staring still. Believe me or not, I didn't.

"There's eight of the top boys taking a five years' rest in Kingston penitentiary. Yeah. And there's a few agitators still creeping around under phoney names, running cover organizations like this fake unemployed outfit today. *And* we've got our eye on a few young punks in the University." He looked carefully blank. Gordon waited. A whole world of intrigue, violence, prejudice, I know nothing about. He was taken with irrational longing to belong to it—but not on this man's side. Ass, dont ever get in a jam like this again. But I am innocent. Ah, but who led the booing? They'll fire you out of graduate school. In the distance he could see a dark police van, Black Maria, halted where a path met the highway; a figure was being lifted through a knot of uniforms into its open back. The shank of the crowd had stopped on the far side of the road to watch. Gordon, his anger ebbed, felt a great desire to be there too, anywhere else.

The detective put his notebook back. "Look, mister, maybe you're a democrat, maybe this is a democracy. But right now Queen's Park is closed; you'll have to take your democratic walk somewhere else." Serene, virtuous; he believes utterly in what he is doing. But he's letting me go. "And next time you see police officers performing their duties, button your lip and go back to your books." He nodded a dismissal, then had an afterthought, "And if it makes you feel better, there wasnt any baby." He gave a little sniff of what might have been amusement, then nodded again, toward the highway and Knox College.

Gordon wheeled and walked quickly away, head down with embarrassment, over torn placards, past a solitary brown mitten, a windrow of trampled leaflets. In one place he made a detour to avoid a little smear of bright red on the scuffed grass.

Across the highway he hesitated. The Black Maria was already moving off, and only remnants of the crowd could be seen, scattering through the adjoining campus in the direction of College Street. Angling to the right he could re-enter Knox.

You have half your seminar paper still to do. "The Influence of Boethius on Chaucer's *Troilus*."

I couldn't have drawn a staler subject. Professor Jefferson's book said it all ten years ago.

All? You must find something new, you want to be a scholar.

All—except that prisoner Boethius could think and think and be a bore. My aseptic cell above the deserted quad. *What sholde he studie and make hymselven wood?* The locked diningroom where nothing is served on Sunday afternoons because that is the day out-of-town students are expected to have high tea with friends or relatives, and if we have neither we can walk, take exercise. Or sit in the common room, chill mausoleum, empty, or—worse—filled with Missionary MacManus lurking to re-tell his two fatuous adventures in China and quote Longfellow. How long before one makes a friend in Toronto. If I'd had one, this wouldn't have happened to me today.

The fault is yours. You went to tea last Sunday at Professor Smith's and insulted your hostess.

I didn't. Middleclass Anglocatholic prude.

She asked you a polite question about Utah and you got yourself angry defending nineteenth-century Mormon polygamy. You're a fool. You can't keep your mouth shut. You antagonize those who could help you, and now the police even.

I will have my friends on my own terms. I want people whose beliefs are not negations, who desire, imagine, will, create. Bergson, not Boethius.

What about that girl teaching-fellow?

A frump. I am homesick.

What, for the Great Salt Lake?

At least it had Sunday movies, and Oscar, and—

She does not even write you. And you do not dare. What are you going to do then?

Time for you and time for me, and time yet for a hundred indecisions.

He veered left and caught a glimpse of the blue baby-carriage, down toward College Street. He glanced around. No one is following; I'm going to find out what he meant.

As he overhauled them, walking rapidly, he saw that the leather-jacketed girl was with the little fat woman in the black raincoat, and two men. Suddenly shy, he started past with a sidelong look. There was not even baby bedding! Only a stack of scrambled leaflets and pamphlets. Library on wheels. I have been victimized. No, you just jump to conclusions.

"Squad from the garment verkers, we shoulda had," the dumpy woman was saying hoarsely. She would be in her fifties, probably, and Jewish, though with an almost comically wide Slavic nose. She shot Gordon a look from snapping dark eyes. "Congradulations, comrade!"

Me? He paused. They were all staring at him, curious but friendly.

"Yes." It was Leather-jacket joining in. "Those were goddam good boos." She spoke with an authoritative flatness, appraisingly, almost without humor. They had stopped beside him.

He was dumb, caught in a strange succession of emotions, deflation, self-laughter, caution, and then even an odd pride. The roly-poly woman was looking at him like a fierce acquisitive mother. These people want to be friends.

"What did Dirty Dirkin say?" asked the younger of the two men, a youth with a freckled pear-shaped face..

"Who?"

Dry laughter, except from the older man, who kept a little ahead, silent, as the rest fell into step with him. Arched nose, swarthy, intelligent, bored. The two youngsters are not Jews.

"The dick," said the girl, "we had him spotted." She tossed her head, perhaps only to free her left eye from a limp strand of her tar-black hair.

"He—I gave him my name—was that wrong?"

"So what?" How flippant she is! A strange lanky, limby creature. "The Criminal Code says you bloody well have to. Name and address. You dont need to answer anything else unless you're booked and in court."

Has she been? This is a new kind of girl. Tough, a little like the detective herself, coldly violent. "Will he make trouble? He found out I live in Knox. I—I'm a graduate student," he added, almost miserably.

"Oi vay, university!" The woman trundling the carriage sounded gloating.

"You dont belong to any organization?" The older man looked at him sharply, speaking for the first time and in a quick peremptory way. They had come to College Street and were turning east toward Spadina.

"O, no. I was just passing by."

The man raised his eyebrows. "An honest citizen," he said dryly. "you'll be all right." He looked fast and oddly at the freckled youth, as if signaling.

Gordon stopped. I am just tagging. But the others had halted as well and the younger man suddenly shot out his arm awkwardly. "I'm on the campus too, uh fourth year Ec. Name's Wilf. This is Kay, she was on last year." Are these Dirkin's punks! He seems almost timid.

"How havent we seen you around?" She gave him a hard little hand.

"I guess I spend most of my time in the stacks." He was introduced to the older woman, a Mrs. something that sounded like Shimshop, and the other man, Roberts.

"Look," said Kay offhandedly, "we're making for coffee at Morrie's. Join us?" Her eyes, grey, explorative, backed the invitation.

"Thanks very much." I am beginning something. My cause?

Snug behind a cloth-checked table in the farthest booth of the warm little Jewish restaurant, a pot of coffee and a bowl of dough nuts before him, Gordon began to enjoy himself. He had always wanted to explore this quarter but, lacking companions, had shied away from it, conscious of his lone Gentileness in its streets. Now, escaped from the raw wind, the faded daylight and the generally dismal exterior of Toronto stricken by one of its Sundays, he found himself excited even by the stuffy air, heavy with the smells of unknown foods, spicy and farinaceous, and by the sight of a shining seven-branched candelabra on a sideboard near the kitchen door. The fact that its middle holder pointed mathematically up to a color print of Joseph Stalin did not detract from the atmosphere. From the front of the café, where Roberts was lingering to talk with a group at another table, came the strange and rapid gutturals of what must be Yiddish.

Questioning Wilf and the two women Gordon tried to understand what the meeting had really been about, but they spoke in such an offhand political patois, with so many little slynesses and syncopes, that he found comprehension difficult. Nor was he greatly helped by the various printed appeals and alarums thumbed for his benefit by Mrs. Zimchuck (it was) and poked under his eyes from a scramble of leaflets she had lugged into the café out of the parked baby-carriage. The affair had been organized, apparently, by something called the Orkwoo or Ontario Relief Camp Workers' Union, which Mrs. Zimchuck described as 'kosher' (translated by Wilf, after some hesitation, as having a 'correct militant policy'). The chairman, however, had come from a much larger and less correct body called Noowoo, the National Unemployed Workers' Union, and he was not kosher. 'Gutless' was Kay's word; he had not rallied the audience around a fighting defense of the platform.

"But," Gordon objected, "the police had batons and had come to break it up. They just seemed to wait for it to get nicely started. If you'd resisted, they'd have clubbed the lot of you. What about that poor guy who *was* hit? Do you think he was seriously hurt? Will they keep him in jail?"

"Ha, I should live so long," Mrs. Zimchuck said. Her eyes snapped with a fierce amusement Gordon could not decipher.

"O hell, that was Lacey," said the girl. Over the rim of her coffee cup she looked sardonically at Wilf. "He's dispensable." All three laughed.

"Trotskyite bastard," she added, with calm venom. "He probably arranged with the cops to get a fake tap on the head so he could look like a real revolutionary."

"O no, he was knocked unconscious, and I saw blood on the grass," Gordon protested. "The cops carted him off in their van. And that dick"—he found himself adopting their language out of sheer courtesy—"called him a trouble-maker, said he started swinging a board with a nail in it. Well, there's not much percentage in that, but from your point of view surely he was right, he was acting the way the chairman wanted him to. What—?" he checked himself, suddenly aware of a collective amusement in their gaze, as if they were listening to a schoolboy who had stopped them in the street—"I'm not even sure what a Trotskyite is."

They laughed again. "You *are* an innocent," Kay said. She had pulled a tobacco pouch from a flap-pocket of her jacket and now proceeded to roll a cigarette. Gordon was impressed; there might be more dash than efficiency to her technique but it was an operation he had seen few women successfully complete.

"Vot are you saying to him?" Mrs. Zimchuck's deep bosom, only half-visible above the table, heaved protectively under the rioting roses of her housedress. "In the States is no Trotshkyites, Americans is too smart. Only up here, comrade, is veels round veels. Lacey! Pfooey, a vite-guard counter-revlootionry. In Russia—" She aimed an imaginary rifle with her pudgy arms and shot Lacey.

"The point about the chairman," Kay spat out a tobacco crumb impatiently, "is the whole ruddy committee knew the cops were bound to bust it up."

"Break up the meeting?" He was bewildered. "Why hold it then?"

"Kind of a propaganda effect," said Wilf, reaching for Kay's cigarette pouch. "There'll be a story in tomorrow's *Herald* anyway, but gosh there'd have been a banner head if we'd staged an all-out resistance."

"O here, wont you all share my tailor-mades?" Gordon hurriedly drew out a packet.

"Thanks, I prefer my own." Kay slid her rakish fabrication into the corner of an incongruously delicate mouth. Wilf also refused. Kay cracked a match on her thumbnail. The image of Joan in

Pedro's blind pig flashed in his mind and disappeared. He felt himself rebuked, as if for a piece of snobbery. These are genuine workingclass people, as I no longer am; I don't need to remind them that they can't afford store-cigarettes.

Mrs. Zimchuck, however, reached nimbly for his outstretched pack. "Sure," she said knowingly, zooping up the last of her coffee, "propaganada."

"But you're against the lad who did fight back?"

"Well,"—Kay blew a jet of smoke at the table, and seemed a little nettled by his persistence—"he broke discipline, once the chairman told us to go."

"Also," Wilf put in anxiously, "he was trying to grab the lime-light for his uh counter-revolutionary fraction by uh—by ultra-leftist putschism." He looked toward Kay. She nodded approval.

Strange young pedants, Gordon thought, but behind Wilf's wide flecked forehead and faded-blue eyes, and behind Kay's bold grey stare, is there perhaps an organized and tested knowledge of what my world is now all about? At that moment Roberts joined them, expressionless, glancing only at Kay. He took the aisle seat between her and Gordon and silently poured himself a cup of coffee. Their logic is not Aristotle's. Nor Planck's. Is it Marx's? I am the only baby here. He grinned and turned to Mrs. Zimchuck. "You congratulated me for my boos, but I wouldnt have let out the first one if the 'counter-revolutionary' hadnt been hit, nor the second one if I hadnt thought there was a baby in your carriage."

"Baby!" They all laughed delightedly, filling the little booth with hard sound, bouncing it off the bright kalsomined walls and up to the portrait of overcoated Stalin, all but Roberts, who suddenly came to life, eyes flashing. "Goddammit, I wonder if Lucy's thought of that."

"What?" asked Wilf.

"Hell, there's the lead for her story. It's good for a streamer. COPS SMASH BABY CARRIAGE. I'd better phone her." He was up and off suddenly through a swing-door into the kitchen.

"Baby!" Mrs. Zimchuck was still wheezing; she reached a grimy hand for another doughnut. "Two dollars of pamplits already I lost. Dat's my baby."

Wilf gave an admiring whoop. "Boy, how that man's mind

ticks!" Then, as if he had checked himself in an undergraduate lapse, he lowered his voice and turned to Gordon. "Lucy's the reporter who covers unemployment sob-stories for the *Herald*, you know, the afternoon daily. It's only uh liberal petit-bourgeois, of course, but Lucy's a, well, she sympathizes with our position and she was there today. Maybe she's thought of it already."

"Vell, vy it shouldnt be in de papers?" asked Mrs. Zimchuck. "De front veel is crooked now." She pulled almost indignantly at her girdle.

"She mightnt have seen it happen," Kay said. Like the men, Kay made it a practice, Gordon noticed, to ignore Mrs. Zimchuck. "He's right to phone her."

"But," Gordon could scarcely follow them, "surely the reporter will only say what she knows really happened. She wouldnt make it sound as if they *had* hurt a baby."

"*You* thought there was one," said Wilf, with a sly air, "and they *did* knock over a baby carriage."

"Christ," said Kay—her vocal toughness was somehow shocking, coming from lips as fine-drawn as willow-leaves, set in a china-smooth face—"anything we can pin on the coppers is all for the good. They're the repressive arm of the state, comrade, and we have to make the thousands of un-class-conscious workers who read the *Herald* aware of that fact. If they dont kill a kid today, they will tomorrow, and plenty of workers too." Is she play-acting, rehearsing for yesterday's barricades, or would she really fight? A long, thinbreasted, humorless pedantic wildcat. Yet she has moments of being almost exotically pretty. And my god, at least she's alive and young—twenty?—and not another graduate student in English. So? . . . *Looking for trouble?*

"Of course the main story will be the arrest of the speaker, the first speaker," Wilf inserted pacifically. "And," he added, "the chairman." Indifferent; another expendable. "The Noowoo will see the *Herald* gives them plenty of space. But you really gave us an idea. Something we can uh develop quite effectively in the *Worker* too." He patted Gordon's shoulder amiably. "Might get as far as the New York *Daily Worker* for all we know."

Veels certainly within veels, greased and secretly turning. Powering what? "Didnt they get the second speaker too?" Gordon asked.

"Him! Not him," said Wilf, proud and reverent, "he's too smart."

"But how could he—"

"Maybe I shouldnt say," Wilf glanced a little warily at Kay, "but—well my guess is he changed hats and coats with a comrade, and just drifted out with the first bunch the cops let through."

"You askin me," Mrs. Zimchuck broke in, bronchial and petulant, "he shouda stayed home. Vastin him on kid stoff. Seffen years is not peanuts, he gets caught. Oi!"

"Shut up." Kay gave her a warning sideways glance.

Gordon whistled. "Then he's one of the top Communists?"

"Who are you talking about?" Roberts came silently from the kitchen, spoke sharply behind him. He turned to him, to the cold waxy mask of his face. He is one too. Wilf and the women were silent, avoiding Roberts' close-set and suspicious eyes, like children caught in mischief. Chaucer's alchemist. . . . *For Catoun seith that he that gilty is Demeth alle thyng be spoke of him, ywis.*

"We were talking about the second speaker," said Gordon calmly. "I dont know his name."

Roberts gave him a snaky stare. "Mr. X, is that good enough?"

"Certainly," Gordon was ruffled. "It doesnt matter to me. I've been assuming, however, from your conversation that you people are Communists."

"It was Zimmie shooting off." Kay looked appealingly at Roberts.

"Vot me? I didnt say nodding." But Mrs. Zimchuck seemed more worried than righteous.

Roberts did not drop his stare. "We're Marxists, Mister Saunders," he said harshly. "Officially there arent any Communists in Canada just now." His eyes were hard and bright as obsidian. "What is your interest in Marxism?" Good Lord, does he actually suspect me of being a police spy! Is that the only reason I dislike him? Well, what is your interest? None, you just wandered in here . . . *Looking for trouble?* No, I want to learn, all this concerns me, concerns everyone. I want to be honest.

"To tell the truth I've never read Marx. Political science, economic theory always bored me, except in Shaw perhaps. But this afternoon rather shook me because I worked in a kind of unemployed camp too once, out west; and it looks like I may be in one again before very long. Also, well, my people were working-class." Respect in their eyes, except Roberts', unfathomable. "I dont like to see people suffering unjustly, and then getting kicked around because they protest against it."

"Vot I tell you—he's a fighter this boy. Got mossels too." Mrs. Zimchuck seemed about to say more but Roberts' aquiline profile swung toward her and she subsided.

"Especially here in Canada," Gordon began again. They are analyzing me as I talk. "I dont know, of course," he went on lamely, "what to do about it. This depression's all over the world so it surely cant go on much longer. Maybe we just have to wait and weather through."

There was a brief curious silence; all but Roberts had their mouth open to reply, but watched him as if for a cue. I've disappointed them.

"A study of Marxism, Mister Saunders," Roberts said with a lazy and contemptuous confidence—he has been careful all along not to call me comrade—"might have convinced you that the present depression is the last one; capitalism will not weather through this one; it will end very shortly, when the workers take over power and create the socialist state. But perhaps," he added tonelessly, "you dont agree."

Gordon indeed felt a hearty wish to contradict, out of sheer dislike of Roberts' assumption of absolute knowledge, but he was intimidated by the man's familiarity with ideas he had never weighed, and now wanted to.

"I dont agree or disagree; I dont know."

"And you would like to know?" The tone was impatient but challenging. All right, what can I say? You talk too much. *You want to go to jail?* Motionless, watching me.

"Well, of course, I could always bone up Marx and—the others, on my own—though I havent much time, and my eyes conk out from all the reading I have to do for my English seminars, and part-time teaching and so on—but in any case I'd like discussing these ideas with—with people like you." He turned appealingly to the others. "I'd like to be able to argue with more than a boo."

"Wilf," said Roberts, with a sudden jauntiness, "you might invite Mister Saunders to your next séance." He nodded almost jocularly, and wheeling went back erect and deliberate to his friends in the front of the café. As if he had thrown a chip on a poker table but thinks so little of the stakes he won't wait to see what happens. Or is he just confident?

"Fine," said Wilf at once, sending the departing Roberts a glance of doggy gratitude, "O.K." He turned quickly to Gordon. "We have a uh a Marxist study-class on the campus right now, called the Social Problems Club. It's not illegal or or anything, doesnt belong to any political party, but of course you can understand we have to be kind of careful about whom we ask."

"It's a oppertoonity," sighed Mrs. Zimchuck. "Vot are you waitin for?" She pried the sugar out of the bottom of her cup with a fat finger. "Me, I'm too olt."

Nuggets on the river-bank. Now is the time for . . . for every man to come—

"Wilf's the chairman," Kay added. She tossed back her hair from her cheeks. "I'm still allowed."

Wide grey eyes. That calm inviting look—to more than a study group? Fragonard face in Lenin's jacket . . . *The romantic moment.* But what is between her and Wilf? Or is it Roberts? Why else would Bigshot take time for their company?

"We meet weekly; tomorrow night's the next," Wilf said. He cocked his little dimpled chin at Gordon. "Would you come along if we called for you—as our guest?"

Perhaps you will do great things. What are you getting into? Say no, you fool, say you have a date.

"Of course," Gordon said.

7

**COPS SMASH
BABY CARRIAGE**

Berlin, Nov. 7 (UP)—German voters threw Adolf Hitler and his Fascists for a decisive loss in yesterday's general election. . . . His percentage of the popular vote went down from 37.7% to 33%, and Communists scored a corresponding percentage gain.

U.S. GIVES ROOSEVELT BIGGEST PRESIDENTIAL VOTE IN HISTORY—BOTH HOUSES GO DEMOCRAT AND WET IN REPUBLICAN DEBACLE

**THIRTEEN KILLED AS
SWISS TROOPS FIRE
ON SOCIALIST MOB**

Hamilton Tigers Victorious

CANADA TURNS PAGE OF MEMORY TO FALLEN HEROES

Man Who Bombed Brokers' Offices Deemed Insane

WHAT PEOPLE ARE SAYING
Charles M. Schwab:
"The very slackness of the recent months is piling up an opportunity for work for the coming year."

**PUT UNWANTED
POPULATION BACK ON
LAND, SAYS SENATOR**

**U.S. WANTS BRITAIN TO
PAY DOLLAR A MINUTE
SINCE BIRTH OF CHRIST**

**British Scientists
Plan to Signal Mars**

**SHAW: BRITAIN NEEDS
DICTATOR**

8

TIME *Monday evening, 28 November, 1932.*

PLACE *The Sunday School room in the basement of the Twelfth United Church, Toronto—a small cavern of grey-painted wood with one hard overhead light and little heat in the radiators. A few coffee-colored benches, center, are spottily occupied by a score of overcoated students, some with little mounds of books beside them. On a rudimentary platform, rear, is a bald table banked with stacks of gleaming new pamphlets: behind it sits the Chairman, with a copy of the Communist Manifesto and an open scribbler of notes. Behind him again, on the grey wall, stretches a canvas streamer:* SUFFER LITTLE CHILDREN TO COME UNTO ME. *The banner arcs over a large poster of Jesus Christ who, bearded like Edmund Spenser, long-haired and bright-robed as a Florentine condottiere of the fifteenth century, and crowned with a quite blinding halo, is patting the heads of three yellow-curled darlings in a garden of calla lillies.*

PERSONS:

GORDON *He also is yellow-curled, though no darling; a mixture perhaps of all; of the scholastic child in his coiled cherubic head and his air of being concerned with some inner conversation; of the Elizabethan man in the supple enquiring length of his nose and the sensual flare of his nostril and lip; of the wandering soldier in the unexpected thrust of his jaw and the set of his muscular shoulders; of the messiah, and the fool, in the lifted half-seeing gaze of his great deer's eyes.*

WILF *the Chairman.*

BAGSHAW
SILVERS
SMEETH ⎱ *other members of the Social Problems Club of the*
ILSKY ⎰ *University of Toronto.*
RAY
ROBERTS

WILF: And now comrades, I call on Comrade Saunders to give us a summary and commentary of, uh on, the greatest fundamental document of Marxism, the basic uh uh document on which Lenin and Stalin, Comrade Stalin, have built the foundations of of Modern Marxism, the uh the *Communist Manifesto* of Marx and Engels, Comrade Saunders.

GORDON (*comes up to the dais and stands by the table clutching some pages of manuscript*): Fellow members. Perhaps I should say 'comrades', but this is only my fourth meeting and I'm still shy of the word. Anyway, I havent the intellectual right to use it, since I dont know yet how much I agree with you.

Last meeting your executive assigned me an exercise for tonight. I'm afraid that what I've got here isnt what they wanted. I really tried to pot the *Manifesto,* but I found that it was already too potted a document. And I was inhibited by a feeling that the assignment was an initiation rite which I wasnt yet ready to take. I began to realize that first I must find out what this ninety-year-old *Manifesto* manifests, today, to me, and if it manifests the same things to you who are Marxists. I hope you'll take what I'm going to say in that spirit and be patient with my confusions.

(*He begins to read*): I have come as a swimmer suddenly beyond the point of the noisy bathing beach into open sea. There are cold waves rolling in, hard and salt to the mouth; my heart pounds and my muscles leap to an ancient challenge: to twist over these alien and profound waters, knife and thresh my way stubbornly through to—where?

Between wave-troughs I can glimpse a long dim island. Its shores seem gentle, tree-ringed; it rises, as I rise on a swell, into blue-hazed terraces crowned by the glow of what might be a strange, magnificent city. Should I strike for it? The tossing heads of other swimmers are near me, but they are few, scattered. I would need to rely on my own strength; the gulf is wide, the tide still against me. Already my body aches from the yielding push of the ocean. Should I turn now, before I've gone too far, let the insistent rolling of waters shoulder me back to the sand?

But it's not as simple as that. I have come farther than I thought, and I begin to remember (seeing now, as the tide washes over the beach, the bright rainbow of bathers bend back and dissolve into the grey town behind them) I begin to remember how it is that I am swimming here. There is an isolated rock near me now, not yet tide-erased; I pull myself up over its weedy yellow flanks and let my lungs ease, while my thoughts reach back, back, perhaps even to where all this began.

I was a child in that town—not the far glinting city across the gulf, but this grey treeless place behind me, into which the peacock bathers have disappeared, this rugged port with the humped steel back and blank cement face, snag-edged with the broken forts of old wars. Yes, I was a child who one day, idling against the base of that half-crumpled round-tower, reached to scratch something in the soft old stone—a girl's name, perhaps, or my own?—when suddenly the torn parapet above me leaned out (I felt it even before I looked up), leaned and curved down upon me. I ran terrified, stone thundering behind.

I remember again that I was in a church; it too was half-ruined, deserted, though somewhere in its loft a dying organ groaned unseen. One thin saint, fallen from his niche, lay broken-necked by the altar, and a wooden Virgin, leprous with peeling paint, trembled in the choir-screen at each vibration of the indecipherable music. Through a gap—a shell-hole?—in the dim roof, water dripped on the tumbled prayer-stools of the nave. And I ran once more, looking for a way into sunlight, sensing that this roof, too, was in the act of falling.

Later, sometime, I was the inhabitant of some vast vault, iron-walled, steel-pillared. An oiled rag in my hand, I was polishing the smooth casing of an enormous machine, I one of hundreds who passed their hands, as in ritual, each over the endlessly trembling back of his own cold monster. It seemed I had been there a long time, and might be for ever. Each day food came silently on an endless belt, enough for that day, and the next day for the next. Beside our glittering charges were the dun cots where we slept. I had already forgotten what it was like beyond the one door, blankly shut in the far blank wall.

But as I looked, one morning, the great portal trembled and slid open, and a man came walking, grey-overalled like my companions, like me, though with a peaked and shining cap. Most of the machines he passed without a glance, but here and there he stopped, touched some hidden switch on a metal pillar, stilling the sleek beast beside it. At each pause, still unspeaking and expressionless, he beckoned the attendant to follow him. And I was one who was chosen.

We trailed, a funereal file, out the iron door and suddenly through dream miles of an endless bright-lit factory, where coats and coins and bottles and cogs, books and toys and pistols, spilled in confusion from the chattering mouths of machines. We passed then into dim warehouses piled with crates, where other greycoats went about obscure episcopal tasks under the shadows of soaring cranes, or waited over the smooth entries and exits of giant trucks. But then, still following the peaked cap, we glided through a tenantless crypt where long machines like ours lay rusting in death, and came into a domed hall, empty also of men, but piled to its cloud-vast roof with pyramids of apples and sliding hills of fish, with terraces of loaves and the raw quarters of cattle, and with all the jumbled outpourings of earth and ocean. As I looked I saw that a green film crept over this arena of food, and the air above it was a black quivering of flies. With each heavy breath I smelled the stink of death. Suddenly the man before me cried out—or was it I?—and a convulsion ran through our line as each of us fought to escape.

Then, as I remember, we were in the open air, grouped calmly by the shaft of a monument. The guide—but it was a new one, tall, with a craggy Lincolnesque face—stood near us beside a stack of wide wooden bowls, oddly carved. He began to speak, his face taking on a noble and persuasive air. It was really the face of—of a man I know—but it was not his voice, not deep, but high, dry, remote, like a crow's.

"You Greyboys have been brought here," he said, "because the Bathers do not at the moment need you at your machines—an unfortunate but temporary hiatus. Meanwhile, you, and you, and you—" he pointed curiously, his first two fingers wedded, the others held curled by the thumb—"will each take a bowl and stand at an entrance to this park. Any entrance—you have the right to choose. The Bathers, whom you will see eating here, may, if they wish, drop

72

food in your bowls as they leave. You may smile, or cry, as your dispositions move, but you may not speak. If nothing is dropped in your bowl, go to the permanent ruins on the town's edge and find a corner out of sight to sleep or wait in, and return for the next meal of the Bathers. For this is the only way, at the moment, by which you can live."

"Can we never be Bathers?" a man asked timidly.

The guide smiled. "Someday, I am sure, provided you behave yourselves, show initiative, have pluck and luck. Meantime, notice that these bowls are valuable; the carving is medieval, they are especially lent by the Bathers from their museum. They have been signed out in your names and must be returned undamaged. Do not attempt to sell them; there are heavy penalties for theft of this kind."

The men to whom he had pointed—it seemed blindly—took their bowls now and scattered wordlessly through the park, walking between ordered rows of statues which radiated from the tall shaft under which the rest of us were still grouped. The park, I saw now, was only a great treeless field of high granite statues, identical except for the names flashing golden from their pedestals. On every stone block stood a bronze Bather, in torso heroically moulded, but the face of each only a blank moon of greening metal. In the cool shadows of these statues living Bathers reclined, men, women and children also with moon-like faces, but clothed in bright swimming suits and beach robes. They were of every age, but many very old, and of many shapes, though I could see none who had the Greek bodies of their statues. They rested in soft chairs around tables bright with food, and were being attended by dexterous Greyboys.

"You and you," the guide was saying in his high gull's voice, his two long fingers wavering, then pointing behind and beside me, "you are to wait on the tables of the Bathers. You have the privilege of eating what they leave, and sleeping in the Park when they have gone home. You—?" he regarded vaguely the only man left with me—"Ah yes, you are to be taught to cast statues. This is a great honor—for they are memorials to the longest-lived among Bathers now dead." Then his fingers quivered at me, as I stood alone with him. "You—you are getting the greatest chance of all. Go at once to the beach. At its rocky end you will find a row of cement cabins. The last one is now vacant. There you will live. You are to be taught swimming."

"I am to be a Bather?" I asked surprised.

He gave me his benign smile. "Theoretically everyone can become a Bather; but if you are not born one, it takes time, patience. Pluck and luck, you know. And enterprise. Meantime you must spend many years learning to be a Swimmer."

"Is swimming so difficult?"

"To be a Swimmer for our Bathers, yes. It is a sacred trust. It includes the ancient offices of Lifeguard and Coastal Warden. Also, you will come to know and pass to others the joy of swimming, which those who have experienced it say is the greatest pleasure of life."

"Then the Bathers do not teach each other?"

He smiled remotely. "You must understand that the Bathers have no desire or need to swim. They spend their days on the beach or in the surf, returning to eat here in the park. But it happens that this, our only beach, is not safe; there are currents, sudden storms, undertows, cold pockets that bring on cramps. There have been tidal waves, each one bigger than the last. There must always be Swimmers to guard the Bathers, and to pass on the knowledge of guarding."

"And this takes years to learn?" I asked, still puzzled.

He hesitated. "There are other things. Bathers sometimes disappear suddenly, pulled under perhaps, or—" He did not finish.

"By sharks?"

"No." He fixed me sternly with his strange blue eyes. "Remember this, but do not repeat it: you must also learn to protect the Bathers from each other."

"But why?" I asked, seeing the Bathers stretched now at peace in the park, under the shade of their heroic ideals.

He did not answer but went on: "There is one more thing. Beyond the beach is a gulf and beyond the gulf there is said to be an Island. It is a foolish legend of an impregnable Utopia where everyone is both Greyboy and Bather—equality, food dropping from trees, peace and the like, the old stale stuff. It is supposed to be inhabited only by those who swam out to it."

"It is not true, then?"

"We have had Greyboys who believed it, and plunged into the sea. Most were drowned by the shore, or were shot, or brought back. But a few, who had learned somehow to swim, got beyond sight and did not return. It will be your most sacred duty to ensure that no Greyboy enters the water without permission."

"I do not understand," I said. "Are there not already too many of us Greyboys? And whether or not the Island exists—"

"It does not exist! But sometimes their bodies do not float back, and the legend is strengthened. Too many Greyboys, often the most valuable, slip down at night to try the Gulf. Even some of the Swimmers—" He broke off.

"But how have the other Greyboys learned to swim?" I asked, looking up to my guide. Suddenly he was not there, though I thought I could hear his high voice floating down now from the top of the great central shaft under which I stood.

"Do not teach them or we will kill you, kill you."

My eyes traveled up the granite and paused, halfway, at gilt lettering. No names, only: *To the Collective Swimmer who has kept our Beach safe for the Bathers.* Above stood another statue, great-muscled, bronze-stiff. "Kill you, kill you," came the voice, and I saw, teetering and flapping on the figure's pate, a great glaucous gull whose creamy ordure ran down beneath its convulsive wings over the blank bowl-face of the Swimmer.

And that was years ago, or so it seems, in that life from which I have not yet escaped, which tugs at me still, as I lie cold on this narrowing weed-bright rock. The white tongues of the waves lick my ankles, the night is sifting down over the gulf, the stars shine cold and irrelevant. I cannot make out where the Island lies now, though beyond me rises and falls the dark head of another Swimmer. He shouts something I do not understand, and gestures. Has he found the direction, or is he in trouble with a current? Behind me stretches the horny glint of my town. The Collective Swimmer is poised still over that wheel of statues, down whose spokes the drab-coated servants must even now be jostling each other for the scraps on the tables. The hulks of the factories, some diamonded with light, some blank, stretch to the snaggle-toothed ruins, in whose rubble some of my old comrades are searching now for their sleep. Then the white fringes of the villas of the Bathers; the long blobs of the Greyboy tenements; and the great dome of that warehouse over which, even in the darkened air, I fancy I can see quivering a furious and immortal smoke of flies.

I must slip from this rock, now, down once more into the give and thrust of the waves. I see at last that I cannot go back. But I do not know how to go on. (GORDON *gathers up his manuscript and sits down abruptly beside the chairman, hands trembling a little.*)

Scene Two

There is a brief baffled silence, then clapping which, despite a few enthusiasts, dies quickly and is succeeded by coughing, murmuring, and the flexing of the bottoms of an audience which has sat long and expects to sit longer.

WILF (*looking around with the sick smile of a chairman begging for a lead*): Well, comrades, I'm sure we'll agree that that was a very, uh very (*he shoots an appealing glance at* ROBERTS, *the only Elder Statesman present; but the latter, at the far side with arms folded, looks ominously blank*) unusual and, and sincere commentary on the *Manifesto,* though (*hurriedly*) I'm sure there are many who wont altogether—yes? (*he leans delightedly toward the first waving hand*) Comrade Bagshaw?

BAGSHAW (*a flat-faced, button-nosed round-spectacled girl in a brown overcoat*) I think that was really *poetry.* (*One or two feminine murmurs of assent*) I mean, it sounded really *beautiful* and kind of sad, and it was very symbolic. (*Unfortunately she has an infantile, piping voice*) It reminded me of Coleridge; you know, the man that ate opium, or was it Poe?

SILVERS (*a crophaired nobble-cheeked engineering student, snorts, and there is a sudden release of laughter in which* GORDON *joins. Everyone feels better, except perhaps* BAGSHAW).

SMEETH (*an English Honors with her hair in buns, who did not laugh, tartly*): You're probably thinking of De Quincey, who wrote *Confessions of an Opium Eater.* But that's not poetry. And what the speaker read was more like a paraphrase of Thomson's *City of Dreadful Night.* (*There is an intimidated silence, since none of the comrades has heard of this work.*) With perhaps some influence from O'Neill's *Dynamo*. (*She has a natural undergraduate desire to score against a graduate student in her field.*)

SILVERS (*he has a sardonic bass*): Yeah, but what's it all about?

WILF: Ah, that's the question! What do *you* think, Comrade Silvers?

SILVERS (*visibly drawing his head in*): Haven't the foggiest.

WILF: Yes, Comrade Pilsky?

PILSKY (*an earnest and careful young man in the front row; he wears steel-rimmed glasses and is from the School of Social Work*): I think that, as you said, Comrade Chairman, it was unusual and subjectively sincere, but it hadnt much to do with the *Manifesto*, or with Marxism at all.

BAGSHAW: O, it has too! The Bathers are the plutocrats and the Greyboys are the protelariat—I mean the proletariat. (*More laughter, but she keeps serenely on.*) And the island is maybe the U.S.S.R.

SMEETH: It *shouldnt* be. It should be the *world* socialist state. But it reminds me more of something old-fashioned like Bacon's *New Atlantis*. (*Another short uneasy silence.*)

PILSKY (*he speaks with the air of a gentle, sad but unswervingly just man*): You see, you cant be sure. And what about the swimmers? At first I thought they were going to be the repressive forces of the capitalist state but then it looked as if they were the revolutionary vanguard. I'm afraid Mr. Saunders hasnt clarified his position. (*There are growing murmurs of assent.*)

WILF: Perhaps Com—uh Mister Saunders would like to reply to that himself?

GORDON: Personally I feel like that character in a Shaw play who says he has no Bible, no Creed, and is thoroughly frightened, but knows just the same he's damned well got to find a way of life for himself or—or *be* damned. I quite admit my own allegory isn't clear, because, as I said at the start, I'm not clear. Perhaps if you'll just let me listen to the discussion I'll acquire some clarity.

KAY (*rises from the back, hands shoved in a manly way in her inseparable leather-jacket. One eye is concealed by a hank of dark hair*): Excuse me, Comrade Chairman, but I dont think we should let the speaker off that easily, especially when he's been quoting the Fascist leader, Bernard Shaw, at us. (*She is not smiling and her usually flat voice has a feline edge she has not presented to Gordon before*) This allegory, or nightmare, or whatever the hell it is,—it's certainly not the summary he was asked to do—is supposed to be an explanation of one of the great classics of Marxism. For the sake of the newer comrades present, who are getting a very false and confused notion of what Marx and Engels said, I think we ought to get right back to the text of the *Manifesto*, and get Mister Saunders back to it. What he read may be O.K. as poetry, and worth an A in his English Department, but it wont be a bloody bit of help in bringing about the Workers' State, comrades. So I'd just like to ask the speaker, Comrade Chairman, a few straight questions as to what he accepts and doesnt accept in the *Manifesto*. (*She flutters a paper; she was taking notes all along.*)

WILF (*his bulbous forehead wrinkled and his little soft chin retracted—was this the line he should have adopted at the start?*): Why, yes, of course—if the uh speaker is willing?

GORDON (*determined to stay calm*): If you think it will help, fire away.

KAY: Do you accept the first sentence of the *Manifesto*: "The history of all hitherto existing society is the history of class-struggles"?

GORDON: I'd say it's *one* obvious pattern of history, but—

KAY: Then you dont.

PILSKY: Excuse me, Comrade Kay, but there's Engels' later footnote to that sentence, providing an exception for primitive society, which we now know to have been based on primitive communism and therefore classless and without struggle and—

KAY: I know, but—

GORDON: I certainly wont buy that! Engels swallowed a theory of Morgan's which has long since been discredited in anthropological circles.

PILSKY: In *bourgeois* anthropological circles. They dont want workers to learn that communism was once natural to man.

GORDON (*warming to this particular class-struggle*): I find that naive. So was cannibalism. We dont resume a culture-pattern simply because the Aurignacians had it.

PILSKY (*growing cautious*): Did you take anthropology?

KAY: Comrade Chairman—

GORDON: No, but I have friends who are anthropologists. They've always seemed to me more interested in evidence than in anti-Marxist propaganda.

BAGSHAW: Well, I think Comrade Saunders is right about Morgan. In my Anthropology 322 class we—

KAY (*shouting*): Comrade Chairman!

WILF: O yes, I'm sorry. We must get back to uh to the point of Comrade Kay's question.

KAY: Put it this way: do you agree that the history of *recorded* times is one of class-struggle?

GORDON: Yes, Kay. But it's also one of bubonic plague, exploration, population pressures, famine, love—and other matters either classless or class-collaborationist. What names do we remember from the history of the Slave Trade? Not those of the traders or even of the revolting slaves but of the liberal-reformers—Wilberforce, Lincoln—

PILSKY: That's because the bourgeoisie have re-written history to emphasize bourgeois heroes. Lincoln only wanted to free chattel-slaves to make wage-slaves out of them.

BAGSHAW: O, I dont think that's *all* he wanted. He—

KAY: Comrade Chairman, do I have the floor? (*She is still standing intractably on it.*)

WILF: Yes, yes, Comrade Kay.

KAY: At least you condescend to admit there is a class struggle. Do you admit that it must go on till there is what the *Manifesto* calls a revolutionary reconstitution of society?

GORDON: Just a minute, Kay. (*He flicks through the Manifesto*) Or until there is "a common ruin of the contending classes"—that's the way the sentence ends in my edition. One or the other, sure—we take a great moral risk when we aid and abet a class-war, any war.

KAY (*contemptuously*): Sure. The revolution's no place for the gutless.

SMEETH (*pertly*): "When torches are carried, beards are singed." Voltaire. (*She is ignored.*)

GORDON (*a little amazed*): Look, Kay, you've got me wrong. I reject the stupidities of our *laissez-faire* society as much as you do; it's an outdated and destructive system and it must change, because change is the law of life. But there are choices in change and in

79

methods of change. The British pulled a General Strike not so long ago; did it get them anywhere? I want first to be sure of the right choice—because when I *am* sure I'll be willing to give my life for it. (*A murmur or two of approval.* BAGSHAW *puts up her hand but is not noticed.*)

PILSKY: I think Mister Saunders means well, comrades, but what he says shows he is in a stage of Hegelian dialectical *idealism* whereas Marxism is the science of dialectical materialism.

SOMEBODY *whistles stunned approval.*

SILVERS: That's tellin im, Pil old boy.

KAY: Whether the speaker means well or not is beside the point.

GORDON: What *is* the point?

KAY: The point is you're preaching petit-bourgeois individualism here, while pretending to explain Marxism. You're talking as if the class-war was something you decided to start or not. The present class-war, my bourgeois friend, started a hundred years ago and more and it's not going to stop for the likes of you. Honest workers know that; they shed their blood in it. And they damn well wont stop until the final victory. The miners of Estevan know about it. They saw their comrades shot down and killed by the goddam Mounties just for walking in a parade under the Workers Unity League banner. It's only the declassed intellectual who tries to stand on the sidelines—

GORDON (*attempting irony*): You mean the non-existent sidelines?

KAY (*not absorbing it*): Exactly. You're either helping the imperialist bosses or you're helping the proletariat, whether you realize it or not, and whether you like it or not.

GORDON: Who is not for me I shoot? But is there any proletariat left?

KAY: Any left!?

GORDON: If I have Marx right, a proletarian is someone who's forced by the owners of the means of production to sell his so-called labor power for just enough to live on and to proliferate more proletarians. Are there any in this club? Seems to me we're all rather unproliferate students.

SILVERS (*suddenly aroused*): What's wrong with being a stoodent?

GORDON: Nothing. That's my—

SILVERS: There's lots of guys here do plenny of *real* work too, every summer, mister, with their *hands*; and anyway we got proletarian backgrounds. Which is more than some would-be profs could say.

BAGSHAW: O, I dont think that's fair!

PILSKY: There are two million urban workers in Canada alone.

GORDON: Maybe we're all from workingclass families—not that I think it matters—

SILVERS: O no?

GORDON: —and maybe we all know what it is to be underpaid wage-workers—

SILVERS: Oh yeah?

GORDON: —but right now we're students trying to short-cut wage-slavery, escape into a world of well-paid specialists; we're the very petit-bourgeois intellectuals Comrade Kay despises. Comrade Silvers here, I know, wants to be an electrical engineer—

SILVERS: I gotta make a living, see!—

GORDON: —and some of you hope to be doctors, social workers, teachers—people who are surely neither proletarians by Marx's definitions nor exploiters of them. Yet it's we who've come together voluntarily to study Marxism, of all the half-million people in Toronto.

BAGSHAW: I think that's very true. It's like—

KAY: The workers dont need to study it. They learn it through their sweat!

SILVERS: Hear, hear. You tell 'im, Comrade Kay.

GORDON: But do they? (*He has to raise his voice against murmurs of the indignant and the tired*) Wait a minute. I made some notes when I was working on this assignment. (*He digs them out of his pocket*) I took down the figures of the last Canadian general election.

KAY: O nuts, who cares about that? (*There is laughter again. She sits down reluctantly, throwing a scowl at Wilf.*)

GORDON: All right, I do. Two years ago, with the Depression already in full swing, and a second Labor Government in the Home Country, Canadians voted the present Bennett government into power, the most reactionary big-business junta we've had for fifty years. They voted in 138 Conservatives and 87 Liberals. And they refused to elect a single Socialist or Communist. In other words, the vast majority of Canadian workers, and even of our one million workless, are still voting for free enterprise, for the four big banks, and the trust companies, and the insurance outfits.

PILSKY: Ah, but the *Manifesto* doesnt say the proletariat acquires class-consciousness immediately.

GORDON: Granted, but—

PILSKY: The speaker is reflecting the unconscious ultra-left impatience of the intellectual isolated from the workingclass movement.

GORDON: Maybe, but—

PILSKY: Also a petit-bourgeois illusion about the importance of bourgeois parliamentary machinery.

KAY: Exactly. You're mighty careful not to say anything about trade unions. We've got three hundred thousand workers in trade unions now—

PILSKY: —The preliminary organs of class struggle!

KAY: And we—

GORDON: Hold on a minute. At the last meeting of this club we had a trade union speaker who told us that that figure marked a decline in membership since the war, that it was split among four rival federations, and that 85 per cent of the industrial workers had still to be organized.

PILSKY: Ah, but the comrade who spoke last week proved that the unions had fallen into the grip of reactionary petit-bourgeois bureaucrats and that it's now necessary to build separate Red Trade Unions.

KAY: All you're trying to do is sow pessimism.

GORDON: No, realism. You're trying to have it both ways. Look, I didnt bring up the subject of unions. But who elects and re-elects these so-called bureaucrats? The workers themselves. If the Canadian worker is in the grip of anything, it's of his own desire to be a capitalist. And as for voting, a lot of them in Canada still vote the way their fathers, familial or clerical, tell them to—despite the assertion in the *Manifesto*—back in 1848!—that capitalism had long ago reduced the family to a mere money relationship and had cynically dispensed with religion.

BAGSHAW: I think Comrade Saunders has a point there—

KAY (*sharply, up on her feet again*): Comrade Chairman, the speaker has been given plenty of time to demonstrate that he's here to attack Marxism not to learn it. I move we get on to the rest of the agenda.

SILVERS: I second. We had enough speeches.

GORDON (*angry now*): Just a minute; that's what I originally proposed—but now—

WILF (*pedantically*): There is a motion—

ROBERTS (*rises for first time.* KAY *and* WILF, *catching sight of him, immediately subside.* ROBERTS *speaks with venomous smoothness and lordly clarity amid a general hush*): Comrade Chairman, before any motions are put, I suggest that we let Mister Saunders get everything off that pigeon chest of his. He's had a lot to say already, it's true, for so recent a recruit, and none of it to the point, but there's a value for the newer comrades in seeing just how stupid a self-styled petit-bourgeois intellectual can be when he starts rehashing Marx and Engels so he can smoke them in his opium dreams. I'm not worried about the political health of our Club members; they've shown tonight they're quite capable of seeing through Mister Saunders' little Mosleyite tricks. So let's have them all, Mister Professor. (*He sits down and, assuming a fixed contemptuous smile, leans back with studied casualness. But down the dark arch of his nose he is staring at* GORDON. *Silence.* GORDON *pales.* WILF *looks bleakly out from his soft pear-face, staring at no one.*)

WILF: Is—is that agreed?

PILSKY, SMITH, SILVERS, KAY (*whatever* ROBERTS *says*): Hear, hear!

GORDON (*fluently angry now*): All right, I *will* go on, not to please Mr. Roberts here but because there are still some in this room whose minds havent been quite waxed round with dogma. In the first place, I say that we are the very people Marx mocks in his *Manifesto*, people who have a little toe-hold on the mountain of the ruling classes, but see themselves in danger of being precipitated into the valley of the ruled. But for that very reason *we* are the natural revolutionaries, we, not the work-drugged, half-educated machineworkers and the crestfallen workless of North America. It's we who are in the tradition of the law-students Karl Marx and Nikolai Lenin, of that intellectual landowner Friedrich Engels, that petit-bourgeois student Leon Trotsky—(*he is interrupted by a sudden outcry of laconic cheers, and oh-oh's*).

ROBERTS (*for him, excited. He rises and levels a finger as if it were a pistol*): Trotsky! I thought so! That's what you've been leading up to! The leader of the world counter-revolution!

GORDON: Any historian knows he was one of the leaders of the Russian Revolution and the creator of the Red Army.

ROBERTS (*shouting, as he stares unrelentingly, finger accusing*): He was its saboteur and arch-traitor!

GORDON: All right, for the sake of argument, let's leave him out—

KAY (*ironically*): Yeah, let's!

SILVERS: Let's leave *you* out!

ROBERTS (*sits, arms folded, again staring*).

GORDON: All I've been trying to say from the start is that I believe with you people that social action of some sort is the only hope out of this decadence of individualism we've inherited, and I will assume with you that the industrial workers can be the historically appointed grave-diggers of free enterprise, if ever they agree to accept the appointment. But I still maintain they must be led, sensibly led by people of education, intelligence, and moral principle, or—

KAY: Like you? (*There are laughs.*)

GORDON: Potentially, perhaps, like any of us. But first we must know how and where to lead, or the end will be worse than the beginning.

ROBERTS (*unmoving*): The workingclass creates its own leaders; it doesnt need your kind. The humble captains of mass action today are the generals of the armed insurrection of tomorrow.

GORDON (*passionately*): My God, cant you believe I didnt come here to lead but to learn? And one of the things I have learned from the *Manifesto* is that Marx did not aim to—I think I can remember the phrase—set up "sectarian principles by which to shape and mould the proletarian movement". He thought of Communists as people who pitched in to help half-starved workers get more food and win a decent parliamentary system!

PILSKY: Ah, but as immediate aims only! For what purpose?

GORDON: So that we may all lose our economic chains and win the world for peace and the brotherhood of man.

ROBERTS (*laughs drily and rises again*): That's all very eloquent, Mister Saunders. But it's the eloquence of Trotskyist fascism. Let me ask you a few questions about practical politics today. (*Rapidly, rapping it out*) First, are you on the side of the AFL and the ACCL and the other reactionary trade unions in Canada today? Or are you on the side of the new Red Trade Unions?

GORDON: I dont know much about it but I shouldnt think anything would be gained by setting up separate unions splitting the workers' ranks.

ROBERTS: Exactly. You are a Trotskyite. (*He smiles around at his flock.*)

GORDON (*genuinely astonished*): Am I? I didnt know.

ROBERTS: Second, do you maintain that the social-democrats, the war-mongering parliamentary socialists, still play a progressive role in the workingclass movement?

GORDON: Still? In Canada they *will*, I hope, when the workers come to understand them.

ROBERTS (*leading him on, eyebrows arched in sportive hate*): In Germany?

GORDON: Well, there perhaps they're underestimating the need to use force to stop Hitler's party now. But if they and the big Communist Party in Germany could, well—

ROBERTS: —could form a United Front?

GORDON: Yes! To defeat Hitler. Otherwise he'll ride in between them and smash them both, and everybody else.

ROBERTS (*looking confidently around once more*): That, comrades, is also treacherous Trotskyism. (*He assumes an oratorical stance*) As Comrade Stalin has tirelessly pointed out, the real enemy of the German workingclass is not fascism—in a few weeks the workers, under Communist leadership, will dispose of Schickelgruber forever —it's the *social*-fascists, the defectionist Social-Democratic Party, the pretended socialists, the *kulaks* and the petit-bourgeois pacifist traitors who are plotting to betray the workers' movement, hand it over hogtied to Hitler—just as this Trotskyite-imperialist teller of screwball bedtime stories is seeking to do. (*He sits again.*)

GORDON: No! No! Why do you want to drive me away from you, when we all have so much in common? You and I, all of us, surely we all want to make an end to this dreary succession of crises and depressions and unemployment and despotisms and war that we are sunk in; we all believe some form of international socialism might end them, whatever new problems of government it might create—

ROBERTS: Ah—what new problems?

GORDON: Well, good Lord, socialism wont produce angels. Even Russia has problems.

ROBERTS (*his dark eyes flashing—the lead-horse in a march-past*): The only problems that exist in the workers' state of Soviet Russia are those created by capitalist spies and white-guard saboteurs under the leadership of your friend Trotsky.

GORDON: O Lord, what drivel! Why always do you drag Trotsky in? I dont know anything about him, about his present role. But I dont believe Russia has either political freedom yet, or economic equality. She's building socialism, so far as I know, yes, but she's building a privileged bureaucracy of politicians too.

ROBERTS (*rises once more, speaking now in consciously ringing tones edged perhaps with a little genuine fanaticism*): Comrade Chairman, let us put an end to this farce. This bourgeois student did a very clever job of worming himself into our group to spread his White-Guard Trotskyite filth. But not clever enough. He is no Sergeant Leopold. None of us are taken in, and he has exposed himself with his own lying lips as a distorter of Marxism, a supporter of the social-fascists, a hater of the workingclass, and an agent of counter-revolutionary Trotskyism. I move that we expel him at once from our Club.

KAY: Seconded! (*There are shouts of agreement, a little embarrassed, from* PILSKY, SILVERS, *and* SMEETH. *The others preserve an intimidated silence, except*)

BAGSHAW: Shame! You cant—

WILF: It has been moved and—

GORDON: Dont bother, friends. (*He stands*) I dont want to stay. See some of you again perhaps—on the Island? (*He walks slowly out, as* WILF, *at a triumphant wave from* ROBERTS, *continues his putting of the motion.*)

9

WHEN HE CAME VAULTING UP THE BASEMENT STEPS, THE SOUR taste of unspent anger in his mouth, he was shocked by the fresh night on his face, as if he had dived into cold lake-water. The pavement was cottony with inches of dry new snow and the air, between the street lamps, alive with sifting flakes. He stopped, in childlike amazement; this had been going on all the time, this utterly alien and natural descending of snow, without regard for the dialectics of Marxism; and it would shimmer as unconcernedly down on the roadways of a Soviet Toronto, or on the ridged earth where Toronto had been.

Nevertheless, he was unable as yet to face the anti-climax of his college room and, turning up his collar, he began walking toward the fuzzed light of a coffee-shop on Bloor Street. I have escaped again. The lightning over the canyon. Or is this only flight? His hand brushed the scrambled papers of his commentary, still sticking from his overcoat pocket where he had thrust them; he pulled them out and, almost mechanically, tore the sheets into quarters, quartered them again, tossing the fragments into the air to fall with the endless falling of the flakes. My public.

But he had gone only a few yards when he heard a muffled voice behind, and turned. Someone, a girl, was padding after him, stopping only with strange anguished little cries to rescue from the snow-fluffed gutter the shreds of his allegory. It was Comrade Bagshaw.

"You shouldnt have done that." She came panting up to him, shoving back, with a distraught and ludicrous gesture of her arms, the strapbag of books which had fallen over her neck as she stooped in the ditch. "Did you keep a copy? I wanted to—" she stopped for a breath, clutching absurdly between podgy mittens a cold sundae of snow and smudged manuscript—"read it for myself." Her voice was still high and hesitant.

He began laughing, but the earnest upthrust of her snub nose somehow checked him. "I'll write you a better one sometime. Here, chuck it."

"O, will you?" Her naivety was evidently bone-deep, and yet he felt himself relaxing to it, felt bitterness dissolving. With a queer reluctant motion, as if she were casting flowers on a grave, she let her treasure drop back into the snow.

"Has the meeting broken up already?"

"No. I walked right out too." She peered at him through cotton-flecked glasses. "I wanted to catch you and tell you how sorry I am. I agree with everything you said. I'm just ashamed I—I didnt say so in there."

"But you did. You were my ally all along." It was foolish, he told himself, to encourage this puppy devotion; she was simply a ridiculous homely creature, friendless, romping out here in the snow to wag her tail at him. But he, too, at the moment was friendless. And cold.

"Let's get out of the weather. I'm going to have a coffee. Will you join me?"

"O yes!" Her eagerness was comic, and yet, as they walked on and she piped out her indignation at the course the meeting had taken, he wasn't sure she was so silly as she seemed.

"You're not really a Communist yourself then?" he asked, when they were sitting, warm at last, over coffees at a table-for-two in a Bloor Street cafeteria. "Why have you been in the club?"

She looked at him calmly through her round lenses. "I started coming with a boy when the term opened. But he quit college and went to Hamilton, to be a YCL Organizer. I—dont hear from him any more."

"YCL?"

"Young Communist League." Her pale eyebrows arched. "Sort of junior Party. Like being a Cub before you get to be a Boy Scout. Gee, you know so much I thought you'd know about that."

"Look," he said, "I dont know anything. Except that the rock's awash and I thought I wanted to swim somewhere." Waiting to drown. "Are most girls in the club because YCL boys bring them?"

"Of course." She sounded surprised that he should ask. "Sort of what they call Camp-travelers," she looked uncertain, "or is it Camp-followers? That's why they're kind of—" she gave him a quirky smile—"quiet. Like me—" she put out the tip of her tongue—"until tonight." If she were a pretty woman, he thought, her naiveties could be captivating. *That of her smyling was ful simple and coy.* "Not Kay, though," she added suddenly.

"What's eating Kay?"

She glanced sidelong at him in a way which, for her, was almost sly. "You wont tell anybody?" He shook his head, resignedly. "Well, she's really *in* the YCL—she joined after she flunked out in Ec. last year—and she's got a crush on Roberts."

"Roberts!" Of course. Eternally refusing to see. *I am the only baby—*

"O yes. He's the Big Noise, of course." She had a way of pronouncing certain words so that they began to write themselves in his mind with initial capitals. "I guess he's the only real Party Member who ever attends the club, and he never comes except, well, on nights like tonight—to make sure things are going the right way. Kind of like Al Capone."

"He made sure all right."

"Yes—except he lost two members." She gave him a look a little too comradely for comfort. "Anyway, he has a wife who's a Party Member too, and they say she was even in Jail. Kind of a heroine. But she's a bit old now, and he's giving Kay a whirl."

"I thought Wilf—"

"O, I think she just sleeps with Wilf enough to keep him interested."

He choked on a mouthful of coffee, but Bagshaw regarded him as sedately as if she were explaining invisible mending. "You see he's still only in the YCL though he's old enough to graduate into the Party. But they dont think he's Party Material. He knows all the long words but he *is* kind of a Rabbit, dont you think? And Rabbits, well they couldnt swim far enough to make your island, could they? Anyway they just use him for club-chairman and Joe-jobs. He sort of hero-worships Roberts so maybe it wouldnt matter what Kay did, he'd hang on."

"I see. Tell me," he said, his voice taking on the tone of a respectful student to a professor, "what is the explanation for the, wouldnt you say, rather precipitate training of the big guns on me tonight?"

She looked indignant all over again. "Because they're awful fools! I think Roberts really decided you're a Trotsky Agent. And Kay and the rest are just too scaredy-cat not to follow his lead. Anyway, she flunked out of Economics last year."

Suddenly she put down her cup. Her eyes, remote behind thick lenses, seemed half-hopeful, half-fearful. "You're not a Trotsky Agent, are you?"

"Good God," he said, suddenly impatient, "I'm nobody's agent, not even my own. Why should Roberts think—?"

She giggled. "I didn't really believe you were. I guess maybe you were just a Straw-horse." He looked blank. "Or is it a Straw-man, in—?"

"In the wind?"

"O you know what I mean. After all, if he could make everybody think you were a Trotskyite he'd get the credit back in the Party for showing you up early, and the same time he's educating the Club against—well, against Trotskyism."

"Then there *are* Trotskyites?"

She seemed amazed and then delighted by the implication of the question. "I never thought—maybe there *arent*. I never saw one. But they have to *have* Trotskyites, dont they?" she argued vaguely.

"Who have to have?"

"The Communists. They must have *somebody* who's leading the Counter-Revolution against them."

"But if they cant find real ones to show up?"

"They invent you!" She clapped her hands.

"Seriously though, I'd like to meet one now. And there *is* at least one in Toronto," he told her.

"But maybe he's only one like you are," she said, "somebody to blame for everything that goes wrong, and give them all the ideas they dont want people to have. It's like I said, a Stalking-Horse."

He sighed paternally. "Yes. It's like you said."

"Also," she went on softly, "Roberts was down on you from the first, I bet. He'd be afraid you were Interested in Kay."

"Me!" He was getting dizzy trying to keep up with her. "Look,

I only met this bunch three weeks ago. It's true Roberts was always stand-offish but, till tonight, Kay's been, well, very friendly. Though I swear I never made a pass at her." Liar. But it was she who tried to—

She shot him a happy little smile. "I'm so glad. But then of course," she went on thoughtfully, "if you didnt and she made one at you and it, well, didnt come off, that might explain why she turned on you tonight, mightnt it?"

"It might," he said, casting her a glance of almost fearful respect.

"Hell hath no scorn, or something like that." Her glasses flashed enigmatically. "Anyway she'd be afraid Roberts would stop her getting into the Party unless she proved she could get tough with you when you werent taking a Correct Line." She pursed her little fat lips wisely. "I knew something was going on right from the start because from where I sat I could see she was watching Roberts' face and when he looked sort of Thumbs-Down on your allegory, that's when she—"

"Speared the slave."

"Yes! O, you're making fun of me."

He reassured her. "It's just that I'm lightheaded after all that ponderous nonsense tonight, or maybe emptyheaded. This afternoon I thought I was practically being drawn into the brotherhood of the world revolution. And now I'm nothing again, not even a Trotskyite." No brother he, no father either. Someday, my darling, you will—She never writes.

"Yes," she said, "we're both kind of starting from the Scratch-Post again. But of course we wont be able to just lapse behind."

"What? We wont what?"

She picked up her cup in both hands. "I mean we'll have to find another political Channel for our Needs. Because, well, naturally our Conflicts wont let us stop." She peered at him over the cup-rim.

"No?" '

She set the cup down and shook her head. "Not yours, anyway. Not with all those falling towers, and having to swim—and—and—statues with blank faces."

He stared at her, beginning to see a glimmer. "You mean you've got me psyched?"

She returned his gaze modestly. "Well, only a bit yet, of course. But I take Psychology 402."

"Is there anything," he asked, fascinated, "you dont take?"

"Of course, silly. But I'm going to be a Social Worker, and Psychology 402 is a Prerequisite. It's Abnormal, you know."

"O, not necessarily," he said hurriedly.

"I mean it's Abnormal Psychology. So naturally it brings in Writers—"

"Ah? Naturally. Go on."

"—and Artists, and it shows how they betray their Unconscious Needs in their choice of Symbols, just like everybody does in Dreams, and since what you wrote was really a Dream too it, well, it made it easier to analyze because you'd really done a lot of the work for me."

"I—I see. Dont stop." That gull was a magpie.

She shook her head. "I was just getting my breath. Well, to begin with, you have very great Native Endowments—O yes, you have—and they create a Need for you to influence others and to—to Fulfill yourself. It's your Ego. Like water wants to rise above its level, isnt it? But because you've been Economically Blocked you've developed Doubts, and Fears of Failing. And then"—she blushed faintly—"well, we all have to Substitute our Sex Urges. Or is it Sublimate? And this kind of turned your Libido inwards for a while, if you know what I mean."

"I'll be damned," he said, surprised, "if I dont think I do." He toyed with his spoon. *I have measured out my life with coffee spoons.*

"Well," she said shyly, "I'm not doing it as well as Professor MacGillicuddy could, but anyway, now you've started turning Outwards, which is Healthier, though maybe you still feel a good deal alone. Then of course there's your Guilt Complex," she added simply, as if that had been taken for granted all along.

"Have I got one?" he asked startled.

"You must have." It was as if they were discussing his colon. "That's what I was talking about at the start. It's what makes people go into Self-Sacrificing Movements. Like Communism or—

or nunneries perhaps. It makes you want to hurt yourself. It's your Super-Ego that grew too big."

Man of Sin!

"Have you a Guilt-Complex too?" He found himself speaking with capital letters now.

"O yes. I got mine because when I was twelve my mother caught scarlet fever from me and died."

"I'm sorry," he said. "But doesnt it go away when you find out what caused it?"

"Well, Our Textbook says it doesnt always, but I've forgotten just why now. Maybe you get to *like* having it. Like a Pimple— only that's not big enough."

"Well, I havent enjoyed squeezing mine." But he was aware that she was more serious than he now dared be, and that in her childish maze was a thread he would not pick up.

"So?" She looked at him.

"So it looks as if I'm not going to be joining any of the new orders, the political Friars."

"O you will," she said placidly, "after you've had a Rest from tonight. Everybody in Politics has to have Rests every so often. Just like you pulled up on that Rock. But you cant stay for always. It's too late. O that reminds me," her chubby face lit with pleasure of her sudden thought, "have you seen a wonderful book of poems called *New Signatures,* from England?"

Gordon had to confess he hadnt, though he'd heard of it.

"You should," she said. "There's a poem that begins 'Oh young men, my comrades, it is too late now to stay in those houses your fathers sold'. It's by somebody called W. H. Stephen —or is it W. H. Spender? I'll lend it to you."

"Thanks," he said, "I hope you do. But tell me, are *you* going to have a Rest now too?"

She put her hands together and regarded the table, considering this, and then looked up. "No, I really *have* been Resting, ever since Nathan—that's the boy who went to Hamilton—left. I've just been going and listening and, well, kind of adding up my Doubts. Now I *know* I couldnt even be a YCLer. I'm just a Social-Fascist Type after all, sort of peace-loving. Like Mrs. Sidney Webb or, or Florence Nightingale. So—" she nodded her head as if at that moment reaching a decision—"I'm going to see Professor Cathcart, you know, the one who gives Social Economics 372. He has a private group too that meets in his house informally every week to discuss Evolutionary Socialism. That's like the British Labour Party, only, well, faster. And it brings in the Alberta cowboys too. He asked me once to come."

"I think that's a very good idea."

She broke into smiles. "You'll come too? They're studying Cole now, you know, G. D. Something."

"I meant—for you," he said hastily. "No, I think I'll—just stick on my rock for a while."

She offered him a long and unfathomable look. "Well, when you decide to start Swimming again, if you'd like to try my way, I hope you wont hesitate letting me know because of any— Personal Reasons."

He searched her flat, earnest face but could not be sure what she meant. "Personal?"

She gave a small, dignified tilt to her head. "I mean that anytime you want to try this other club, dont stay away because you're afraid I'd be expecting you to Go To Bed with me. 'Cause I'm not."

On an impulse he reached over and took her primly clasped hands in his. This is no Joan. "I think," he said quickly, "you're the thoughtfullest infant I've met in all my days and if I ever dip my feet in political waters again I'll consult you first. Where do you live?"

"Annesley Hall," she said with a little sigh. "I'm a Victoria College Type. And it's time I got in before the door is locked."

"I'll walk you over. But before we go—what's wrong with the Communists?"

He expected an answer from Psychology 402, but she surprised him with a question. "Did you notice the banner there tonight, the one left over from Sunday School?"

"Suffer little children?" Always the children.

She nodded. "I kept thinking it was a pity it couldnt say anything to them."

"I'd thought it had a certain ironical aptness." Yes, always—

"I mean," she said, "they have a Religion without any, well,

Ethics. Like having a Longer Catechism and no Bible. Or is it a Shorter? Not that they *ought* to be Christians. After all there are more Buddhists than anybody else, or maybe Mohammedans, arent there?"

"I suppose so." He was beginning to lose track again.

"It's like if I were to spend all my time becoming a Woman Wrestling Champion," she prattled on earnestly, "and then at forty expected to be a Great Pianist." She gathered up her coat.

"That," he said, helping her on with it, "I do *not* follow."

"I mean they start off to make the world better but they make themselves worse trying, and so even if they get on top they cant do much to Improve people because, well, they're so in the habit of being Unimproved themselves."

"Ah," he said, "I think I've caught up. They've forbidden the little children?" So have you, so have you. Awaaag—away!

"O you do understand," she said gratefully, picking up her strapbag of books, "but of course maybe I'm prejudiced, because, well, Nathan says I'm pretty childish myself."

"You!" he said. "I'm going to take you home before I start calling you Mother."

They came out into a Christmas-card world; the feathery snow had ended its falling and rested now, an airy and sugary icing, over the hushed trees, the bowing telephone wires, and the improbable Tudor of Trinity College. It seemed exactly the right setting through which to be walking Comrade Bagshaw home.

10

IT WAS ALMOST A WEEK LATER WHEN GORDON SAUNDERS, COMING past the dormitory letter-rack on his way to breakfast, saw his name on an envelope. It was postmarked Salt Lake City and he snatched it from the rack. It was only Oscar. He opened the envelope and began reading as he walked into the draughty dininghall. But he did not sit down to breakfast.

29 November, 1932

Sir and Quondam Colleague,

There is a centre-forward in the Freshman team this year who believes, though by now I may have persuaded him to the contrary, that Shakespeare is a contemporary American author. No, "contemporary" was not the sticker because I had defined the word to the class in terms that even a centre-forward understood. It was simply that his highschool teacher up in Panther Creek had not found it necessary to warn him about Shakespeare, and he had associated the rather odd name with a billboard now on the campus advertising the advent of the touring Stratford-on-Avon Players. I think I will pass him, for he has obviously an observant and retentive mind, and a sense of time which can be easily defended. What after all is more contemporary than a billboard?

But your pardon, friend, you asked for news. What budget I can assemble, as I pause for an anaesthetizing if fattening beer between themes (I now ration myself to a pint every five freshman essays, or seven sophomore, and am holding the line at 210 pounds) is neither fat nor soothing, particularly to send a man who suffers unaccountable Heimweh for the funereal mountains of Deseret.

Weather: It is cold enough this morning to force me into heavies and it is ten above nothing tonight, with the usual wind off the salt-flats. There is widespread discomfort even among brass monkies.

Deaths: Yesterday there was a rather sudden one, which may distress you. Anne Barton, after a few days of some kind of blood poisoning, died in hospital. There is mystery about the matter and campus gossip of an abortion that went wrong, but until the story reaches the papers or the courts I must infer either that it is not true or that a doctor of more power than skill is involved. Personally I should be at a loss to find a motive. Granted that, having given birth to two such guppies as the Barton smallfry, one would take thought before conceiving a third. But, conception begun, an abortion would be for me, and I think, sir, for you, a gesture more painful and less discreet than letting nature take her brattish way. But then we are not women. A happy thought. Unless of course—but even Miss Clutts of Household Ec, who was the loudest whisperer in the campus coffee-shop today, does not suggest that the tragic flaw was any other than an illegitimate desire to limit a quite legitimate family. She feels, of course, that it is a judgment on poor Professor Barton for not having married within the Saints. I rather fancy she hopes soon to help him correct that error . . . Anyway, that is the most sobering piece of intelligence I have for you. A pity. She was good to look upon and seemed a warmhearted wench, though I didnt know her as well as, perhaps, you did.

What else? *Scholarship*. The Head of Geology is circulating autographed offprints of an item he published in one of the learned journals, on the stratifications of the Uinta Mountains, with dating. There is a footnote on page one, however, explaining that the dates were computed in deference to current scientific theory and that, according to the *Book of Mormon*, all strata continue to be of the vintage 4004 B.C.

Economics: Even in the polar fastnesses of Toronto you have probably heard that our depression continues. How is yours? I see Canadian wheat being quoted at 38c; if my memory is right, it was around $1.60 three years ago. We Americans are refusing to pay Mr. Hoover's board after Christmas, and even Utah has gone Democrat, but so far I have not noticed any effect on my salary. The ullulations of the university's Regents grow louder as dividends shrink—it becomes plain that their financial crisis was not solved by your escape to Canada; the rest of us in the English department simply teach more students, having absorbed your sections. We walk around muttering prayers to the new Saint Roosevelt, who is going to fix everything, come New Year's. He has a stout Dutch name, and got all the Van Bome vote. And now that Congress seems about to pass 3.2 per cent beer, my faith in the Republic is reviving.

I think from what you say about Toronto that you had better wander back here. Seriously, Crump does not bear you any ill-will; perhaps he is a forgiving sort, or he may even have a conscience. And I gather you sent him some sort of verbal ointment. At any rate he inquired gravely and paternally about you in the hall last week. Despatch him at once a Yule card, with sleighs and French-Canadian red-toqued trappers and a noble message; and express the hope at the bottom that you will see him next year.

I continue to hold the bachelor fort you have deserted, though recently I have been making the odd sortie into the heterosexual plains, where I sit down and play a rubber or two of conservative but not unprofitable bridge. Somewhat in this connection, I have been seeing a little of Joan Krautmann. She asked me to tell you, when I wrote, that she hopes you are well. I have pointed out that you would assume she hoped so, but women apparently attach importance to the transmission of optative phrases. I think, by the way, that you have underrated the lady; it is true that she has a name like something out of Ben Hecht, and she will never be Utah's Sugar Beet Queen, but the name can be changed, and her bridge is practically adult.

I have the honor, sir, to be etc.

Oscar

P.S. I note, in your own postscript, that you have encountered a girl in a leather-jacket who is teaching you Marx. I hope the lessons prove profitable, but I could have wished for you, sir, as I continue to wish for myself, that you might meet a girl in a mink cape who would teach you Veblen.

O.

11

MANITOBA FARMERS
KIDNAP REEVE, BURN
TAX RECORDS

WORLD WITHOUT PRICES,
DEBTS OR WAGES COMING

**Technocrats Say Only
People 25-45 Will Work**

HUNGER MARCHERS
IN WASHINGTON

TOGETHER!
THE
  LOVERS
    INCOMPARABLE
Clark GABLE—Jean HARLOW
IN
RED DUST
NOTE: This is not a film about
communists.

BRITAIN TO ABOLISH
SLUMS BY PAYING
BUILDING SUBSIDY

Chaco Territory, Bolivia, Dec.
10 (UP)—Attacking with bay-
onets and machetes, Bolivian
troops today dislodged besieging
Paraguayan forces at Kilometer
7 in the Fort Saavedra sector
in one of the most desperate
battles of the Gran Chaco war-
fare.

MAPLE LEAFS SMASH
OTTAWA 4-1

---

*WINTRY BLASTS SHOULD
REMIND YOU OF CITY'S
POOR: GIVE NOW TO
HERALD'S HARK-
THE-ANGEL
FUND*

**Prosperity Returning With
Beer, U.S. Wets Believe**

**Brewerymen Planning to
Spend $360,000,000 and Pay
As Much More in Taxes
When Sales Begin**

JAPS DEMAND
BIGGER NAVY

RUSSIANS BUILDING
GREATER NATION DESPITE
SETBACKS SAYS WALTER
DURANTY

POLICE FIRE ON
STRIKE MOB
AFTER MINE LOCKOUT

12

THE OVOID BULK OF MRS. BARSTOW ROLLED FROM THE KITCHEN coal-range. First she lowered the coffee pot to the oilclothed table where her two darlings sat, and then her own two hundred and eighty pounds into the armchair at the table's head.

Thelma, beautiful Thelma, with her hair in curlers and her dressing-gown awry, raised her innocent eyes subtly from her porridge. "Mom, is it all right if I ask a professor for dinner tonight?"

"A professor!" Jack, roguish Jack, whose hair curled naturally, laid down his spoon and looked satisfactorily astonished. "You mean the one we met last night?"

"Yes," said Thelma, smug and strokable as a kitten.

"He's no professor, he's just a teaching-fellow."

"He is not!" Her teeth flashed, such white and even little teeth. "That's what he is here but he was a professor in a big American university." She spoke with the exaggerated but rather amusing indignation of the fifteen-year-old. As it happened, she was twenty.

Jack gave his special older-brother groan and wrinkled a nose as bland and straight as any nose in a shirt ad. For a moment he too looked barely sixteen. He was, however, twenty-two. "You're blowing it up as usual. He just said he was an instructor in some cow-college in the Rockies. You—"

"Pull-leeze," said Mrs. Barstow in her great sighing contented male voice, reluctantly halting the work of her own spoon. "I suppose you ast him already."

"Well, kind of."

"Then he's comin. Dont forget Leo is too—"

"And Ronnie and Bobbie and Hymie," Jack chanted. "The Sunday night suitors, faithful and unrewarded. It's like the *Odyssey*—without Ulysses."

"So long we got enough food." Mrs. Barstow sighed placidly. "Lucky, Uncle Harry come by last night." Uncle Harry was Mrs. Barstow's cunning brother, cunning and generous brother, who worked as a shipper in a local meat packer's and found ways, so far undetected, of helping his relatives. "We got a nice ham."

"What's wrong with Leo—and the others?" Thelma pulled her dressing-gown over a creamy shoulder and went over to the offensive.

"Did I say there was anything—?"

"They're all nice boys," Mrs. Barstow murmured vaguely. "Even if they *are* comrades."

"Leo's no boy," Jack said.

"That's why they *are* nice," Thelma said stoutly.

"Mebbe." Mrs. Barstow poured herself coffee. "I suppose this perfesser's one?"

"No," said Jack.

"He is too," Thelma flashed.

"He's a political muddlehead."

"Last night you thought he was terrific. Now you dont like him. You're just mad because I had the gumption to ask him here and you didnt."

"Look, I do like him. He's an honest dope and he sees through the Stalinites. Also he's got brains and college degrees and if we could make a Bolshevik-Leninist out of him he'd really be a shot in the arm for the League. But if you get your hooks into him first he'll just be another scalp-lock hanging around that scrawny virginal neck of yours." He helped himself to bacon.

Furiously Thelma pulled her dressing gown back on her soft shoulder; it had slipped off again. "My neck is *not* scrawny," she shouted.

"Shush up." Mrs. Barstow brought her fat paw down on the tabletop. "Both of yuh." Her great bosom shook. "Virginal! A nice man dont talk to his sister like that." She sounded shocked, but then she had the faculty of being easily and lustily shocked, where matters of sex were concerned. "Your sister's gonna stay single a long time yet," she said fondly. "All her life if she wants to. I wish I had. Pass up the bacon."

"But then," said Jack reasonably, passing it, "you couldnt have had us."

Mrs. Barstow helped herself generously. "I wouldnt have had *him,* either." She cast her eyes, once as big and blue as her daughter's, eloquently at the ceiling, and her face, so far as it was capable of it, hardened. Mr. Barstow, the only other member of the family, did not go to work on Sundays, being a postman, and had not yet appeared from his separate attic room. She took up her knife and fork as if for murderous intent but fell only with rippling bosom upon the bacon strips. "You take alla time you want to look em over," she resumed, serene again, "'cause if you do marry it's gotta be some good Christian man who'll take me in when you-know-who has drunk hisself to death. Have some bacon."

"I wouldnt marry anyone who wasnt an active comrade." Thelma suddenly contrived to look prim as a March snow-drop. "Just coffee, Mom."

"That's all right so long as he dont get into any trouble," Mrs. Barstow rumbled vaguely, filling her daughter's cup.

Jack groaned again. "He's got to be a bourgeois, a Methodist, and a Bolshevik-Leninist all in one."

"Why not?" Mrs. Barstow raised a round earnest face and regarded her son stolidly. "That's what I am." She spoke a form of truth. "And in two years we'll be burying *him*." She tilted a ham-shoulder wearily at the ceiling.

"Dont worry, Mom," said Jack, in the effortless voice of an actor running over a well-known part in the wings, "we'll look after you." It had indeed become that sort of conversational drama which families tend to invent for their own torture and entertainment and which they rehearse with variations over the years without ever achieving a public performance.

Mrs. Barstow came in on cue: "Who's we? I dont want Thelma goin out workin for me. And anytime the bank finds out about your politics you aint gonna have a job either."

"So what. I'll be turfed out with the next staff-cut anyway. They're throwing out ledger-keepers right and left."

"Sure"—it was Thelma's turn—"you know there's no future under Capitalism, Mom. I'll be glad when he loses that job and then he can work full time for the League. I bet our Trotskyists could pay him as much as the bank."

"Yeah." Mrs. Barstow reached for the toast. "And how much is that? I gotta go and humble myself to *him* to get the money to buy you two clothes still."

"Maybe I'll get a job with real money," Jack came in. "Maybe Sarah will—"

"Sarah," his sister interrupted, switching roles in the wink of an eye, "she'll only help if you turn bourgeois."

"That's what you think," Jack said haughtily. "For all you know I might make a Bolshevik out of her and bring the League a fortune. Dont I get coffee?"

"Her? A Bolshevik?" Thelma shrieked. "That big dumb Junior Leaguer? You've been going with her six months and she still buys the *Reader's Digest*."

"She does not!"

"She does too, and she believes in the Oxford Group."

"That's enough," Mrs. Barstow passed her son's cup. "Sarah's a nice girl. She dont drink or smoke. And you oughtnt to talk like that, Thelma, she might be your sister-in-law some day."

"Good-bye to another Bolshevik-Leninist then. She'll convert him to Technocracy or something, you watch. O, why does everybody always have to talk about marrying! I dont think revolutionaries ought to marry ever."

"Thelma!" said Mrs. Barstow reprovingly.

"Ah, ha! Free love!" Jack smacked his lips.

"Jack!" His mother was so agitated she set down her toast.

"I dont mean that at all!" Thelma, beautiful Thelma blushed. Then her eyes began to take on a dedicated look. "Rosa—"

"Dont tell me!" her brother cut in, clapping his hands to his curly head. "I know it by heart. Rosa Luxembourg didnt marry except to get a passport and she was the greatest woman revolutionary. She just had a Platonic friendship with Karl Liebknecht —yeah! Only I dont think Saunders is the Platonic type."

"O, Mom, make him shut *up*!" Thelma reverted, as she easily could, to a plaintiveness that had been even more piquant in girlhood. "I'm not interested in him or anybody except as a *convert*, and that's why I asked him here today, so you and Leo and the others can *work* on him. And if you'd had any intelligence, smarty, you'd have asked him here yourself."

"I did," he said calmly. "Last night."

"You—you did! At the party?"

"Sure. He told me you'd already asked him."

"Then you knew all along—"

"I was just watching how you explained it all to mom." Roguish, roguish.

"O," she said passionately, "I hate you." She sounded almost as if she did. She stirred the sugar in her cup with her long tapering fingers and whanged down the spoon. "I'm twenty— and you're still trying to make me look ridiculous and—and you even shadow me around when I go to a party!"

"Now, now, you two," Mrs. Barstow murmured. She had really let her attention slip while pursuing and crunching the last curlicue of bacon-rind on her plate.

"I shadow you! You just tagged along."

Thelma tossed her head, forgetting her curling pins, which rattled. "It's just like Leo said, you've got some kind of Orestes Complex about me."

"A *what*? Leo said that? I bet you dont even know what that means."

"I do so, you smug—"

"Shush." Mrs. Barstow, spreading jam on her fourth piece of toast, looked amiably at her children. "What kina party was this?"

"Just one of those pinko bunfights," Jack said. "Not even beer, if that's what you mean. At Cathcart's. He's an economics prof mixed up with the League for Social Reconstruction and the new social-reformist outfit, the C.C.F. He's got some kind of student club that meets in his home and they threw an open-house. I met Cathcart's daughter at the Labour Rally last week— she's somewhere Left of her old man—and she asked me to drop in and bring a girl. I dont think she knew I was a Trotskyist."

"She does now, I bet." Mrs. Barstow stirred more sugar in her coffee.

"Yeah, I made the mistake of taking little Bigmouth along."

"O it was wonderful, Mom!" Thelma, suddenly enthusiastic, ignored the insult. "Gordon, that's Mr. Saunders, was fairly new there too and he was telling some of us about being bounced by the so-called Social Problems Club the Stalinites have down on the campus. Can you imagine? They threw him out for being a Trotskyist and he told us he'd never met a Trotskyist and he was still looking for one but he'd come to wonder if they really existed!"

"Sometimes I wonder too," said Mrs. Barstow.

"Wait, Mom. And then I said, 'Well I'm one and I exist!' and I dragged him over to Jack and we worked on him the rest of the evening. Why, he's practically a convert already."

"Convert to Thelmaism," said Jack.

"That's not true. He listened to you more than to anybody."

"Yeah, but dont forget the Stalinites have him soured on all Marxists. Also he's full of idealistic bushwah. He's still sucker-bait for social-democracy."

"We'll fix that. Wait till Leo's had a workout on him." Thelma's baby eyes glowed with anticipation.

"Sure," said Mrs. Barstow, as if all this had been irrelevant. "Is he a nice boy?"

"Boy!" said Jack. "I'll bet he's thirty."

"He's only twenty-eight. I asked him."

"You would."

"And he's a Master of Arts already."

"O.K., O.K. . . . So he's tall and handsome, Mom, with real shoulders, and he thinks Thelma's the most wonderful woman he's ever met."

"I dont think he's so handsome." Thelma pointed her nose in the manner of Myrna Loy. "Anyway, he was there with a girl."

"That frump with the glasses and a voice like Baby Snooks? Bagshott or somebody? She couldnt get within five feet after you'd shone those goo-goo eyes on him."

"It dont matter," said Mrs. Barstow, pursuing her own slow thoughts, "if he aint goodlookin so long as he dont drink. All that beer in the States now. On purpose to dope the workin-class."

"Well," said Jack, "I doubt he's a Methodist. Still," he grew speculative, "he's an odd fish. I dont think he's very happy—kind of restless and haunted-looking. Got eyes like a scared deer."

"He's just had a bereavement," Thelma said solemnly. "He

wouldnt say much about it except it was a very close relative and her child both, and it was very sudden."

"That so?" said Jack. "He sure took his hair down for you. But anyway, I dont think he knows what he wants to do."

"He told me," Thelma spoke defensively, "that there's nothing that he wants to do more than dedicate his life to the good of society. And that he longs for action, for *intelligent* action. And O, he quoted a wonderful poem for me, something about always thinking of those who were truly great and—and making trips to the stars or something."

"Yeah, that's what I mean. The guy's neurotic."

"Well, maybe if you were more neurotic," Thelma burst out, "you'd spend more time in party work and less running around with—with girls whose fathers are exploiters of the workingclass, and—"

"Nuts!" Now Jack was angry. "I spend my time working for a living, while you sit home and moon over Rosa Luxembourg, when you ought to be boning for that Matric supp you havent written off. Twenty and still not graduated from high school! When are *you* going to join the workingclass?"

"O you—!"

"Shush—here he comes!" Mrs. Barstow began heaving her soft mass out of the chair. As the flip-flop of Mr. Barstow's slippers came sounding down the staircase, Jack rose automatically and slid into the livingroom out of sight. Round Mrs. Barstow went proudly, pot in hand, to the stove and poured fresh water onto the coffee grounds.

"I heard you, I heard you." Mr. Barstow's tremulous and jeering voice preceded him into the kitchen. "Rosa-Luxembourg and join-the-workin-class and here-he-comes. Jabber, jabber, jabber. Fight, fight, fight. Marxy-barksy-Trotsky-snotsky. Aint you made that World Revolution yet? No blood on the streets this mornin?"

He came shuffling into the kitchen, a thin small bald man with a pair of baggy trousers, their fly unbuttoned, hauled over his winter-underwear. His head seemed cocked permanently at the floor but the little green marbles of his eyes, with their rosetinted corners, flickered and darted through the kitchen and up over the great round body and the little round face of his wife. Her eyes, sunk in fat, cold and unwavering with hate, stared back at him from their fort of flesh.

"Lo, Dad," said Thelma calmly, and went on sipping, with Cupid lips, her coffee.

13

IT ASTONISHED GORDON, WHENEVER IN LATER YEARS HE TRIED TO
send his memory back over that first supper at the Barstows, and
the long fateful evening of talk that followed, how little of it he
could with any fidelity recall.

He must have ridden an hour at least, on two changes of draughty
streetcar, out to the far windy edge of that depressing and depressed
suburb. But he would not have been aware, that first time, of the
rows of sagging verandahs and the squat façades of liverish brick,
for it was already late in a dark December day, the houses dimly
snowmantled and blurred in the frugal streetlighting. He could
remember only that he had, until the moment he was fumbling
for the first icy step on the Barstow porch, been on the point of
doubling back, of jumping from the car at its every halt, or wheeling in his steps in the destined street itself, and running, taking the
road back, even though it could lead only to his private hell, the
room of his self-torture in the Sunday-deserted dormitory.

Had it been a fear of being caught, this time perhaps irretriev-
ably, in yet another dubious and even more sinister dance of
politics? Scarcely—for surely he had been impelled toward that
evening by the anguished conviction that he could atone for his
manifold crimes, more real again in his mind than all the little
Bagshaws of his world, only by abandoning the role of watcher,
and whirling, to the end of his strength, in the wildest dance that
would have him.

No, the dilemma was only that for dancing he needed a partner,
and feared what he would do to her. Had not his guilt been visited
invariably upon those whom he chose, out of sheer physical greed,
to step mirror-fashion with him? And whom he then abandoned?
Had not the worst of his deeds, the Sin against Life itself, been
the murder (for he had come now to feel it was nothing less) of
the one woman for whom he had ever declared a love, and of her
own child, which was also, for all he would ever know, his child?

And what were those wronged ghosts saying to him? Saying, undoubtedly, that he was rushing to drive them from his mind less than a month after their deaths, at the first smile of the next pretty girl. The wistful voice of Anne echoed in him more urgently; some day you must do great things; for it is the only way you can provide dignity and meaning now for the sacrifice you made of me, of me and my children, our children! But, he told himself, she knows, she can see, that there's no career for me in the old world that was already crumbling around us, nothing for me by Toronto's flat fouled lakeshore nor, even if I could face it, in the mountain-ringed valley where once we moved as secret lovers. Greatness is hidden away, he told the accusing phantoms; somewhere the measures of it are being rehearsed by just such serious youthful dancers as I met last night; would you have me avoid them because I am not worthy of a partner, and yet you would have me dance? Your own dancing is ended, my poor lover.—Ah, and who ended it? It would have been that question, in the staring eyes of the listeners he had conjured, which kept him on the point of flight until the moment he walked up the Barstow steps.

But then the porch light flashed, the door opened, and improbably out from that dingy frame stepped Thelma, a smiling green-frocked reality, Thelma, stretching out to him, as he mounted, her soft living arm.

They would have sat down to supper in a room just big enough for the table and themselves—there must have been eight of them. The cloth would certainly have been frayed and none too white, and the blotched wallpaper relieved only by thumb-tacked prints, banal and overcolored, salvaged from calendars. But such things, if he noticed them at all that first night, only intensified the strange ardor that took possession of him, and that now began to still, for the first time, those silent images of guilt and loss which, from the moment of Van Bome's letter, had been rising and turning relentlessly within him like floating corpses in a tidepool.

What heartened him, at the beginning, was perhaps simply and absurdly that he was once again, after what seemed too long an absence, in somebody's home. Moreover, it was a real workingclass home, he told himself, innocent of phony proletarianism, and containing, because its inhabitants were also alive with intelligence and vigorous with purpose, the seeds of that power which, he had already come to believe, might quicken the whole torpid world.

For it was not only the glowing presence of Thelma on one side of him, and her gay-hearted brother competing flatteringly for his attention on the other. It was also their extraordinary parent, who sat almost in and filling the kitchen doorway at the table's other end, huge and serene as a Buddha in a niche, yet with a little Picasso dollface from which her eyes peered with a blue almost as intense as her daughter's. From her shoulders her flesh billowed down through arms that began like thighs and tapered into surprisingly small hands, nimble hands that served great slices of whatever it had been—ham, perhaps, and probably undercooked—from a platter as oval as herself and washed almost beyond her reach by the tremendous tide of her own bosom. A veritable Earth Mother she had seemed to him that first night, saying little, but what she said folkwise, gentle, practical. Even the fact that she made no pretensions to grammar was, in the mood of the evening, a charming proof of her authenticity.

And if any speculation flickered in his mind, looking at her, as to what the years were plotting for the Aphrodite body of her daughter, he would certainly have suppressed it at once; it would have been as disloyal and trivial a thought as to have wondered why Jack did not carve (one simply did not think of that shining-faced youth as the head of the house, and there was evidently no Mr. Barstow) or why Mrs. Barstow did all the fetching and carrying and—later—the washing-up.

But above all, of course, it was Sather who had set a spell on him, Sather, the protean and inimitable leader of the group and, as he began to realize before the evening was over, of the whole Trotskyist movement in Canada, whatever its size—it was not defined and Gordon was not brash enough to ask. Sather sat on Mrs. Barstow's right, a man in his early thirties who, for all that he wore the usual funerary suit and white shirt of the Toronto male on Sundays, contrived somehow to give the effect of being raimented in a Jacob's coat of silks. He was a macaw, a glittering tropical bird; he even had a trick of listening like a bird, fork in right hand and the left clutching the table's edge as if it were a perch, one eye half-closed and the other cocked across his high keel of a nose. And when whoever had been speaking paused for breath or thought, he could, apparently at will, be silent or set down his fork and launch an addendum with such a dry knowing air that the conversation would be willingly surrendered to him like a tray of seeds to peck at. Then, when he had tired of it and nosed it back with one last comic squawk to his admirers, he would toss a dark glittering wing of hair from his forehead, and return to his fork.

An exhibitionist? Sather had not seemed so, then, but simply a man turned properly outwards. "I am," he told Gordon, "the kind of smalltime lawyer who takes on just enough business to keep alive, and saves his energies for politics. Being by chance a bachelor," he added with a lugubrious cock of his eye, "I have a fair amount of energy, at least, to donate to the capital cause."

It was a way of life Gordon was ready to respect; that night, he had also envied Sather. For here was surely a happy man, in full use of his powers, a man he was quite sure was neither haunted nor sex-ridden, a being at once subtle and bold, who would not easily be defeated and who was yet basically indifferent to what ever consequences, public or private, might result or had resulted from his actions; he knew what he wanted, and was being extremely shrewd in his efforts to obtain it; and above all he *believed*, in the goal and in the method. Quite apart from this, Gordon found himself, in common obviously with the whole group, caught up in impartial admiration when Sather would pass from retort to serious debate. His voice then would lose its macaw quality and take on a sonority, still perhaps half-jesting and yet compelling, resonant with the cadences of his synagogal training, and sharp with the convictions of his political faith.

So dominant indeed was Leo Sather's personality that it was not until after supper, when they were crowded in the tiny livingroom in unsparing and yet goodhumored argument, that Gordon began to separate the identities of the three other guests present, who seemed indeed not so much visitors as extensions of the family. He had begun by regarding them unconsciously with a jaundiced eye, for were they not all male, single and young—younger, that is, than he but older than Thelma—and quite obviously in pursuit of her? Yet as the talk grew he found himself warming all the more to the three, not only because Thelma inflicted on them equally a careful sisterly affection less encouraging by far than what he himself was receiving, but because they made no attempt to form a bloc against him. Instead, each seemed intent on friendliness and on a flexible and civilized exchange of ideas which, after his recent experiences, warmed him with an almost absurd gratitude.

Of the three, Ronnie Mandell had been the slowest to emerge for Gordon as a person. Sallow, slight, quiet, his round spectacles following the flittings of Thelma whenever she moved about the room, Ronnie had been drawn into the conversation only when Gordon had rather deliberately made some slighting remark about "proletarian literature". To his surprise, they had all leapt to agree with him, though for different reasons.

"Proletarian literature!" Sather's eyes brightened. "You mean those Little Elsie Books for Stalinist *Kinder*?" No true worker, he went on, could write one, nor would be seen dead reading one. Then he tossed the ball to Ronnie, "the only Trotskyist poet".

Ronnie, serious and a little stammery, protested that he tried verses just to let off "a little p-private steam. They're for myself and—" he glanced with unwitting obviousness at Thelma—"a few friends. Maybe, if I spent my life at it I could become a writer, if I didnt starve first, but all the time I'd be getting farther and farther away from the lives of most people, w-wage-earning people, and less able to write about them, wouldnt I? And," he went on less haltingly, with gentle honesty which somehow reconciled Gordon to his pedestrianism, "until the revolution I'd have to sell my books in a p-price-and-profit world and be conditioned by its values like anybody else."

They had indeed been not only cynical about contemporary art but indifferent to it. Gordon's feeling of shock at this was lessened, however, by their reasons, which, though he branded them Philistine, were actually, in a twisted way, idealistic.

"It's because we foresee," Sather said, "the absolute need to struggle wholeheartedly against gigantic destruction, in the years immediately ahead, that we are impatient, my dear Gordon. We must use only the most rapid and direct methods of swaying human minds. We're an in-between generation of little Davids, my friend, and we've got to occupy ourselves single-mindedly with our slingshots, because we have to bring down with them not only every looming Mussolini and Hitler, but every murderous Stalin. Otherwise, the Goliaths will reinherit the earth."

"But where the devil does the artist fit into all this?" Gordon asked.

"Our times can only make an artist by accident," Ronnie answered, "and even then by a kind of waste of a good revolutionary."

"Waste!"

"O yes," Ronnie went on, staring first at the carpet and then, with a kind of gentle intransigence, at Gordon. "I think a great writer could be quite good at other things; I dont think he's all that limited."

"Limited!" Gordon felt professionally outraged. He would not let this humorless youth shake his whole hierarchy of values.

"Rosa Luxembourg was a great writer too," Thelma said then.

Jack snorted and Ronnie skirted the remark tactfully. "P-political writer, yes."

"She didnt live in Canada in any case," Sather interjected. "Let us distinguish between Writing, which even Canadian college professors occasionally find time for, and Literature, which is carried on in other countries by persons who inherit money or marry it, or who die young."

"You just wait until we get a socialist state and literature and, and, everything will really blossom like never before," Thelma said eagerly, and Ronnie agreed.

"You dont mean," said Gordon dubiously, "as in Soviet Russia?"

"Ha!" Sather gave an explosive laugh. "Peace to the ghost of Mayakovsky."

"The Soviet poet?" Gordon asked.

"The only Russian poet since Pushkin. He had to become Stalin's court jester or stop writing. So he shot himself. Soviet art today is just another cement dam with statues of Commissars along the parapet and no water behind, you know that, Ronnie."

"O, but of course Thelma meant the *world* socialist state," Ronnie had amended calmly, and the others had nodded agreement. For all their warnings of disaster, they were capable of referring to global socialism as if it were something no more tricky to arrange than the election of a progressive mayor in Toronto. " 'They dream of the world state,' " Ronnie in fact suddenly now began quoting (and Gordon recognized with some astonishment that it was a poem by little Bagshaw's esoteric Stephen Spender), " 'with its towns like brain-centres and its pulsing arteries. No more are they haunted by the individual grief nor the crocodile tears of European genius, the decline of an era wept by scholars who dream of the ghosts of Greek boys.' "

"Can you guarantee we'll get that state?" Gordon had asked, after he had recovered from his somewhat envious surprise (since he himself had recently tried to memorize and had already forgotten the poem).

"O no," Ronnie said. "That's just why anyone who wants it ought to pitch in and work for it and forget about being an artist or anything else till we've got it."

"But that would mean sacrificing a whole generation of artists, even revolutionary poets like Spender himself, whom you've just been quoting, or W. H. Auden. If you break the precious tradition of art, it wont be so easy to bridge it again."

"There'll always be enough artists who dont agree with me, to carry on," Ronnie said, allowing himself a smile, "right through the revolution."

"It's true," another of the young men, dark, intense and hollow-cheeked, broke in. "But if too many people disagree with him, there'll be no revolution, there'll just be war again and again and again, because capitalism lives by it. There'll be war with more and more deadly weapons until we kill off the species, or revert to bushmen."

"Or at the best," Sather added, "lick our wounds under some kind of universal fascist-Stalinism."

"And then," Thelma rounded it off, "art will really stop."

Their logic was as full of holes as a gillnet and Gordon had seen the apertures even then. He thought of little Bagshaw—wrestlers expecting to emerge as pianists. And yet he had been drawn to them, to Ronnie especially, if for no other reasons than because this unpretentious youth had quoted with aptness and feeling a poem in Comrade Bagshaw's anthology, and because he could face the possible "common ruin of the contending classes".

But there was a profounder attraction. Deep and acknowledged within him must there not have been a curious self-destructive urge to accept this boy's negation of art? Gordon had always secretly thought of himself as an author, even perhaps an important writer, who had, through circumstances unfortunately beyond his control, not yet written. But could he? Could he bear the tortures of discipline and loneliness, could he risk the shame, if after all what he sweated out was rejected or, worse, printed and rightfully damned? And indeed, if he felt such qualms, was he by nature a writer at all? What, after all, had he achieved by his ponderous sermon to the Social Problems Club except the awakening of contempt and hatred in all whom he had most sought to convince?

It was many years before he came to acknowledge that there had been these divisions, wise or craven, within him, but when he did, he knew that they had been whispering within him that night, helping him to tolerate, and later to accept, the immolation of his own creative spirit.

Yet on the surface he gave battle, and none too fairly. "You're some kind of inverted aesthete," he told Ronnie. "It's only the over-protected child who wants to play at games of death, because, because he knows too little about life."

And he seemed in fact to have driven the sallow little poet from the field, for the latter shortly, while attention had shifted back to Sather, got up and was stuttering out his good-byes from the door, before Gordon had even noticed his retirement from the general argument. He felt a moment of triumph, but it was gone, grotesquely and sentimentally knocked from under him, when, as Ronnie's feet sounded down the porch steps, Mrs. Barstow remarked that she hoped he wouldn't be late for work.

"He's got a job at last, on night-shift," she explained to Gordon.

"What does he do?" he asked, surprised.

"He's a hoseman," she said serenely. "In the slaughterhouse up the road."

"He washes blood off the floors," Jack said bluntly.

"Aint he a real nice boy?" asked Mrs. Barstow.

Yes, Ronnie Mandell was a Real Nice Boy and no doubt he had

remained one up to that moment when the last of his own blood ran unregarded between the cobblestones of a prison yard in Spain.

They had all been Nice Boys. There had been Bob Fournier, with the sunken cheeks and smoky brown eyes; half-French, almost self-educated, and now unemployed, he had come recently from piece-work in a Quebec textile factory where, he told Gordon, he had averaged four dollars a week for a seventy-two hour week. He had perhaps an understandable interest in economic theory, the first Marxist whom Gordon had yet encountered who seemed to know what Marx meant by "surplus value". The air around him quivered with such formulae.

"Competitive production . . . consumption by waste and by war . . . expanding dole and the permanent crisis . . . ownership of the means . . . industrial patriarchism . . ."

How impressive and urgent the phrases had seemed. Was it because they came from such a youth? Or because he himself was intellectually too shortwinded to chase such arguments beyond the second syllogism? Bob Fournier breathed them easily, more easily than he did the physical air—another Nice Boy, while he lasted.

And there had been Hymie. One always thought of him at the end. What was it Meredith said about every Beauty having her Dog? Hymie Wolfit, with his black sorrowful bull-pup's eyes and his flat broken nose and his thick curly pow, was undoubtedly Thelma's devoted dog. Gordon could not remember a Sunday evening at the Barstows when Hymie had not been there, ready to define the Permanent Revolution again at the hint of a question-mark. He was a tailor's apprentice, like Bob with little formal education, and like Ronnie a trifle understocked in *persiflage*. But he was, as Gordon came to realize, a Freudo-Marxist philosopher of sorts, and one to whom Gordon, who was perhaps no philosopher at all, could not close his ears.

But before that, before they left the supper table, they must have talked about himself. The Barstows would have made sure of that. It was just a day or two after Pellat, the young Englishman who conducted the Medieval English seminar, had stopped Gordon in the hall and told him that Gregor, Dean of the Graduate School, had refused to support Gordon's application for a Royal Society traveling scholarship. Pellat was apologetic, because it was he who, liking what beginnings Gordon had so far made on his doctoral thesis, had suggested he try for the fellowship. It was the only one possibly available to him since what he now had was not being offered next year—Toronto's budget continuing to shrink as rapidly as Utah's. And it was exactly the bursary which could have taken him from the inadequate libraries of Canada to the medieval riches of the British Museum itself.

"Dean Gregor!" Sather had exclaimed with jovial scorn, when Thelma had drawn the story out from Gordon, "that fugitive from a Manse. Gregor's a Great Canadian of the League of Nations Society who gives an annual oration on the brotherhood of man, and refuses to have Jews on his staff. One of our fine old liberal minds. But dont tell me he's objecting to Aryans now too!"

"I'm afraid I quoted with a little too much relish some of Tolstoy's reservations about Shakespeare, in a seminar paper I had to write for him," Gordon explained. "Gregor wrote on the cover that my judgments were 'dangerously close to Marxism'."

"Ha!" Sather flung back his wing of hair, "but 'out of this nettle danger we pluck this flower safety!' Now if you can only get *close* enough to Marxism—though I doubt if Dean Gregor is a good judge of distance here—perhaps our not so universal university will throw you completely out on your ear and we'll have a candidate for the job of a professional revolutionary."

But this drew a reproachful murmur from Mrs. Barstow. "You oughtnta say such things, Leo. You should tell Mr. Saunders to keep mum till he gets a real perfesser's job. Then he can help the revolution with money." At the time, he had found it refreshing that Mrs. Barstow referred to the revolution as naturally as if it were the local Community Chest.

This had started another argument. Jack, offhandedly charming and adroit as Gordon had found him on first encounter the previous evening, and as he would always be, had remonstrated that they were embarrassing Gordon.

"Gosh, Mom, you cant take it for granted just because Gordon doesnt like the Stalinists' ideas he likes ours, let alone wants to join us."

This in turn led to a discussion of what he, and they, did believe. After the cryptic and dogma-laden air of the Social Problems Club, and the cagey and tenuous attitudes of Cathcart and his Fabians, Gordon found the Barstow brand of discussion frank and illuminating.

He had already gathered from Jack and Thelma, at the Cathcarts the night before, that the Barstows considered themselves the true Communists, the historic Left opposition of the Third International—the Bolshevik-Leninists, to use the ferocious sobriquet which from Thelma's petaled lips sounded only like good clean fun. This did not mean, as he was beginning gladly to find, that they were not surprisingly critical of doctrinal approaches to Marxism, insofar as it was a body of fallible and historically conditioned writings, and they were far harder on official Communism than he had ever thought to be.

"But what's wrong with it," Hymie said, "isn't Marxism, only Stalinism."

"The Stalinists are the new Thermidorians," Sather broke in. "From 1924 on, they've rapidly and systematically perverted the first bastion of world socialism into a nationalist police state, into the private farm of a privileged and murderous bureaucracy. In Russia, Stalin has already jailed or shot the original Bolsheviks. In the rest of the world, his boyos have expelled from the Communist Party any who stood up for Lenin's ideals. Consequently, without proper Marxist leadership or principles, they got themselves caught in the wings of a possible British Proletarian Revolution in 1926. And they sold out a Soviet China to Chiang Kai-Shek the very next year.

"The once glorious Third International, my friend," Sather summed it for him, "is now, under Stalin, simply a syndicate of mutually treacherous yes-men misleading a shrinking flock of famine-starved innocents and fanatics down the dead-end lane of 'Socialism-in-a-separate-country'."

How turgid, obvious, how mild even, the Barstow conversations were, looking back at them, but for Gordon in 1932, the year of the proclaimed fulfillment of the First Five Year Plan, their strictures seemed both too pat and too devastating, and he remembered resisting them.

"You're sideline critics," he taunted them, smiling—though it was balm to his soul to hear his Stalinist accusers themselves accused of treachery and sabotage.

"Nothing of the kind," Thelma said roundly. "If we were on the sidelines, the Stalinites wouldnt be so worried. We're out in front fighting their battles for them." She tossed her golden head and sent him a look half-haughty, half-appealing.

"Thelma's right," Sather came in. "We have in fact such a nice regard for proletarian solidarity that we continue, though admittedly with a wry face, to support the Stalinites in their current agitation for the release of Tim Buck and their other stalwarts from the hoosegow."

"Why?"

"Because they are class-war prisoners, jailed by our common enemy for 'criminal syndicalism' against the capitalist state of Canada."

As they talked, Gordon was startled to learn that three of those in the room with him had been active members of the Communist Party, and the other three (one excluded Mrs. Barstow as a Party all her own) would enter it tomorrow if they could, solely to work from within' (it was one of their magic phrases), to unseat the very bureaucracy they wanted the government to release from jail. By this strategy they hoped to reform the Third International.

Sather indeed, Gordon realized now, had been one of the founders in 1921, when he was a mere teen-ager, of the Workers' Party, the original Canadian communist organization. He had been in the glorious barn in Guelph at the First Meeting. And years later he had been expelled, with éclat, at the same time as the fabulous Trotsky himself, for supporting, from the distance of Toronto, the Red Army's original Commissar in his battle against Stalin. He could be all this, Gordon thought, and an unashamed 'petit-bourgeois intellectual' too!

"And Fournier here," said Sather, turning to the dark boy from Quebec, "was excommunicated by the Young Communist League nearly two years ago for disagreeing with the precise doctrine of social-fascism which you, my dear Gordon, have been butting your head against in that abysmal Social Problems Club."

And Hymie the tailor? He had recently been driven from the adult Party—which he laconically referred to as 'the Synagogue'—for refusing to connive at a 'red split-off' which it had tried to effect within his own union.

It was such enforced exilings, Jack now insisted, which had led the Trotskyists everywhere to set up a separate international organization, something which, on this side of the Atlantic, went at present under the name of the Communist League of North America.

As for Thelma and Jack, though they seemed to have leapt by some arcanic process directly from Methodism into Marxism without suffering a Babylonish captivity among the Stalinists, they appeared at least, Gordon had to confess to himself, more at home in the tangled chronicles of radicalism than he was in the plays of Shakespeare. And even in the latter Sather could certainly outquote him.

"Do you have a comrade named Lacey?" Gordon had interrupted at one point, at last remembering the name of the little man who had been carted away in the ambulance from Queen's Park that fateful Sunday. He described Lacey's battle.

"That guy!" Sather laughed somewhat sourly. "Hell no, he's just a Lovestoneite."

"A Love—?"

"A right-international deviationist," Fournier added solemnly. "A Bukharinite."

Sather went on to define, and to dispose of Lacey, with more finesse than Mrs. Zimchuck, but with scarcely less firmness. Yet listening, Gordon had decided only that he was himself a political illiterate.

And so being for a while content to listen, he heard with new ears many old deeds, which were for his tellers no casual affairs but Acts of the Apostles along the bitter road to power. In 1919 they reminded him, five regiments of Imperial Guards had mutinied and a whole camp of British soldiers had formed themselves into a Soviet in Calais. In 1920, the London dockers had refused to load a munitions ship sailing against Red Russia. Sacco and Vanzetti, he learned, were now admittedly innocent and their execution a frame-up. The Winnipeg General Strike, which he had almost forgotten about, had, Sather assured him, set up a veritable proletarian dictatorship in Canada's third city so firmly that it had been broken only by thousands of troops rushed all the way from Ontario.

Compared with any of them, except perhaps Mrs. Barstow—who inclined to regard all Stalinists as hell-bound drunkards and betrayers of women, and all Trotskyists as the chosen forerunners of a Puritan kingdom on earth—Gordon felt himself a child again at school, as he had never felt under the tutelage of Roberts and Kay. What the latter had flung at him was true—the workingclass creates its own leaders. And here they were!

Yet he had that night—or was it on one of the many other Barstow nights?—earnestly and painfully spelled out his instinctive objections, and got their ready answers.

"How do you know that bureaucracy isnt an inevitable product of violent revolution?"

"All modern democracy is the fruit of bloody revolution."

"But force always ends in force, it's a perpetual-motion machine."

"Dogmatic Tolstoyism. The universe is Force."

"All right, but supposing Trotskyism *is* divine truth, and the Church of Moscow is in the claws of Satan, can you Protestants convert the devil and his kin? I dont think an organism is ever healed by what it has purged itself of."

What better questions could he have asked? How did it happen that he felt his own makeshift house of arguments being slowly cut from under him by the small droning saw of Hymie, the Marxist tailor?

"Thought and action progress only by the shock of opposites . . . ideas are created dialectically . . . Hegel . . . thesis, antithesis, synthesis . . . the Heraclitan flux . . . life lives on death . . . the evolutionary appetite . . . Trotsky's Left-Oppositional faction . . ."

. How important and bizarre and even exciting it had all seemed, the real food and drink of revolution, the wisdom of the past rifled to feed the future. And yet he had not given in easily, had not, truly, given in at all that first night. Or had he?

"Why, why," he remembered he had burst out once, asserting that hope which perhaps, even later in the nadir of his fanaticism, he never quite abandoned, "why can't we try first, in Canada, in North America, to get socialism cleanly and gently, and in the peace of the ballot-box? How else than by democratic means can we possibly hope to arrive at democratic results? The means dont justify, they *determine* the ends. Surely it was your Apostle Engels who said that!"

"You tell me," said Sather, looking comically puzzled. "Why did Norman Thomas get nowhere in the last election down south, or in the one before, or in any election the dear big gentle galoot has ever run in? Or tell me why the Canadian Socialist Party is only now trying to get born?

"I don't know the answers," he went on, in that voice which could charge the most hackneyed dogma with exciting and hypnotic resonance, "but I know the reality when I see it. Peaceful Socialism, my dear Gordon, never has and never can be anything but a big shiny unhatched egg. It's been sat on and sat on and warmed and coddled and addled by every old hen from Lasalle and Keir Hardie down to the Reverend J. S. Woodsworth. But the little bird inside—if indeed it ever had a bird—has never got itself out, not even when it was a great fat turkey like the German Social-Democratic Party, feathered already with six million votes. And believe me, if the U. S. ever develops a third party or even a truly liberal Democratic party, the power of money will frustrate it by throwing the whole world into another war or by backing some national American fascist. And dont forget we're only a tail to the American comet, all three million seven hundred thousand square miles of us. They've got four billions invested in us. Socialist pacifism, my dear Gordon, is doomed . . . And why?"

Sather paused and threw an arm out rhetorically, looking happy and wicked. "Why? Because every fowl that ever was born had to *peck* its way out. It had to commit what to our parliamentary friends is a dreadful, not to say unimaginable thing, an act of violence. It had to sit inside the dark shell of capitalism and say to itself: It's not enough that there's a world of sunshine outside waiting for me; it's not enough that I *should* in all fairness be liberated into it; it's not enough that I am big and ready, with all my bones and six million pin-feathers in place; it's also necessary that I draw back my soft little head, however difficult it is for me within the cramped gloomy space in which I find myself, draw it back and strike with all my might at that bland and completely useless shell, and break it—or else what began as my armor will end as my tomb!"

Sather had said more, but it was never possible for Gordon to recall the elusive magic by which he made everything he uttered sound utterly logical. That one metaphor he did remember; it seized somehow on his memory and on his will, compulsive to his thoughts as had become also the chanting phrases of Spender that little Bagshaw had brought him—"O young men, my comrades, it is too late now to stay in those houses . . ." Why had a mere figure of speech seemed so cogent to him then? Was it the man who made it?—it had not really shaken him when, a few weeks later, he discovered that the maestro had borrowed it from Trotsky's *Whither England?* Or was it some need of his own to believe it? —because to believe it was to fit himself at last into a rolling and armored machine of ideas, and move within it, a trusted and powerful soldier?

Looking back, he knew it had not been at all like this, had been neither simple nor intellectual, this capitulation of his mind to an idea. There had also been the two phantoms, turning still somewhere in the dark waters of his being, waiting then (as they would always wait) for the moment when he should once more be alone and marooned in the darkening gulf, waiting to twist their drowned faces toward him, staring with the gentle eyes of a woman already dead and the blind sockets of a baby never born.

Had even this been all? Who, groping back in the always darkening twilight of memory, can touch his strange hand on any one of the shadowy evasive beings that were himself? There was this time and this place, and a Gordon Saunders who was already many people; who was a grown child drawn to willful children; a solitary man stung by the flesh and gnawed by the spirit; a pedant who was also an adventurer, swimming out to the most adventurous of all the world's pedantic utopias; a being of grandiose thoughts and microscopic cares, a blocked teacher, a reluctant martyr, and a self-betrayed poet. Yet the Gordon Saunders, who sat in the draughty Barstow livingroom that night in December, would have denied bitterly being anything but an entirely rational man of twenty-eight who was beginning to find, to his immense satisfaction, that he had fallen in at last with others almost as rational as himself.

And so, fallen thus happily together, what had they decided? What in particular was he, Gordon, to do—since the others had already come to their decisions?

It was Thelma who had returned to that subject with one of those impulsive remarks of hers—something to the effect that he was 'an instinctive Marxist'—which fitfully reminded him that she was some years younger than he.

He looked up at her, perched shimmering on the edge of the only morris chair, and her reckless innocence frightened him.

"No," he said abruptly, almost urgently, "I'm still a teacher—looking for something honest and integrated to teach—and somewhere to teach it."

There was a soft wheeze from Mrs. Barstow, whose seated bulk blotted out the rest of the morris chair. "That's right," she said seriously. "You git a good steady job. This League wont go nowhere without more dough."

"O, Mother," Thelma had leaped to the floor and faced her great parent in a pretty girlish passion, "that's not being Marxist! We'll get money other ways and why should Gordon throw his brains away and waste years learning to teach Tennyson or somebody to little bourgeois swots just—just so they can do the same—when the whole future of—of the universe is at stake!"

Wynsynge she was as is a joly colt. He had been too conscious, that moment, of the delectable rounding of her breasts under the green, fresh frock to look into the implications of her argument. But Jack had rescued him.

"Look, goofus," her brother had said, brotherly rude, "you're being ultra-leftist again. The woods are full of jobless and black-listed radicals ready to lead the charges. Yeah, and they havent anybody to lead but themselves, and not enough food in their stomachs to fight a cat. We need Fellow-Travelers, as well as hunger marchers, and not just because they can give us a few bucks but because they can stay outside the Party and look natural and give us prestige."

"Bourgeois prestige." Thelma's magical teeth, white and even, gleamed between soft scornful lips. "That's a Stalinist trick."

"Nuts," said Jack. "We can learn from them too."

Sather laughed and cocked an eye at Gordon. "You see what we mean by the dialectic? Before the Barstow fraction begins to multiply itself by three, may I suggest that everybody's right? Sure, you should complete your doctorate, if the gods of free enterprise allow. You should snaffle on to the position and influence in the educational world to which you're entitled. And of course you'll be tainted with bourgeois lucre and bourgeois prestige. But does anybody know any other coinage that can be passed these days? If your money stalls off our *Militant*'s printer another week, and your prestige herds one more lamb into our fold, why, the great Lord of Burghers bless you. It's been worth it. *And*, my friend—or my dear comrade, as you prefer (I've always thought the term a little sentimental)—you can, if and when you come to understand and accept fully our position—join our ranks *sub rosa* as an honest-to-Marx Bolshevik-Leninist-Trotskyist as well."

"You mean," said Thelma, subsiding, "he could under another name?"

"Another?" Sather threw out his arms. "We can give him a new one every week, if he likes. Not that at present we'd need to, for I fear that we're not yet a sufficient threat to Canadian capitalism to have merited the flattery of police spies. In any case, why should he come to meetings? Our sessions I am bound to believe are less boring than those of other parties, but they're still boring at least ninety-five per cent of the time. Gordon, if he became one of our anointed, could write pamphlets for us in the dead of night —I believe that is the hour in which they are written in proletarian novels—or he could hold his own Problem Social Club. My God, let him boot the big fat football of capitalism with either one of his feet or bunt it with his head if he likes—so long as," and the dark rich voice suddenly rang out in seriousness as he turned to Gordon—"you kick it toward our goal, and accept our rules and our playing-season."

Sather paused, and let his voice sink. Debater's tricks?—or was it that for a lawyer such mannerisms were natural? "Just being vaguely on our side isnt enough, like the League for Social Reconstruction or the pinko professors at Victoria College. There's a flock of professors in Germany," Sather went on slowly, "who've been pumping one watery kind of socialism or another into their students for years. Cooperative commonwealths and revolution-in-the-head and jelly-in-the-heels. Meantime, as you'll have noticed from the papers, a lot of other students have been picking up very wrong but rather clear ideas from a paranoidal ex-corporal. And those fine feckless whitebearded *Professoren* who could never quite make up their minds what kind of social paradise to head for, or what train to take to it, are now—if they are very lucky—wandering around on their uppers in a Paris backstreet. Or they are in a concentration camp getting their dreamy faces kicked in. Or they are very dead."

It had been in the moment of intense silence, after the sudden pause in Sather's ringing voice, that steps had sounded uncertainly on the porch, and faint querulous singing. Jack got up at once and slid quickly into the little hallway; Hymie rose and silently followed him. Gordon was aware that the others were deliberately ignoring the interruption. Thelma was staring, lips parted, at the carpet. Sather and Fournier, heads rigidly turned to Mrs. Barstow, seemed to be waiting her lead. And, just as Hymie closed the livingroom door, huge and unmoving in her morris chair, she spoke:

"Leo, you tell Mr. Saunders about them Stalinites he met, like, well like Roberts. He dont know jus' how bad they are."

Her voice was calm but it carried an order, and Sather leapt nimbly into a fulfillment of it. His biography of the Grand Inquisitor of the Social Problems Club was illuminating, and further ointment to Gordon's wounds; yet he found it difficult to concentrate on it, for over even the deliberate loudness of Sather's voice, and from beyond the closed door, floated curious echoes of some *contretemps*. The stranger was undoubtedly drunk, and was apparently being led or shoved not out but in, and up the stairs, against his expressed will. There was confused clomping, some indistinguishable droning appeals from Hymie, and plaintive protests. "Won' go," Gordon heard, and there was something "not your house" and "vipers".

"I should have remarked earlier," Sather was saying, "that Roberts began this life as Rabinowitz." ("Trotsky-rotskies," came the furious and drunken voice.) "I mention this fact not to deride him for changing his name but to suggest that he is middling resourceful." Everybody laughed, a little too promptly. "He showed, as I remember, a rather early distaste for the proletarian life, unless you would include phony bookmaking and ward bootlegging in that ambience."

At this point there was a thumping from what was probably the stairtop, and a wail that sounded like "goddam reds", but Sather did not falter. "I understand that he was converted to communism by his wife Betty, whom he contrived to meet in the prison laundry. She was at that time a class-war prisoner, which he was not, and honorably immured for having assaulted a police officer in the course of her duties as a strike picket. Ah, Betty!" Sather grinned fondly, "she was a fighter from away back—" there was a distant upstairs crash which made the little house quiver slightly—"*and* a good Bolshevik. In consequence she was thrown out with the rest of us when she refused to mumble the required exorcism over the diabolic apparition of Trotsky. Rabinowitz, however, recanted and, to make his loyalty to Comrade Stalin doubly clear, he deserted Betty. She has now, I regret to say, given up the revolution and is working as a *masseuse* to support her two children. Rabinowitz still finds the revolution a paying proposition (there are rumors that the Red Trade Union business is not unmixed with the numbers racket in one of our city wards) —but I should judge that he still deems it wise to be the loudest hound in the Trotsky-hunting pack. After all, he was once nearly mistaken for a hare."

Again the laughter was a little heavy. The noises upstairs had stopped but Jack and Hymie had not returned. Gordon hastened to ask Sather about Kay.

"Kay? Kay? That's Rabinowitz's new doxie, isnt it? Dark and lanky, in a shock-trooper's outfit? . . . She's of no political consequence. A young *epigone* who equates proletarianism with dirty fingernails."

"Her father," Thelma added, "is a filthy-rich coffee importer and she doesnt get on with him, so she's paying him back with a big act of being radical."

Sather laughed. "Comrade Thelma, as usual, goes to the heart of the matter. I should guess too, if Mrs. Barstow will forgive my diverging into such a subject, that she's also an unconscious lesbian being a conscious nymphomaniac."

"O Leo, you're terrible," Thelma said, with a giggle which had jarred Gordon for the moment, it was too coy, but then she flashed her blue anxious eyes at him and he instantly forgave her. She was obviously troubled, listening, as they all were, for the next sound from upstairs. In any case, was her occasional naïveté not a guarantee of her purity, political as well? She certainly was no Kay, no Joan, no—

"Now you shush, Leo. I dunno what them words mean," Mrs. Barstow's heavy voice was poised between enjoyment and disapproval, "but I bet it's sex." Was it then, or not till later, that he noticed how very remote and dirty she always made this word sound?

At this moment Hymie and Jack came in, without speaking, the latter a little flushed. Sather drew them quickly into the conversation, but the spirit had somehow gone from the evening and Gordon remembered that the hour of the last streetcar was approaching. It was when he stood up to go, and the other guests with him, and there was the usual noise of leavetakings, that the halldoor suddenly flew open and a wildeyed little man stood in its frame. His bald head was angled belligerently, and his knobbly body was clothed in nothing but a suit of long woollen underwear.

A sound almost a sob came from Thelma, and there was a concerted rush of Jack and Hymie toward the weaving figure.

"Long lif Hitler!" the little man shrieked, poised like a bedraggled rooster. Then he slammed the door in their faces. Before Jack had it open again they could hear his bare feet pelting up the stairs.

"Muss'lini f'rever," came a dying wail from the upper storey.

And so the evening had ended, in unintelligible farce and awkward good-byes. Jack and Hymie, who had disappeared up the stairs again, did not come down before he left. Meantime Fournier, who had lived nearby, paid his respects and hurried off on his own. Gordon found himself with Sather at the door, saying his thanks, the whole fantastic interruption unacknowledged. But when Mrs. Barstow, who had struggled out of her chair and rolled behind him into the hall, put her fat little paw into his hand, she looked up into his face with enigmatic calm:

"You come from a workin class home, Gordon, so maybe you'll understand sometimes people got temp'rily to live with people they dont want." It was the first time she had called him by his Christian name. Gordon started to stammer something reassuring but she went on, "Anyways I hope it aint upset you too much to come and see us again often. Sunday nights is open house for us, you know, and you're welcome anytime."

He would have returned for that alone, solely to demonstrate to this indomitable creature his loyalty and sympathy. But in addition, Thelma, standing uneasy and vulnerable, like a slim green tree beside the round rock of her mother, gave him once more her white miraculous hand, gazed at him from eyes alight with appeal —and asked him for dinner the next Tuesday. "Just the family," she said. He leapt like a boy at the invitation, and went down the steps in a happy daze.

Sather, whose flat lay in Gordon's direction, caught the first streetcar with him. He seemed tired and their conversation was desultory until Gordon, still puzzled, asked Sather how the Barstows were able to put up with such a roomer.

"Even if they need the money, couldnt they get one who wasnt a drunk and a—well, a fascist!"

"Roomer!" Sather had laughed and looked at Gordon with amusement. "Well, to begin with, he's only a Hitler fan when he's drunk—that's to say, in the evenings. Daytimes he's one of Canada's soberest *fonctionnaires*. He's able to boast, as a matter of fact, that he's the honest-to-god proletarian of the Barstow menage, since Jack's only a junior bank clerk. Yes, in the daytime he earns his living by the sweat of his feet, carrying His Majesty's mails; rather naturally he supports His Majesty's Government. Come nights, he drinks dago-red; I envy him his constitution.

That bibulous gentleman is the head of the family and, so to speak, the basis of its economy."

"*Mr. Barstow!*" Gordon watched Sather's head bob in ironic amusement. "Mrs. Barstow's husband! I thought he must be dead. Jack's father?! And—"

"Thelma's."

Gordon was reduced to astonished silence.

"I should add, in the interest of accuracy," Sather went on—he seemed rather to be enjoying the task of rattling the skeleton—"that Old Tom has lately been reading Major Douglas and wants to start a Social Credit Party in Ontario, all on his own. An independent character. And politically, for all we can be sure, farsighted. You might even get to like him. You're not a Jew. Well, anyway, now you know. And here's where you transfer."

Gordon had ridden the rest of his way alone. And what had he seen, the only passenger on the last citybound car, staring through the reflection of his own unregarded face on the windowpane, into the blank of the night? His preposterous Island, perhaps, shining in that darkness, and himself slipping at last from his dubious rock to swim for it? Behind him certainly was nothing now that he wanted. Only ahead in that emptiness might be stability and a justification for existence, only out there escape from the beggar's bowl, a possible fulfillment of his energies, a challenge at last for whatever courage and intelligence and steadfastness he had. And in the long strange voyage there would be certainly companions, even friends, lively and amusing friends, who already treasured his virtues, who would take them and give them back, and whose wisdom, however untutored, was alive and at work on the world's destiny. There was no return to the soft libertine shore; and for a long time there would only be waves. But even if he drowned in them it would be good, and he would go down purged and body-clean from the touch of the reproachful dead who nudged forever against him on this rock in this tide-pool.

Yes, he must have thought in some wild and desperate and quite reasonable and happy way like that. No doubt there were ambiguous sounds and sights of the evening's past to weave themselves into the glint and rattle of that lonely streetcar—the round spectacles and the stuttering nihilisms of Ronnie and the rolling cadences of Sather; the bright tubercular cheeks of Bob Fournier and the sorrowful drone of Hymie Wolfit; the old enigmatic doll's face of Mrs. Barstow and the cockerel shrieks of her husband. But when Gordon Saunders' head touched the cold pillow of his bed that night, there was only one vision investing it.

Thelma—perched momentarily in a kind of sparkling quiet on the faded arm of the morris chair and swinging a long vision of leg—or leaping tomboyishly to the floor in righteous argument; or letting her eyes rest momentarily on his with surely some message of admiration and desire dancing out of their incredible blueness; Thelma—with something of the clearskinned childlike quality he had always liked, had admired even in that absurd little Comrade Bagshaw (but thank God how different, and how glad he was that he had not entangled himself there); Thelma, who was not only fresh and malleable (how could he have thought of Bagshaw in the same breath with her!) but who also gave promise of an informed and confident and beautiful woman.

He thought with pity of Oscar's tawdry wench in mink who would teach him Veblen. Here was a Renoir, who could quote Rosa Luxembourg—somebody he'd never even heard of. It was too much, too wonderful. And—shutting out, as he could not before have shut out, both the reasonable thought that it was indeed too wonderful, and the unreasonable fear that he deserved the love neither of this nor any woman again,—he admitted to himself, with almost fatuous relief, that he was once more totally and incontestably in love. And so admitting, he fell asleep.

14

**FRANCE & BELGIUM DEFAULT WAR DEBT PAYMENTS:
GOVERNMENTS OUSTED**

**QUEBEC UNEMPLOYED
FUNDS SQUANDERED**

SOVIET COAL BARRED

---

*CALLS TO COURAGE
FEATURE MESSAGES FOR
DAWNING YEAR*

**ONLY 75 had Million
Dollar Incomes in 32**

**Dean Inge Sees Little
World Progress in
Last 40,000 Years**

**LEADING CANADIAN
CLERICS WELCOME
OXFORD GROUP**

**WORLD WORSHIPS AT
BETHLEHEM TODAY**

**EMPIRE THRILLED
AS KING'S VOICE
WAFTS OVER AIR**

**WORLD PLANS WHOOPEE
ON BIG SCALE TONIGHT**

**Champagne $20 Quart
At NY's Waldorf**

**18 Unemployed Girls
Arrested For Leap Year
Marriage Parade**

HITLER IS CHANCELLOR

RECOVERY NOW SAYS FORD

Ottawa, Feb. 3 (CP)—Debate centred yesterday on the resolution of J. S. Woodsworth (Labor, Winnipeg North Centre), calling upon the government to establish a cooperative commonwealth in Canada.

GLOBAL FIGHT FOR GOLD SHARES

ALL MICHIGAN BANKS CLOSE

Ottawa, Feb. 15 (CP)—Dangerous organizations are operating throughout the length and breadth of Canada, Hon. Hugh Guthrie, Minister of Justice, told the House of Commons today. The minister complained that he was receiving long petitions to which were appended "nothing but the names of foreigners, no French or Anglo-Saxons, most of them unpronounceable."

Miami, Fla., Feb. 16 (AP) — A bricklayer who "hates all governments" tried to assassinate President-Elect F. D. Roosevelt last night and failed as the five shots struck five other persons, one of them Mayor Anton Cermack of Chicago.

STORES DISCOUNT RELIEF SCRIP
Police Threaten Action

GREAT WAR IMMINENT IN ORIENT

Oxford Students Vote "Under No Circumstances to Fight for King and Country"

POLICE CLUB RIOTERS BESIDE "SCAB" SHIP

JAP DELEGATE WALKS OUT ON LEAGUE OF NATIONS
War Risk Rates Up In Pacific

BANK PRESIDENT DODGED TAX BY FAKING $3,800,000 LOSS

15

Sir and Colleague,

There is a chronically generous gentleman in this interminable novel I am now concocting who keeps falling into arguments with his wife because every time he gets squiffed on a party he wants to lend her to whoever is his best friend that night. No sir, he is not out of Hemingway but out of our chemical engineering laboratory, a hollow-eyed young demonstrator whose fortune it has been to meet me recently. This improbable youth, whom it is now my lonely endeavor to make probable, quietly invented some sort of sticky ichor which, applied to fuel oil, increases the efficiency of a diesel engine by ten per cent. I will leave you to calculate the possible market value of his little potion, and then ask you to consider the unlikeliness of my nine-hundred-bucks-a-year acquaintance when I tell you that he insisted on presenting the patent to his department, for free, for its dubiously general welfare. Oddly, though this was several months ago, the College has not got around to a public acknowledgement of the gift. Old Man Rumor says his department head has been offered a job with the Mallon interests. I am wondering if the story ends here; the young demonstrator's, I mean; the curtains of mine are snarled in the wings.

And you will ask no doubt if I intend to make over its royalties to the English department, supposing it is ever finished and there are royalties. As it happens, even this could be. For I have news which may startle you, as indeed they still do me, and may others when they are public. (The plural is a concession to a citizen of that farflung empire of Fowler's *Modern English Usage*.) Joan Krautmann and I are to be married come June, the day after whenever exam results are due. It appears that we spend the summer in Europe, unless all banks fail. In September, having assumed the fate you perhaps rejected, I enter into a respectable but I trust unlaborious post in some streamlined outpost of my father-in-law's modest empire, probably in Honolulu.

Farewel my bokes and my devocioun—but your friend Chaucer was only saying *au revoir* while spring sprang. I intend an act of Prospero. I shall take out a full length of chalk to the fetid shores of this inland sea and solemnly break it into the brine. Even if she divorces me in a week, I shall never tramp into another classroom. I shall not, however, toss my novels in too; what the hell, maybe now I can publish them myself.

There it is then—I am decamping from teaching, which I do not like, while you are clamoring to reinlist, because you do. I have not, my friend, been inert to this paradox, nor has that really thoughtful and, if I may say so, forgiving person Joan, who, I must admit, first suggested that I should not give notice, nor should we announce our engagement, until I had exchanged signals with you. We suggest then that you airmail Crump at once, and our hoary President, formally asking for reappointment in September. As soon as I've heard from you that you've done this, I'll tender my resignation and suggest, independently, that you be asked back. This of course will only be a light finger at the back of the scales, but at the same time Joan's father (who is still, by the way, Chairman of the Board of Regents) will—for he has already fallen, amiably for him, into this little conspiracy—speak to the Prexy who will perforce speak to Crump who will etc. In other words your job, or something close to it, is again yours if you want it and can still sign a decipherable hand.

The wind is howling off the saltflats and testing the dubious carpentry of my windows. Our indestructible brewer's yeast caught a chill and died in the last batch of beer. There are a hundred bluebooks under last week's *New Yorker* on the table. I cant get anything on the radio but Bing Crosby. You will not be too disappointed in old bachelor Van Bome if he seems to be looking forward to summer.

I gather from your last that you too are becoming marriage-minded, having abandoned the leather-jacketed Amazon for a veritable dryad of the Canadian snows. If this as is serious as it sounds we must exchange congratulations.

Your continued interest in the finer points of Marxism I put down to the astonishing power of the *Zeitgeist*. But I am assuming that the obdurate archaism of this Land of the Mormons will prevail when you return—with or without the belle of the barricades. I shall be, as you can see, in a position to defend with happy zeal a Man of Sin, though better Sin Legitimized—but a Man of Virtue, a Tamburlaine of the ultra-left—well, that could be a different matter. This is not yet the Western Oxford.

One of my more polysyllabic sophomores has set it down that the artist must be more omniscient than God. Do you agree?

I am, sir, your etcetera as ever,

Oscar.

16

MR. BARSTOW FISHED A PENCIL STUB FROM THE COAT OF HIS
uniform on the seat by the bed. He blew his breath to see the
vapor form in the attic air.

Downstairs Mrs. Barstow filled her morris chair, mending socks
and listening vaguely as Jack read titbits from the late paper.
It was a little after supper, the last day of February.

"So if it's just a parliament, this Rye-stack, why do we care if
it burned up?"

"*Reichstag*, Mom." Jack was sloped against the mantelpiece
beside the hissing gasfire. He stood because he wanted it clear he
was going out soon. "The point is Hitler said the Stalinites did
it, and they say he did. To work up a pogrom against the Left.
Listen. 'Virtual martial law reigns in Germany. President Paul
von Hindenburg signed a decree tonight completely disbanding
all constitutional safeguards for freedom of speech, press and
assembly. One hundred communist members of the Reichstag have
been ordered arrested.' Whee!"

Mrs. Barstow grinned comfortably. "We should worry if he
gits rid a all them Stalinites." She looked askance at a sock.
"Yotta cut your toenails more."

Jack shook his *Herald* impatiently. "O, Mom, you're being
ultra-leftist again. There's millions of honest deluded workers in
the CP and we Trotskyists have to defend them against fascism."

Mr. Barstow softly raised the sash, slowly slid back the movable
pane in the storm-window, reached his bony arm out into the
dark.

"So how are you gonna do that in Toronto?"

Jack sighed, looking up. "We have to take a position I mean.
I dont see how we can defend terrorist methods if the Stalinites
really did burn it. The Central Committee ought to meet. I'll have
to write an editorial for the *Spark* on it. I need a *line*."

Tenderly Mr. Barstow drew in the snow-slippery bottle, set it by his bed, made tight the double window again.

"They give you any money for another *Spark*?"

Jack folded the newspaper and threw it on a chair. "I got to be ready to print one if the Party does raise enough." The phone began ringing in the hall. "Anyway we have to have a position. Maybe we even ought to call a big anti-fascist rally to—to interpret the German events to the workers."

"It'll be Gordon," Mrs. Barstow murmured.

"I'll get it." Thelma's voice trilled from the stairtop and her feet came tripping down.

"What workers?" Mrs. Barstow wormed her plump little hand into a brown stocking and waved three fingers through a hole in the toe. The top of the sock bulged like a funnel around her forearm.

Jack sat abstractedly on the chair's edge, without removing the paper. "Now dont *you* be cynical, Mom. Anybody we can get out to listen, of course."

"Hel-lo," said Thelma with impersonal melodiousness and then, more archly, "*lo*-o. Just a minute."

"The League aint paid you yer four dollars for last week yet, how they gonna hire a hall?"

Thelma closed the door and scampered back to the phone.

"I know, Mom, but maybe things will pick up soon. When the Canadian workers realize what's happened in Germany they're going to swing away Left. Our Party'll get mass-support." He didn't sound too convinced.

Mrs. Barstow probed an itch in her scalp with the blunt end of her darning needle. "Mebbe. But that dont mean you oughtnta have a real job again. I dont like you being a profeshnul revolution' at four dollars a week specially when you dont even git it. I dont pry enough outa Him to much more'n pay the rent, you know that, an if it wernt for your Uncle Harry we wouldnt be eatin and that's God's truth."

Mr. Barstow, wrapped in his overcoat, his long grey-green undies beneath, sat up in bed and let the sharp red wine chug from the bottle's cold neck into his gullet. Then he set the quart on the chair, feeling the familiar comforting dryness on his tongue.

He wriggled his toes in his two pair of socks and flipped another page in *Sun and Health Magazine*.

"Well criminy it's not my fault the Bank cut staff down, I told you it would. And anyway, I'm still looking."

Just then Thelma popped her auburn head into the livingroom. "Dont go out," she said to Jack, her voice important. "Gordon's coming up. He particularly wants to see you. *And* mom," she added, waiting to be asked why.

"Me? I've got a date." Jack stood up hastily.

Leaning supple on the doorhandle, one slender foot in the air, she swayed and smiled her prettiest, looked at him as she might look at a lover.

"You phone Sarah you'll be late. Gordon's on his way up."

"Nuts. I saw him last night. He was even still here when I went to bed. He just wants to unload some more backsliding and deviation. He'll be all mixed up again after reading about the Reichstag."

Thelma abandoned her smile and stood righteously straight. "Gordon received an important letter from Salt Lake today which he wants to discuss with all of us. He wants Leo too if we can get him to come over."

"He got a job?" Mrs. Barstow asked, peering eagerly around.

"He didnt want to explain over the phone. But he says the letter raises problems about the future and we all have to help him decide." Her mouth curled. "Look who's talking about deviations!"

"Well, you get Leo to come and maybe I'll wait in a while," Jack said cautiously. "Leo I do want to see."

"Then you phone him. I've got to get dressed."

"You are dressed."

"And Sarah too." Thelma, suddenly serene again, skipped to the door. Then a thought stopped her and she turned. "Do you think *we* did it?"

"Did what, goofus?"

"Set fire to the Reichstag?" She looked devilish, adventurous. "Our German comrades."

Jack groaned, picked up the paper again, sat down. "This family's just a bunch of terrorists." He looked at her pityingly.

"Of course not, stupid. What for? It's against our principles. Anyway I'll bet we didnt have more than fifty Trotskyists in all Germany and already most of them are probably bumped off."

"Fifty! For all you know we might have thousands. Still, a big underground organization. Who's backsliding now?"

"Aaarrh."

"Jack, you better phone Leo right away," Mrs. Barstow said.

"And Sarah." Thelma slipped humming into the hall.

"Company sent a registered notice," Mrs. Barstow rumbled. "Gonna take that phone out next week."

Mr. Barstow heard steps thumping up the stairway. He whisked his magazine under the pillow, set the bottle under the bed and scrambled up. Coat flaring out, he tried his door to make sure the lock was holding. He listened while Thelma's feet stopped at the stairtop, by lazy Jack's room; they tripped on down to the other end, where she and her wicked mother slept. Then he tiptoed back to his cot and took another swig. When he had set the bottle gently down he resumed work with a pencil stub on the photographs of the great-thighed girls of the nudist camp, delicately restoring their pubic hairs wherever the printer's engraver had smoothed them away. *O we sing we sing we sing of Lydia Pinkham.*

When Jack came from the phone Thelma was downstairs again, standing willow-lithe in her slip beside her mother. "Leo can come," he said.

"Yer vyelit dress," Mrs. Barstow was saying, "the new one. Course I ironed it. It's hung up your side the cupboard front a your eyes."

But suddenly Thelma turned, demure as a squirrel, and held her left hand drooping out to her brother.

"Aint you showed him yet?" Mrs. Barstow looked reproachful. Thelma giggled, watched Jack, said nothing.

"My God, a ring!"

"Shush, that's swearin," Mrs. Barstow said fondly. "Aint it lovely? A real dyemont with little seedy-purls round it."

"But the guy's supposed to be practically broke." Jack bent suspiciously over his sister's hand without touching it.

"Well. Dont you say anything?" Thelma stepped back and

clasped her fingers below her smooth throat. Eyes, teeth, stone sparkled in concert.

"I thought you thought engagement rings were bourgeois."

"It's a hairloom," Mrs. Barstow interposed softly. "Belonged to his mother. He's been carryin it round all these years just lookin for a girl like Thelma."

Jack went back to his chair. "Yeah."

Thelma's eyes flashed. "Well you might at least wish me happiness!"

Jack sat wearily down. "I did. I did last week when you hinted you were engaged to him. And two months ago when you definitely said you were engaged to Bobby Fournier. And last year—"

"She never got—" Mrs. Barstow began.

"—when you announced you were engaged to Ronnie," Jack raised his voice.

"—a ring before," Mrs. Barstow finished unperturbed.

Thelma faced him proudly, slim hands behind her back now, firm breasts full beneath the silk of her slip, the accused and innocent queen. "You know perfectly well that Bobbie made me break it off."

"O for gosh sake," Jack shouted, nettled, "you were just leading him on to put the heat on Gordon. You never intended to marry the poor guy. And now that he's in a t.b. ward you've dropped him."

"Now, now," Mrs. Barstow said. "She goes to see him once a week, doncha Thel?"

Thelma padded to the door on stockinged feet and turned, furious. "I hate you. Ever since you lost your job and started pretending you're a Revolutionary Leader you just cant say anything that isnt mean and —and cheap." Her voice broke.

"Stop it now." Mrs. Barstow reached for a sock fallen by her chair, grunted, failed. "Pick it up for me, Jacky-boy."

Thelma nipped over and retrieved it maliciously before he could get off his chair. She sank on an arm of the morris, turned a square of cream-white back to her brother, huddled herself against the ballooning shoulders of her mother.

Jack shook out the paper in front of him. "You could have

waited a few months till the poor guy died," he muttered behind it.

"O Mom, did you hear what he said? O, that's an awful thing to say." Thinking indeed how awful it was she burst into tears. "Bobby isnt going to die," she wailed down into her mother's shoulder.

"Now see wotcha done." Mrs. Barstow probed in the vast regions of her bosom, found a handkerchief, passed it up automatically to her daughter. "Course he aint gonna die. Now you apologize, Mister Jack. Thelma couldnt stay engaged to a boy with t.b. I wouldn' let her. And Gordon's a nice boy and you oughta wish her happiness."

"Happiness!" Goaded by the word, Jack hauled down the *Herald* with a rush. "O.K. O.K. O.K. I do. But she isnt really going to *marry* this time, is she? Why in three months he'll just be another unemployed."

"Mebbe not," Mrs. Barstow said. "Dont fergit he's comin up about a letter. Mebbe he's got his job back in Salt Lick."

"He will not anyway be unemployed." Thelma lifted her head, patted an eye, spoke as if from a sickbed. "He's going to be a professional revolutionary."

Mrs. Barstow quivered, looked up shocked. "Thelma. He is not. That's enough of that. You go on and git dressed before somebody comes."

But Jack was laughing with theatrical irony, and had flung down his paper. "He *is*? Like me? You're going to live on the four bucks a week he wont get?"

"*Gordon*," Thelma said with hateful emphasis, "can always find part-time teaching or coaching, or even writing, and—"

"Writing what?" His little straight nose was shrunk with unbelief.

"Articles and—and stories. You'll see, and besides"—she got up, recovered, and sauntered toward the hall again—"I'd be working too."

Jack laughed brokenly, as if he had a pain in his chest. "That'll be the day!"

"No you wont," Mrs. Barstow said flatly. "You aint marryin

Gordon till he gits a real good job, like Leo said he should git, and kin look after us both."

"Both?" Jack grinned. "You got a ring too?"

"O you shut up!" Thelma stood in the doorway and stamped her pretty stockinged foot. "Mom goes wherever I go. And you wait, Gordon'll be a *real* revolutionary. He wont sit around moping and snarling. He'll go to Vancouver and organize a new branch for the League. Leo said he could someday. And I bet in no time he'll have a movement big enough to support us and mom and put out a paper too. And that's more than you can do, you—you Tired Radical."

"That's not fair." Jack got up, redfaced. "You're just an incurable little babyfaced romantic. Anything Leo says is gospel to you, it's—"

"I'm not babyfaced! And you leave Leo out of—"

"It's Leo you've really got a—"

"Shut up, both a you," Mrs. Barstow leant forward, as far as she could, and hissed the words; she jerked her head at the ceiling. "You wanna git *him* down?" She scowled at them both.

"He staying in?" Jack asked, sobered.

Mrs. Barstow lifted a great shoulder. "So far. But he aint got nothin to drink, less he got a new hidin place. I searched his room when he was down makin his supper. Now you go on up and git dressed."

Thelma went.

"He dont hide it in the coal-shute no more," Mrs. Barstow added with a kind of gloomy triumph.

Jack sat down again. "But look, Mom," he said, meek yet frowning, "this is serious. Is Thelma going with him to Vancouver?"

"Course not," Mrs. Barstow soothed him. "Gordon says he's willin to wait."

"Wait!" Jack's whisper was dramatic. "But he may never get a good job, a bourgeois job, which is what you mean, Mom. You've got to remember that capitalism's maybe collapsing. Or the Japs may start a war."

"Then all the better she should be in her own home here with us," Mrs. Barstow said, fond and sturdy as a mother-bear.

Jack shook his head in resignation. "He'll get tired waiting."

"There's lots of other nice boys." His mother held a sock up serenely to the light. "Taint as if she were really set on gittin married. She jus likes bein ingaged."

Busy Mr. Barstow did not hear her stockinged feet, for he was bent away over, chucking and huffing in a corner of his room, scrambling through his little heap of paperbacks and scruffy magazines piled on the floor. He was looking for a blank page, a flyleaf, anything to scribble on, for his head was crackling with phrases. He'd write mebbe a ballad, somethin like "The Cremation of Sam McGee", only it'd be about the Bolshies, he'd show 'em who was the clever one. "There are strange things done," he crooned, "by her commie son." He laughed, so loudly he almost upset himself. "There—"

"Father?"

He peered around straightening, frightened. There was a stuttering little knock on his door. He froze—but at once lost his balance and, clutching *Astrology for Everyone*—it had an empty page at the back—bumped noisily against the wall. Detected, he leapt into a new mood, began walking recklessly toward the locked door. It was only Thelma, it was his poor li'l misguided daughter, the only person who really loved him and he was gonna have a long talk with her, soon, this very night. But he stopped again. He couldn't let her in just yet, there was still nearly two inches left, he'd have to hide everythin, and anyway she'd start sniffin—

"You all right, Daddy?"

Ah, but her voice was false, she wasn't really concerned, oney trying to find out did he have a bottle. He stared, bent, at the brown blistered door. How did she know? She didn't, the old sow sent her up, tiptoein, spyin. Thelma, li'l Thelma, to do that to your daddy. He swayed again, feeling a belch coming, had to put one hand on the dark doorframe, another on his mouth, but he managed to hold it down. Ah, ah, she was even turnin the doorknob, not makin a sound, the sly one. But he was smarter, smarter than all of them. Fallin for that red junk, that was only for Russian hayseeds, the chumps, it was the old hippopotamus of course, she and that dirty yappin Jew was he comin up again tonight was that it—the crockery knob turned back again—was that why they was makin sure about him; or that new fellah, the perfesser, with his big calf eyes what kind a perfesser was that to get mixed up with a bunch a out-of-work kids, kids and yids— he heard her go tip-tip down to her room. They ought a put em all out on the land.

A half-hour later Gordon sat in a little semicircle around the gas-fire with Mrs. Barstow, Jack and Thelma, giving them the gist of the letter. He had been careful not to bring the document itself; it would need too much bowdlerizing for Mrs. Barstow's ears. Sather had not yet arrived.

"The first problem is whether I should take the job at all."

"You'd be a sap not to," Jack said at once, sitting beside Gordon on a chair's edge, thinking my god that wouldn't be a problem for me, and perhaps I can still get to Sarah's in time for the last show.

"But—but it's almost a sneaky way to get it back—just through a woman!"

"Ooh, Gordy!" Thelma, a velvet vision opposite him, almost squeaked with shock. "That's anti-feminism. What would Trotsky say if he could hear you!"

"I didnt mean that, but dont you see it's using nepotism and— and the power of money behind the—" She was wearing his ring. At last!

"You have to eat," Jack cut in. "And maybe you could save a few bucks a month to send back to the *Spark*."

"But dont forget our American Section would have first claim on him," Thelma said with an air of virtuous firmness. Gordon half-wanted to nod agreement but his head refused; he had been assuming that the first claim was hers.

"Whatcha mean claim?" Jack said, wrinkling his smooth face at once into a veritable relief-map of impatience, "he isnt even a member of the League yet."

"All right, smarty, he's going to join at the next meeting, arent you, Gordy?" Her enchanting great eyes were on him, conjuring affirmation. Even they had darkened to violet with the new dress.

"Well," he said, a little faintly, "that was the idea. Or at least until this letter came." Consciously he looked away to Jack. *Your eyen two wol slee me sodenly.* She could never remember that he disliked being called Gordy,—even if she *was* wearing his ring.

"Well now it's different," his future brother-in-law said briskly. "He'll have to wait till he gets to Salt Lake and can analyze the political situation there. The Americans havent even a branch in Utah yet. He'll need to get New York's advice. Maybe they'll just want him to be a fellow-traveler for a while." He got up and crossed to the fireplace, looking covertly at his watch.

"Fellow-traveler." Thelma's eyes followed him with scorn. "He'll organize a big new branch in Salt Lake this fall,—wont you, Gordy?—after he's sewed up Vancouver. *He'll* show New York up."

She never says 'we', Gordon thought, more and more uneasy.

"Then," she went on, eager and pugnacious, flawless teeth flashing, "if he got it going right away he could be its delegate to their national plenum in New York next Christmas and then maybe he'd be able to help get the Cannonites out of the leadership of the American section and—"

"Whoa, whoa!" Jack shouted, "for jeeper's sakes, that's inner-party factionalism. Remember the poor guy's not a *member* yet and for all he's supposed to know the Trotskyists are just one happy family. Be tactful, cant you, just once?"

"But look!" Gordon found himself shouting too. "How can I organize a single branch even? I told you Oscar expects me to stay out of trouble, out of politics that is—"

"O, so he wouldnt care about other kinds of trouble," Thelma caught him up, piqued. "I'm beginning to think he's a bad influence on you, Gordon Saunders, from all you've told me. Why should you worry so much about him? He's just a fortune hunter. A déclassé intellectual. Trying to buy you off, that's all."

"He's the first man who's tried to *get* me a job, not *lose* me one," Gordon said, flurried. "And he's one of the best friends I've got. And if I get branded as a Red at Wasatch College it'll rebound on him. He'll get into Dutch with his wife and his father-in-law. I owe him, and them, certain loyalties."

"O, so you care more about being loyal to a big capitalist than to the Movement?" Thelma stormed back. "Or being loyal to me." Her eyes were tragic pools of violet blue, the dimple in her chin quivered.

"I didnt say that." He strove for calm. "I began by asking whether I shouldnt refuse—"

"You said—"

"O fer gosh sake, Thel." Jack banged on the mantel. "Let me get a word in. He doesnt have to barricade the campus and run up the red flag. He can play it smart, get through a year at least, work undercover. His pals will be away and he doesnt have to go telling the Board of Regents every time he has a Marxist thought."

"That's all very well," Thelma lowered long eyelashes and continued to look both beautiful and unappeased, "maybe he could, but he oughtnt to talk about being loyal to those bourgeois reactionaries. A Bolshevik-Leninist has room only for loyalty to his Party."

"To the Party's *principles*, dope, you ought to say," Jack corrected her. "At that rate we'd all still be Stalinists."

"You're twisting what I—"

"Shush." It was Mrs. Barstow, who had so far sat in unruffled silence, and who spoke now, so matter-of-factly it was as if nothing had yet been said. "How much they gonna pay yuh, Gordon?"

"Fifteen hundred, I think, Mrs. Barstow."

"You grab holt of it." She spoke with such breathy emphasis that, after her little round face was placid again, a wider ripple of energy was still running down through her bosom and losing itself in her midriff. "There's four of us livin here now on less'n that."

"Yes," said Gordon, catching at least part of her meaning, "and that brings up the reason—" he suddenly floundered, looked across to Thelma—"if we agree it's the right thing politically .and—and morally to take the job, then," he went on in a rush, "let's be married first and go there together."

He was mortified, first to see Thelma slowly sliding her gaze down into the lovely swell of her bosom as if he had made an indecent proposal, and then to feel himself pointlessly blushing. My God, is she going to be a Saint Cecelia and come to the wedding with a hair-shirt under her bridal dress?

Why did he have to say it out like that, so crude, she was thinking, making them look at me, he's always wanting to rush me, last night in the hall, O yes I like kissing him but the way he held me,

I could feel—O is it something wrong with me it frightens me to think of getting into a bed with him, with a man—

"Well supposin you went there first on your own, Gordon," Mrs. Barstow said, after what seemed an age, "and mebbe you found a place big enough, then Thelma and me'd come out and join you Christmas time."

And me? Gordon thought. The old girl had pulled him out—and dropped him in deeper water. He sat, too surprised to answer, while Jack leant against the mantel, knowing better this time than say anything, and Thelma was silently thanking her mother and thinking that's the only way I would go, with her along, and maybe I will because I do like him even if he is old, and he has lovely hair and he's the sincerest man I've ever known and almost as smart as Leo, I like older men, they're—but why can't he just stay here and—

"What do *you* say, my dear?"

He was trying to make her look at him but she wouldn't, not at any of them, only reproachfully, like a wistful princess, up at the window curtains now, and Gordon thinking I'm not going to be scared off by a stock mother-in-law situation, I *am* fond of this mountainous old girl, and after all she *is* Thelma's mother and a comrade and if this has to be another one of the prices of the marriage I'll pay it too; *I assent* (something he had that day been reading in *Piers Plowman* began to echo in his head), *I shall work as you will have me while life is lasting. . . . I shall put on, said Perkin, a pilgrim's garment, and—*

"You're all just trying to rush me," Thelma burst out, addressing the curtains. "I can't decide right away like this. Besides," and now she turned her eyes, lake-beautiful and pleading, not upon him but upon her mother, "Gordon promised me he'd join the League and go out and organize Vancouver."

"Dear God!" Jack strode over to her, stung by this inanity, "that was when he didnt have a job in sight. You're just making up silly romantic excuses, I told you you werent serious, you shouldnt *get* engaged like this all the time if you dont want to get married."

"Stop it now, Jackie," Mrs. Barstow growled but already Thelma had her face in her soft slender hands and from under them, under

148

the flashing of his ring, came a desolate sound like the mew of a kitten. "Now you got her bawlin again."

Gordon, feeling the guilt upon himself, sprang up and squatted awkwardly beside his coiled and unpredictable love. He tried a protective hand on her golden head but she shook it off and wept louder.

And I shall go with you till we find Truth.

"But look, Thelma, darling," he said, feeling utterly naked and knowing that he was being very silly, "I can still go to Vancouver first. And I will, for the summer, unless you and—and the other comrades think I shouldnt." *Go on pilgrimage as a palmer, to get pardon for my offences.* He waited, crouched painfully, and appalled suddenly to see Anne's face rising in his mind.

"Now you see, Thel," her mother said soothingly, "you got no reason to cry, nobody's makin you do nothin. And soon Leo'll be here and we kin see what he thinks."

At this Thelma's sobs rose to a wail. "I dont care what anybody thinks."

"Baby," Jack muttered, redfaced and disgusted. He had retreated to the fireplace.

"Now you hush up," Mrs. Barstow rolled her head at him. "You said too much already."

Gordon, wishing fatuously he had never come, and by now very uncomfortable on his bent knees, made the error of trying to separate Thelma's hands, still tight over her face. She jumped up, nearly bowling him over, and stood, arms stiffly bent, disclosing a mottled and abandoned countenance.

"I'm never going to marry anybody, never, never," she screamed, dancing on her feet in a tantrum. She snatched at her fingers and something bounced glinting over the carpet and rolled by Jack's feet. It was Gordon's ring. Before it had come to rest Thelma had wheeled, a violet swirl, and fled up the stairs.

Jack automatically picked up the ring and was about to hand it to Gordon when he stopped, perhaps feeling the action carried a symbolism he did not intend. Just then there were steps on the porch and the bell rang.

"I'll go." Jack rushed away in unashamed relief, shoving the ring in his pocket without looking at it or at Gordon. "And—and dont worry about this."

"Perhaps—" Gordon began, stranded on the carpet, "perhaps I ought to leave, and come back tomorr—"

"You sit right down," Mrs. Barstow said, soft and rapid, "taint nothin you did, those two are just a coupla kids in a lotta ways yet." There was an odd note of pride in her voice. "Thelma'll be over it an back down here in a minute or two you watch, and anyway here's Leo. You just relax. Thel aint the kinda girl you can rush about anythin."

"I know," said Gordon, though he didn't know the half of it, "but I do have to answer this letter." Joan Krautmann and I . . . Yet hearing Leo's voice in the hall—and somebody else who had evidently come with him—and an anxious query of Jack's if there was any late news on Germany, Gordon had a sudden moment of self-contempt that he should be so filled with the banal problems of his own soft life. Bourgeois prestige. . . . There was the noise of much shaking of coats; it must have started snowing again.

"You tell em yes," Mrs. Barstow was rushing on vigorously while they were still alone, "and as fer this summer if you kin git enough coachin round Toronto to keep yerself and mebbe find a dollar for the *Spark* dont you go off to that old Vancouver, and Thelm'll git time to know yuh better. Then mebbe we'll all go to Ohio or wherever it is together in the fall." She gave him a fat crafty wink. "An me an Jack'll git her outa this notion of you bein a professhnul revolution dont you worry, the idea," she hurried on, puffing, "that's fer when comrades cant find nothin else to do." She turned her head. "Well, Mac, aint you a sight fer sore eyes."

Gordon got up; it was MacCraddock, whom he'd met once before, the old trade-union warhorse of the Trotskyists and chairman of its Canadian League, twin power with Sather, who was its secretary. Like Sather, he had helped to found the Canadian Communist Party, had in fact been its leader until he too was exiled for heresy, to be succeeded by Tim Buck. MacCraddock was a big-chested man with great eyebrows and heavy cheekbones and black stumps of teeth. Behind him came Leo, alert and dapper though oddly quiet. Jack had not returned with them, was on the telephone.

"I'm sorry to brreak in upon you this way, Mrs. Barstow," Mac-Craddock said in his soft burr—he was a Maritime Scot—shaking hands with them both. "Leo and I had some things to talk over errlier on, and he made me step in since it's on me way home." His voice, deep, grave and gentle, would have served him well in Church, Gordon thought, remembering that MacCraddock had been sent as a boy to a seminary and had run away to work in a coalmine.

"I thought," Leo was inserting rather perfunctorily, "that Gordon might be glad to have Mac's advice too, in case his problem involves, shall we say, Local Headquarters."

"Why yes, that's fine," Gordon said, but it wasn't. For all the fatherly cadences there was a remoteness in MacCraddock's manner that did not impel Gordon to frankness, and he suspected that this redoubtable leader, whom he still admired and had been prepared to like, had never taken his revolutionary candidature seriously. Cautiously then, dryly almost, Gordon summarized once more the message from Van Bome. He found himself glad, now, that Thelma was out of the room.

"Well, what do you say, Mac?" Leo asked when Gordon had stopped. He spoke with surprising offhandedness, his macaw's head perked at neither of them, as if he, too, were preoccupied. Was it the German news that had upset everybody tonight? MacCraddock's rocky features did not relax, but the two grey tufts over his eyes raised and lowered themselves silently.

"I canna see but what it's a perrsonal matter," he said at last. "If ye want my perrsonal advice it would be to grab the jobe."

"Jus' what I been tellin him, Mac," Mrs. Barstow said comfortably.

"But if I take it on the terms implied by the letter—that is, a kind of gentleman's understanding that I wont be engaging in left-wing politics—I shant be of much use to the Party down there, especially if I'm married." *Dangerously close to Marxism, Mr. Saunders.*

MacCraddock had been looking sideways, as if only politely hearing him out. Now he glanced at Sather. "He'll no be a grand help to us here wi'out a jobe would ye say Leo?"

Leo hesitated, seeming, for him, almost embarrassed. "Gordon had thought, Mac," he said, setting his words down cautiously, as a cat puts his feet on a roof-ridge, "that he could ride the freights to Vancouver in June and try to organize a branch for us out there."

MacCraddock wrinkled his forehead, his eyes on the floor. He said nothing.

"This was of course," Gordon spoke, feeling the silence, "on the assumption that I was to be taken into the organization first, at, well, at the next meeting."

MacCraddock raised upon him a long extraordinary look from eyes powder-blue and faded, a regard at once questioning and indifferent, as a man might bestow from his deathbed upon a strange well-meaning visitor. But he said nothing, and his silence, which at first seemed to be a searching for words, came gradually to be realized as willful, as MacCraddock lowered his gaze again to the floor.

Gordon paled, realizing that the wordless act was a refusal, that MacCraddock might always vote, and by that one vote prevent, his entry into the movement. The thought put him in turmoil, for did not MacCraddock's hostility provide him with a last reprieve from the fate he was demanding for himself? In Canada at least he would be, perforce, a reasonably safe fellow-traveler. Or he could try the CCF. But what if Thelma rejected him in consequence? *The whole future of the universe. . . .* And my God, what was wrong with him if he was not fit to belong to something Hymie the tailor and—he was suddenly angry at MacCraddock, but before the emotion found words Mrs. Barstow had spoken.

"Now Leo there aint no reason why everybody gotta join the Party, and Gordon and Thelma could do a lot jus bein in a college and sendin money in to help."

"Maybe not," Leo said with high unexpected harshness—he seemed to have shed tonight all his flamboyance—"but we need a branch in Vancouver." He was no longer the macaw but, in the unsmiling asperity of his features, some small sharp bird of prey. "That town's crying out to be organized, Gordon knows the place, and he's given me to understand he's willing to make the try. I for one am all for it. As to that, he can perfectly well do it and still go on in the Fall to his college job."

Gordon glanced quickly at the others. MacCraddock's face seemed sunk in apathy, as if he were scarcely listening, and Mrs. Barstow sat expressionless as a Buddha. Jack, who had come silently back with his hat on, was sitting by the door, evidently hoping to get away. Gordon turned to Sather and caught again something (was it only the hawklike poise of his face?) something cunning, ruthless, inimical, which, despite all his reason, he could have sworn was directed against himself. And it was a little odd, surely, that Sather too, like MacCraddock, seemed deliberately to be avoiding any reference to his engagement, or to Thelma at all. He felt deserted—even by Jack. *It is too late now to stay in those houses. . . .*

It was true that MacCraddock was paying little attention, thinking *I should never a stopped by for Leo'd never have asked me to if he'd thought I wouldna fall in with his plans. But I canna say yes, the League's bad enough off without havin such kittle-kattle, though Sather'll do what he wants as soon I'm gone, and I'm no much carin, for it's too late, it's a soft generation that'll no give us a Wurrkers' State, a fascist one more like. Ah weel I mun make a move and get away home.*

Mrs. Barstow, then, was beginning to say something but she had only got her mouth open when there was a thin high laugh from the hall door, and Mr. Barstow sidled in on skewgee carpet-slippers, out of which his legs, sheathed in dirty gray-green undies, rose like asparagus stalks and disappeared under the brown buttoned-up overcoat.

"Bourgeois? Bushwa?" He mimicked Sather's voice. His little pink-rimmed eyes flickered over them, on guard, ready for a fight or a welcome. "Supprised yuh eh, dint hear me come down them stairs?"

"How arr ye Tom?" It was MacCraddock who spoke almost at once, friendly and unperturbed.

"Ow's it Mac?" Mr. Barstow asked, suddenly lapsing into the cheerful and ordinary, but just avoiding a hiccup. Sather and Gordon essayed polite greetings, which Mr. Barstow began to acknowledge with an ironic bow to the room in general but, starting to go off balance, he plopped down quickly in the nearest chair. This was Jack's, who had jumped up speechless when his father entered. Gordon had meanwhile been rising and making a belated gesture to his own softer seat.

"O dont trouble yourself, dont trouble yourself perfesser," Mr. Barstow fumbled at his ear, produced a shapeless butt of a hand-rolled cigarette and poked one end of it into the corner of his mouth, with a little imp-glance at the round stone staring image of his wife. "It's only me, you know, only Thelma's old nogood pappa." He began feeling awkwardly in a pocket of his greatcoat.

It's God's judgment on me, Mrs. Barstow was thinking, where's he been hidin it this time?

"You needin a light there, Tom?" MacCraddock got up and went over with a box of matches.

"Light? O sure, sure." Mr. Barstow held two yellow fingers around the butt in his mouth and, sucking at the flame, peered slantwise up at MacCraddock. "You fellahs allus ready with a light, eh?" he said. "Like in Berlin, eh?" He snickered. There was silence. "Ah well. Doin any carpentry these days, Mac?" He leant back puffing.

"Not much, Tom." MacCraddock shook out the match. "How's things with the postal wurrkers?" he asked easily, going to the mantel over the gasfire to look for an ashtray. There wasn't one Mrs. Barstow discouraged smoking.

As MacCraddock's figure moved between her and her husband Mrs. Barstow sent a stage whisper toward Jack. "Go see what's happened to Thel." Mr. Barstow heard her.

"O Thelma's all right, all right, dont you worry old girl." He grinned up at Mac, who was laying the burnt match abstractedly on the dusty mantel, but then, as Jack edged toward the hall, Tom Barstow swiveled sharply. "She dont want you," he said contemptuously. Jack paused. Mr. Barstow removed his butt—it had already gone out—and spat a flake of tobacco at the carpet.

"Pig-hog," Mrs. Barstow breathed, not stirring, but her husband spoke at the same moment, did not catch it.

"Thel and I been havin a nice little confab and she tole me I was to come down and take her place in this little meetin a yours." He cocked the butt back in his mouth and grinned piratically at them. "Dont mind a—" he hiccupped suddenly—"father in at th

154

mbly council, do you, dont mind if I got somethin to say about
ᵔe own daughter gittin married huh?"

"Yer lyin," Mrs. Barstow said, loud and ruthless. "Thel dint
ᵉnd you down and what's more yer drunk."

Mr. Barstow squirmed out of his chair and, pulling his butt
ᵒm his mouth again, pointed it waveringly at the great target of
ᵢs wife. Jack seized the moment to slip out. "Now you listen to
ᵉ, you ole bag a wind—"

"You go on back up them stairs and dont make no scene," she
ᵢd unmoving. Her eyes, deep in her tight dollface, were little cold
ᵘe stars.

"I aint gonna do nothin of—" he began, but MacCraddock was
ᵃ his feet now too.

"I'm sorry, Tom, but ye'll all have tae excuse me."

"Now see wotcha done," Mrs. Barstow said righteously.

Tom turned, uncertain, fuddled, and Gordon looked up surprised
MacCraddock; it wasn't like him to run away.

"I just dropped in by chance the while, ye know, and I must
ᵉ gettin on home to the wife. I've a big day tomorra." He spoke
ᵢf unaware that he was in the midst of a family quarrel. Yet he
ᵃt a big hand gently on Mr. Barstow's sloped back, pressing into
ᵉ cloth of his faded overcoat as if holding the little man straight.
ᵉ ken I'm no mixin in yer family affairs, Tom," he went on
ᵢetly. "All the counsel I've given the night, and I'll grant ye—"
ᵉ smiled and lifted his eyebrows—"twas no worth much, was that
ᵢ a perrsonal matter that doesna consairn me."

"O now dont you git me wrong," Tom began, stuttering, quite
ᵒn over. "My—my affairs is your affairs, Mac, you know that,
ᵧ-anytime, dont you go now, you sit right down an' tell me what
ᵤ think, I—"

"I'll tell ye what I think for the now, then," Mac cut him short
ᵢsily, "and that's that ye go straightway to your bed and sleep
ᵒn the proablem and have your talk in the mornin. And I've
ᵃ proablem or, two I mun do the same with." Thinking, as the
ᵒw ache spread deeper into his right jaw, that's a new hole,
ᵉy're all rotten and what will they do will they yank em out for
ᵉ where I'm goin?

"Ah?" The little man seemed dashed, but trusting. "Mebb
that's right then, Mac."

Mac gave him a pat and looked canny. "And if ye've a dra
left in yer boattle I'll be glad of a nip for the road."

Mr. Barstow dropped his head ludicrously, the boy who had eate
all the candies. He clutched at MacCraddock's coat-tail as th
latter turned with his hand out to Mrs. Barstow. "Honesta go
Mac, you know me, f'I had a drop in the house it'd be yours yo
—you know that, but they wont let me have any Mac, they—" bt
MacCraddock was busy saying his farewells.

"You comin wi' me, Leo?"

There was a pause and Gordon noticed an indecipherable ex
change of glances between MacCraddock and Sather.

"No," said Leo then, "Jack wants to talk to me. But I'll g
straight back to my flat from here. You, or Mrs. Mac, can phor
me if—"

MacCraddock nodded, moved into the hall, with Mr. Barsto
anxiously in tow.

At that moment Jack came down the stairs. "Thelma's O.I
but she's gone to bed," he said shortly, "and I'm late for a date
He had his hat and overcoat on. "I'll walk down to the car wi
you all." He stopped. "Isnt Leo coming?"

"No," Sather called from the livingroom, "I'm staying a whi
I'll give you a ring about the editorial tomorrow."

Gordon looked up at Sather startled. He just said he was stayir
to talk to Jack. He doesn't want to go with Mac. Why? There
something wrong between them.

If MacCraddock felt surprise he did not speak it, perhaps becau
Mr. Barstow was hovering at the halldoor, distracting him. "Yc
can take a joke, Mac," he was saying urgently, fiddling with
scrap of paper he had fished from his overcoat pocket. "I mac
up a pome," he added hurriedly, "all about you fellahs, Mac, a
about Trotsky."

"O, Dad, for God's sakes," Jack said, agonizing at the door, "v
have to go."

"Yah, yah, beatin it. Cause he knows I got him in it, donc
Jackie lad?" He waved the paper delightedly, thinking it's like
had a snake and they was little girls runnin away. "And wotc

talkin about God fer anyway. Yer supposed to be a natheist."

"Next time," MacCraddock said vaguely and hurried out, Jack on his heels.

And now the door was shut Mr. Barstow felt suddenly betrayed, standing lonely and lost and needing a drink, listening to the listening silence in the livingroom and yes, even catching out of the corner of his eye the dim malevolent shape of the old sow waiting to grunt and squeal at him from her chair. He was tired, his feet hurt, and everything that he hadnt said was whirling still in his own ears but now not in shape to say, as if he'd tuned into two radio stations at once and couldnt get either of them loud and separate. And upstairs under the bed was only an empty bottle. Then he noticed he had his poem in his hand; he turned and shuffled hesitatingly back into the livingroom, to where she sat, she and her bigmouthed sheeny lawyer, and was he her lover too? and that dreamy-faced perfesser only he wasnt even a perfesser— (alla them clammed up, and only she watchin him)—jus' another long nosed commie for all his fine airs, the big gowk, wantin to marry his little Thel, and that pair helpin him, tryin to git her out of the house, because—because they knew she still loved her old dad, that's why.

"You wanna hear it?" he asked, but of course they didnt, it was just to see what the damfools would say. No one spoke.

"All right, I'm gonna bed, sure, sure. But I'm gonna tell yuh somethin first—" hands thrust deep in his old rusty overcoat he swayed toward them—"I'm gonna tell yuh Mister, Mister"—he was hunting, watching with his little green eyes Sather's averted face, hunting for the annihilating word—"Mister Rabbi, Mister Jehovah-interferin-Sather—"

"Dont you start yer jew-baitin in here." A sound that was half shudder, half growl, came from Mrs. Barstow and she heaved on her chair-arms; but she was too suddenly swept with rage to manoeuvre herself up. "You git to bed like you promised Mac you would," she said, thinking God make him go before I git up cause if I put my hands on him I'll choke him I'll choke him till he's dead.

Gordon sat wondering whether there was anything he could do

that would be better than the nothing he was doing. Sather's unprecedented silence persuaded him to keep his own.

"Mac," Mr. Barstow was saying, his thoughts all helter-skelter and his body urging a retreat, "Mac's a good man, see, Mac's all right, even if he is a Red, you leave Mac outa this, Mac and I unerstan each other, cause we're real workers see, Mac an I—" he swayed, voice tailing off—"we're real workin class." His eyes wandered, hesitated over Gordon, who was in turn staring at him in fascination and suspense.

"Go on," Mrs. Barstow grunted, straining on her bulging forearms, "before yer sick on the carpet."

He was stung, drew himself up, desperately trying not to wobble, to be the dignified suffering man he knew he was. "Dontcha worry bout me, yaint never worried about me, yuh wickit ol woman, yuh —yunnatural—I-I aint nobody I'm jus a postman, sure, perfesser, jus a fellah pays fer alla bills, fer"—his eyes darted at her—"fer keepin that barrel a lard there filled up with—"

Mrs. Barstow rose quivering from her chair. At the sight her husband began backing, speaking frantically, knowing he had only a few more seconds.

"Lemme tell you this, Thel got too much sense to marry one a yer Reds an what's more I ain gonna let her an if she does I'll— I'll go t'the p'lice that's what yes yuh bet I will—" Mrs. Barstow was rolling relentlessly forward, the shanks of her arms crooked, while Leo and Gordon rose silently behind them—"so you put that in yer pipe and smoke it, all a ye, yuh—yuh firebugs!"

"Git," said Mrs. Barstow succinctly and crowded him through the halldoor.

"Dont you touch me," he cried at her in sudden panic in the hall, and Gordon and Leo moved awkwardly toward them. But Mr. Barstow was plowing up the stairs. "Touch yuh," said Mrs. Barstow with soft and terrible scorn from the stairbottom, "I aint touched you fer twenty years an I never will."

"Ta hell with yuh, ta hell with yuh all," Mr. Barstow yelled, still reeling upward, almost sobbing. "You take *her* to the States, perfesser, an that bastard son a hers, an all her dirty sonsabitchin jewboys with her, but you leave my Thel alone."

Mrs. Barstow came, purple-faced but proud, back to her living-room.

"You set right down, the two of you," she said, as if they had just arrived, "and I'm gonna make us a nice cup of coffee." She turned, panting, and rolled off through the tiny diningroom into the kitchen without waiting for an answer.

Gordon and Sather exchanged glances. "There," said the latter with a touch of his old manner, "goes a very gallant gentlewoman." But he sounded distraught and, sitting down, stared at the floor. Thinking there goes the goddamned Canadian workingclass, I've had enough, I should have pulled out long ago and now it's too bloody late, for all Mac's mess will be down on me tomorrow, tonight even, and this half-pint group will splinter over it whatever happens, and the Cannonites will have the laugh. The Third International's dead and the Fourth will never get born. I'd walk out of it all if I could take her off with me but first I've got to get *him* as far away as possible. And that means I must tell him at once, this instant, that he can join, that Mac doesn't matter. But if I explain about Mac, will it scare him? Well fine if it does, it'll queer him for good with her if he rats. Now how shall I put it?

Before he had decided, Gordon broke the silence, for there were things he too had to say before he could lie down with his own misery. "Am I to take it, Leo," he said tonelessly, "that Mac-Craddock wont let me join your ranks?"

What luck! He couldn't have asked for a better lead. But Sather looked up blankly to mask his relief. "Mac?" he said slowly, "I dont think Mac's going to be in a position to decide for a while." He paused, looking away with an unconscious narrowing of his dark eyes that once more made Gordon think, though he reproached himself for the thought, of some medieval bird of ravine. "And as for me," Sather went on carefully, "and I think I can speak for the rest of the Central Committee, I'm prepared, as I said a while ago, my dear Gordon, to welcome you in—provided," he added casually, "youre willing to take on the Vancouver assignment, for the summer at least. But I wonder, after all this, are you?"

Gordon laughed dryly. "All Thelma's family, for rather various reasons, have warned me not to. And Thelma seems to be warning me that I'd better—but also that I probably havent a chance with her anyway. Which all makes it easier for me to decide on my own and for honest political reasons. Yes." He took a breath, as on a diving board. *Kick it toward our goal and accept our rules.* . . . "I'm ready and willing—so far as Vancouver is concerned. Though what I do in Salt Lake—"

"Is a matter to decide then," Sather finished quickly for him. He seemed pleased, and with a manner both jaunty and serious, put out his hand. "Welcome, my friend."

Gordon clasped it awkwardly. What am I doing?

You're surrendering your identity into his hands, fool.

"But Leo," he said, "I still dont understand about Mac, what you've just said—" He stopped.

Leo cocked an eye toward the diningroom, thinking I'll tell him now while he's full of his romantic resolutions. "There's no reason, I suppose," he replied then, low, "why I shouldnt let you know tonight, though it's strictly between us and I dont want Mrs. Barstow upset with the matter at the moment—the fact is that I expect Mac to be arrested, tonight or tomorrow."

"Arrested!"

"The Stalinites engineered one of their phony united-front rallies yesterday, protesting Section 98 again, and—"

"The criminal syndicalism law?"

"Yes, the one that put Timmie the Buck and their other opera stars in the Kingston pen. Well, Mac managed to get delegated to it by the building-trades federation, and put over a speech. Apparently there was a stool taking notes. And Mac perhaps got carried away a little."

"But—but didnt Mac *attack* Buck and the CP?"

"He attacked their politics but he defended their right to have them, correctly, and naturally he lambasted the Bennett government for jailing workingclass leaders. Dont forget that we still share, even with Buck, the common class enemy. Anyway, he got tipped off this afternoon that the Mounties are going to charge him—under the same statute."

Gordon sat thinking, this is the reality already and this is what will happen someday to me, now that I am burning my bridges, this happens under democracy, and if a Canadian Hitler comes

I'll be jailed too, tortured, killed—"But cant we help him to lie low till, well till it blows over?"

Sather raised one eyelid. "Where do we hide a man with a wife and three kids? We discussed the whole thing in Central Committee earlier this evening and agreed the best thing is to make it into a propaganda trial. It's what is known as a political opportunity, the first we seem to have had, as Trotskyists, in Canada, for a public platform—with Klieg lights."

"You'll be his lawyer?"

"Naturally. We'll do our best to put over our whole international position."

"Which means," Gordon said softly, "he'll be convicted. He can get seven years." *A revolution's no place for the gutless.*

Sather made a grimace. "Buck's in for five. But I'm hoping for less." He glanced sharply at Gordon. "I might even get him off." But he didn't sound convincing.

"And Mac? He wants it this way?"

Sather gave a tired shrug, thinking *it might be even smarter if I scared him right off now. If he goes west, and does anything, she may like him all the more. Let him rat and he'll lose her for sure, the poor bloody innocent; if I were in his place, if I had a choice again, I'd run, I'd run hellbent from everybody's politics.* But he only said: "Mac accepts the executive's decision. Personally I think he's a little numbed at the moment, as which of us mightnt be?" He seemed to think about this briefly and then went on. "Mac's been a fighter in the radical movement for about thirty years now, my dear Gordon. He had six months in hospital once, ·after being clubbed in the mouth on a miner's picket line. He spent most of the war in jail as a resister, and was in stir again after the Winnipeg strike. He was thoroughly beaten up two years ago by our friends the Stalinites. And lately he's not been well— teeth, I think, or what stumps he has left—and maybe he's not been getting quite enough to eat. Anyway, Mac's about ready to call it quits. But—" and Sather's face tightened—"he's going through with this. This is what we'll all have to go through, sooner or later—and maybe worse."

"I see," said Gordon slowly, but seeing less than was there, seeing only what his wish and his precious new faith did not instantly erase from his vision.

"Perhaps now," Sather flicked him with a look half-challenging, half-jeering, "you'd like to reconsider our little agreement?"

Gordon flushed, feeling suddenly that he could never again live with himself if he turned tail now, at this moment, under Sather's dark and appraising eyes. *Every fowl that ever was born. . . .* "Certainly not," he said, "I'm more determined than ever."

"Good," said Sather with almost heavy heartiness, but his eyes did not change.

"Comin up," said Mrs. Barstow, rolling in through the dining-room with a rattling tray. "I thought you boys might like some cheese san'iches too."

There was a rustle in the hall, and an arch voice in the doorway said: "Do I smell coffee?" Thelma, twinkling in a blue dressing-gown and little satin slippers, all smiles and forgiveness, stepped gracefully into the room. *More blisful on to see, than is the newe pere-jonette tree.* She was once more, he saw, wearing his ring. But it was toward Sather that she walked.

17

HITLER PROMISES NEW
LABOR ERA—TO BE
DICTATOR ONLY TILL 1937

Girls Recant Story
in Scottsboro Case

BANK HOLIDAY PLAN
SPREADING

WORST OF DEPRESSION
OVER, SAYS BENNETT

GERMANY MAKES
WOODEN BREAD

BANKS CLOSE THROUGHOUT U.S.
AS ROOSEVELT INAUGURATED

"The only thing we have to fear is fear itself," said the new Chief Executive of the United States in his inauguration speech today.

MANY CANADIAN
HIGH SCHOOLS MAY CLOSE
FOR LACK OF FUNDS

Britain Fears Only Miracle
Can Prevent European War

RAMSAY MACDONALD
TO ROME TO MAKE
FRIENDS OF IL DUCE

SENATE CUTS BEER TO 3.05

Nazis Torture Jews,
Reds, Refugees Claim

LEAGUE SEEKS SANCTIONS
AGAINST JAPAN

STORE MAGNATE FINDS
PEACE FOR FIRST TIME
IN OXFORD GROUP

DOLLFUS BECOMES
DICTATOR

U.S. HOUSE PASSES
BEER BILL

SOVIET CHARGES
HUGE SABOTAGE BY
BRITISH VICKERS
ENGINEERS

MUSSOLINI READY
TO DISARM

No Tortures in Germany;
Goering Says Press Unfair
Some Jewish Shops Picketed

SCIENCE GUIDING WORLD
TO GOLDEN ERA
SAYS DR. TORY AT
PACIFIC SCIENCE MEET

Vancouver, April 12—Fees for Teacher Training classes will be increased, and members of the university staff will receive another salary reduction when the University of British Columbia session opens this fall. The Faculty have already had cuts ranging from 5% to 25% but . . .

EASTER REPTILES ARE HERE

JAPS RUSH ARMY TO SIBERIAN BORDER

Unemployed to Work on Roads at 20c Day—Dominion Taking Over All Camps

JEW REFUGEES STORM PARIS

Many of World's Great Books Burning in German Bonfire

London, May 11 (From our Special London correspondent) —Sir Francis Goodenough, one of London's public utility kings, sees prosperity ahead for all the world. The stalwart, rubicund baronet, when I lunched with him in his Club this week . . .

HAPPY DAYS COMING AS BRITONS BUY FEWER USED GOLF BALLS

U.S. Wage Volume Now Only 40% of 1929 Figure— Business Running at Yearly Loss of Five Billion

GOVT. CONTROLS CAPITALISM NOW SAYS BRAINS-TRUSTER

Kingfish Says Brother a Liar

Americans Bow Before Queen at Court

U.S. OFF GOLD STANDARD

Wall St. Stocks Boom; Pound Up 30 Per Cent

Science Growing Pink Chicks for Easter Eggs

Calgary, Alta., April 25 (CP) —Relief strikers in a mob of more than 1,500 clashed with fifty police today in the suburbs of this city. No police were injured but several . . .

MILLIONS IN EXILE UNDER SOVIET EDICT

Mystery Surrounds Garbo as Her Ship Nears Coast

Ottawa, Ont., May 6 (CP) — Publication of the names of those in receipt of incomes of $100,000 per year or more will not be permitted, Honorable E. N. Rhodes, Minister of Finance, told the House today . . .

I SPEARED MAN-EATERS IN MALAYA

Europe Feels Easier after Hitler's Speech

Saskatoon, May 9—Inspector L. J. Sampson, commander of the local R.C.M.P. detachment, was thrown from his horse and fatally injured yesterday afternoon when leading a squadron of mounted officers into a rioting mob of single unemployed at the local relief camp. Twenty-eight occupants of the camp have already been placed under arrest and . . .

MORGAN PARTNERS PAID $51 MILLION TAX SINCE WAR DESPITE EVASIONS

18

AT MAY'S END, WHEN EVEN THE MOST CLOISTERED ELM IN THE
darkest quad of Toronto's winter-scarred campus was risking green
leaves again, Gordon packed his lecture notes, his album of snaps,
and his birth certificate into a suitcase which he chucked in a corner
of the Barstow basement. His books he sold to a secondhand dealer,
his own scruffy suit and his watch he pawned, and keeping back
five dollars for the trip, he mailed thirty-two more, the sum of
his wealth, to himself at the Vancouver Post Office. The six com-
pleted chapters of "Carnality and Idealism in the Fifteenth Century
Scottish Chaucerians" he deposited with Professor Pellat, who still
hoped to find his pupil a fellowship to finish it, sometime.

But not this time, when Gordon borrowed an old rucksack from
Jack and stowed a blanket, a tin cup and a twist of tea in it, a
toothbrush and a change of sweat-shirt, four packets of raisins,
a pair of socks, a piece of soap in a metal box, and Marx's *Criticism
of the Gotha Program* (perhaps at last he would understand what
Hymie meant by The Dialectic). And not this night, when, pack
strapped snug against Hymie's gift of a faded turtle-necked sweater,
a brace of Mamma Barstow's ham sandwiches in the hip pockets of
his old campus corduroys, and his five-dollar bill flattened between
the sock and sole of his right foot, Gordon, by blind luck evading
the yard cops, caught the cold rungs of a freight rumbling slowly
out of the Toronto yards, and swung aboard for British Columbia.

He lay belly-flat, fingers clamped on the swaying catwalk on the
top of a wind-tormented boxcar, fighting numbness. Almost at
eye-level a jerking yellow light began swelling toward him and
his fingers tightened in a rush of fear as he recalled Bob Fournier's
tales of brakemen so tough they would literally kick a hobo off a
moving train. But this one mutely led him to the hollow clangorous
shelter of an ore-gondola and, at the first halt, showed him where
to climb down and hop into an open boxcar. So many wandering

Canadian workless had descended on the freight trains in the spring of 1933 that trainmen had in fact grown helpless, then indifferent, and some at last friendly—provided they did not suspect a company 'spotter' in the vicinity. Empty boxcars had become traveling bunk-houses (and latrines), foul, lawless, sometimes lethal, but in a sense free. Gordon shared his the next day with a growing colony of fellow-amateurs and a few professional transients, whose ages ran from a dubious sixteen to a manifest seventy.

In later years the sequence of the next three weeks blurred in his mind. Somewhere certainly, even before Northern Ontario, he had learned how to jump from a moving way-freight. The first time coming into a yard, he had kept his rucksack strapped to him; when his momentum pitched him on his face and rolled him head-over in lacerating cinders, the pack pivoted him toward the train. One leg, arcing down, had actually glanced off the side of a boxcar. A split-second later and it would have come between two cars and under the grinding wheels.

From then on, whenever they began clanging and screeching in past the first houses, and the old stiffs predicted cops ahead, Gordon threw his pack off first and hunted for it after. That is, he did until that day on the prairies when scrambling up from a ditch he saw a yardcop, arms folded, a club poked out from under an armpit, uniformed legs straddling Gordon's possessions. There was another railroad policeman coming down the cinders toward him. Gordon plunged through willows, rolled under the barbed railway fence, and hid half-drowned in a swamp until the hunters disappeared after more visible game.

Then he made his way, by luck, to the local 'jungle' between a garbage dump and the river, and tried to dry his shoes and corduroys at a fire of cardboard cartons, along with a recent Bachelor of Science in Civil Engineering who had also been in the swamps and had never found a job since he graduated but was still hoping, he said, standing in frayed BVDs mechanically toasting his armorphous jeans. He had a bony, skull-like face, a death's head, Gordon had thought; even the chattering of his teeth had a skeletal sound, and his eyes remained drugged with the torpor of a man who slept and ate too little and too seldom.

There was a sudden rainstorm and the two of them endeavored

unsuccessfully to keep their semi-dryness by crouching in an empty 'jungle-hut', a hollowed brushpile floored with dirty wet excelsior and sour rags. Hours after, directed by the snag-toothed oldster who had been tending the fire, Gordon and the B.Sc., both as wet again as ever, hit the ties for two miles to a watertank where there were no bulls and the next freight might stop. It was, as it turned out, the next freight but two which watered there, fourteen hours later. After he caught it, he discovered that the two dollars left of his original five were no longer in his right shoe, nor in his left. They were back with the yellow-toothed old man in the jungle. He had thirty cents in his pockets, no pack, and half a continent still to go.

In the going, he learned many things which never proved of much use to him in academic life but which he found at the time to be axioms of existence. Hogheads, or engineers, are all right if you leave them alone, but some brakemen are 'sour shacks' who will pretend to ignore your presence until a cop is in sight; then they'll boot you off, as the train slows, into his lap. Empty flat-cars are to be avoided; they are afflicted with shrieks and palsy, and leave you with bellyache and deafness, temporary but dangerously incapacitating. Loaded lumberflats, on the other hand, offer the quietest of all rides, but on fast curves the load may shift and brush you off at any speed up to fifty miles an hour. He found that no one actually 'rode the rods' any more; the newer cars in fact had understructures so designed as to leave no cranny for riding in, and even if oldfashioned affairs were available, the danger of detection or injury was too great. Empty boxcars were the warmest and least conspicuous solutions, and the safest—provided you wedged the sliding door to prevent it jamming shut and leaving you to starve or suffocate, to freeze or thirst to death, banging your heels unheard against dark carwalls on some lonely siding.

It was also wise, he learned, not to get sentimentally attached to even the friendliest of trains. Most of the transients hopped off even a through-freight, if they were nearing a divisional point, —where mounties reinforced the railroad police—or any fairsized town. There was always the chance that yardbulls would be there, one on each side of the cars, ready to tramp the length of the train, thrusting tenfoot poles into the farthest corners of a boxcar;

if the probe struck flesh, the flesh would be goaded out; then it would be beaten up, or its owner charged with railway trespass. If the pole missed, you were nevertheless afraid to stir till the freight pulled out—when your chance was gone to get food, and flex aching muscles locked from everlasting bracing against the sway and shudder of the train.

So you jumped off, however cushy your nest, as soon as the speed was low enough to make your action something less than suicide, and swabbed your face in the cleanest available ditchwater, or in almost anything that would remove the top layers of greasy trainsmoke from your wind-peeling skin. If, of course, there was a 'Y' in the town and you found it before a policeman found you and charged you with vagrancy, you got a wash and a shave free. Or if you were both lucky and nimble you might once in a while sneak unobserved as far uptown as a Salvation Army hostel and get a meal of sorts, a bath, and a bed for the night.

But there was an afternoon, a few days after he had hid in the swamp, when, in order to hang on to whatever handhold he might snare on the next freight, Gordon knew he must have food and if possible a blanket; to earn them he had gone knocking down a whole street of houses on a town's fringe, offering, as he had on other days in other towns with equal lack of success, to cut lawns or split wood or do anything useful in return for a sandwich, and getting only mumbled words and frightened stares and slammed doors, and going on down the next street until he was too faint and sat on a curb. And then, since he had not eaten for two days, he had asked flatly for a dime from a blue-jowled man in an immaculate Stetson who was locking a Buick—knowing that a dime would buy a coffee and two buns, and that if he were given two bits he could eat something called a three-course meal in a Chinese restaurant down by the tracks. He got nothing but a silent hangdog brush-off and went back dizzy-headed toward the yards, because a freight was due, but on the way through an alley he passed a garbage can by the backdoor of the town's hotel and lifted the lid and found a whole roasted potato and a fresh drumstick, only half-eaten, and ate them, and felt better, far better than when he had been panhandling for the dime.

Eating out of scrap cans and stealing train-rides were at least actions his comrades could approve, part of the inevitable pecking of the revolutionary chick through the bourgeois shell. But a *lumpenproletarian* odor clung around panhandling, and perhaps he never would have begged even that one time if the possible penalty had not been so severe as to create a challenge for any apprentice rebel. The owner of the Buick could have turned him in; and there were magistrates willing to hand out jail terms—the maximum was six months hard—for panhandling, though they might sentence a man to fewer days than that for theft or wife-beating. In one Manitoban town, in which he found himself simply because a tough brakie had booted him off a freight running through its yards, he had been stopped in the first block from the station by a deadpan town cop and warned, because he could not give a local address or show that he carried money, to get outside the municipal limits and catch the next freight or be booked for vagrancy. He got out. He had talked with many a stiff by this time who had struck a hot spot and been vagged, sweated out fourteen days hard in the fetid local jail and been given a boot in parting, and he was not curious to experience the ritual. Most magistrates, however, not wishing to add to the board bill of the local taxpayers, gave tramps, panhandlers and even petty thieves alike a 'floater'—a sentence suspended for twenty-four hours to give the criminal a chance to leave forever the town he had victimized by his presence. But it was a sentence, an initial entry in a police record, and something to be concealed if ever again in his life a man, whether bourgeois teacher or professional revolutionary, wanted to cross an international border.

It was astonishing, nevertheless, how many hundreds were daily taking such risks in order to wander over the barren richness of Canada. Before he had got through half his journey Gordon knew that he himself would never again willingly board a freight train and lie drugged with insensate noise and violent motion, watching an endless idiotic stutter of poles and glittering wires and blank landscape. Yet, though he had met many on his journey who talked the way he felt, there were others, of whom Sam Archibald, a Nova Scotian who shared an empty stinking cattle car with Gordon through most of Alberta, was typical.

Sammy, a lanky loose-jointed man in his middle twenties, told

Gordon he had been a pulpmill worker till the plant closed two years ago. Since then he had three times made the 8000-mile return-trip by freight between Atlantic and Pacific.

"I jus got the bug to keep goin, I guess," he had murmured, scratching his grimy head when Gordon asked him why. "Old folks is on relief, I aint no use to em. If I git a job its oney for a few days. Last summer I even made some dough harvestin on the prairies. Two bucks a day with a thresher gang, we was lucky we had good weather, worked every day nearly, but jeez it's like the feller says, a bead a sweat frevery ear a wheat, and you cant hang on to what you save. Frinstance I come out to Vancouver after and there was a job jus posted up at a employment agency, cookee wanted at a upcoast loggin camp. So I nip in and pay them blood-suckers ten bucks to git the job, and another twenty boat fare to git to the goddam camp, and ten days later the outfit goes phut and shuts down and we all hafta fork out passage back to Vancouver. Dont pay to try settlin no more. If they is a job around, you gotta have letters of recomm'ation no less, even for pickin berries. Anyways, most towns you can oney stay twenty-four hours in, and git a charity bed and a mug of soup, then you gotta move on. So movin on is what guys like us got to do. Until we git that golden age them science fellows is talkin about, anyways. Lucky it's a kinda interestin country anyway, Canada I mean. Fulla scenery, that's fer sure."

Sammy had been, in his lugubrious way, a cheerful companion and Gordon regretted that he did not meet him until after Regina and lost him soon after in the Ogden yards at Calgary when ten of them scattered into the darkness at the shriek of a police whistle. It was more than regret. Gordon never grew so old that he stopped feeling enormously in Sammy Archibald's debt. For it was long, dirty, feckless Sammy, of all his fellow wanderers, who offered a blanket when he saw Gordon had none, offered from his store of two and insisted he accept, shoved his grey grubby old second blanket into his arms and even cut the hank of binder twine, that tied his bundle, into equal lengths so that Gordon could packroll it, and sleep again for more than half an hour at a stretch.

19

SENEATE COMMITTEE TO PROBE MORGAN

Montreal, June 6 (DP)—The swastika symbol of Hitlerism was hoisted in Montreal today when members of "The Foreign Friends of the Hitler Movement, Inc." gathered at a temporary headquarters. The Society claims a total membership of 298 and has petitioned the government for letters patent.

TOO MUCH WHEAT GROWN IN WORLD SAY SCIENTISTS

Japs Demand Abolition of
Aircraft Carriers—
Another Disarmament
Conference Setback

Anglican Clergy Bless
Barrie Crops in
Unique Ceremony

Belleville, Ont., June 8 (Special)—Mackenzie King, leader of the Opposition, in a speech here today, charged that since the Conservative Government took office three years ago unemployment has grown from 117,000 to 800,000, with a total expenditure of $116,365,000.

GERMANY DECLARES DEBT MORATORIUM

CAFE FINED $100 FOR MINIMUM WAGE BREACH
Waitresses Getting $5 Week

OTTAWA TAKES OVER RELIEF CAMPS, PUTS GENERAL IN COMMAND

Control of provincial Relief Camps passed today to the Dominion government under an administration headed by Brigadier-General J. Sutherland Brown, C.M.G., D.S.O. According to General Brown the single unemployed men in the camps will in future be used only for "work of national importance," including labor on the Trans-Canada Highway. All camp men will now, the General stated, receive food, clothing, shelter, tobacco, and "a small cash allowance" in return for "fair dealing and a certain amount of work".

World Economic Conference in
Lavish Setting—Claridge's
Luxury Astonishes Delegates

Maclean's Magazine Authors
Advocate Exclusion
from Canada of
Unabsorbable Races

**ESSEX TERRAPLANE—
FIRST AWAY IN TRAFFIC**

CANADA RE-ENTERING
ERA OF PROSPERITY—
REPORTS ACROSS COUNTRY
SHOW SLUMP OVER

Toronto, June 9 (CP) — Reports presented this week at the annual general meeting of the Canadian Manufacturers Association prove the current depression to be definitely passing, according to B. G. Buncombe, retiring president of the association. Even lumbering, which had been lagging behind because of British and U.S. barriers on imports, is now on the verge of making better headway. Mining, however, . . .

RELIEFEES DEPORTED

Vancouver, June 8—The number of deportations of persons on city relief rolls rose to seventeen during the last two weeks of May, according to the latest figures released at City Hall yesterday. All were foreign born being returned to countries of origin, namely Ireland, Australia and Great Britain.

ZION CHURCH
11 a.m.
"Jesus the Revolutionary"

WORLD JOBLESS
TOTAL ESTIMATED
32 MILLION
At Least 10 Per Cent
May Be unemployable

**BAER KAYOES
SCHMELING**

PARKS BOARD BUDGET
CUT 51 PER CENT
Gardeners offer to set out
30,000 plants without pay—
but unemployed protest

Vernon, B.C., June 13 (CP)—Nineteen men were arrested by provincial and city police here late on Monday as they dropped from an incoming freight train. Several more evaded the officers and escaped into the woods . . . Chief of Police A. N. Clarke expressed the belief the men were transients probably gathering for an unemployed demonstration.

OPPOSITION LEADER SAYS
GOVT. SPENDING LIKE
DRUNKEN SAILORS

Victoria, B.C., June 14 (CP) — Opposition Leader Bowser, speaking in the Legislature today, charged the Tolmie government with wholesale waste of public funds. Over a million dollars worth of road machinery, he claimed, had been purchased without public tender and at inflated prices. This equipment, in turn, had displaced hundreds of workmen, throwing them onto relief, to the further cost of the taxpayers. Now the machines too are idle, operating funds having vanished. Despite a $29 million dollar budget, Mr. Bowser went on, the government is now having to throw its own clerks out and cut relief grants still further . . .

MONEY KINGS
MEET QUIETLY IN
BANK OF ENGLAND

———

Victoria Trade Unions
Will Join CCF

———

LITVINOFF WILL BUY
MILLION $ MORE IF
EMBARGOES WITHDRAWN

———

CANADA WHEAT SURPLUS
NOW 350 MILLION BUSHEL

———

Did You Know?
Today's Interesting Facts
About Your Own Country—

11,787 persons paid taxes last
year in incomes over $10,000,
for a total of $21,733,464 tax
paid.

UNITED CHURCH
CONFERENCE RESOLVES
AGAINST CAPITALISM

Advocates socialization of
banks, industry, transport

———

WORKLESS YOUTH SHOT
IN BURGLARY

James Gull, 17, Dying
from Stomach Wounds

———

Bride of 1933 Wears Short Veil

———

Wave of Terror Sweeps Austria

———

COURT ORDERS YOUTH
LASHED FOR BREAKING
AND ENTRY

———

TRAVEL POSTERS DEPICT
ATTRACTIONS OF MEXICO

———

FIRST ROOSEVELT CONGRESS ADJOURNS—
NEW DEAL FIRMLY LAUNCHED IN 3 MONTHS
4 Million More Men at Work by Fall

———

Merritt, B.C., June 17 (Special to the Planet)—Arthur H. Evans, trade union organizer, in court here today, charged he was kidnapped by 25 men at Princeton on April 28, who took him to Coyle, a flag station six miles from here, and placed him on the train at 2 a.m., warning him, under threats of violence, not to return to the Princeton mine area.

Albert Keene, past president of the Butte, Montana, Business Men's Club, was a guest of Vancouver Lions Club Thursday noon and spoke on conditions in Russia. Russia, he said, covered one-sixth of the globe, had 160 million people who spoke 147 different languages and represented 182 different nationalities. President E. S. Robinson thanked Mr. Keene for his address.

20

THERE WERE OTHER COMPANIONS GORDON WOULD HAVE BEEN happier to lose than Sammy Archibald. On the very next freight, puffing up into the Rockies, on a sun-golden afternoon, a quarrel broke out in his crowded boxcar between a hard-eyed, crop-headed Detroit youth and a black-shirted slum-boy from Montreal. They disputed the lie of a cocked dice in a crap game played for money the two of them had acquired with odd suddenness in Calgary (they had been broke on the previous freight). The wrangle went on for miles while the green rollers of the foothills swelled into waves of mountains and broke into a spray of peaks beyond the boxcar door; it began with words and spit, and went to fists and boots, and then to a kind of strangling tussle, and had graduated to knives before enough of their fellow-travelers felt impelled to interfere to make intervention possible.

That same night, as their freight dragged itself in darkness over the hump of the Great Divide, an overalled Indian girl, dulleyed and gum-chewing, in the light of a stolen yard-lantern and after prolonged negotiations by a scar-faced male companion with saintly white hair, began to exchange her grimy favors in a corner of the bouncing floor in return for a packet of Bull Durham, a tin of canned heat, and four dimes, the combined offerings of the only two customers who could scrape up both the taste and the capital.

A half-hour later Gordon and all of them were dropping into the chill black mountain air·as the train began shuddering and tolling to a halt in the cop-infested divisional yards at Field. He remembered hitting the cinders with head back and eyes closed, and thanking God it was cinders and not a pole or a siding-rail or the yelping wheels that the darkness he leapt into had found for him.

But when the authorities were duly circumvented and the freight regained on the other side of the sleeping town, there were long hours of cold still in the thin high air before dawn, and rain and a near-wintry wind all morning that shook the box-car as if it would hurl it over the cliffs perpetually receding from their feet. Then, running down into Revelstoke in the bright gay sun once more, and under the dancing fabulous peaks, there was sudden horror.

A long, thin, adam's-appled kid had scrambled into the car at Canmore, splay-footed in frayed brown sneakers and with half his shirt-tail out; he was plainly on his first freight and from then on had had his ears filled in consequence by the old stiffs with tales of the murdering yardbulls and the nightmarish jails awaiting him if ever he were caught. And now, as they came jerking and rattling into Revelstoke, the American who had been in the fight, and who was now keeping lookout, pulled his bullet head in suddenly and yelled "Yellowlegs". The train was still running fast but the American leaped, and his erstwhile pal from Quebec close behind him. They had good reason to take the risk, no doubt, but the rest of the boxcar stayed back, waiting for the speed to drop, all except the Canmore kid who, moving suddenly from Gordon's side before he or anyone understood his intentions, shut tight his eyes and leapt like a poor frightened jackrabbit straight out from the car door. Gordon, reaching ineffectually, was in time to see the long body spin along the cinders, arms outstretched, and to hear, and never to forget, over the wheel-shrieks of the slowly braking train, another more piercing screech of the boy whose arms had disappeared under the overhang of the cars.

One of the rear trainmen must have seen him, too, and signaled the engineer, for almost at once the full fierce power of the brakes went on and the train began grinding to a convulsive halt. From the caboose a man came running, gripping a bag marked with a red cross.

"Poor punk," said one of the old boys. "Must a got the bull-horrors."

"By jeez I'm pilin out while there's still time, we cant do him no good," said the pimp with the saintly hair. He jumped and the Indian girl after him and the others after her, and Gordon with them. They raced to the end of the nearest car, scrambled over the couplings, through the fence and into the woods. What else was there to do?

He did not even see what had really happened. But two months later in Vancouver, he heard, from a man who had just passed through along 'the main stem'. The Canmore boy was alive, and still in Revelstoke, an up-patient at the local hospital. The man whom Gordon talked to had seen him in fact, for the boy, having nothing else to do, liked to walk down in his free hours and watch the trains go by, waving sometimes at the stiffs on the flatcars, standing by the track still in his old brown sneakers and waving at them with the stumps of his lost hands.

It was early on a flannel-cloudy morning, almost three weeks after he left Toronto, that Gordon dropped, now with an old stiff's wary dexterity, from a lumber flat rolling and tolling toward the New Westminster yards. He washed his hunger-pinched face in the flooding, muddy Fraser. Then he thumbed his way on to a fruit truck and into Vancouver.

21

O come let us sing unto the Lord: let us make a joyful noise to the Rock of our salvation. (Ps. 95:1)

Canadian Gold Reserves
$72 Million

GRANDVIEW THEATRE

K
I N G
G
N O
K

FREE TO LADIES
Your choice of dinnerware with every 25c admission!

EDITORIAL

We have contractors in Ottawa advertising in vain for men to cut wood. And we have loafers in Victory Square interfering with the honest gardeners who would plant the flower beds without cost to the city . . . Vancouver's pride matters a good deal, and Victory Square has been a symbol of Vancouver's pride. If it is allowed to go to ruin, it will become a symbol of Vancouver's defeat. Can Vancouver afford to proclaim to the world, in her most prominent park, that the Depression has beaten her?

DEROCHE RELIEF WORKERS QUIT CAMP

350 March on Mission City

Mission City, B.C., June 17— The parade of men is orderly so far but about thirty-five police officers of this district and the coast are on hand in the event of trouble.

The men, who are reported to be objecting to regulations under which the Camps are now conducted since being taken over by the Dominion Government, left their camp Friday afternoon and spent the night on the floor of the Community Hall in Deroche village.

It is reported that, when the men refused to go to work Friday morning, they were not fed, but that food was obtained for them sometime Friday evening. It is also stated that the telephone wires from the camp were cut.

Manhood—How Regained Take Our Remedies

. . . Sir Henry Deterding has a huge round table in his Park Lane apartment with a map of the world inlaid in wood on the top. He spends a lot of time here watching and changing the colored pegs on the map. Each peg is an oil-drilling centre. One color is for those that pay; another for those that do not pay . . .

U.S. PREPARED FOR NEW ERA OF ISOLATION

RELIEF CAMP MEN INVADE VANCOUVER

Vancouver, June 19—Refusing to return to their unemployed relief camp at Deroche and work for bed, board, twenty cents a day, free medical care and tobacco, between 300 and 350 men left Mission City Saturday afternoon for Vancouver. They began entering the city at various times yesterday (Sunday), some having traveled part way by freight, others in autos and trucks provided by sympathizers; a few late arrivals claimed to have walked the thirty miles from Mission City.

Inspector Cruickshank of the Provincial Police, met the men at Mission City Saturday with forty officers, who diverted the parade from the Main street to a sidestreet. Mission citizens eventually provided a meal which was eaten by the men in an old gravel-pit a mile west of town. Major E. Champbers, in charge of the camp, then addressed the men but they refused to return to Deroche.

Civic officials were not yet available for comment this morning as to what disposition will be made of the invading strikers. Most of the men spent last night in the Ukrainian Labor Temple.

SOCIALISTS OUTLAWED BY HITLER
Join Communists in Hiding from Nazi

WILL SERVE WITHOUT PAY
City Teachers Willing to Give Services After Board's Funds End, November

EDITOR, THE PROVINCE
Sir:
While sitting in my garden I noticed a tom-tit with a tin band on its leg. . . .

Prairie Doukhobors Stage Nude Parade

CHINESE VISITOR GUEST AT TEA BY AUTHORS' ASSOCIATION

Seldom has the Vancouver Branch, Canadian Authors' Association, enjoyed such a pleasant time as on Saturday, when they were entertained by Mrs. A. Roll-Smithe of 3280 Marine Drive. Punch was served in the garden by Chinese maids in colorful native costumes. Iris decorated the summer house, while on the porch pink lotus flowers blossomed in Chinese urns . . . The guest of honor, Dr. Kiang Kang-hu, said, in his address, that the two things important in authorship had been invented by Chinese, namely paper (in 105 B.C.) and printing in the fifth century . . . Chinese held the record also for the three largest books in the world, and the first rhyming dictionary. A presentation was made to Dr. Kiang of a long free-verse poem written in his honor by Mrs. Annie Charlotte Dalton entitled "The Chinese Phoenix".

CCF SEEKS BALANCE OF POWER

Thanks to Life Insurance—
They Can Afford
a Second Honeymoon!

NUDE DOUKHS GET 3 YEARS, WOMEN 2

Century of Progress, Chicago, June 21: Disintegrating the atom may unlock new energy to construct a new world for mankind, said Dr. Niels Bohr, world-famous Danish physicist, at the formal reception to members of the American Association for the Advancement of Science at the Century of Progress Exposition . . . The star Arcturis, which opened the World Fair, was one of the many evidences of the mysterious new powers which . . .

STORM TROOPS
THROUGHOUT GERMANY—
OTHER PARTIES BANNED

MAYOR WIRES OTTAWA
FOR HELP—OTHER CAMPS
THREATEN STRIKE

Vancouver, June 20 — Mayor Louis Taylor today telegraphed the Dominion Government that up to 1,500 men are reported to be deserting government road camps and planning to join the Deroche strikers in Vancouver . . . Most of the Deroche visitors congregated outside the Relief Hall at Hamilton and Dunsmuir yesterday where they were told by Mr. A. S. Tutte, superintendent of the special relief commission, that he had definite instructions not to grant relief to any man who had refused to go to or to stay in a camp . . . Civic authorities also refuse to grant the men any assistance beyond the forty cents per man food allowance which Mayor Taylor authorized when the men arrived Sunday.

It is reported that the men plan to erect a food depot on the old Recreation Grounds at Smythe and Homer, and a delegation met aldermen this afternoon seeking authority to canvass for food supplies and distribute them at this centre.

It is reported, however, that aldermen have no intention of granting such permission.

22

FIVE YEARS HAD MADE LITTLE DIFFERENCE TO THE LOOK OF HIS city. The mountains, under the soft June clouds, presented their shaggy and indifferent backs, as ever, to the upstart town. The latter's untidy skyline was less smoke-dulled than usual for a Friday morning, probably, Gordon realized, because many of 1928's sawmills were now silent and deserted shells. No doubt he would find other changes across that fouled estuary, in the Rat Portage area, where he and his mother had lived. But he did not at present propose to wander in that direction, nor even to visit the chestnut-shaded cemetery where her bones lay now, nor the university from which he had once been graduated (with professional ambitions somewhat different from those he now entertained). His present aims, in fact, required him to quarter himself as far from his old haunts as he could, without removing himself from the field of his mission.

Consequently, after visiting the familiar scabby old Main Post Office and drawing on his savings at last, he turned his face to that part of the crowded dockside known as Skidroad, and exploring dilapidated Powell Street, found himself a room at the top of a three-story brick flop-house, the Hotel Universe, which rose, naked and narrow, between the striped pole of a cut-rate barber (who kept a pool-room behind, and a blind pig behind that) and the three balls of a pawnbroker (below the placards of a palmist and of an instantaneous pants-presser).

It was not the worst hotel in Vancouver. Indeed it began with something like a lobby, or at least a widening of the dark hallway big enough for two cracked leather chairs barricading the Japanese proprietor's cubbyhole. One had to be careful, however, in skirting them, not to run one's crown into the surprisingly rigid muzzle of an ancient and mangy moose-head, relic of the hostel's jauntier past, whose senile and enormous lips seemed everlastingly curled to spit sideways down into the porcelain cuspidor on the blotched linoleum floor. But it was really the peg-legged old bachelor, trying to live and drink beer on his army pension and a bit of touting, who sent the daily contributions of tobacco-juice splatting into the bluebottle-haunted spittoon, as he exchanged grumbles about the rain or about Ottawa with more transient travelers, with a hawker of ichors, perhaps, of opiated cough syrups and fortified javelle water, existing apprehensively on his last commissions and waiting for the week-end boat that would carry him to some godforsaken upcoast cannery town, or to some string of Indian villages forsaken too by their gods, though not by the missionaries, nor by him.

Such were the ground-floor aristocrats of the hotel's clientele. In each of their rooms was a radiator, a radiator that sometimes in midwinter would be found warm to the touch, and two taps, from one of which there occasionally dribbled enough tepid water for a shave. And their rooms had once been papered, and still held furniture, of a kind, and were on the same floor as the proprietor and his family and the one ammoniacal and rat-haunted toilet. But to possess such grandeur one paid three full dollars a week.

On the second floor the rooms were only two dollars, or thirty cents per night; there was no radiator, and the solitary tap ran colder than the bare board floor. To these abodes came loggers, at the end of their rolls and at the end of sprees begun in more glittering streets and on fleshier mattresses, to sleep it off. And there were three permanents on this floor too, three comrades and rivals, three slackbreasted anxious poxed old girls who toiled together along the sidewalks and in the beer-parlors nearest to the Hotel Universe, dodging the flatfoots and pursuing the lush, their grey hairs dyed yellow and red and black respectively, three old autumn leaves tacking and sailing in the western wind. And they brought to these darkfloored boxes what aging waiters or ancient mariners, callow dockhands or lonely Chinese laundrymen they could stop and in soddenness persuade to their unkempt and swaybacked beds.

Persuade them they must, since four clients together would merely cover the weekly rent (in advance) of any one of their rooms. And though it was true that half the rent was paid, and meals too of a kind (now that they were all properly registered as single unemployed females and drew their scrip money regularly from the City Relief Office), there was no telling how long that would last, nor meantime were there any free tickets for beer, nor relief scrip for high-heeled shoes or yellow, red or black silk stockings and hair-dyes, nothing for these nor for many another need of their upsadaisy old lives, no way out but through daily and Sunday tramping of sidewalks as hard and uncertain as the times.

Yet the times were not yet so hard, thank God, that they had ever to consider moving to the third floor. Happily for them, for at the top there were no taps at all, no blinds, no lights, no chairs—though chairs weren't vital—nothing whatever but a nailed-up disused storeroom and two leprous kalsomined cells, each with one smutted draughty attic window and one clothes-hook on the back of a lockless door. And a bed, of course, or rather the iron frame of a bed, with boards laid across for springs, and a mattress, a size too small, thin and lumpy and dank as a slice of old lawn, and one stained blanket thrown over it for bedding, sheltering possibly a few hungry fleas from its last possessor. The mattress, however, the urine-scented mattress, concealed nothing but a permanent and cunning colony of bedbugs.

But then, such life was not confined to the top floor—and where, if you searched the city, would you find handier shelter for a dollar a week, or furnished abodes of any kind for less? Or more? For all the worst rooms in the town, indeed, had been fixed at this price by a quiet arrangement between the city fathers and the hotel-keepers when the former had been reluctantly compelled to issue rooming coupons of that exact value to the growing swarms of homeless, jobless, wifeless males, on the understanding, of course, that the recipients were not voluntarily unemployed, did not belong to someone else's city, were too unhealthy to be worth shipping to one of the work camps in the bush, and were properly and gratefully destitute.

Gordon paid his dollar in cash, for he was, from the point of view of the relief rolls, a foreigner, required to starve or fatten on his own devices until such distant time as he was duly registered, and transported quickly to some less conspicuous part of the Evergreen Playground, to swing a shovel in a camp. This he had no intention of doing, however, since only in Vancouver could he hope to organize a permanent cell for the party hive. To remain would not be easy; true, he had thirty-two dollars in Postal Savings, enough to pay the rent for the rest of the eight weeks he had ahead in Vancouver, but not for all the food he would need. Try as he might, he found that he could not, without a morning cup of coffee and a noon hamburger, get through a day, and even with these by night he was so ravenous nothing less than a twenty-five cent special (spud soup, hash, prunes and coffee), would stay him. And there were all the rest of his summer needs, party literature, postage, carfare, all the costs indeed of the founding of the first branch in northwestern North America of what was to be the great regenerated Third International, or if necessary even the Fourth, which would bring at length to this whole weary globe that true socialism which the Third had so far missed bringing even to one-sixth of the land-mass.

He had insisted that the Toronto group was to send him nothing; its members were all in debt as it was, and in danger of losing their broken-down mimeographing machine to their creditors. Any promises he might have got them to make they would not be likely to keep any more than they had for Jack. No, he would live on what he had and what his new comrades, when he found them, could supply. In a tight hole, of course, perhaps when he had to find clothes and fare in September to get back to Utah, he would have to borrow from someone like Doc Channing, his favorite professor—though he would not let him or anyone else of the undergraduate days know he was in Vancouver until such necessity forced him. Bourgeois contacts must be avoided as long as possible, for they would not only be embarrassing all round, they would destroy his incognito. He had registered in the Hotel Universe under the name of Paul Green, and Paul Green he wanted to stay that summer, living the life that the world of 1933 had arranged for its single unemployable males along the skidroad of Vancouver. And this was not only because he felt in truth now almost one of them but because he hoped to make some of them one with him.

But with what in him? What was it, he would ask himself later, that had both goaded and tamed him for the strange drudgeries of that now misty summer, what kind of bit had he willingly clamped in his mouth and what load had he tried with all his harnessed and blindered energy to pull? What was the source of that dumb and desperate intensity which had made him oblivious of all other considerations, of his precious 'career' that the betrayed ghost of Anne still mourned, of his very physical liberty and life?

There had been horror, certainly; horror and disgust at the mere sight, faced properly by him for the first time, of the dark side of his own planet, darker, colder and more tortured than any scene the moon hides from us, the black seamed countenance of man's intricate injustice, calculated cruelty and natural indifference. And the realities faced from under an elm tree in a park, and from a boxcar door in mountains, had, through his scholarly habits, driven him into wider and wider readings of the documented villainy of his age, the long venial tale of modern imperialism, of mass wars, and their stupid motivations. And out of these again, perhaps, and from the frustrate urge of the muffled artist within him, had there not sprung his furious urge to act, to work quickly, cunningly and if necessary violently, to be prophet and writer by deeds, to work in any way that might provide, in this last breath of opportunity, the leadership to divert the dumb hordes of driven humanity from streaming over the cliffs of yet another and worse and perhaps final disaster? Or even to act out of sheer rebellious despair and in spite of any evidence that such a disaster was certain. "Strike then"—there had been a couplet of Julian Bell's, from the little book of verse Comrade Bagshaw had lent him, another cry echoing in his mind—"Strike then and swiftly; if the end must come, may war, like charity, begin at home."

There must, of course, have been something else, something more tenuous and yet more powerful, which had kept the fire in him long after his reason told him that his flame was unregarded and dying. Had it been simply the conviction, the logical and absurd and true and impossible faith (all the stronger held because he had lost any other faiths) that socialism, *some* kind of socialism, *was* the complete solution for all of man's man-made ills, the magnetic mountain of Day Lewis, the natural lodestone of the human universe? And that the race was indeed capable, once headed from the destroying cliffs, of settling into upland valleys of contentment and reason and beauty beyond anything yet imagined?

Granted even these grandiose but surely not ignoble romanticisms —was there not also still to be confessed that most ancient and banal of all motives without which he might never have been led to Vancouver at all in that long-gone hazy summer? Had he not been stubbornly still and with deliberate self-deception, in love with a girl playing Let's Pretend in her own backyard but directing the game with such realistic zest that at least one of her playmates found himself three thousand miles from her, on a Bolshevik-Leninist dare, acting out the reality? It was only half-true, for it was also true that he had sensed, before ever he had set his foot on the rung of the freight in the Toronto yards, that the game was somehow false, that he was being sent away into dark woods to hide with no certainty that, while his hands were over his eyes, the other children would not drift away, forget him, and begin a new sport.

Perhaps he would never know himself well enough to be sure where, in the tangle of his emotions, love and fear of his fellowmen ended and desire and distrust of Thelma began—nor how he might have disentangled either from love of himself. Perhaps after all what had stung him had been only the ubiquitous wasps of every man's summer, the stabbing need to be heard and reckoned with, and to have followers and admirers, and to be judged valuable and wise, and to triumph or die in a good cause, and be loved, and above all to be forgiven.

It was a curious summer's manhunt. There was no time, or there did not seem to be then, for proselytizing the naive, wooing the unpolitical to politics, shocking the contented into reformism, encouraging the reformer toward socialism, or steeling the socialist to revolution. He must quickly find men who had already passed or leapt all these stages, who thought of themselves as Marxists— and yet who, for that very reason, were discontented with official Marxism. They must be men able to reason and willing to act, reckless and secretive, obstinate and flexible, enterprising and disciplined. In advance he had thought of his prospective converts in terms of the heroic youth that the new poetry of Auden and Spender seemed forever to be addressing, the young comrades who would "step beautifully from the solid wall". They would "advance to rebuild" with him. They would be ready to suffer, determined to, even. And some day they might all—who could say? —be listed among the Truly Great.

The hunt began, indeed, before even he was ready for it, a few minutes after his arrival in the flophouse room. Gordon was lying on the pillowless mattress, collecting his energies for the next move, when a face poked into his open door, a doughy middle-aged face above sagging shoulders. Watery eyes appraised Sammy Archibald's twine-bound blanket on the floor and then Gordon on the bed.

"I'm in the next coop," the visitor said, with a bronchial wheeze. "Got a match?" He wore a dirty grey workshirt, patched dungarees too small for him, and boots whose broken seams showed the dull flesh of his sockless feet.

Gordon sat up and produced a box. "Glad to meet you; my name's Paul Green." He gestured down the bed. "Want to sit?"

The stranger, however, taking the box, backed to the wall and leant against it in a curiously automatic way, as if he had hooked himself to it, like some beast of burden who had found a way of standing that was also a way of rest.

"Mine's Bill Smith," he said softly.

Gordon, feeling guilty in his own strange *alias,* instantly suspected his visitor, and must have shown it in his eyes. For the man went on laconically: "No, it's real. I got nothin to hide, the dicks know me, Bill Smith, old Wobbly Bill, Bill Smith from Deroche. Smiths of the world arise yuh got nothin to lose but yer names." He looked again at Gordon's coal-stained blanket-roll. "You been ona boxes, eh. Main stem?"

"Yes. From Toronto."

The pasty face showed some surprise but its owner merely poked open the matchbox, studied it. "Y'aint got the makins too?" he asked hopefully.

"Sorry, I gave up smoking. Cant afford it."

"Dont mind then if I take, say three matches, case I pick up a snipe or two?"

"Go ahead." A wobbly, Gordon was thinking, thankful now of the long meticulous coachings from Ron and Hymie in the chronicles of radicalism, a wobbly is a survivor of the Industrial Workers of the World; in the west nearly all the leftist loggers once belonged to it or the Canadian equivalent, the O.B.U. Debs and Heywood founded the I.W.W., Joe Hill was one of its martyrs, the man Dos Passos wrote about; One-Big-Union idea, anarcho-syndicalist, weak on politics; they sparked the Winnipeg General Strike; and the Communists rose from their bones. So this wheezy old wreck had been a fighter. Still was, for Deroche was not merely a town, it was the relief camp where the workers had struck last week and marched into Vancouver. One of Gordon's boxcar mates coming out of Revelstoke had a discarded Vancouver *Province* with the story. The grapevine had news of it too; and it was supposed to have been engineered by the Stalinites. Was Smith one? Well, to earn further frankness he would have to begin giving it.

"I'm a teacher—without a job. Vancouver's my home town, so I've floated back. Also I'm a Marxist and I want to get into the unemployed movement here. I heard about Deroche. How can I help? I'd be glad if you'd tell me how to get started."

"I can tell yuh this much," Smith said promptly, chucking the matchbox on the bed and easing himself toward the door, "there'll soon be a stool in every flophouse."

Gordon got up stung. "Well, I'm not the one here."

Smith stopped in the doorway, looked at him, then opened his hands in a gesture both indifferent and conciliatory. "How yuh know I aint?"

"I dont. I dont know anybody here. I've been away five years."

"You let the cops know what yer after they'll git yuh started in a movement. They'll move yuh right out to the limits and kiss yuh goodbye with their boots in yer balls."

"O.K. Suppose they do. Meantime maybe I can help."

"Yuh married?"

"No."

Smith shrugged lazily. "You kin always git sent to a camp and then organize it, or join what's there."

"I aim to stay in town."

"Yuh got any dough?"

"I've got—" Gordon started, wanting to establish the fact that he was scarcely a capitalist, but checked himself, thinking that Smith might be fishing, for reasons less honest. "I've enough left to tide me over July—in a Postal Savings account," he added lamely.

Smith grinned. "I dont steal, n'I dont stool. I eat like most a the boys, on twenny-eight cents a day meal scrip, and what I can bum. The Canadian Noo Deal."

"Well, that's less than I'm budgeting. So I ought to be able to stand two coffees now if you'll join me."

Smith hesitated, plainly tempted, almost exasperated. "Look, who the hell are yuh? You aint a pigeon, they wouldn waste one on this flophouse because I'm the only Red in it, and yer not a Black Monk."

"Black Monk?"

"Yuh see, y'doan know nothin, y'doan even know what they call the Commies."

"Maybe we've other nicknames in the east."

"Mebbe. Mebbe in the east people go around tellin strangers they're Marxists. Y'talk like a schoolteacher alright. But even a down-east schoolteacher'd look up the local hotshots, if he was a commie, and git the score before he settled down in a flophouse. Commies dont go round on their lonesome askin bindlestiffs like me the way to the little boy's room." He stopped, breathless, then added scornfully: "Commies dont ask questions period. They's too busy givin phony answers."

"So?" Gordon stared at him, concealing his pleasure. A Red who isn't a Stalinist.

Smith put the end of a match in his mouth, rolled it between yellow gapped teeth, and stared back.

"All right," Gordon said, thinking this is worth taking a chance. "I'll tell you what I am, I'm a convert to Marx. And to Lenin. But not to Stalin. I belong to the Communist League of North America. I suppose you'd call me a Trotskyist."

Smith looked at him with a widening startled grin. "Well, I'll be goddamned. A *real* one?"

Then there *are* Trotskyites? Gordon thought of Bagshaw. Smith's tone seemed friendly but he decided to go slower. "I didnt pack a party card on the freights."

"Y'seen the June first *Militant*?" Smith asked then.

It was Gordon's turn to be surprised, for the *Militant* was the New York newspaper of the League, a heavily theoretical and bombastic organ chronicling the weekly misdeeds of the Third International and the daily heroisms of the Almost-Fourth. Since it was banned by the Canadian Customs, both Gordon and his eastern comrades had assumed it had never been seen in Vancouver. In Toronto, copies had to be smuggled in between layers of the Sunday edition of the *New York Times*.

"June the first!" Gordon said. "I left Toronto before then. Have *you* got one?"

"Sure. You can borrow it after I'm through."

"You—you *like* it?" The average worker could never make sense out of it.

Smith merely gave an asthmatic sigh. "A great little scandal sheet."

Yes, it was that, Gordon thought reluctantly, but it was also meant to be a call to battle.

Perhaps Smith had heard the trumpets in it too for he added now, almost slyly, "I git it on loan from a guy—a guy mebbe you'd like to meet."

It had been that easy, at the start. He went with Smith slowly along the sour-smelling sidewalks, between the greasy gutters and the dreary succession of run-down or empty shops, to a lunchcounter neither as wide or as long as a streetcar, on a windy paper-littered corner of Cordova. Here the mugs, though cracked, were big, and Smith could daily exchange his foodtickets for a morning coffee, a noon bowl of uncategorized soup, and an evening plate of stew, with perhaps a thin slab of fly-specked pie to follow. They sat on the wobbling stools and Smith talked, and Gordon began to learn the pattern of a jobless bachelor's life in Vancouver.

When the weather was poor, Smith explained wheezing (he seemed to have some sort of bronchial trouble), he'd always found it best to sleep or at least to lie in bed as long as possible.

"In the kind of beds we've got?" Gordon asked incredulously.

Smith brushed a bluebottle gently away from his coffee and groped for a toothpick in a dirty tumbler on the counter. "Yeah, the bugs is bad. Mebbe I was thinkin more about last time I was in town. But they ain't as hard's a doorway, and no flatfoot to boot yuh out. Or a marble floor. Y'ever been on a siddown in one of these here public buildins? I dreamt I slep on marble floors. Yeah. Besides, yuh git up yuh git hungry. An yuh move aroun yuh wear out shoe-leather." He tilted on his stool and brought up one of his gaping boots to view. "I wanna save mine fer the nex' Hunger March. Them Dooks got the right idea, though. Nood parades."

"But isn't there a Relief Stores office or something like that here where you can get at least another pair of shoes?"

"The Pogey yuh mean?" Smith gave him a condescending grin. "Sure. The Men's Instittoot, they calls it. Some stiffs line up there for a week at a stretch, I hear. Once in a wile mebbe they git somethin—if they's good boys."

"Then they haven't got much stuff to give you, you mean?"

"Hell they got duds in there stacked to the rafters, but they dole it out like it was munitions. Nobody tole them boys yet ol' Bennett's ended the depression. Anyways they know the holes in my soles was made walkin in from Deroche. I'll never git a Pogey pair unless we raid the goddam joint." He paused as if taken with his own thought, took the toothpick out of his mouth and looked sideways up. "Saay, that's kine of an idea too!"

A thin spectacled girl in a dingy brown suit came in from the street with a sheaf of leaflets under her arm. She slipped one on the counter deftly beside each one of them and went wordlessly out. Millions Now Living Will Never Die.

"But isnt there anywhere else to go and sit, somewhere warm and dry that is, when it's raining?" Gordon persisted. "And I dont mean the British-Israelite Hall," he added seeing Smith gesture sardonically at his leaflet.

"You got dough there's the movies."

"Free, I mean. And apart from meetings and churches. What about—what about station waiting rooms?"

Smith took his eyes off the leaflet beside him and shook his head. "Even there they got yardcops now; you try to sit down and they spot yer Pogey gladrags and you git the bum's rush." Smith spoke without rancor, between thoughtful probes with the toothpick. "Like today, though, when taint rainin, most of us boys'll be settin in the Sun Parlor—Victory Square to you—it's close and the oney park they leave us alone in jis now."

They strolled there, after the coffee, since it was a likely place to encounter the owner of the *Militant*. Gordon remembered the Square as a small steep quadrangle on the edge of Hastings Street's noise, an island of grass and scraggly trees and flowerbeds and a few benches, centred by a more than usually ugly and gull-spattered war memorial. Seeing it again he suddenly recalled his abortive allegory for the Social Problems Club (it seemed a long time ago he had written it), for it was clogged now with humanity—at the Beggar level. They were, however, beggars to whom even bowls were forbidden, except on special tincan tagdays, and who were isolated from their Bathers, relaxing elsewhere. The Blueboys, meanwhile, hurried ceaselessly, as always, around the park's grimy edges, in cars or on foot, noisily getting and hotly spending. But now, in 1933, the respectable almost automatically avoided the square's interior, even though its paths provided shortcuts to their parked autos. For it had become a dump of human litter, one of the myriad impromptu disposal heaps for a civilization mired in its own waste.

Some men lay unshaven, snoring, odoriferous, on the sunlit grass; others, the neat and the ragged, the dirty and the clean, crowded the hard benches, arguing; others again merely stared down, slack-handed, from the ornamental stone parapet of the war memorial into the foreign hurry of Hastings Street. Clusters of old men, some with veterans' buttons in their faded lapels, squatted cross-legged on the turf playing endless cardgames with decks too decipherable from use. "Wastage as never before"—a phrase of Ezra Pound's came to Gordon as he walked beside the heavy-breathing Smith. These, however, had not died for a botched civilization, they were merely living in spite of it. Knots of younger workless stood under trees, listening blankly to some impromptu speech, some argument or dirty joke or ordinary bicker. Others lounged by the *Province* building across a sidestreet, reading through plateglass the headlines of the noon edition pasted out of reach on the inside of the window. Nearer to him, still other jobless sat, their backs against clipped shrubs, reading, often in twos or threes, from the same broken-spined book or discarded journal. Gordon, as he wandered with Smith, peered to see what papers were favored. He identified several copies of the Toronto *Worker* and even a New York *Daily Worker* and other Stalinist and some socialist newstracts, but nothing, he saw mournfully, reflecting his own esoteric politics.

"The posies look well nourished anyway," Gordon said, as they stepped around a bed of freshly planted geraniums.

"Them's union flowers." Smith gave a wheezy chuckle. "Just put in last night. Goddam Parks Board tried to make their gardeners plant em fer nothin in their spare time but a Deroche fellah, guy named Hughes, y'otta meet him, he rounded up a bunch of us boys and we come and squatted on the beds till they buggered off." There was a kind of professional pride in his voice. "Parks Commissioner coulda paid us stiffs to plant em outa his own pocket and never missed it, but O no. We made em agree to pay the gardners to do it, anyway, union rates. I see they's all pink or white. Think we oughta demanded red ones?"

They found a discarded paper, spread it over the still damp grass and sat. Smith, under Gordon's prodding, resumed his slow commentary, the talk of a man for whom words were still important though time was not. He had been a sawyer with one or other of the big logging companies until 1928, when his camp was closed for the winter; it had never re-opened and he had been jobless ever since, though not idle. "First we dreamt up a Unemployed Council," he said, "a hundred of us about."

"What did you do?" Gordon asked, shouting against the clanging of a passing streetcar.

"O the usual buggerin around—protest marches, siddowns on the main drag, letters to the papers, beef p'rades to the Council. The public was kinda on our side an the Unions give us a pat or two. One thing and another we made the bastards fork out a dole for a while. But when we yelled for relief jobs the TUs got the wind up we was tryin to cut in on what little work there was, an they shied off. Then the Black Monks—they'd come hornin in once we got a going concern, naturally—they started beatin their breasts for us and so a course the boss press howled we was Reds. And with the Unions scared, the cops knew we was orphans and they broke us up, run every mother's son of us out a town."

From over the dowdy roofs of Hastings Street came the long *wooob* of some big steamer moving in the concealed harbor.

"Where did you go then?" Gordon asked. He was learning things. Smith looked amused at the question. "Back in. Wernt nowhere else, winter-time. I holed up in a squat-shack on the Fraser with a old Wobbly sidekick till I used up the few bucks I had. That winter, a course, we all thought there'd be jobs again forever in the spring." He dug his boot-heel reflectively in the moss-cankered grass. "But come May jobs was scarcer'n hen's teeth. I hit the freights over the Hump and all the buckin way to Fredericton. And never even seen the rear-end of a job. I aint got a build them farmers like." He cast an ironic eye at his scraggly frame. "Anyways they growed too much wheat down there already it seems. So I come back here, and by then they'd got a new Unemployed Council started with a lot of married outaworks in it. Went up to about twelve hunerd, enough to make a noise in the street—about all mosta them would do a course—so the City give us some sewer-diggin and we even got the wage scale up to five-and-a-half a week. Then the Monks got control of the exec again and shoved us all into Noowah. Mebbe you heard of it back east?"

"Yes," said Gordon, remembering the day he first met Kay and Roberts. "The National Unemployed Workers Union." Another front for the Thermidoreans, invented to produce shouts, make headlines, provoke police action, impress the party bosses back in New York and in Moscow—even if it used up the last flick of energy in the workless.

"Yeah," Smith said, as if reading his thoughts, "phony as they come, but was all we had to raise a rumpus with, and we had to raise one or starve." So they raised it, a mass demonstration on the Powell Street grounds which, according to Smith, so frightened the Provincial Government that, with Ottawa's help, it invented Relief

Camps, a string of them, "all over the friggin bush from Yahk to the Yukon". They hustled most of British Columbia's single unemployed into them—thirty thousand men, by now—and a few hundred who were married but were also known to be Reds, hustled them into the remote corners out of deviltry's way.

Smith, who qualified on both counts, single and Red ("I never got a chit to show fer none of my marriages") spent the last half of 1932 in a camp in the Interior helping to build the great mythical Trans-Canada Highway. He pushed a barrow eight hours a day—"though I didnt often have anythin in it," he added, as if afraid Gordon would accuse him of scabbing. "Grub like garbage, nowhere to go at night except back to the bunks, and flies'n skeeters everywhere. Not a beer parlor for fifty miles. By God, the Yanks aint got banks any more but they got beer at least." The pay had been twenty cents a day—with unfailing deductions for soap, towels and broken crockery. Some men left owing the Government money. Most hutments had been put up hastily for summer weather; by Christmas camp hospitals were crowded out, crews in revolt. The scheme was abandoned and the men carted back into Vancouver. They were at once jobless and, within a week or two, broke again.

"We had to git out on Hastins in the rain and rattle tin cans and bust a few windows and land on the blotter before they'd put us back on relief." Then it was flophouses and twenty-eight-cents-a-day mealtickets, Smith said, through the rest of the winter, and renewed panhandling, at the risk, somewhat tempting now, of jail. Until spring, this spring, when the province counted up sixty-five thousand unemployed, and Ottawa decided to take over the camps. Out the single boys went again, except the medically excused, and they were few. "I seen a sawbones was as big as Maxie Baer himself, an' he was sendin old buggers up to the bush with asthma or ulcers so's they could hardly handle their chow—dint matter so long's they could walk."

But this year the men had organized. In Calgary, in April, fifteen hundred of them rioted. The next month, when the Mounted Police tried to "skim the Reds off a camp" in Saskatoon, there was a battle whose fame had already reached a self-occupied Toronto when Gordon was there; the leader of the police squadron had been killed when his horse shied, bolted, and dragged him. And then, last month, Smith's own camp, near the Fraser river village of Deroche, had struck, the whole three hundred and fifty of them, struck for union wages, for medical care, and for decent food.

In reply the Provincial Government had simply dispatched a truck to cart off the food stores, and a posse of Mounties to close down the camp and deal with the mutineers. The latter, now without food or shelter, had set off, only the previous Friday, to march over a logging road and down the river to the highway and Vancouver, thirty-five miles away.

"The yalla-legs was doggin us, swingin their quirts, keepin us ona move," Smith went on. "Wouldn even let a guy walk over to a farmhouse and git a drink a water. And when night come it was too goddam wet to bed down in the woods so we jis kep movin, excep the guys that folded—some a them had shoes come apart and feet bleedin. Course the Monks sent out cars for their own comrats, and a few others grabbed a freight when the yella-legs was herdin us aroun Mission City to make sure we couldnt git no food there. But most of us hoofed it to here." He got up, coughing. "They's a empty bench, let's grab it, this grass is jim dandy fer asthma."

"What's happened since?" Gordon asked him when they were seated again.

Smith shrugged. "Las week-end we was pratically Heroes of the Soviet Union First Class. Other camps started strikin and threatenin to march. The Mayor give us emergency relief tickets. And the Black Monks dremp up a reception, saxophones, speeches, free hotdogs, vasseline, bandages, even a barrel a beer. They got their Ukes to let us sleep on the floor of the Ukrainian Labor Temple. Yeah, we was heroes—fer almost two days. Now it's all busted up." Smith reached then into the inner pocket of his coat, where most men carry their wallets, and brought out a soiled wad of newspaper clippings. "I'm keepin a file on it; here, you kin bone up on it."

Thumbing through Smith's file, and listening to his running commentary, Gordon began to see the Deroche story in some kind of perspective. The Communists, it seemed, had wanted to keep the strikers indefinitely in town as shock troops, demanding the abolition of Slave Camps, making trouble. They hoped the strike fever would run through all the camps until a whole unemployed army was concentrated in Vancouver. "Mass agitation" was the *Worker's* phrase for it. But not only had the Government no intention of allowing this to happen, most of the Deroche men themselves were willing enough to return to camp provided wages and conditions were improved.

So they had begun arguing among themselves about what they should demand; an extra two dollars-a-month clothing allowance at camp—or full cash relief in town—or union wages and public work projects—or the moon. The Trades and Labor Council, to whom they sent a delegation, expressed sympathy and solidarity, but did not offer to feed them or share jobs with them. The Communists, as soon as they found their own line rejected, locked the Deroche men out of the Labor Temple, and ran out of hotdogs. The same day the City refused them further food.

"Vancouver operates on a Pay-as-you-go policy," declaimed the Mayor.

"Relief costs must come out of current revenue, by reducing other expenditures," intoned one newspaper.

"No raising of taxes," chanted the other.

If the men didn't like it here, the aldermen suggested, the city would be willing, as a gesture, to chauffeur them back to Deroche.

An invisible spokesman of the Provincial Government, however, pointed out that Deroche was in fact closed, although the strikers might be permitted to summer in any of a hundred other camps—at the old twenty-cents-a-day, of course. He had added that the relief workers were actually going to a sort of free trade school, were actually being taught how to placer-mine ("wash in criks the oldtimers starved on," Smith explained). Had not the Dominion Government, indeed,—though it could not be reached for comment—already declared the camps to be activities of national importance and sent the militia in to run them? ("With a million and a half outa us ten million Canucks on relief it ain't no time to fool.")

Meanwhile, the only folk who were systematically doing anything about the Deroche boys were the Vancouver police, who were whacking them over the head with riot sticks and tossing them into patrol wagons for begging on the streets or going to sleep in the doorways of alleys, activities which Gordon remembered Voltaire had remarked are forbidden by the law, in its magnificent equality, to rich and poor alike.

"Some of the stiffs are even gittin themselves spliced so's they kin git onto married relief—fifteen bucks a month and stay in town. Hellva lot smarter, my thinkin, if y'aint that desp'rit, is to git yerself a ailment tough enough for a Physical Reject for camp. Like me. Oney reason I'm baskin temp'ry in the luxury of the Hotel Universe, special privilege of the bronchial. Trouble is I git to worryin I mus be ready to cash in my cheques if that sonsabitchin relief doctor was willin to certify me even fer another munt."

Others from Deroche had, of course, already hit the freights, heading east, looking for work. "But they'll jist have to bum or crawl into some other camp—I never heard of no one gittin a job once he hit the skids these days, less it's in stir. Yeah, there's a few of the young sprouts from Deroche doing hard-time already fer trying a little strongarm stuff last week-end, and there's a ole sidekick of mine comin up for a shop-and-grab tomorrow." He grinned. "Crime dont pay much now either. Or does it?"

Smith told him more—of the public collections raised by two liberal preachers, the fund turned over to the strikers' committee, and already spirited away by the Communists who controlled it. Some of it had reappeared this morning,—and from another pocket Smith fished out and unfolded a handbill. *Support the Deroche Boys,* it was headed, but the text was devoted to glorifying the Stalinite line—"plenty of guff about tradin with Russia and the Scottsboro boys but not much in it fer our guts. An lookit the bottom, they want we should stage a tag-day. Mass panhandlin, wit tin cans." He spat. "Brother kin you spare a dime."

"Maybe that's a good idea," Gordon said, "it could draw public attention."

"Police attention, yuh mean. It's the one stunt them stooges on the City Council already told us they wont buy. Any character turns out fer tag-day is gonna git tagged for the hoosegow, by way a the hospital. That's all right, see, that's fine, if you kin start a real scrap. Nobody never said Bill Smith dont like a fight. But taggers gotta keep separate. Mebbe that's what the Monks want though, come to think a it, cause now we're jist a disappointment

to em. I bet they aint none of the Deroche boys faces Moscow
tonight wen he says his prayers."

Yet they face no other direction with certainty, thought Gordon
later, sitting once more on his lumpy mattress, footsore and des-
pondent. Smith, who had slid away to find the mysterious *Militant*
man, had never returned. Gordon had gone wandering through the
Sun Parlor on his own, talking, listening, looking. It is only, he
told himself, that they do not know yet what to do.

And you do? asked his mocking inner voice. Only you?

Others too, he muttered half-aloud in his empty room.

But those who know are not doing, only sitting, like you. Or if
they have acted, on what tawdry levels. That hulking ex-trapper
you talked with, what was his boast? That he shoves pick-handles
now, slyly, under the wheels of backing trucks; a schoolboy saboteur.
Is this where you hope to forge heroic resistance to the iniquities
of a decadent civilization?

But the concept of struggle persists, and of liberty.

Liberty! They've got themselves permanently drunk on the idea
of it, as underdogs always do, without any notion what to do in
their euphoria except to scream, in freedom's name, against a
passing cloud for raining on them. These narrow-eyed, thin-lipped,
belly-angry men, they're content with the dark abstractions of
hate and conquest. And deep within themselves what are they
unconsciously dedicated to? To the destruction of all liberty, all
individuality, including their own—and yours.

It's true, Gordon thought, agreeing with his own logical devil or
angel, he did not know now which. Some of them seem to have
stopped thinking individually at all, once having hatched their first
bitter negations in the frightening newness of being unemployed, of
being separated from the tending of the accustomed desk or
machine. In a mere rejection of the 'boss papers' and the Sunday
preachers they've expended their whole lifetime's energy for intellectual rebellion. But still there are those who have thought through
to Marxism.

Marxism! Stalinism, you mean. These, your precious 'politicized'
few, they're just working for a new boss and mouthing a new
religion. Everything, for them, has already been thought and

written down somewhere by Saints Marx or Engels or Lenin or Stalin or one of their attendant priests.

But through this road they may come to me.

You! Are you a Christ? You're only an imp of Trotsky, their Anti-Christ.

I'll make them read Trotsky.

They won't. They read only to be confirmed. They don't *read* at all.

It's true, Gordon thought, picking aimlessly at his lumpy bed, they read little and remember less, for all their solemn passing of pamphlets and poring and disputing over print. He got up. I suppose if I had the money I would now get drunk. Instead he went out and had a cup of coffee.

Yet it was among all these, about whom he despaired, that Gordon the next afternoon found his second disciple, as he wandered again with Smith through the littered Sun Parlor, listening and not listening to the voices, the ceaseless rising and falling of human speech, to the mesmeric passionate droning of religious cranks, the self-righteous intoning of grizzled and stoical socialists, the bitter barking of their adolescent opponents, the mutterings of the timid and the cynical, the casual bravados of the healthy, the weary boastings of the frail, the swearing out of swearing's sake, out of habit or desperation, the words thrown as filth, as stones or as smiles, or set like picadors' darts in the flanks of some conservative old bull, or tossed like a smothering blanket over the fire of some lonely logician.

One of such fires refused to be quenched. Calm, his back immovably against a maple, sat a knobble-cheeked man with thin sleek hair the color of laundry soap. He was dressed in a faded checked logger's shirt and the usual misfit castoff pants and broken sockless shoes which was almost the uniform of the unemployed. Directly facing him, among the dozen lounging listeners, was a youngish man conspicuous mainly because he wore a coat, and it matched his pants, and both seemed to have been made originally for a man of his size. His feet were apart, his cap cocked back, and his swarthy little face thrust out. Smith muttered to Gordon that this was McNamee, an executive of the Workers Unity League, a Black

Abbot no less. And the blond logger against the tree was Hansen, the man they were seeking.

"Yoost a bunch of tieves is all you fallahs is," the latter was saying calmly to McNamee, as they came up to the group.

"Liar!" the dark one shouted, leaning down still farther over Hansen with his flatnosed angry face. "Dont think any honest worker will ever believe you again, you're finished. I warn you all," McNamee wheeled on his toes, speaking rapidly and sweeping his arms around rhetorically to embrace the stolid scattered group, "this man Hansen is a traitor, a renegade, you can read about him in the last *Worker,* a counter-revolutionary, the Workers Unity League threw him out a month ago for trying to sabotage the unemployed fight, but we're on to him, arent we boys? He's a bloody stooge of Trotsky, he is, he's a paid agent of the greatest mental prostitute in history."

McNamee stopped for breath. There was the passion of conviction in his voice, despite the oratorical stance. Gordon sat down, watching the masked, silent faces around. Impossible to know what they thought. At least it was a casual group containing, obviously, no avowed supporter of the Monks. Meantime, Hansen was back in, unruffled, stubbornly continuing a monologue begun before their arrival.

Listening, and recalling what Smith had already told him, Gordon began to piece together Hansen's story. He was another ex-lumberjack, ex-wobbly, ex-Communist. Until recently he had been in charge of the Party's bookstore. "Too bad for you fallahs," Hansen was saying in his slow cadenced accent, "ve can read a bit too." Reading, he had noted the changes in communist pamphlets and classics, from edition to edition; the deletion of whole sections, the additions of corrective footnotes, the silent suppression or revision of awkward phrases in a passage of Lenin—the innumerable tinkerings and bowdlerizings of Marxism which went on in all the party pressrooms after each change in the line of the Third International. Hansen had been awkward enough to ask about these matters at cell meetings. And he had also been downright foolish. He had discovered that certain funds, openly collected for rescuing the Toronto *Worker* from one of its periodic collapses, had been diverted to raising the 'expense accounts' of certain Vancouver party leaders. Hansen declared that he had brought paper proof of this to the Agitation-Propaganda Committee and read the figures. He was, of course, immediately denounced by the chairman (one of those who had profited) as a liar, forger and Trotskyist. Next day he was expelled. Next week all the party press organs carried the routine photograph and denunciation of him as a police spy.

To all such denunciations, repeated pitilessly now by McNamee as Gordon and Smith listened, poured out indeed in a rush of brutal verbiage from his leaning contorted face like dirty roofwater spouting from a gargoyle, Hansen replied now, as no doubt he had the first time, with ponderously patient denial and the unemotional counterposing of facts and reasons and historical arguments. And it grew evident to Gordon, from the sullen muttering faces of those sitting like a jury around, that, whatever their political conclusions, none of these believed Ole Hansen to be either a liar or an informer. It was evident, too, to McNamee who, with the air of a Messiah withdrawing from publicans, turned without further words and stalked inflexibly off. Gordon and Smith moved over to Hansen's tree.

By the end of that day Gordon's spirits were soaring; he was sure that he had found in Hansen what he had been almost hopelessly seeking: a Vancouver radical who had already converted himself to Gordon's precise political position and was simply waiting to be 'organized', a man who would at once become the loyal lieutenant of his still shadowy regiment and a comrade utterly fearless and dependable. Moreover, with Hansen making common cause, Smith would join too, and perhaps dozens of their friends, responding to their lead.

He came back along the fetid old sidewalks of Skidroad to his room and, opening the rough five-cent scribbler that served him now for all writings, penciled long and gleeful letters to Thelma and to Jack, and a brief urgent note to Sather.

23

McLARNIN WINS WORLD WELTERWEIGHT CROWN

U.S. REFUSES PLAN TO STABILIZE WORLD CURRENCY

Threatens to Dump Glut Wheat Stores

Nanaimo, B.C. — An Oxford Group platform of "absolute honesty, absolute unselfishness, absolute love" was announced today by Hugh Savage, Independent candidate in the Cowichan-Newcastle riding . . . The only remedy for the Depression will come by the individual altering his views, said Mr. Savage. Friends must finance his campaign, he added.

Rush for Divorces
Before Vacation

DISARMAMENT CONFAB POSTPONED

Revival of Confidence
Seen as Prices Improve

POLITICS TABOO NOW AT VARSITY

Governors Refuse Summer School Appointment to Former Liberal Candidate in B.C. Elections.

No. 5 Car
"Daniel and Christ Discuss the World Economic Conference"

at
Second Presbyterian Church
7.30 p.m.

CHINESE WOULD RECRUIT NEWFOUNDLAND BATTALION TO BATTLE JAPANESE

PICCARD PREDICTS PLANES WILL TAKE TO STRATOSPHERE

Sees Ultimate Speeds of 450 MPH

PRINCE OF WALES 39; SEES FILM RECORD OF HIS LIFE IN 5 PHASES

Co-Motional Motion Will Restore Prosperity To World
(Advt.)

Honoring Mrs. Constance Chiselhurst, who is leaving shortly for her home in Leeds, England, members of the Tennyson Reading Circle and Fellowship were guests of Mrs. and Mr. J. B. Fox in their beautiful home and gardens on Capitol Hill, Sunday afternoon. A tour of the garden was enjoyed by all and tea was later served. During the afternoon Miss Zenobia Green presented Mrs. Chiselhurst with a teaspoon from circle members with a totem pole handle in honor of Pauline Johnson, the immortal Iroquois chieftainess and poetess.

Vancouver, B.C., June 26 (CP) —A mob of 200 unemployed men raided the Men's Institute, 1038 Hamilton St., yesterday at 4 p.m., manhandled four police officers who endeavored to stop them, and damaged furniture and crockery before being driven off. They paraded from the old Recreation Grounds, Smythe and Homer Sts. . . . The door of the Institute, at present used as a storehouse for relief food and clothing, was opened to the men by some person inside and the rioters entered shouting that they would help themselves to the food and accommodations.

The officers seized one man who was apparently the ringleader and ordered the others to leave. "Let's all go," shouted a voice from the crowd, and seizing cups, plates and other dishes, the invaders laid down a barrage on the officers. During the scrimmage the prisoner escaped. . . . No arrests were made.

24

THROUGH SMITH, GORDON GOT HIMSELF ENROLLED IN ONE OF THE unemployed squads formed around the vestigial core of the Deroche strikers. But it was necessary for him (Sather had enjoined on him) to gain entry into as many other left-wing groups as he could, if possible the Communist Party itself. The next Sunday morning, on Hansen's advice, he set off to reconnoitre the Stalinite cover organizations. These maintained offices over a store on upper Granville Street, and made a point of staying open on the Sabbath.

Arrived in this dusty warren, Gordon first located the Left Library, from which Hansen had recently been expelled, and the Workers' Sports Association and the Friends of the Soviet Union, whose cards were clustered on one dark doorway; across the hall he saw the stenciled signs of the Vancouver Committee of Unemployed Councils and the Workers' Unity League. Walking past these down an empty dirty corridor whose walls were splattered with posters, including an elaborate, colored chart of the Second Five Year Plan, Gordon entered an open door marked Workers' International Relief, Workers' Holiday School and Canadian Labor Defense League.

He gave the name of Paul Green to a thick-haired youth, the musty room's only occupant, who regarded him suspiciously from behind a desk cluttered with pamphlets. Gordon explained—he had been coached by Hansen—that he was an unemployed schoolteacher and 'a sympathizer' and that he would like to offer his free services as an instructor in the Workers' Holiday School that was advertised to begin next month on an island upcoast. The youth heard him out blankly.

"What kin yuh teach?" he said sharply.

"English. Marxism. Diving. Courtly love. What would you like?" He grinned, but the desk's occupant regarded him with paralyzed solemnity. He unfroze sufficiently to take Paul's address, and make the routine remarks about getting in touch, then tried to sell him some of the varicolored pamphlets spread out on the desk; but he plainly regarded Gordon as a police spy, another Sergeant Leopold in mufti.

Returning down the corridor Gordon noticed a small red-faced woman in clashing orange sweater propped in the open doorway of the Friends of the Soviet Union, etc. She stared at him with large sullen eyes but backed in and shut the door as he drew opposite. He could hear other doors opening and muffled voices, but saw no one else.

He had not gone three blocks down Granville when, happening to turn his head, he glimpsed the orange sweater. He stopped and looked in a jeweler's window; the sweater turned toward a storefront too. Gordon hurried his pace, wheeled onto a sidestreet at the next crossing, and halted just beyond the corner. In a moment the lady panted precipitately around; she stopped, her flushed face going pale and then redder than ever, and she crossed her hands behind her like a schoolgirl caught in mischief. Obviously, thought Gordon, she has not learned from Stalin's *Problems of Leninism* what a shadow does when confronted with its body.

He smiled at her. "Sorry, I really do live in that flophouse address I gave your friend. And it's quite a long way. If you have to trail me why not let's walk together?"

Her round eyes were alarmed and stricken upon him, and her sweater, grease-spotted, heaved and sank visibly. Left-librarian, Athlete or Soviet-Friend? He decided he did not care for her in any category. Nor she for him, evidently, for without ever having spoken a word, she went pelting back around the corner. Gordon stepped after her into Granville Street. She was running, convulsive and flatfooted, toward the offices like a little orange house-cat on whom a mouse has turned. Unexpectedly he felt loneliness descend on him. Even a shadower was a form of company.

It was the Sunday Blues again, and he could face his flophouse room on this gleaming June day no more easily than he could his Knox College barracks that cold afternoon (so long ago) last November. He resisted a yearning to hunt up someone from the past, from his undergraduate days, Doc Channing perhaps; instead he set off through the leaf-dark streets of the West End to English

Bay, where the season's first bathers were splashing in the green waters. Though he had neither a suit nor the money to spare for renting one, the sand was free to sit on. He took off his shoes and socks. Blown along the beach by a wind's puff, an oversized handbill came to rest by his bared feet. An Oxford Group meeting.

> It's not an institution,
> It's not a point of view,
> It starts a revolution
> By starting one in you.

Gordon put the leaflet on the sand, laid his head on it, and slowly went to sleep in the sun.

In this way he missed, as on that November day he had encountered, a fracas. Back at the Hotel Universe he was surprised to find redhaired Theda from the second floor up in Smith's room. She and Bill were sitting side by side on the bare mattress and from an enamel basin at her feet she was swabbing a cut over Smith's eye and mournfully humming *Easter Parade*.

"Class-war wound," he wheezed, peering proudly at Gordon from his one open eye. "We raided the Pogey. You sure missed somepn!"

"What happened—why—why didnt you tip me off?"

"Su'prise raid. Dreamt it up this morning—that feller Fred Hughes come back in town, he got us goin. Decided we'd bust in and git some duds."

"Yeah yuh dumb bat," Theda stopped humming and pursed her thin lipsticked old mouth enigmatically, "an all yuh git's a tin mug." She pointed the cotton swab at a galvanized cup on Smith's bed, his only loot. "And a shiner." Her legs, bare and varicosed below her short tight skirt, seemed incongruously female in this barren loft.

"Christ they's all I need ta set up as a firs' class perfessional beggar," Smith protested.

She cut a strip of tape and pressed it with surprising lightness and deftness over the cut. "Aincha jist the poor girl's Jimmy McLarnin?" she said, mournfully mocking. "Perfessional troublemaker more like. Though mosta time it's other bastards you git into the soup."

Smith, elaborately paying her no attention, went on to give

Gordon a loving account of the affray. It had been sparked by still another refusal of the city council, the day before, either to issue clothing allowances or to dispense, to the Deroche remnants at least, any of the charitably donated stores piled in the Men's Institute. The raid had been broken up by two squad cars full of police swinging billies and threatening tear-gas.

"Was a honest-ta-god show anyways," Smith concluded, "and we dint let the Monks in on it. That boy Hughes, Paul, we gotta git him on our team. You'll hafta meet him. Trouble is he likes bein a lone wolf."

Theda, who had been rounding up her first-aid kit spread on the mattress, smacked the swab in the basin and sniffed. "Lone wolf. Only wolf I see round here's the one I'm keepin from my door." She got up, staring at them unsmiling from her glittering old whore's eyes. "Ask me aint none a you more'n ki-yoots. Nutless yappin chicken-stealin ki-yoots at that. Someday you'll git us all into trouble." She grabbed her basin and kit and headed for the door, stiff-hipped and pigeon-toed, but turned, before leaving, with a grimace. "You keep that plaster on till I give it another look."

One morning a few days later Gordon, sleeping late, was unexpectedly wakened by Hansen's great bony hand on his shoulder.

"You like to come on soo-prise party, Paul?" Ole's weathered expressionless face hung over him. "Ve goin to raid Red Tape Hall." There was as much casualness in his lilt as if he were suggesting only a walk to the corner.

Gordon slid from his mattress, rubbing his eyes—a hardened bedbug, survivor of a week's assault by exterminator powder, had fought him half the night. "Red Tape—you mean the Relief Office! What are you going to do to it?"

"Nobody get hurt, yoost de files," Hansen said serenely.

Gordon dragged on his corduroys. "I cant miss this! But how come I didnt hear before? Are the Monks running it?"

"Naw. No Monks. Dat fallah Hughes. He round up some of us boys raided the Pogey. Ay tole him you wass good man, he say you can come."

He shoved his feet into his shoes, noting with a childish irrelevant pride of belonging that they were now nearly as broken-arched and skew-heeled as Hansen's standing before him, or Smith's. "Then Smitty must be coming. Did you wake him?" Smitty made a point of sleeping in.

"Hughes say not Smitty, not dis time." The Swede's voice, blank and dreamy as his face, ignored Gordon's lifted glance.

"He'll be sore if we go without him. Maybe Hughes thinks he's still laid up from that last affair, but his eye's all right now."

"Ve got to hurry," was all Ole said.

They came out onto a sidewalk wet with new rain and slithery with old dirt. Something that was half-mist, half-drizzle immersed them, and blobs of fog drifted over the grey rooftops. They crossed Hastings, snarling with nine o'clock traffic, and cut through deserted Victory Square, no sun parlor this morning. Entering at length an alley behind Hamilton Street, they began to converge with other little groups of silently moving unemployed.

There is violence ahead, Gordon thought. What am I getting into? Adventurism with no political value; because they hate Relief they want to wreck the Relief Office. But he hurried on beside the silent Hansen. I don't know enough about what's afoot to argue, and if I drop out Hansen will think me a coward. Besides, this is my chance to meet Hughes. There was also a part of him, Gordon realized, that was responding with happy irrationality to the sudden strange atmosphere of action.

The knots of nondescript men moving into the rendezvous from every side coalesced almost suddenly into a tight whispering crowd in the narrow lane. This was no garrulous aimless cluster of time-killers; though there must have been nearly thirty men pressed together, there was not a raised voice among them. The only sounds rising above the susurration of the rain were an occasional choked cough or the scrabble of shoes on stone.

Gordon and Hansen had scarcely been merged in the little army when, over its collective heads, appeared the top half of a man, mackinaw coated. He seemed to be mounted on a garbage can by the back gate of a paintless slumhouse looming on their right. The man's hair, uncovered, thick-matted over a great round skull, glistened jet in the rain, and drops ran like tears over a face sculptured and dramatic as an actor's.

"Hughes," Hansen whispered.

"All right boys," the leader began. His voice was low, resonant, with a faint Welsh magic of cadence in it, for all its tenseness. Now even the small murmurs and shuffles stopped. "Everythin's O.K. so far, boys, but we got to work fast. Fast it is. Cops may get wind any minute. So here now's the plan. There's another twenty of us round the other side of the Hall, look you, but we go first. Soon as their scout sees us hittin the front door, in through the back they come. And a third squad is behind Dunsmuir, in reserve see, ready to start a rumpus at the corner and lead off the po-lice from the scent, supposin they turn up before we're finished our little job. But mind, boys, we're not aimin to fight, not with cops, not this mornin, not with anyone. I want that clear to every man of you." He paused and his eyes moved with cold fire over them.

"The idea, look you, is to get in fast before them sour-assed clerks bar the doors. Then we yank every goddam one of their files out and spill em on the floor. Jumble them up we will, scatter em till it takes a year to put em back. But mind now—that's all ye do. I've told off already the boys that're set to keep the clerks from interferin, to handle the phones, all the strongarm stuff. They go first, with me. The rest of you stick to your job. Keep close behind us, look you, and wreck them files. Any hotheads here can bugger off now; just one man starts a fight, and, see, we'll all be doin a stretch in college." His gaze traveled over them again, fierce and righteous as a preacher.

"When it's time to get out, I'll whistle twice, and everybody leaves, look you, whatever he's doin. And when you're outside again, boys, scatter, scatter, and keep scatterin the rest of the day. Now then, anybody got a question, ask it low and make it short."

The vibrant, urgent words stopped. In the brief silence Gordon's gaze roamed over the faces near him. There was a strange eager quality in these eyes narrowed under the dingy cocked caps, eyes in which he was accustomed to see only dullness or cynicism or defeat. Slack mouths were thinned now with tension. Yet they were, most of them, the faces still of youths, faces that for all their truculent air were tilted with pathetic trust into the sifting rain. There were no questions.

"All right. Now one last thing. Ye *know* why we're raidin this place?" There was a low exasperated murmur. "O.K., once again.

It's got nothin to do with the clerks. They're a pack of surly ward-heelin flunkies, that's all. They'll only holler. Let them. It's the files we're after, look you. The files we'll smash, for there's cards there on every man of us, on every workless man in this town. And the cards say whether they think you're a Red or not—never mind if ye *are* or not—or a troublemaker or you been in the jug or they dont like yer face. The *cards* say if ye get relief or get turfed to a camp. The cards say if yer married or not. If yer not married on them cards ye get single relief, no matter how many wives ye got or kids either. The cards is lyin and informin and buggerin up every one of us. We're goin to fix them cards, look you, and that's all. Right?"

There was almost a shout of approval, which Hughes gestured angrily into silence. This is how an infantry officer talks to his soldiers at zero hour, Gordon thought.

"Bodyguard up!" Hughes' voice came hard and quick. There was a movement near him. "Follow me, all." He leapt down.

Within seconds Gordon found himself swirled behind the lead-group that rushed, heels treading on heels, down the little passage-way and poured into Hamilton Street. It fanned into the roadway, bringing a startled autoist to a squealing halt. Now a ragged, panting column it veered toward the hated Hall, at the nearer corner. An overgrown house, converted to less domestic ends, its bald clapboard walls rose yellow-wet and dismal before them. Hughes' black bobbing head disappeared into its street door. With a sudden throaty vengeful cry, the human pack funneled in behind him.

The next few minutes were an utter confusion of yells, tramplings, the vindictive shovings of bodies, the rip and crash of furniture. The moustachioed doorkeeper, a former company-sergeant-major, caught off guard, tried belatedly to resist. He was heaved bellowing into the air and passed almost jovially out over the invaders' heads into the street. At the same moment the rest of Hughes' husky body-guard leapt the office rail and tore the telephones from the walls before a single one of the panicky warren of clerks and stenographers had found presence of mind to lift a receiver. Some who tried to escape through the back were blocked at the doorway by the second squad roaring in.

Meantime, the mass of the raiders were assaulting the tiered cabinets of files, yanking out drawers and spilling their contents—little blue cards, and bigger green ones, and great square white ones.

Gordon, swept up in the schoolboy excitement of destruction, and seeing Hansen wrestling with a towering oak letter-file, grabbed a corner and they tilted it, sending a yellow snow of duplicates flaking and flying onto the oily board floor. Whole compost-heaps of the Depression's bureaucracy began to mount between the desks and the sprawled cabinets and the hopping feet of the pale clerks who, huddled against the walls, alternately shouted in fear for the police or stood speechless and pop-eyed with clerical outrage.

Box by shiny box, steel file, overstuffed cardboard case, the records were uncloaked and assaulted. The revolting slaves, for want of the means to reach the palaces, had broken into one of their oppressors' minor sanctuaries and were raping the temple virgins. The workless, working and sweating again, if only for these few glorious moments, shoved and elbowed each other for the pleasure of trampling with their broken muddy shoes the spotless symbols of their bondage. They jumped and stomped and squealed on the heaps till the cards flew like parti-colored feathers in the long dingy room, and one of the girl stenographers fainted, or seemed to, and another shrieked "Murder!" But no sound they uttered could be heard above the din of the pillagers.

Suddenly Gordon saw a swarthy boy near him draw flame from a matchbox in his hand. Before Gordon sensed what he intended, the youth touched it to a paper crumpled in his other hand.

"Stop that bastard!" Hughes' voice rang out from across the room. Gordon lunged but the burning paper dropped on the nearest mound. He felt himself caromed aside. The little leaping fire disappeared under the great spreadeagled body of Hansen, self-propelled upon the heap. The pile slithered with his weight and the old logger, with surprising litheness, rolled clear and leapt again to his feet, slapping at his chest, and wheeling to stamp at the pile. But the flame was out, the remnants quenched under the heels of Gordon and of Hughes who had come vaulting across in the wake of his own shout. There was a brown singe across Hansen's old checked shirt, but Ole was evidently unhurt and certainly unruffled.

Hughes glared around but the swarthy youth had managed to disappear. He put two fingers in his mouth and blew an astonishingly shrill double blast by Gordon's ear.

"All right, boys," he shouted. "The job's done. And there's a stool been in here tryin to start trouble. Time we got out. Take it easy, the cops aint here yet. Out the back way we go now, all of us. Dont crowd. Follow me."

Miraculously, within another two minutes, everyone had trampled out through the ankle-deep discolored slush of tabs and slips and cards and memos, and had scattered and vanished down the city's backstreets before the first squad car came wailing up Hamilton. It was a complete and bloodless victory.

It was also, of course, a somewhat pointless one, as the Communists, because they had not led it, were quick to emphasize. Its chief effect was to give the newspapers another excuse to write editorials denouncing mob-violence, and the trade unions another reason for disassociating themselves from the anarchy of the workless, and the respectable public another justification, through fear, for its apathy. As for the files, they were reassembled and repaired within a month, and on certain cards there were fresh notations, wherever the clerks could match names with remembered yelling faces.

Hughes' fame, it was true, was increased among the unemployed. Also with the police, who began hunting him in earnest. But he had become invisible.

A strange *putsch*. Neither Sather nor MacCraddock nor the Barstows would have approved of it. Nor did Gordon, theoretically. Yet the most disturbing afterthought that came to him, when he had won back undetected to his skidroad home, was that, from start to finish of the raid, he had been thoroughly and unthinkingly happy.

25

Lady wants loan $500 urgently; repay $75 per month, 10% interest or arrangement. Box 2241 Planet.

U.S. FEDERAL RELIEF BILL NOW $3,300,000,000 Needed Pump Priming, Says Keynes

HAPPYLAND DANCING

Victoria, B.C., June 25—Protest against the Federal Government's new physical examination of single men entering roadcamps was lodged yesterday by the Union of B.C. Municipalities at their conference here yesterday. It was stated that nearly one-third of the men were being rejected as a result of the increased stringency of the examinations and that these men at once became municipal charges. This, the municipal representatives said, was most unfair.

Vancouver Agog to Play Host to Northwest Pacific International Race and Regatta Beginning Today.

7.30 P.M.
"Would the Carpenter of Nazareth Work for 25 Cents a Day?"
Hear the Rev. Andrew Roddan

Washington, June 28—For the past three years, Otto Kahn, N.Y. banker and lavish patron of the arts, has paid no income tax. Later, he will be asked by Ferdinand Pecora, counsel of the Senate investigating Committee, to explain . . .

RICH WOULD GLADLY PAY TAXES IF LAWS WERE JUST, KAHN TELLS SENATE COMMITTEE

MCLARNIN GETS KEYS TO CITY WORLD CHAMP WELCOMED HOME

RUSSIA BLAMED FOR
LUMBER MARKET SLUMP

AUTO MAGNATE
SHOOTS SELF

Lenglen Sets Rouged
Knees Fashion in Tennis

"Our anxiety," said Colonel Spry, "is to speed up getting these men back to camp. There is accommodation for 3,500 in the Province but so far only 1,200 are in occupancy. In other provinces we understand that long queues waited outside employment offices for opportunities to go to the relief camps but in B.C. some wrong publicity had been given and a certain element is afraid of military discipline."

There were even single men over twenty-one who were living off parents at home although of course not eligible for relief so long as they did so. Only transients over 21 are eligible.

HOLLYWOOD IDYLL
ENDED: MARY & DOUG
TO SEPARATE

OVER THE HUMP OF SLUMP
SAYS ROTARY PRESIDENT

Unemployed Jumps
Into False Creek

Vancouver, July 6—Important plans for the development of the Canadian Radio Commission station in this city are stayed for the present, said Mr. Hector Charlesworth, chairman of the Commission, who reached Vancouver this morning. Lack of public funds, said . . .

BIG CROWDS FOR
FIRST DAY OF RACES

STOUT HEARTS &
EXCELLENT BANKING
SAVED CANADA IN
DEPRESSION SAYS
LONDON POST

Baby boy, healthy, white, ten weeks.

JOHN BARRYMORE BRINGS
BACK ALASKAN GRIZZLY

Middle-aged man wants work—will do anything. Box 3492 Province.

Loretta Young, shown in a Los Angeles court today, as she obtained approval of her new motion picture contract calling for $1,731 per week for the first year.

26

NOW GORDON BEGAN ATTENDING OPEN MEETINGS CALLED BY THE various radical organizations, behaving as every man did who had his own little hatchet to sharpen. He proposed loaded queries at question-time, spun them into speeches if he could before the chairman stopped him, grabbed at chances to fulminate in open forums at the end of other people's harangues, and kept hinting that he be asked to give an oration himself. He never was. His participation in the Hamilton raid had given him standing in such circles, but not that much standing.

Moreover, in the inevitable arguments after such meetings, when the little knots of men drifted back to the Skidroad, or, the next morning on the grass in the Sun Parlor, Gordon had soon been drawn into the stock Stalin-Trotsky controversies and was not adroit enough to avoid revealing his position. Nor had he even been able to abandon the feeling, despite Sather's coaching, that honesty was at least a tactical necessity. The news quickly spread that Paul Green was a hundred per cent Trotskyite and had converted Smith; before many days he found himself almost as much a political oddity as Hansen and in consequence quite misunderstood and almost powerless.

The Trotskyite label was indeed thoroughly and publicly pinned on Paul Green by McNamee. The latter came on him suddenly as he lay on the grass in the Parlor one hot afternoon, and deliberately baited him before a politically mixed assemblage.

"Come on, Mister Green, or whoever y'are, tell us the truth—if you know how." He poked his cap back cockily. "Which one would you rather see leading the Soviet Union today, Stalin or Trotsky?" Flanked this time by a half-dozen henchmen, the secretary of the Workers' Unity League leaned confidently down, his pouty lips twisted in a movie-gangster's sneer. Gordon looked around at the young puzzled faces of the men on the grass. Some of them did want the truth and if he didn't give it he'd never win them from McNamee.

"If you put it in terms of leadership—Trotsky, by a mile."

"Told you, boys," McNamee crowed, wheeling and then turning savagely back to Gordon, all the more savagely perhaps because there had been no spontaneous protest from the listeners at Gordon's reply. "You fascist scum! We ought to run you out of the Square. Mr. Trotsky's the biggest paid agent the international bourgeoisie ever had, he's a White Guard spy, a pal of Otto Kahn and John D. Rockefeller. He's out to wreck the Soviet Union and the Third International."

"The Third International's already wrecked. I'm out for re-building it with a new and honest leadership." Gordon stared up at him. "And save your name-calling for the real fascists."

McNamee looked around, smiling, his voice now deadly soft. "You heard, boys. Now you know how a police spy talks." He whirled again on Gordon, dirty finger pointing. "In a couple of years from now, Mr. Paul Trotsky Green, we'll have a Workers' State of North America and you'll be one of the first to be stood up against a wall and shot—if some honest worker doesnt bump you off sooner. And I hope to Christ I live to have the personal pleasure of helping to blow out your dirty brains."

Lying there still on the grass Gordon had a momentary sensation that he had already been shot, and partly to break the spell of McNamee's melodramatics he stood up and confronted the man, glaring into his glare, arguing back hotly and rapidly. But McNamee thrived on such melodrama, for he not only believed in it as a technique. He projected himself into it, assumed himself the impersonal avenging force of history (Gordon thought, even as he shouted), identified himself so hysterically as to be incapable of listening. McNamee simply yelled Gordon down and it was someone else who got the lead.

"Aw you goddam commies wotcha allus wantin to shoot people?" On the nearby stone parapet a puffy-eyed old-faced youth had stirred. "Shoot people." He shrieked the phrase with a spasmic energy as if he himself were firing a gun.

"That's tellinum," said a big fellow in a ragged mackinaw beside him. "Hell with politics, all we need's jobs."

McNamee turned on them, but his voice was now carefully conciliatory. "Brother, that's what we all want. But—"

"You're doin all right. On Moscow dough." It was another commentator, glancing up from a blackjack game on the grass.

"But—" McNamee ignored him—"we wont git it without an organization, you fellahs know that, and soon as we organize and start demandin our rights the bosses call us Reds. They use their own boss-parties to outlaw ours; it's the goddam capitalists that force us to have our own outfits, comrades, aint it the truth?" His voice was folksy, cajoling. "You think we gonna git the laws we want from a govermint run by R. B. Bennett, the world's Match King?"

There were mutters of approval, a shifting of loyalties.

"McNamee's right." But it was one of McNamee's men.

"Nyaah, he's still a comic." The boy on the parapet wriggled and spat. "Gangster comic."

"And what ta hell are you, a Oxford Grouper?" One of McNamee's henchmen, a thin man with a scornful sooty face, moved over to him. "What's wrong with bein red? We're the only ones fightin fer jobs fer guys like you right now."

"He's right."

"Nyah! The CCF's done more in a coupla months than—"

"Cor, the CCF's just another gang a ca-*pit*-alists, comrade," came a cockney voice. "Supportin Bennett's slyve-lybor camps and war on Russia."

"That's a bloody lie, you read the Regina Convention report—socialized banks, public—"

"Social fascist promises!" McNamee shouted. "The role of the CCF is to prepare the way for Canadian fascism and Trotskyism."

"Prepare the way for you horse-thieves, yuh mean. Commies Come Fishin, that's all CCF stands fer."

"Shat," a silent old codger on the grass said unexpectedly, pushing a yellowed crown-broken panama back from his forehead. "Belly-reds, that's what y'all are. Coupla full dinners in yer guts and you'll be yellin God Save the King as loud as any of em and dreamin of sleepin with Carole Lombard."

"That's what *you* think—"

"Fightin each other," the puffy-eyed youth resumed, encouraged.

"S'all y'ever fight. Each other." He looked around anxiously for approval. "That's—"

"Lissen, fallah." McNamee's surly-faced companion shoved his fist up at the youth on the wall. "You tryin to tell us they aint no pigeons nor no Trotskyites nor no fascists round here?"

The big man in the mackinaw put an arm out between them authoritatively, and scowled at the questioner. "Yuh keep outa politics and keep yer paws to yerself and yuh dont need ta worry about none a them. This feller and me we aint doin nothin the police gotta worry about. All we want's work and it'll come along. The govamint'll do somethin, you watch. An we dont need no Stalins or Trotskies to tell us. Pensions, Social Security, we'll get em." He had the air of a chairman winding up a debate. "If Bennett dont do it, Mackenzie King will. We'll get a New Deal, the right ta work; that's all any square-shootin guy is askin for."

"Yah vell but maybe ve ought to tink about right to be lacey tew." It was Hansen, who had quietly strolled into the group.

There was derisive laughter, led by McNamee.

"Right to be lazy!"

"Key-riced, that's what we got now."

"That's the only right us buggers have got."

"Now you heard Vancouver's other Trotskyist," McNamee shouted happily. "And these pigeons pretend they know Marxism!"

"Maybe you is better Marxist as me," Hansen retorted in his lilting serene way. "But I yoost sayin what that fallah Paul Laforgue say. Right to be Lacey. Book you fallahs wass sellin, by French comrade was sidekick of Karl Marx. He talkin about real Vurkers State tew, when everybody got time to enjoy life, money tew, workin big wages maybe ten hours a veek and den have right to be lacey any vay he can, sailin yachts mebbe even, in English Bay, not yoost sit on his ass on grass like ve is doin."

There were laughing cheers at this, but their sound did not suggest understanding or belief.

"Yachts! Pie in the sky," the old codger said. "You commies is all alike, Trotsky, Stalinsky, Tim Bucksy—nyaa, why doncha go back to Moscow all of yuh y'dont like it here. Yuh fulla canned heat."

"Yah, go jump off a bridge."

The argument became an almost aimless shouting and lost its focus. McNamee, with a gesture of sour superiority, turned and, followed by his three supporters, performed once more one of his lordly retreats. The Parlor was restored to its dozing, grumbling, the rustle of shuffled cards, the patter of bet matches.

Depressed, Gordon wandered without conscious purpose alone up Pender Street, resuming his ancient argument with his other half. You see, surely to God you see now, the mass of mankind is determined to remain ignorant.

Nevertheless, he reminded his shadow, a few months ago I too was a political ignoramus. And there's still the precious few who at least have embraced the socialist ideal.

Embraced the McNamees, you mean, running after the stupid arrogant neurotics of their own class.

There are true leaders somewhere; the men who fought and won the Russian revolution were not McNamees.

How do you know? A little smarter, no better. The same sort, simply magnified in the minds of this gullible new generation, blown up by distance and success. Wrestling champions still; remember Bagshaw? They'll never be pianists.

No, no, the Soviet achievement exists, is a fact.

A fantastic stroke of luck scored by a few vicious fools. Unrepeatable. Because what have they been doing ever since? Betraying. In Germany now, in half a dozen countries before Germany, tomorrow a whole continent. They'll always betray, betray your precious suffering masses, lead them to defeat.

But they can't be that foolish; it would mean their own torture and death!

Would it? They'll turn torturers first, cannibalize on their own, to stay in power. You see it in Russia. And if they see they're losing, they'll rat away. That's the way the world wags, has always wagged. The Middle Ages continue. *Inconstant warld and wheill contrarious.* And what about your side (his invisible companion's whisper went rushing on), what about your microcosmic army? Nobody joins it, not even the few Marxists who do chuck Stalinism. They prefer to create a new sect for themselves so they can lead it. They only rebel because they have a psychopathic need to be leaders. Do you remember that burning gas well on the prairies you watched from the boxcar door? That's what your sacred Marxism is, an uncapped flame consuming natural power, wasting it, releasing its pressure violently and spectacularly—to no end.

No, no, he shouted at himself as he plodded mechanically along the street, it can't be. My Toronto comrades—

Comrades! (He heard his Doppelgaenger laugh within him.) Not one of them's so much as written you, not even darling Thelma. *She* can't be dead too, like Anne; *she's* not given you a chance to kill her, as you killed—

O Christ, why doesn't she write? She promised me.

Ah but "Gordon promised me he'd organize Vancouver." Remember? She's waiting till you do.

He had walked several blocks and stopped, without realizing it, outside a bookstore. He went in. Perhaps his feet, he thought, would always, given their way, lead him back from forums to the homes of books. Generally he avoided this part of town because someone from his undergraduate past might recognize him and ask embarrassing questions. He was still dressed in the old corduroys and rollneck sweater he had put on when he left Toronto; indeed he had now no other clothes.

His eye caught sight of a glistening new 'art' edition of *Leaves of Grass* on the nearest table and aimlessly he turned its pages, thinking in fact not of what he saw, but of Thelma. Was his mail being intercepted?

"I speak the password primeval," he heard softly at his elbow, "I give the sign of democracy."

He turned and found a domed head, white with fuzz soft as a rabbit's tail, at shoulder level beside him.

"Doc!"

Professor Roger Channing fixed him with blue merry-grave eyes, and quirked a Punchinello chin at him. "You dog," he said elegantly, "you long yaller snuffling graceless hound. When someone told me yesterday they saw Gordon Saunders two weeks ago walking in Victory Square, I called him a liar. I said you would have come to see me long ago."

Gordon found himself struggling against falling into the old role of the naive and abashed sophomore before this knowing and lordly little man.

"I'm—well," he made a gesture at his dirty corduroys, "I've been thinking of it but—"

"You've been thinking, have you?" Professor Channing reached and seized him by both ears, glaring with an indignation that seemed alarmingly genuine. "This is indeed a new Saunders. You will drive home at once with me and show me how you think." He pulled on both ears. "It may be that I will give you a small rye." Gordon grimaced acceptance. "And a bath," Channing said fiercely, releasing him. "Certainly a bath. I think perhaps the bath first."

He had gone gladly, for Channing's insults were, as always, blows of affection concealing a tact and loving-kindness Gordon had almost forgotten the sound and sight of. He went knowing that he need tell Channing nothing and could leave in an hour; in fact, he stayed to supper, left after midnight, and told his old professor almost everything.

Channing, once Gordon had convinced him he was serious about whatever he was doing, and had promised to ask for help if trouble overtook him, did not argue against his politics. The old Hardyan aloofness, Gordon realized, had also undergone a depression-change, and though Roger Channing was too much an individualist ever to be a Marxist, he had always had a leaning to the underdog, and was now, it appeared, at least an ardent reader of John Strachey, an occasional public baiter of the Bennett government, and a secret supporter of the CCF. "Dangerously close to Marxism"—Gregor's stuffy phrase, and Sather's ridicule of it popped into Gordon's mind. Was the Doc just another pseudo-liberal Puritan? They would no doubt have come to disagree about Trotskyism, and violently, if a rather innocent undergraduate had not come in. Channing's wife had immediately seized the opportunity for a foursome of bridge.

When the little professor finally shoved him out the door into the darkness he had pressed into Gordon's hand two ten-dollar bills— "a loan, you doe-eyed *sansculotte*, for which I shall exact full repayment in Canadian rubles."

27

First Mine-Laying Submarine Has Successful Trial Run

JOHN D. ROCKEFELLER 94

Penticton, B.C., July 7 — Charges of kidnapping against seven Princeton citizens, including two provincial police constables, were dismissed Thursday by Justice of the Peace Hooper of Merritt when neither Evans, red union organizer, nor his attorney, appeared in court. Allegations in a communist-front paper that the two had been terrorized by local vigilantes into staying away from the trial area were dismissed as leftist inventions by local police.

ORANGEMEN REAFFIRM LOYALTY
Thousands across Canada Celebrate Battle of Boyne— One Flag, School, Language Emphasized

---

SILVER CREATES MONETARY STRUGGLE AT LONDON PARLEY

Powell-Lombard Divorce Poised

WOODSWORTH PLANS RED DICTATORSHIP WARNS CABINET MINISTER CCF'S AIMS SAME AS MOSCOW'S
Only Bennett Stands for Order

BANKER HARRISON PLEADS INSANITY— MADE FALSE ENTRIES FOR $1,713,225

ITALIAN AIR ARMADA COMPLETES GREATEST MASS FLIGHT IN ALL HISTORY
Balbo Lands 24 Planes In Chicago

Victoria, B.C., July 12—Relief figures released by governmental sources here today indicate that, at May's end this year, there were 22,800 married and about 30,000 single men on relief in this province. This represents a decline of 12,000 over the March figures, which officials attributed to seasonal summer employment, chiefly logging.

Minister Greets Musso's Airmen in Montreal Today

Vancouver, July 12 — Aldermen today declined to endorse demands of the central local of the Vancouver Unemployed Councils for upping wage rates in relief camps from 20 cents a day to 40 cents an hour and for abolition of alleged "militarism" in these establishments.

28

LATE THE NEXT MORNING, PAUL GREEN AND OLE HANSEN CARRIED
into the former's room a man dripping from a scalp-wound that
had parted his thick black hair from crown to forehead into blood-
clotted and dirt-soiled halves which quivered like a wig when they
laid him on the bed. It was Fred Hughes and he had been stretched
on a Hastings Street sidewalk a few minutes earlier by the butt end
of a quirt brought swinging down on his head from the height of
a provincial policeman's horse. The officer, one of a posse engaged
in "dispersing an illegal demonstration", to use the *Daily Journal's*
phraseology, had at once ridden on along the sidewalk into the
scattering shoppers since he had spotted still another 'ringleader'
and presumably felt that Hughes was in no condition to move on
until he could be gathered into the Black Maria. Hansen, Smitty
and Gordon, however, had been near him and managed in the
general excitement to drag Hughes into a nearby alley-mouth before
the police van had leisure to find and garner him in. Then they
manhandled him the two blocks to Gordon's flophouse. It had
not been easy, because Hughes was unconscious.

Fortunately, Fooki and the rest of the ground floor were down
the street watching the shindig and, using Smitty as an advance
scout, they were able to cart Hughes through the lobby unobserved
by any eyes except the glassblack orbs of the bull moose, and get
him up the stairs.

Hansen, who had acquired a St. John Ambulance certificate in
logging-camp days, took charge and sent Smith out to scrounge
court-plaster from the corner drug-store while Gordon woke up
Theda on the second floor. Grumblingly she lent him scissors and
disinfectant and came padding and swearing up later, still in her
spotted old dressing gown, with hot water she had heated on a
spirit stove. With these, a razor, and the tail torn from Gordon's
one clean shirt, Hansen silently cut back and shaved the caked hair

around the long wound, washed it and taped the gaping sides together.

"Sonsabitches," said Theda softly; her eyes, glittering still with last night's mascara, rested on the round Welsh face pale now under Hansen's lumpish turban. "If they'd give you bums ration-tickets to my room and leave *me* to do the layin-out, there wouldnt be no goddam Depression."

"Yoost you lay out Fooki if he start comin up here," said Ole. After she had shuffled out, now drearily whistling *The Last Roundup*, and Ole had returned to his own hostel, Gordon and Smith took turns sitting on the floor, backs against the dark peeling wall, waiting to see if Hughes would come out of his concussion. He lay unmoving on his back all that afternoon and evening, snoring with a hard unnatural steadiness. Olsen had said they should give him until morning; if he were still unconscious they must call a hospital. This, of course, would mean trouble for everybody—for Gordon, who had sneaked him into his room, for anyone who could be shown to have helped him, and most of all for Hughes himself.

A delegation of unemployed had started up the steps of the City Hall (an old office building on Hastings Street) to interview the Mayor. They had been promptly and quite literally kicked down the steps again into the midst of alarmed pedestrians, by a cordon of forewarned police. Immediately a 'mass reserve' of about two hundred workless in the nearest alley, led by Hughes, seeing the repulse of their chosen, had rushed into Hastings to the rescue. This in turn had been the signal awaited by a mounted police-squad ranged up a sidestreet.

The police spurred out with quirts whirling, charged up and down both street and sidewalks, scattered passers-by into doorways, knocked down shoppers who got in the way, and deliberately sought out for clubbing any flying figure which looked dirty and ragged enough to be one of the workless. Some of these began fighting back with stones they had stowed in their pockets for just such a contingency. One man found a long stick and fixed a razor blade in its tip and laid open the quivering flank of a policeman's horse. Panicky storekeepers rushed to lock their street doors against the inward press of escaping street crowds, and the crowds, in turn, shrieked in anger at the storekeepers and cursed in fear of the police.

It was obvious from what had happened, Hansen and Smith argued, that the police would be more anxious than ever to sweep up as many who could be made to look like ringleaders as possible, and that the magistrates would make an example of them. They knew that Hughes, if conscious, would take the same risks they were taking with him unconscious.

"Wont be no thirty-day incite-to-riot if they git him this time," Smith said with a sort of mournful satisfaction, "specially after him leadin them two raids before. Crimnul synaclism more like it —five years."

But what to do with him? If he had been a Stalinist disposal would have been easy. The Faithful were said to have their own secret emergency-ward and genuine doctor-sympathizers who would minister freely and privately to any of the flock laid low in honorable class-war. But Hughes, though a tireless writer of agitational letters-to-the-editor and a flamboyant speaker at United Front rallies, had kept clear of political tags and party cards. The Communists, Hansen knew, feared Hughes' Celtic tongue, which had not spared their follies, and feared more his ascendency to independent leadership. They would merely give him a kick for luck if they found him in the gutter. As for any ordinary doctor, he would immediately call the hospital if shown such a patient, and the hospital would call the police. There was nothing to do but take a chance and wait.

It was while waiting, squatting on the bare floor of his own room, his ears obsessed with the frightening rasp of the stranger on his bed, his eyes automatically following the path of a cockroach up the wall, that Gordon suddenly remembered—and with utter astonishment that he had for a half-hour forgotten—what he had seen, as he staggered through the lobby holding one end of Hughes by his dusty boots. There was a fat envelope in the rack addressed to him! In the frantic strain of rushing Hughes through the hallway, he had not dared to free a hand and reach for it. Now he went leaping down the stairs, wondering if at last it was a letter from Thelma. It was.

29

July 10th (I think)

Dear Gordon,

Writing the first time to somebody who's practically a proffessor of English isnt easy even if I am sort of engaged to him. Maybe that's one reason I havent written before that you didnt think about, smartey. Why Ive never even got it straight, where commas go. Its certainly time you had some kind of scrawl though, Gordie, after all the exciting dispatches from the battle zone you've been sending me. Two converts the first two days is really zipping along even Ronnie and Hymie are impressed, though of course when I told Leo he muttered some old Jewish proverb about apples that drop off when you touch them being too ripe to keep, but you know Leo. You have to admit though you've still got to convert some employed with union cards who can pay regular dues before you can set up a Branch with a library and everything. And you'll have to do some writing or coaching in between organizing to pay for a Press and a secret headquarters maybe. Still its good to know you've been getting the breaks so far and Mom was very happy you hadnt got arested yet. What a kick she is, she was sure you were going to lose both legs on those freight trains even before you got there. Of course I keep reminding everybody I was the one, who said you could do it right at the start. You're a real proffessional revolutionery now even if the League is still too poor to send you that measley four dollars a week they promised. Jack doesnt get his anymore either, you know but then the only League he's working for is the Junior League. He just went out the door shouting at me to tell you he'd answer your letters tomorrow but I wouldnt expect anything from that Big Noise til you get it, he's even worse than me. I guess we Barstows all talk so much we cant be bothered writing though he certainly should too because you write so *amusingly*, Gordie everybody enjoyed reading them.

Well I've been studying for that matric supp in English you

know but I've decided I'd just get plowed if I tried it this month so I'm not even bothering now, anyway I'm not interested in a bourgois education any more, I havent even time to read all the books Leo wants me to. I'm learning to type though you'll be happy to hear. I go down almost every day to Leo's office and practice on his machine. Next letter maybe I'll type for you! Its the only way I ever see Leo anymore, he wont come here because it makes dad so crazy mad its too embarrassing. Then I was going away out to the San to see Bobbie and that takes nearly a whole day every week, though lately he's too sick even to have visitors isnt that *awful* Gordie? And that brother of mine keeps saying I should get a job and just worrying about that takes time.

I guess the revolution is running in secondgear just now too, maybe it always does in the summer. With Mac in jail and Leo not appearing at any more public meetings and our Spark not getting printed Toronto isnt exactly Petrograd in 1917. Come to think of it though even the Bolsheviks didnt get power till October anyway did they? I dont blame Leo though, he's given up a lot of time to the League and the comrades just lean back and take it for granted he always will, he says what the League needs rite now is money and he's in a position to earn it providing he is allowed to remain low politicaly.

Perhaps I oughtnt to tell you this because Leo doesnt want it known, but he's now doing consultive work in labor relations for a huge company, dont tell anybody because if the Stalinites heard it they'd say he was selling out to the capitalists or something. I just hope he gets a fulltime job with this firm and then he could really put the Toronto branch on its feet and send you money to organize all Western Canada, eh? He might too because this firm knows who Leo is but they dont care so long as he stays out of trouble; the fact he knows radical politics so well is all to the good for them. Anyway you can see why Leo couldnt possibly follow you out on a freight like you sugested in your last letter, and speak in Vancouver. He's too important to be used that way, Gordon, and after all you'll have to learn to stand up and holler for the League yourself—a proffessor shouldnt be worried about public speaking. And as Leo says if you keep on reading Marx and Engils and Lenin and Trotsky you'll know what to say, wont you?

Anyway first you'll have to form a Workers Defence Squad to defend the platform otherwise the Stalinites will just break up any meeting you try to hold in Vancouver, they can still do it here even sometimes. Gee politics is awful complicated Gordie isnt it? Our kind I mean. And slow too—sometimes I wonder.

You asked about Mac. He doesnt write any of us not even Leo, though of course the Prisen Governor or somebody would read his mail, wouldnt they? so he couldnt say what he really thought except in code and anyway Leo says the Mounties would check up on any one Mac wrote to but I kind of wish he was smuggling out secret letters to us through a wardor or somebody, like Rosa Luxembourg did. Did you ever read her Letters From Prison? I wish I could write like her. Mrs. Mac is kind of hostile to us so we dont get news through her. I think she really blames the League for Mac being in jail. Still she might be more greatful to Leo, after all Mac might have got seven years instead of three if he hadnt had Leo to defend him.

It seems I havent much cheering news to send you, Gordie, but I guess my revolutionery temprature is below normal just now, what with the latest splat going on in the League here. They had a meeting at our place, of course I wasnt allowed to stick my nose in because I'm still secretary of the Spartacus Youth Club and you cant be in that and belong to the adult organization too isnt it *rediculous*!! But between you and me I heard most of it from the top landing—do you think that was awful of me? But wait, I knew they were going to discuss moving me up into the adult League so do you blame me for listning? After all it was my own house. Anyway what I missed I wormed out of Jack and Leo the next day; what happened was that super intellectual Willie Baumling spoke against my admission as you might guess saying Rosie Romanuk—you know, the flatfaced one—ought to go ahead of me because she was "more mature", imagine! and "idealogicaly, sp? more stable". Bah! you know what that's all about Gordon, that dummy and Willie are living together, everybody says so and I think that's terrible we should leave that kind of morals to the Stalinites. And anyway it makes him predjudiced. Of course Leo spoke up for me, and Ronnie and Hymie naturally they said some really sweet things the smoothies, you'd have been pleased, I hope but Willie's gang all raved about Rosie. Leo says Willie has a secret fraction right in our group that's tied up with the Fieldites in New York of all things, that bunch of bohemeans, and Field is really Bauerite, you know that ultra-leftist they expelled in Paris and Trotsky had to write a pollemic against because they kept bringing up a lot of hair splitting points about theory though all they really want is to get the leadership away from the Old Man and set up a 4th Interntl rite away, isnt that terrible? And the worst is the Baumlingites are so strong in our League now Leo says all he could do was get both Rosie and me refered to a Standing Membership Committee rather than force a vote and maybe have a split which would wreck the organization, after all there arent more than about twenty active comrades left in Toronto now even counting the Baumlingites. Anyway Leo thinks I can be more good to the cause just learning to type and helping him so I'm not too worried.

Guess what? Mom is staking me to a new suit for my birthday (July 27), it's navy with tight sleeves flaring into fur puffs above the elbow (Alaska Mink shade coney) and the cutest row of buttons straight up from waist to neck, and a tam to match, wish you could see me in it.

About the other things you ask me gee Gordie I'm not good at writing about how I feel, not the way you are but you know I still like you and I'm very proud of you. Mom thinks she and I might be able to come to Salt Lake some time next winter perhaps, if you can raise the fare but gosh I dont want to plan so far ahead just yet because after all you and I know there's no future under capitalism anyway. Though I sure would like to escape from this house sometimes with everybody raving at me for one thing or another all the time. Anyway please write me as ever, how you are making out and I wish you every success this summer. If you dont hear from me soon you know it's just that I'm busy too and have to look for work as well as learning to type. Mom sends her love. Up the rebels!

Your comrade Thelma

P.S. Dont you think it's sinester all those fascist Italian planes visiting Canada? And Leo says the Prince of Wales is a Musolini fan.

P.S. again. You'd better write. This letter took me two whole days.

30

GORDON READ THROUGH THE STRANGE CURLICUED SCRAWL TILTED
every whichway over the crowded pages, read without moving from
his cramped seat on the uneven floor, as the small light faded and
the stranger snored unmoving on the bed—read searching in each
phrase for the warm and vivacious and beautiful woman he had
fallen in love with, and who had set in motion the events that had
brought him here. But I have never known her; where is she? This
is the dull babble of an adolescent.

Snob, it's you who are being adolescent. You're put out because
she doesn't write like George Sand, and hasn't showered you with
praises.

But dear God, she could have written something more generous
than—what was it? (he looked back at the page)—"it's good to
know you've been getting the breaks". Damn her.

All right, but she's telling you truths you've never faced. She's
a woman, practical after all. You haven't recruited one employed
man. Look at that liability on the bed, what kind of leaders are
these you're choosing, ass, *déclassé*? You've forsaken your own
kind to rummage in this ragtag and bobtail for the heroes of a
new social revolution.

It's not true. Think of Hansen. Hansen is strong, intelligent,
lionhearted.

Hansen's an aging outcast, undernourished, penniless, introverted,
a dreamer. He's in worse shape even than Smith. Smith's only got
asthma; your lionheart has stomach ulcers, chronic. Otherwise
they'd both be back in a relief camp and you'd never have met
them, even them. Thelma's right; she's the realist, not you.

But this is not the point. Why does this letter leave me with a
terrible sense of loss?

Loss of something you never had. Death of another of your
illusions. You're simply admitting at last that your romantic inno-

cence has played an obvious and enormous joke on you. The Thelma you loved never existed.

She did, she does, I must cling to that. I will make her into what she can be.

This lazy feckless creature? You've been spellbound by an *enfant terrible*, a selfish shallow gabby child, an incorrigible little rationalizer.

It's not true. I will remember what she is, not what she writes. She is young.

Too young—for you. But not for Leo. He crops up on every line.

It's because she's intelligent she goes to him. He is her leader, her true father, nothing more. She will come to love me.

She loves neither you nor the cause she and he converted you to.

So passionately converted me.

Fool—and she can't even spell.

Nevertheless, I believe in what I can make her into. I will still marry her, I—

It was at this moment that Hughes suddenly shifted, breaking the rhythm of his dreadful snore with a quick groan, coming back to consciousness and pain, and bringing Gordon back to the challenge he constituted.

All next day he fed his patient aspirin and milk, nursed the slow renewal of his strength and kept him in bed till the depth of the following night. Then, since they dared not shelter him longer, Smith and Gordon got Hughes down the stairs, along the back alley, and under waning moonlight to the docks. There, following the Welshman's murmured directions, and with many stops for rest, they shuffled a mile under the black shadows of pier-sheds to a dim floathouse in Coal Harbour, the squatter home of Fred's half-brother, Harry Dack.

Dack was almost employed. He owned an ancient warped row-boat and a few feet of frayed net, with which he occasionally caught shrimps in the waters of the harbor. He and the half-Indian girl he lived with took Fred in without question or thanks, giving up their one narrow bed and sleeping on the plank floor till he seemed well again. Meantime Gordon, Smith and Hansen paid almost nightly visits to the floathouse, partly in the hope of extending their mission field, partly out of sheer professional interest in the success of their surgery. This by sheer luck proved to have been antiseptic and roughly adequate. Hughes continued to complain of headaches, and it was obvious he would have a welt across his head for the rest of his life, but his hair, when it grew long again, would be thick enough to brush over this and half a dozen more scars, should he collect them. There seemed a likelihood he might, Gordon thought, since Hughes was as militant as ever and began gradually to phrase his scorn of the Third International in ways which gave them hope he would join them in reforming or overthrowing it.

Persuading him was a task Gordon instinctively welcomed. It was a symbolic labor, a demonstration of the continuing validity of his own beliefs, a stubborn assertion of his independence from Thelma or at least from whatever infection, emanating from the breath of the spiritually ailing Sather (as he now began to see it) had weakened, temporarily, the fidelity of this girl whom he still wanted to love. Society, he told himself, would be in no less need of doctors if those who had diagnosed the disease withdrew from the case.

He could not for a week, however, bring himself to write her. During that time he contrived even not to think of her, hurling himself into systematic argument against the lingering individualism of Hughes, or even at times against the fitful deviations of Smith, whose violent schemes might have landed them all in jail if even the adventurous Hughes had not rejected them. Hughes, in fact, seemed to have no natural liking for Smitty, and Gordon had to act as peacemaker between them; and even between Hansen and the others, for Ole, grown tired from licking the old wounds of Stalinism, had begun to argue for a frank declaration of a Fourth International. Gordon himself was now of two minds about this, thinking of Baumling, and Sather and the state of things in Toronto —about which he felt he should tell his Vancouver comrades, but did not yet dare.

Nevertheless, by the week's end, Hughes was their comrade.

Poor and jobless and fugitive though he was, Gordon was jubilant. They had recruited a fighter of prestige and courage and craft.

They had also, by adding Hughes, secured themselves a temporary meeting-place at his half-brother's. Harry Dack was a hospitable man who liked to listen and to have company. He and his girl were too poor to offer them more than a mug of black coffee in the evening, but they encouraged the four to come and sit in their creaking floathouse, under which whispered and chuckled the unseen harbor waters, and settle for them the affairs of money-lords and commissars.

One night they even had an impromptu party when Smitty joined the rest belatedly, wheezing and teetering happily down the catwalk from the shore, the eternal shapeless cigarette rolling in his mouth. Somehow Smitty always managed to possess tobacco. This time he also had a case of beer under his ragged coat.

"Ran into a old logger sidekick owed me dough since a helluva time," he explained. "He was comin out Theda's room an I hit him up fer somepn on account. Theda'd got all his cash though so all he give me was what was left of his beer." He dumped the chunky carton triumphantly on Dack's bed.

"You carted it all the way from the hotel?" Gordon asked in surprise.

Smitty gave him a quick look. "No, I—he gimme a streetcar ticket too."

"What's dis fallah's name?" Hansen asked softly.

"O you wouldnt know'm," Smith said. "He's from Spokane way. You got a opener, Harry?"

Hansen, for some reason, perhaps because of his ulcer, refused to drink, and left early and wordless. But the rest of them made a night of it, shaking the bleak walls of the old floathouse with the roaring of the sentimental and scurrilous songs of old Wobblies. It was a moment of strangely normal good fellowship, remembered because it was the only one.

Yet the most memorable evenings, for Gordon, were those after hot days when they stretched outside on the harbor end of the stealthily swaying boat-landing, smelling above the casual floating garbage the iodine of seaweed and broken mussels on the bird-crowned piles; when they lay idly blinking against the sunset, watching the homing tugs and fishboats come trailing their smoke of gulls, looking away from the brash towers of a commerce that had no need for them, gazing silently toward the strong neutral firs of Stanley Park, and beyond to the molten glow on the high mountains.

There would be this glow on mountains whether Thelma ever sat with him to see it or not.

31

I'M NO POODLE CROONS AIMEE'S IRON MAN

Los Angeles, July 17 (UP)— David L. Hutton, Jr., third husband of Aimee Semple Mac-Pherson Hutton, today announced plans for a divorce from his evangelist spouse . . . .

TRANSIENT BROTHERS DIE ON RAILS

Metal Mining in B.C. Has Yielded Billion Dollars In Half-Century

---

WOODSWORTH PROMISES NEW CANADIAN TYPE SOCIALISM TO CCF CONFERENCE IN REGINA

Ralph Connor's Son Also Speaks —Says Capitalism Ended in 1929

BENNETT SURE U.S. CAN RESCUE WORLD BY CLOSING DOWN WALL ST.

Mussolini Does Know How to Smile

by Hector Bolitho

. . . Approaching this truly great man, who has made a plan for his country, is an exciting ordeal, for no Emperor was ever surrounded by so many walls of care and pomp. The Duce. . . .

WINNIPEG POLICE USE TEAR GAS BOMBS TO QUELL JOBLESS RIOT

Man Hit by Bomb Cap Loses Eye

Winnipeg, 20 July (CP) — Protesting against the closure of the Out-Patients' Hospital here yesterday, jobless. . . .

U.S. FARMERS TO PLOW IN COTTON CROP

ONE YEAR TO RELIEF DEFRAUDER

To Be Deported After Serving

TOM MOONEY DEFENSE COMMITTEE COLLECTED $81,000 IN 4 YEARS SPENT ONLY $2,500 ON DEFENSE

"Salaries & Expenses" Take Rest; Mooney Means Money to Reds—Says Investigator

---

Middle-aged Man wants steady work will do anything. Box 673.

Eight Love Letters of Napoleon Bring Twenty Thousand

EDITORIAL

What is the truth about Germany today? Readers of this newspaper will have asked themselves this question when they saw the recent photograph of Adolf Hitler addressing a million German people, his face obviously alive with tremendous passion. . . . Yet this emotion, however dark and tragic, was somehow lit with a splendid light. . . . You cannot indict a whole nation nor . . .

CCF REJECTS CONFISCATION OF PROPERTY: DODGES FARM ISSUES

Denies it is "Comrades Come Fishing"

FLYING MOLLISONS OVER OCEAN

Canadian Graves in France Kept Beautiful by Children

32

Thelma dear,

From the letter I sent Leo yesterday you'll know that I've been busy too, and that we are four here now, a recognizable Vancouver *cadre*. But this isnt why, for the first time, I've let so many days go by without writing. It was just that your own letter, the only one you've ever written me, forced me to stop and take stock. You've made me realize that my own loyalty has to stand or fall on *my* understanding of the justice of our cause, and the rightness of our method. Believe me I'll never blame you if you retire into a more peaceful private world. And I know you must be as concerned as anyone with all the problems of becoming and being adult, from the dingy trivialities of learning to type and looking for work, to the problem of—of giving a meaning to being alive, alive in the world of Hitler and Aimee Macpherson and Tom Mooney committees.

But, dearest girl, I write you still in the faith that your life and mine will increase their meaning if put together, whether a system that plows in its cotton crops lives another millenium or ends tomorrow. Write me again and reassure me you still share that faith. I'm reading Krupskaya's *Memoirs of Lenin*; it's an 'official' edition, the only one I can get hold of out here, with all the admiring references to Trotsky deleted. But her subtle relations with her incredible husband are still there. They suggest that even one of the greatest of revolutionaries needed the physical assurance of the woman he loved. How much more a fumbling and provincial amateur Marxist like me?

Just the same, Thelma, dont think I wont go on trying, looking for men who were "born of the sun", whatever you do. I want to travel with them a little way toward the sun—did you ever get round to reading that little New Signatures anthology I gave you when I left? I think perhaps the act of traveling is the important thing—whether or not we all turn out to be only fellow-travelers who never "leave the vivid air signed with their honor".

> Your comrade, and your love,
> Gordon

What a priggish bookish letter! All I really set out to say was—I love you and need you. Please please join me in Utah. I can borrow your fare money. Let's be married in October.

33

THE NEXT MORNING GORDON FOUND A LETTER FROM NEW YORK for Paul Green in Fooki's wire letter-rack. It was from the International Organizer of the Communist League of North America who said he had heard—a little belatedly, Gordon thought—from Toronto that Comrade Green was organizing a Vancouver branch. It had occurred to the International Organizer that he might be interested in a long-standing Vancouver contact of the New York office, a Mr. Michael Halloran, who made regular purchases of League pamphlets which, owing to the oddities of the Canadian customs, were being mailed him, one by one, inside old numbers of *Time* magazine.

The address was at least three miles out in the workingclass suburb of South Vancouver and Gordon made one of his rare investments in a streetcar ticket. He found Halloran to be the proprietor of an untidy pintsized corner-grocery. He was a big shaggy-grey ex-Dubliner and still somewhat of a professional Irishman, with a happy-go-lucky air and an open admiration for his own talk.

The New York letter providing a sufficient passport, Halloran put his gangling delivery boy in charge of the fly-loud shop, and ushered Gordon through a rear door into his 'library', a fifteen-foot-square converted storeroom. Dusty boxes and sacks were piled in confusion up the wall that backed the shop, and more of them mounted the end wall except where a rusted screen door opened into a weedy yard. But the side walls were taken over, from floor to ceiling, the left with racks of magazines, the right with solidly stuffed bookshelves. A stack of *Time* rose in a corner, conspicuous as a homburg in the cloakroom of a trade union. Six cumbrously backed benches, which had surely once been church pews, and a home-made rostrum with two Everyman volumes on it, occupied the room itself.

"Well now, sit down there and tell me what d'ye think of me chapel," Halloran ordered, waving at the back pews, and rushing on to avoid being held up by an answer, "the only true church in these parts me lad as you should agree seein as who ye are—and ye should have come to me long ago for I'm its Holy Fadder, and do you know how many I have for a flock? Twenty-two no less and faithful as Papists, bringin their two-bits collection each week and I preachin to them here in this blessed place, and me Bible beside me." He strode over to the rostrum and hefted the two volumes of *Das Kapital*. "And ye see now here," he laid the books down and swept a showman's arm toward the propaganda-heavy walls, "what a feast they get, any night of the week they want to come till eleven o'clock for their measly two-bits, a finer collection of Marxist Masterpieces ye'd scarce find in the Vatican, so dont be thinkin its any racket I'm runnin. What's over is in our treasury and my livin is in me groceries, poor pickins of course, though you'll agree it's unlikely a comrade would be so discourteous now he'd come walkin into me church here and then go shoppin somewheres else, where it's unhandy too."

Gordon, who had been sitting wanting to break in, now asked Halloran what he preached about.

"Socialism." Halloran looked astounded at the question. "What else? Arent me boys all socialists—and I mean socialists, none of yer pie-faced no-confiscation CCFers—and though you're going to tell me never preach to the converted I'll ask you what else do the converted pay attention to but the same thing converted em?"

"What kind of socialism?" Gordon persisted. "There's more than CCFers. Everybody's a socialist these days from Mackenzie King to Mussolini."

"Your kind," said Halloran, suddenly stomping over and slapping Gordon on the back. "Trotskyism! Where have ye been fiddlin away your time ye didn't know about us, look here—" he stalked away and began hauling books from the shelf with great veined hands—"here's Trotsky's *The Chinese Revolution In Danger*, and here's his *German Revolution in Danger*. Any revolution you want, Trotsky puts em in danger, and we pray em out of it." He laughed uproariously and was instantly solemn. "Dont mistake me, I think he's a broth of a lad, Lord God if we'd ever had a fellow like him in Ireland—and mind you now I know them all."

He came back and breathed confidentially over Gordon, "I've been everythin in my time, a good little Mick once, you know, O yes, babblin Hail Marys till I was high as I am now. Then it was the Irish Republican Army I put my money on and after that the Independent Labor Party boyos in London, though I cant think why now, a saltless stew of a party that one. And then like all the lads, of course, I had to give the Black Monks a chance to let me lead them but they wouldnt, no my friend, they had that Beelzebub Stalin. So you see"—his dancing eyes focused on Gordon—"I've been in the First International—the real one that Comrade Saint Paul founded—*and* the Second, *and* the Third, and now you've got a Fourth I dont see rightly how you can keep Mike Halloran out."

"Nor I," Gordon began, "if we had—" a Fourth, he was going to say, but Halloran cut in with glazed eyes.

"Right you are." Halloran folded himself abruptly and sideways on the bench in front of Gordon, without letting his stare off him. "But mind, ye'll have to take the whole twenty-two of us because I'll not have my boys split up for any number of Internationals." Halloran was dead serious.

"Take it easy man," Gordon said laughing and getting up. This was too good to be true. "Are you sure they want to, or know enough? Are you sure we're in agreement anyway? We Trotskyists havent declared ourselves a Fourth International yet. Perhaps we can still reform the Third. Anyway, the time's not ripe. There's not enough of us. You'd better be clear what we stand for because if you come in you'll swamp our little group; there's only four of us, we havent even a branch yet."

"Well, ye've got one now." Halloran was up and had Gordon by both shoulders. "The time's not ripe, it's rotten. First meetin's next Friday at eight. You skedaddle up here and organize us; dont worry about whether we know enough or agree with ye. The South Vancouver Workers' Educational Army knows as much as anybody, me lad, and a lot more than that. *And* we've fifty and more dollars in the treasury." He peered incredulously into Gordon's eyes. "Holy Saint Bridget, d'ye think the four of ye's enough for a Party? Or are ye frightened now I'd take the leadership **away** from ye?"

"Certainly not," Gordon tried to stare back with dignity but was caught in the Irishman's eyes like a deer by headlights, "I'm not staying here any—"

"Because of course I will." Halloran grinned and shoved Gordon off balance with a playful push. "The boys'll not come in if I'm not General Secretary or Reichskancellor or President of the Presidium or whatever ye call your local Cardinal. I'll have to run it."

"Look," said Gordon almost fiercely, "there wont be a damned one of you come in who hasnt satisfied the four of us he understands our program and that he hasnt any principled disagreement with it and—"

"Ye mean," Halloran grinned and lapsed suddenly into sing-song, "the first four Congresses and the corresponding Plenums of the Communist International and nothin after them but the writins of Comrade Trotsky and His Majesty's Left Bolshevist-Leninist Opposition so help ye Marx?"

"Well—not quite as bad as that," Gordon said, beginning to feel he had a lion by the tail, "we're not dogmatists, we're simply scientific international socialists and—"

"So ye tell me and it sounds dogmatic as Genesis to me but I was never one to think ye can keep lollopin toward a Promised Land without gettin a good shot of dogma in the behind every few miles."

"But it's not all—all dogma and talk, I mean it's not dogma at all," Gordon was shouting, aware that he must somehow master this great barking Airedale. "We demand action from our comrades, planned and disciplined action. We dont want führers, we believe in internal party democracy. And we're not looking for evangelists nor for armchair socialists!"

Halloran slumped in the nearest pew again, head in hands. Gordon thought for a moment he was physically stricken.

"To think," Halloran began slowly swiveling in a fixed stare, "that Mike Halloran should come to the day when a sprig of a boy should accuse him and his comrades of being arm—" he could scarcely repeat the phrase—"armchair socialists! Mike Halloran, who—" but after peering desolately first at his magazine racks

242

and then at his books, Halloran gave up speech and turned on Gordon the novel and shattering weapon of his silence.

Gordon involuntarily took a step back toward the store, as if he had been caught profaning the Church. "All right, I'm in no position to judge really. I must take people on trust as—"

"As I do you," Halloran said with mournful irony. "And how much have you in *your* treasury?"

"A dollar sixty-seven."

Halloran got up, walked around to his pulpit, picked up again one of the Everyman *Capitals* absently, as if deciding whether after all it was worth its weight in blood he was prepared to shed. Or the money. He turned. "Is it nothin to you—" a great agonized H appeared between his eyebrows—"that at our last meetin we almost decided to ask your New York office for a charter to form a branch here?"

"Almost?"

"Yes, and the reason we didnt, my uppitty bankrupt friend, was only because one of the boys heard a rumor there was a branch here already. But he hadnt heard twas a four-man sect." He looked sideways at Gordon, waiting.

A whole tree of apples. If I dont pick them, they'll fall on my head. *The man that will nocht quhen he may, Sall haif nocht quhen he wold.*

"My God," Gordon said laughing, "if you really have this group ready to join, what are we waiting for? Friday at eight, as you said. But it all seems too good to be true. And you'll have to present us with a written declaration of your political solidarity with the International Left Opposition for transmission to Toronto."

Halloran reached his bony hand over two pews and Gordon was gripped in it.

Back in the flophouse, Gordon went leaping into Smith's room to tell him the day's news. But Smitty wasn't in. Gordon walked to the back-end of their narrow corridor and, opening the fire-escape door, poked his head out to see if he were on the rickety wooden platform that hung suspended over the wall-dark lane. Here Smitty occasionally retreated during an asthmatic spell in hot weather. The hotel's dead end, it was no exit from flame since the iron ladder once fastened under it had long ago rusted and fallen into the stony alley and been carted away, no doubt, by some quick-eyed junkman. It was not even big enough to set a chair in comfortably, supposing either of them had had a chair, but by sitting balanced on its one reasonably firm rail Smitty had found it possible to poise in an air which winds had brought from regions less heavy with the rot of back-lane garbage, an atmosphere a degree cooler than that which welled from the nearby shambles of warehouses, tenements, shunting-tracks and pier-shacks that sprawled between the hotel and the fouled harbor.

Deciding to walk over to Hansen's flophouse, Gordon went back into the corridor and started down the stairs. As he came to the next landing he was startled by the sight of Smitty's sagging figure. He was in the act of emerging from Theda's room, closing softly her door behind him. Smitty also seemed startled.

"Taint what you think," he said quickly, before Gordon could speak. "Theda aint in there. I was jist borrowin a coupla asp'rins. She wont mind."

"You not feeling well, Smitty? Anything I can do?"

Smith's rheumy eyes shifted from Gordon's curious stare and, putting a trembling hand to his eternal grey workshirt, he coughed dismally. "No thanks. Jist me asthma. Think I'll—I'll walk out fer a stretch, git some air. You comin?" He began clumping down the stairs, sending back a grumbling chatter as Gordon followed. "Them goddam relief sawbones, Paul, they sendin me back out to camp for sure, nix week, if I dont watch. Had to see em agin today. They really puttin the screws on me."

"Putting the screws—how?"

"O well," Smith finished vaguely, "I mean they dont seem ta cotten I really got asthma, but I'm goin back and see the head doc tomorrah—so wot you been doin, Paul?"

Gordon told him of his afternoon with Halloran. Smitty began to brighten at once, came alive in fact and, as they strolled toward the Square, was not content till he had heard every detail.

The next day there was a hullabaloo in Fooki's flophouse. Theda discovered that ten dollars was missing from under her mattress and demanded that Fooki search the whole hotel. It was plain, however, that she was not too sure one of her own clients had not lifted it, and Fooki refused even to get interested. Gordon said nothing, even when Smitty came home mysteriously drunk that night. What could he say that might not alienate his oldest comrade in this town? What could he think that would not be a betrayal of his own complete faith in the old Wobbly?

34

Peace Pacts Now Cover All
East Europe—War Danger To
265 Million People Abolished

JOLSON KNOCKS WINCHELL FLAT FOR INSULTING WIFE

Facts and Figures

U.S. insurance companies in
1931 paid out $13,974,282 on
33,351 suicide policy claims. In
1929 the same companies paid
out only $6,606,965 on 2,234
claims.

MACKENZIE KING SAYS
CCF WOULD KILL
ALL LIBERTY

Would Need to Resort to Violence

MILLION TO GO TO WORK IN U.S. TODAY

Blue Eagle Flies in Every Store

REPENTANCE IS NEED
TODAY

Need Money? Bills To Pay?
Cash?

BRITISH BOMB INDIA FRONTIER TOWN

Ottawa, July 25 (Special to
the Planet) — "Everybody is
happier now that the workless
are off the dole," a prominent
member of the government remarked to your correspondent
this week. Fifteen thousand
men are already in relief camps,
the spokesman added, and there
is general satisfaction over the
smooth working of the plan at
a minimum of net outlay. Cost
of the men, who are working on
the Trans-Canada Highway pro-
ject, is now only twelve cents a
day. . . .

B.C. MAN'S ESTATE
OVER MILLION—ALL GOES
TO TWELVE YEAR OLD GIRL

Mellon Family's Sixty Million
Yearly Income Was Tax-Free
Through Mellon's Own Laws

Calgary, Alta., July 29 (CUP)
— Following introduction of
British Columbia's "no work, no
relief" policy, dozens of Alber-
tan cities and towns are being
flooded by unemployed transients from the Coast province,
according to Relief officials here.

A. A. MacKenzie, chairman of
the Alberta Relief Commission,
stated Alberta authorities were
cooperating upon a plan under
which it might be possible to
barricade the Great Divide and
turn back the hundreds of men
arriving daily from the west.

35

Dear Cde:

Trust you received our first report, dated 9 July, informing you of the creation of a Vancouver *cadre* of four members. We are happy to advise that at a meeting held yesterday, 28 July, this cadre was expanded by 22 new members (names and occupations attached) as a result of a mass absorption by our cadre of the South Vancouver Workers Educational Army. We attach a digest, by Comrade Halloran, of the origins and history of the SVWEA, and a declaration of its solidarity with the CLNA (voted unanimously).

The new cadre of 26 members herewith makes formal application for recognition as the fully constituted British Columbia Branch of the CLNA. Please note that the majority of the new members are employed workers who have already commenced regular dues payments.

Subject to your confirmation, our new cde. Peter Merivale, at present a member of the YCL, is directed to remain in that organzn for the purpose of encouraging honest rank-and-file revolt against the Stalinist burocracy and the breakaway of the best elements to the CLNA.

Subject to your confirmation, it is agreed that the new cde Lennard, at present a teacher at the Quick-Matrick Institute, Vancouver, and a member of the new Vanc. CCF, will not be requested, because of his difficult economic position, to identify himself openly as yet with our movement, provided that in public pronouncements he abstain from criticism of the policies and platform of the ILO & the CLNA. He is instructed to remain in the CCF to encourage honest rank-and-file revolt against the social-reformist burocracy.

The following executive was unanimously elected:

Branch Chairman & Western Organizer: Mike Halloran

Agitation-Propaganda Director: Will Lennard

Youth Organizer: Peter Merivale

Treasurer: Ole Hansen

Temporary Corresponding Sec.: Paul Green

Unemployed Activity Co-ordinator: Fred Hughes.

It was unanimously agreed that the immediate tasks of the Vancouver Branch were, in order of priority,

a: establishment of sales outlets for New York organs & pamphlets on a cost plus 20% basis.

b: utilization of profits & dues arising from (a) to found a local mimeographed propaganda organ to commence a wider fund-getting program.

c: utilization of funds arising from (b) for rental of a hall & presentation of the program of the International Left Opposition to gain mass recruitment.

Awaiting your comment and advice, and with warmest comradely greetings,

Paul Green (Temp. Corr. Sec.)

———————

As it happened, this missive, snug in one of His Majesty's roaring eastbound mailcars, met and passed a similar west-bound vehicle embracing a bag containing the following:

28 July

Dear Gordon

I guess you wont like my news Gordon and I hate having to be the one to tell you but Jack says I should and he will write soon, my little Thel has run off yesterday morning right after her twenty first berthday and got herself maried. She went out in her new suit I got her with the fur puffs and it looked lovely she said she was going to Leos to type but she didnt come home for lunch and next I knew she was on the phone from Oshawa she and Leo was maried. They was on their way to Muntreal to live in a new car he bought she said I am just hartbroken Gordon I dont think thats anyway for a desent girl to get maried without her mother there or

248

anything just bearly of age, how can I visit them so far away when Leo took only a oneroom appt so Thelma told me on the phone. I know it will be quite a supprise to you too Gordon I still wish if she had to get maried it was you but a girl must chose herself I guess Thel never rely wanted to go way out there to Salt Lick and may be you and I was wrong trying to talk her into it, she alweys was a mulehead that girl, and lately she got to feeling there wasnt nobody like Leo even though hes nearly twicet her age. Still and all if she loves him thats what matters, hes crazy about her I know he alweys was but I never thought hed do this to me elopeing like that. Hes a good clean man though, he dont smoke or drink and a good ballshevick or he was, Thel said on the phone they were given up polutics because Leo had a big new job with this firm hes been working for. Well thats alrite too any mother wants her child to have the good things of life and I dont blame Leo the way things was going in the Leegue anyway its just Im dissapointed she went and rushed things. Well Gordon I am sory for your sake because were all proud of what a good ballshevick you are turning out to be too and I was looking foreward to spending most my life with you and Thel what with the NRA and all in the States now. With enough time here to look after Jack till he gets maried and make sure old you-know-who dont get us all into trouble like he's trying right now talking about sooing Leo for kidnapeing, the old fool. But now Ill just half to wait till Thel finds out she needs her old ma and I guess that wont be long. Now dont you take this to hard Gordon keep up the good work only dont get into any trouble yourself neether. Me and Jack sends our love and forgive the misteaks

Yours Truly

(Mrs) Mary Barstow

PS Dont forget to tell me when you want your sootcase sent to Utawa also where do I send the ring you give Thel and she left behind

PPS—Poor old Mac is in the Hosspital in you-know-where with Infexous Teeth.

36

U.S. PLACES ORDERS FOR TWENTY WARSHIPS

GREATEST SHIPBUILDING PROGRAM IN HISTORY ANNOUNCED BY F.D.R.

$238,000,000 For Carriers, Subs, etc.

New Fortunes Being Made; Stock Gamblers Reap Profits

ADVERTISING WILL PUT BRITAIN BACK ON FEET

An attempt to address a crowd at Carroll and Hastings Street yesterday shortly after 7 p.m. ended in the arrest of George Drayton, 45, of 27 East Forty-Second, by Chief John Cameron and Dept. Chief Murdock on a charge of obstructing police.

A demonstration was made by the crowd at the time of the arrest. . . . Reserves were called and . . .

TIM BUCK CHARGES GUARDS FIRED AT HIM IN CELL

Vancouver, August 2 — Protests of single unemployed men living with their parents against going to relief camps were unavailing before the civic committee today. A delegation of three claiming to represent "the vast majority" of the estimated 1,500 of such cases addressed the meeting. The delegation declared that if these men are forced to leave town their chances of finding regular employment are ended. All parents were put in the position of refusing shelter to their sons. . . .

Mayor Taylor replied that "the food in these camps is better than I get myself."

GOVT. BOND INTEREST IS SACRED CONTRACT SAYS PRIME MINISTER

HITLER WARNED BY 3 POWERS AGAINST RAIDS ON AUSTRIA

Gandhi Sentenced to Year in Jail

EUROPE AN ARMED CAMP 19 YEARS AFTER WAR

"We'll All Be Sleeping on River Banks If CCF Gets In," Says MacKenzie King in Saskatchewan

SEES HITLER AS JULIUS CAESAR EXPELLING JEWS
(Special to the Star by Col. Robert McCormick)

Lloyds Now Insuring Rich
Against Kidnapping Risks

"I SAW THEM STARVING"
Ontario Labor M.P. Thanks
God He's Back from Russia

NRA NOT NEEDED HERE
SAYS CANADIAN
MANUFACTURER

SCORES HURT IN RIOT
BETWEEN JEWS AND TORONTO NAZI CLUB
10,000 in Free-for-All When Fascist Youth
Display Swastika Emblems
"Keep Toronto Beaches Clean of Jews"
And Other Slogans Provoke Donnybrook

37

Hi Gord,

Sympathies (belated) and all that, pal, tho I think it's Leo I really ought to send them to. To think it was Sather the Kid was stalking all the time and we were too dumb to notice. Anyway you're free to concentrate twenty-four hours on politics now, eh? Freer than me—it begins to look like I might be spliced ahead of you, after all, if you can bear it. Officially engaged, as of this week, to a honey too; met her recently through dear old Jan. Sally Phelps, dont think you ever met her, her old man just about owns Imperial Motors no less, and I've started working as a salesman in the downtown showrooms. Commission plus thirty smackers a week, but the sky's the limit, Gord. The old coot's in the Market too, and I'll be cleaning up in Wall Street yet. Unless of course the Rabblelution rolls round first. From the way things have gone here though I'll be hawking sedans for a while. The Canadian Sec. of ye olde CLNA has really gone phut, as you may have twigged already. Mac's TU group all pulled out because they didnt like the way Sather handled Mac's trial; they were Cannon-ites anyway. And with Sather and Thel gone too, that gave Baumling's gang the majority. So they called a meeting right off the bat and forced a vote declaring against the Old Man and in favor of an immediate Fourth, the Field-Bauer line. Ronnie & Hymie and I resigned as soon as the vote was counted, and Ronnie's written a long involved wail of solidarity to Trotsky himself, with a blurred carbon to the Stackmanite group in New York. He & Hymie are talking of hatching up a United Front with the Love-stoneites here for an anti-anti-Semitic rally. The two of them, and the four Lovestonites. I cant get quite that bold and fractional so I've quit the whole so-called movement. From now on I'm looking out for little Jack Barstow. O sure, I'm still a Fellow-Traveler and

I'll be there when you guys put up the barricades, but meantime I'm invisible. I've come to the conclusion we were all being rather romantically in a hurry, dont you think? Seems to me it'll take another imperialist shooting match to get us out of this depression; and if North America wins it, we wont change over to socialism— why should we? And if we dont win it, who cares what kind of revolution we get, life will be stinking. What do you think old Pal? Hope you dont feel I'm letting you down. I really wish to heck you'd get out from under, yourself, while the getting's good and before you pull a Mac or a Buck and snag yourself a police record and get stuck for life with the job of working up a revolution in a country that's strictly non-revolutionary like Canada. We'll always be waiting to see what Uncle does, you know that. If the States wont revolve, we wont; and if they do, we wont need to— we'll just adopt whatever streamlined brand of state socialism or state capitalism they dream up. Only we'll adopt it ten years later, step it down to second gear for Canadian driving, give it a quiet paint job and a Mounted Police escort. Nuts. If I were you I'd forget it, when you get back to the States, and look for a couple of nice Mormon gals instead. Whatever you do, old man, good luck. And Mum sends her best.

Jack

P.S. Hymie just phoned to say Mac died last night in the prison hospital. Peritonitis or something—they'd hauled all his teeth out. Guess they didnt try too hard to be careful. Poor old Mac. Kind of pulls the last blind down on the old Trotsky house here, eh?

J.

38

TIME *7 p.m. Friday 18 August 1933.*

PLACE *The "Educational Institute", rear of Halloran's Grocery. Right and Left, the pictured walls of propaganda; Rear, sacks and shelves of bulk groceries, interrupted by a dusty window and an open doorway framing tall backyard weeds against the soft sundown. Centre, two pew-benches lead Up, facing each other, to a high packing-box and chair.*

PERSONS *The seven members of the Executive Committee of the Vancouver Branch of the Canadian Section of the Communist League of North America of the International Left Opposition (Bolshevik-Leninists) of the Third International. On the left bench:* Hughes, Hansen *and* Green. *On facing bench:* Lennard, Merivale. *Behind box-table:* Halloran.

SCENE ONE

HALLORAN (*redfaced and grim*): Everybody here. Where's Smith?

GREEN: He couldnt make it—flat on his back with asthma.

HALLORAN: O.K. boys. Let's start. The reason for this emergency session, ye might call it, will be clear enough in a shake. Green here has got a long crazy bitchin communication from the East which I'm asking him to read to ye.

GREEN: I'll try to read it, but it's in a kind of Marxist shorthand. (*He stands up, takes a big breath and translates the following*):

12 Aug 33

Cde Paul Green

re orgzl report, Vanc area

1. Yrs of 29 July addressed Leo Sather has bn fwded to u/s & brot attention this Exec

2. All yr cdes warned that Leo Sather now *expelled renegade* this org together with his burocratic-centrist Menshevik clique. New natl. exec elected. Adr further communcns to u/s.

3. You are directed call immed meet yr org to inform mbrs:

a. Yr so-called "Vancouver cadre" was never formally accepted into CLNA.

b. Acceptance this cadre plus SVEA as "British Columbia Branch" is withheld pending signed statements *all* mbrs, including y/self, solidarity with attch *Manifesto for a 4th Intrntl* issued by new Cdn Exec here this week. This *Mfsto* supersedes previous Draft-Program of so-called Intrntl Left-Opposition, whose historcl utility now terminated; continued adherence to latter will be regarded as treacherous centrist compromising with Thermidorean Stalinism and prevent admissn yr cdes in Cdn sec 4 Intrntl.

c. Yr statement "immediate tasks" not acceptable; revise as follows, in order priority:

i: immed intensive educ yr own mbrship in prcples, tactics, strategy 4th Intrntl as set forth in attd Mfsto & previously outlined in recent articles of Cdes Bauer (Paris), Field (NY), Baumling (Tor). Cdn Sec denounces rightist delaying tactics of Trotsky in our intrntl org, declares world situatn now requires immed formatn 4th Intrntl & denunciatn all parties 2nd & 3rd Intrntl as bankrupt.

ii: establmnt immed sales outlet our Toronto *New Spark* (1st issue pending). Yr sales quota 200.

iii: coordtn & dirctn remaining energies to advance prop & fund-raising campaign for visit Cde Baumling, Natl Orgzr, during his hitch-hiking tour Sep next.

4. Re-direct Cde Merivale break immed with YCL, denouncing it as hopelessly corrupt orgzn of counter-revoltry Stalinism & urging all honest workr youth follow him into 4th Intrntl.

5. Re-direct Cde. Lennard break immed with CCF, denouncing it as hopelessly corrupt orgzn of Cdn social-patriotic bourgeois-reformism & urging all honest wrkrs follow him into 4th Intrntl.

6. Direct Cde. Halloran study att. *Mfsto* intensively & revise accordingly his "Origin & History of SVWEA" to reflect proper Marxist self-criticism esp of his own Bonapartist-adventurist ldrship and reformist-pacifist tendencies in past activities this org.

7. Natl dues now 25c wkly all employed mbrs with income to $15 wk, rising 5c each extra dollar-wk income, with special levies (see attchd sheet) for incomes over $30 wk. Unemployed cdes will

now also pay dues 5c wkly. Direct yr Treas to fwd 50% *all* dues wkly to Natl. Treas, now Cde Rose Romanuk, c/o this office. Also $10 cash advance order for 200 *New Spark*.

8. Contingent to successful applicatn a/m program, & after 3 mos probatn, applicatn yr gp for full mbrship will be reconsidered.

> Revolutnry greetings
> W. Baumling
> Natl Sec & Orgzr
> Cdn Sec
> 4th Intrntl (formerly CLNA of ILO)
> Toronto, Ont.

GORDON *drops letter sadly on packing box under wrathful face of Halloran and sits down.*

SCENE TWO

HALLORAN (*flamboyant as ever though dismayed*): Well aint that a goddam peacheroo of a letter!

LENNARD (*a small middle-aged man with perpetually puckered lips and a dreamy uplifted face*): Absolutely shocking!

GORDON (*pale and miserable*): Comrade Chairman, may I—

HALLORAN: Before I hear any comments from you Paul Green *I'm* makin a statement meself chairman or not be the holy Jazus, I want ye to know Comrade and you can write and tell these snotty bastards you've got for friends in Toronto that the good old South Vancouver Workers' Educational Army hasn't pooped out yet and—

MERIVALE (*a lank intense filbert-eyed pointed-faced youth*): Hear hear!

HALLORAN:—begod it's not takin a thing like this lyin down nor puttin itself on probation to some hoity-toity Bumboy down east writin letters like he was Morgan sendin telegrams from Wall Street if ye please, even if you Trotskyists—

GORDON: Please, Mike—

HALLORAN (*bangs a fist on his box*):—are willin to lick the boots of some upstart we never heard tale of before that says we're to be drummin up a visit for him if ye please and—

HANSEN (*poker-faced and seemingly unperturbed so far*): Yoost a minute—(*everybody is now trying to talk at once, except* HUGHES, *who sits silent, scarred head clutched in his hands as if he had once*

256

more been slugged. Whatever HANSEN *is saying is lost in the rise of* HALLORAN's *voice*).

HALLORAN:—sendin him half our rightful dues for God and Marx's sake—

LENNARD (*drums his fingers on his knees*): Completely shocking!

GORDON: Comrades, I want to explain my side of—

MERIVALE: Order! Let the chair—

HALLORAN: All right, all right, explain away! But before ye came wheedlin to us with yer Torontah talk, Paul Green, I'll remind ye we had our dealins direct with the top boyos of New York and it's them we'll go back to—

MERIVALE: Back! We're not going back to any more Trotskyites after this kind of letter! We're—

HANSEN: Iss good idea here because—

HALLORAN (*trying to hold his throne*): As I was about to say, Comrade Merivale, New York's what we'd go back to if indeed we went back at all but I'm thinkin with you our boys will be wantin no more truck with Trotskyites at all, for—

LENNARD: Certainly not! I'm—I'm really quite stunned by—

HALLORAN: For arent we wonderin now what kind of an outfit you Trotskyists have at all, Paul Green, that could have sonsabastards like this—whatshisname? Bumleg? in it?

MERIVALE: Hear hear! Green telling us all about their internal party democracy!! Why, they're worse than the YCL. Reversing the whole international policy over-night without consulting anybody.

GORDON: Oh he's just a stupid kid. Let me ex—

HALLORAN: All right then, explain (*He switches histrionically to a mournful tone*) Tell us now what kind of a trick ye've played on the good old South Vanners, mixing us up with a crazy outfit ye didnt even belong to.

GORDON: I did! I belonged when I came here. It's just that Toronto didnt get round to admitting the rest of us before this Baumling got local control.

HANSEN: Yaw, Paul iss right dere.

HALLORAN: Well, they dont want ye no more then, nor us, so tell us, I hope ye will, just what I'm to say to my own boyos, the honest rank and file of the old SVWEA, Comrade Green, now,

257

just explain what me and Lennard and Merivale here are to say to them?

GORDON: I havent played tricks on anybody, please, believe me. I'm as much the goat as you. More. This Baumling is nothing— if you could see him you'd understand—he's just a goggly-eyed clumsy pedant, a kind of thwarted little Rabbi who thinks he's a new Trotsky. He managed to start a tiny ultra-leftist faction in our Toronto organization last winter. And now somehow, because of Mac's death and—and other things, he's got a majority there— just at the moment when we were organizing out here—and he's apparently staged a purge of those who are loyal to Trotsky. But our international organization's certain to turf him out on his ear as soon as they hear of this. He's just pulling a bluff with us.

MERIVALE (*skeptically*): Yeah? What about Field in New York and that guy in Paris. Paris is your centre, aint it? I'll bet they've shot Trotsky already, and you talk about Russia and purges. Balls!

HALLORAN: And why dont we hear from the great Leo Sather, tell us?

GORDON (*embarrassed*): I hope we will—hear from his group and from MacCraddock's too. But Sather himself is—well, he's temporarily out of the movement too, I understand.

HALLORAN: Holy Mother! Sather too?

LENNARD: Ah, so you've heard from him?

GORDON: No, from—from his mother-in-law.

MERIVALE: Sather out? The Canadian Lenin you kept on boosting to us, *he* is a renegade! Then there's truth in this fellow Baumling's letter after all. And why havent we heard from all these T.U. fellows you told us MacCraddock had? Has Baumling gobbled them too? What does Sather's mother-in-law say about them? And who the hell is she?

GORDON: She's—it doesnt matter.

HALLORAN: Saints and Engels. Will ye hear him now? I'm thinkin there's nothin left this day of all this Trotskyism ye talked us into but a cloud of hot air.

HANSEN (*almost to himself*): Yaw, maybe all of you talk too much dat kinda air.

GORDON: It's not true, Mike, you know it isnt; there's the International Left Opposition still, with the Old Man at the top of it.

258

That hasn't been broken up because of the ructions of a dozen fools in Toronto.

MERIVALE (*sharply*): A dozen! Is that all? And they're the *majority*. For God's sake you made out there were thousands.

GORDON: I made out no such thing and you damn well know it.

MERIVALE: Well, you talked so big—

HANSEN (*judicially*): He never talk no bigger dan you fallahs.

MERIVALE: I wasnt speaking to you—you—

HALLORAN (*bangs on his box again*): Order, order, ye pack of fools. Finish what ye've got to say, Paul Green.

GORDON: O Mike, dont you see, we're falling into a trap when we quarrel like this. This is what little Willy Baumling wants. He's gone and jumped the gun, committed himself to a Fourth International before the rest of the labor movement's ready for it—and the only way he can keep his local prestige is to get rid of the steadier comrades and stampede the rest into following him. If we do that, Trotsky and his whole cause will be lost. I'll make a motion that we wait, that we table this letter. I mean dont show it to the membership, send it on to New York, along with a copy of the original report we sent Toronto. And let New York use this as evidence against Field there and against Bauer in Paris. This way we can start a chain of lightning going that will blast every ultra-leftist out of the Trotsky movement and give us a chance to get on with the real fight, the fight against capitalism and against Stalinism.

MERIVALE: Aw hire a hall. You and your two-bit ILO aint a damned bit better than the Stalinists. You're a bunch of burned-out squabblers spending your time thinking up ways to cut each others' throats.

LENNARD: Quite right, Comrade Merivale. I'm stunned, simply stunned by this letter. Comrade Chairman, how could you ever have led us into the hands of these arrogant foolish people?

HALLORAN: (*full of defensive indignation*) I? What d'ye mean I led ye? Didnt ye all vote fair and square and unanimous to join? Ye want to blame anybody blame Green here, he's led us all up the garden with his fancy plottins, foxin even his own comrades so far as I can see. You now, Hughes, the way yer sittin I'm thinkin ye never knew till this hour that ye'd never been baptized with Toronto's holy water, eh?

HUGHES (*black head in hands, he does not even indicate he has heard*).

GORDON: If I've let any of you down it's because I've been let down myself. I never knew this would happen, and I'm sorry, but the important thing is that *we* still have an unbroken organization. Let's keep it together, whatever happens. And I made a motion—

MERIVALE: Whatever happens! That's an unprincipled approach to politics if ever I heard one.

GORDON: O for God's sake we're all choking to death from a surfeit of principles. I'll give a few of mine up for a change if it's the only way left to keep our group together.

HALLORAN: Will ye give up yer Trotskyism then and help us build up the old South Vanners again?

GORDON: But that's asking me to give up *all* my principles!

HANSEN: Wat you fallahs going to build Sout' Wanners up to? You aint got principles, you aint got no International.

HUGHES (*suddenly jumping up, redfaced at the pew's end*): Shut your stupid gobs, now, the lot of you! Talk-talk-talk and never do nothin. Crocks and has-beens and goddam longhairs you are and that's all, and I'm through with you, with all of you! (*He raises a fist savagely*) Revolution in the head it iss only, and treachery in the belly. (*Suddenly he falters, his eyes uncertain; he moves his scarred head in an odd dazed way, and begins to shake as if with palsy.* GORDON, *seeing this, gets up and gently pulls him down onto the bench again.* HUGHES *sinks his big head once more in his hands, moaning faintly.*)

HALLORAN (*after a startled silence*): What the hell bit him?

GORDON: He'll be all right in a minute. He's been getting these spells lately. Would you like me to take you back to the floathouse, Fred?

HUGHES (*muffled*): Leave me alone.

HANSEN (*still on his own track, as if there had been no interruption*): On odder hand yoost because dis fallah Bauer throws out Trotsky, ve dont have to go tew. Trotsky hafta make Fift' International. Maybe better ve stay in Fourt'.'

MERIVALE (*laughs suddenly, almost hysterically*): Yeah, a Fifth! And then a Sixth, and a Sixty-Sixth! You crazy bastards! Me, I'm sticking with the Third.

GORDON: You cant, you know it. It's too corrupt.

MERIVALE: Well then, for Christ sake, why are you against the Fourth?

GORDON: I'm not against it, but a handful of people cant declare themselves an International.

MERIVALE: No, you're right there, and that's all you'll ever be, a handful, a handful of crackpots. At least the Stalinists have workers following them, thousands here, millions in Russia. But I'll bet there arent more than a hundred honest-to-God Trotskyists in the whole world.

GORDON: I dont know how many there are and what does it matter?

LENNARD: Matter! Of course it matters, unless all you want is a sewing circle. You just said it mattered.

GORDON: I mean what matters right this minute is that we go on together fighting for socialism.

HANSEN: Yaw, but mebbe dis Toronto fallah make sense too. Time ve pulled everybody outa dat CCF outfit, like he said, dey never make a ravvalution.

HALLORAN: That Bumling make sense! What kind of sense is it I'm asking ye when a man writes all the way from Ontario to say that me Mike Halloran been actin like Napoleon out here in Vancouver where he never was and couldnt see me? It's that lad thinks he's Napoleon, and the infant Jesus too I'd lay a bet, they ought to send the dogcatcher out and put him where he'll do no harm to himself. Writin and tellin the old South Vancouver Workers Educational boys we got to start educatin ourselves if ye please, and intensively too it seems, Christamighty it's—

LENNARD (*squeaky with the violence of his disapproval*): What was that *you* said, Hansen? Pull everybody out of the CCF? Out of the coming mass party of Canadian socialism? Pull them into what? It's time you and the rest of you, and you too Mike Halloran, got *into* the CCF with me where I'm fighting a lone battle, as I've told you before. All of you, the whole organization, should be in pushing the CCF toward a truly Marxist line.

HANSEN: Yoost a bunch a skewlmaams.

HALLORAN: He's right. You wouldnt make Reds outa them even if you boiled em.

LENNARD (*rising with over-great dignity*): You—you, Hansen, you're just an anarchist! I've always suspected it. You'd strangle the Canadian revolution in its cradle just to have your own way. You hate organization and you cant take discipline. And you, Green, you and your Trotskyists ordering me to leave the CCF just—just when the whole West End Branch is swinging over toward a Marxist position. You've got no understanding of *tactics*. And you, Mike Halloran, I've had enough of your one-man rule. Either you quit this Trotskyist adventurism and bring the whole SVWEA into the CCF or I'm through with all of you.

HALLORAN: To hell with you. I'm not puttin my boys into any more political straitjackets. To hell with all your parties. To hell *especially* with the CCF.

LENNARD (*buttons his coat offendedly*): I hope we shall all meet on the same side of the barricades (*He heads for the back door*).

GORDON: Dont go, Lennard! There's no reason—(*but he is out the door*).

HALLORAN (*shouting*): Pinko! Reformist! Good Riddance!

HANSEN (*as if nothing had happened and everyone had been agreeing with him*): Time ve pulled comrade Merivale here outa Young Commies too, like Baumling says alla Commies iss a bunch of tieves.

MERIVALE: What!

GORDON: Ole, you dont *agree* with Baumling on this, do you!?

HANSEN: Soore, wy not? Wy keep on pretendin ve iss reform skewl for dose Black Monks? Dey's all criminals for life.

MERIVALE: Who the hell you callin thief and criminal, you big squarehead? *I'm* still in the YCL and I aint no thief. I want an apology outa him, Comrade Chairman.

HALLORAN: Orderr, orderr. Hansen, you sayin comrade Merivale here's a thief?

GORDON: O what childishness, of course he wasnt.

HALLORAN: I'm askin the Swede.

HANSEN (*unemotionally*): He aint one he shouldnt be wit dem.

MERIVALE: That's no apology!

262

HANSEN: Soore, soore Ay poligize. (*He nods serenely at* MERI-
VALE) You iss only Commie aint a tief.

MERIVALE: O. K. but—hey I still dont like—

GORDON: Comrade Chairman, for god's sake, let's stop this, and
pass my motion.

HALLORAN: What motion?

GORDON: That we forward the letter to New York, for guidance.
Fred, you'll second that, wont you? (*He looks appealingly at*
HUGHES *who has begun to sit up since* LENNARD *walked out.*)

HUGHES (*after a silence, begins speaking calmly*): No, Paul
Green, I wont. It doesnt matter a damn what you do now for,
look you, the damage is done. There's nobody here is goin to
trust the Trotsky leadership again after this. If we dont do what
that little Toronto punk says, some other deluded workers he'll find
to peddle his paper out here, see, and we'll all be in it, branded as
renegades from whatever number of international he decides to
name it. And supposin we do string along with him, man, we'll be
renegades to all the other Trotskyists, for sure. And if we keep to
ourselves we'll have to be, as Hansen tells us, a Fifth International,
for every man to laugh at. (*He stops, clasps his black pow and
then, with a sudden change of voice and countenance glances mur-
derously up and down the two benches*) Shit! (*Yelling*) The
truth is there's not the sense or the guts of a single old IWW in
the whole goddam lot of you and I—I've wasted all my time. (*He
begins to fall into a Welsh sing-song*) The truth—the truth is it's
too late for revolutions now. Things are run by kids now, by little
boyscout troops of rattin kids they are, bringin in the age of counter-
revolution, of fascism, fascism black and fascism red, and then war,
ye fools, and more fascism, look ye, and more war till we've wiped
ourselves off this stinkin planet, and good riddance. (*He stops*) I
—I'm not feelin—(*He stops, puts his hands over the long scar on
the top of his head, and holding this pose stumbles toward the
backyard door*).

GORDON: Fred! Wait. I'll go back to the floathouse with you.
(GORDON *jumps up. But no one else speaks and* HUGHES *continues
silently and in silence to the door. Then he turns and glares red-
eyed at* GORDON.)

HUGHES: You. With you I wouldnt walk to the pisshouse again. (*He wheels and stumbles out*).

MERIVALE: Crowstamighty the guy's rum-dum.

GORDON: He's not well. It's that blow—

HALLORAN (*breaking in bitterly*): Hell, what's a slaphappy Wobbly here or there? Now we've got rid of those two, I'll accept a motion, since no one would second comrade Green's, that the old SVWEA reorganize, withdraw its offer to the Trotskyites, and resume independent life.

MERIVALE: Subject to our continuing fractional work in the YCL I'll so move.

HALLORAN: Subject to nothin! We'll keep our skirts clean havent I been tellin ye? Hansen's right, tis time you broke with the stinkin Communists, Merivale.

MERIVALE: Then I resign. (*He stands up and walks quickly to the same door*) And I'll see ya on the *other* side of the barricades.

HALLORAN: Get out! (MERIVALE *does*).

HANSEN (*serene as ever*): Point a order, comrade chair—

HALLORAN (*stands*): Look, the meetin's over, it's adjourned, the executive's dissolved. You can both beat it. I'm not interested.

HANSEN: O.K. (*Stands*) You comin wit me, Paul?

GORDON: Mike! I'm sorry. Let's save what we can, Mike. Let's the three of us stick together anyway. We'll build your group up, retain the SVWEA name if you like, and—

HANSEN: Naw, naw. We call it Fort' International, or I—

HALLORAN: To hell with both of ye. Ye've wrecked the only decent law-abidin revolutionary organization was ever created in this benighted country of anarchists. Ye've left old Mike Halloran sittin wonderin what he can say to his own boyos that they wont all give him the back of their hands for life. I dont want ye. Get out. Get out, get out!

GORDON: Mike! Please—

HALLORAN (*inclines ironically*): Unless you gentlemen have something you want to buy in my store. A packet of firecrackers, maybe, was left over from the King's birthday?

GORDON (*looks at* HANSEN, *then at* HALLORAN): O.K., Ole. (*Exeunt* HANSEN *and* GORDON. HALLORAN *stands alone and proud behind his packing box in the empty crowded room*).

39

IN THE WARM FRESH TWILIGHT HE FOLLOWED HANSEN'S TOWERING
back through the weedy yard and around by the sidestreet into the
suburban bleakness of Fraser Avenue. Failure. You have lost again,
lost your cause now, lost everything. But not my faith. What faith?
You've done nothing more than splash a bucket of dirty paste
over an innocent wall again, because someone didn't pay you your
wages. . . . Is Sather laughing at me somewhere, cocking his smart
treacherous head? The rotten apples fall without picking.

At the white-banded telephone pole that marked the streetcar
halt he caught up and managed to persuade Ole to accept a six-cent
ticket and wait to ride the three miles home to Powell Street. And
now Hansen's presence began to distract him unwillingly from his
own despair. The old Swede was probably this moment in misery
from his ulcerous stomach or he would have insisted on plodding
the whole way lonely back, as he had plodded it up, on his great
flat feet. Hansen never complained of his health, regarding questions
about it as something hovering on bourgeois sentimentality, but his
face, under the street lamp, was rock-grey and rigid.

They stood silent and separate. Fool, he too has betrayed you,
farcically abandoned you, like all the others, like Halloran, like
Hughes, like Sather, Thelma, all the Barstows, everybody. *The
working class creates its own leaders.* Roberts' sneering hawk-face.
But the Roberts clan will not lead either. Who will? *Politics is
awful complicated . . . Sometimes I wonder . . .* She was wiser than
you.

Yet it was Hansen's defection which was bitterest in his mouth,
for it was fresh, and it was the defection of the only man here
whom he had treasured as a friend as well as a comrade. He was
managing already to think of the others simply as failures in an
experiment, men who had, under the stress of too sharp a challenge
to their new-born solidarity, turned back to their old predictable

paths. Ole Hansen, however, had unaccountably lumbered ahead, repudiating Gordon's pace and, by that act, Gordon's fitness to set one.

"Ole," he murmured when they were seated side by side on the creaking wicker cross-bench at the car's rear, "I hope we're still friends."

A fatuous remark, especially to offer Hansen. He doesn't even *answer you. Why can I never learn to be wary about expecting human love? . . . Lovers be war and tak gude heed about whome that ye lufe, for whome ye suffer paine. . . . Fy, fals Cresseid.*

"Soore," the old logger said primly, at last, staring out from his grey face at the empty opposite seat, and said no more while the ancient streetcar hurtled another block. Then he went on: "Yoost now. But ideas iss what matter."

"O.K." Gordon leapt in, "but how can you knuckle under to Willy Baumling? I know about him. He's only an adolescent two-bit firecracker." *A packet of firecrackers, maybe. . . .* And what were the others, the ones you knuckled under to? *My little Thel run off.*

Hansen, if this pricked his pride, spoke as serenely as ever. "Yaw. Baumling iss dumb." He poked abstractedly with warty hands at a loose patch in the knee of his ancient dungarees. "Only right now he iss smart tew, smarter dan Trotsky. Ve gotta make dis International now, today, yoost like he say."

"Make it with what? Who've we got left now, here in Vancouver for instance, except you and me—and Bill Smith?"

"Not Smit'," Ole said with dark gravity.

"Not even Smith!" Gordon laughed for the first time that evening, but not from happiness. "Something wrong with *his* ideas too?"

Ole looked as if he regretted having said anything and Gordon was vexed into prodding him further. He felt motherly still toward the old Wobbly, whether or not he had stolen from Theda, not only because Smith was lying in asthmatic misery on his wretched board bed but because he was Gordon's first and now perhaps only ally.

"Just us two? Or wont you have me, even if I decide not to wait for Trotsky and the rest of the world?"

"Not you eider, Paul," Hansen's lilting voice went gently on. Gordon saw he was not joking; indeed he never was.

"Why not?"

"You is yoost havin holiday. Purty soon you go back to be perfesser. Dat's where you belong. Yaw, yaw—" he added, seeing Gordon about to protest—"you iss good socialist, Paul, and good man tew. You help me tink, but you iss only summer-time rebel."

Gordon, shutting his ears to whatever was complimentary in Ole's summation, was cruelly hurt. The sense of being mocked, uselessly made a fool of, redoubled itself upon him. *Young punk in a university.* The squinting contemptuous eyes of that detective in Queen's Park. What a latter-day Quixote he had been. I have not even kept my Sancho Panza in this semi-literate old Swede. But I will not show my wounds to him. For once I'll outdo Hansen in phlegm.

"Maybe. But I've been an active revolutionary for six months now, even if no one's noticed it. And I've been an unconscious rebel most of my life. I dont think,"—chagrin was creeping into his voice in spite of himself—"that you've any right to doubt my political seriousness just because I—I'm a university teacher. Certainly I'm not silly enough to think I can act like a new international all on my own." You *did* think it, though. *Romantically in a hurry.*

Hansen chewed that over till the next streetcar halt, then, his pale eyes apparently contemplating a lush string of pearls in an advertisement across the aisle, he went on, "Lenin wass alone once; every fallah said he wass wrong tew. Yah, but he wass right."

Gordon, despising his own obviousness, asked Hansen with a grin if he thought of himself as a Lenin?

"Naw." His face was unchanging. "Yoost a Hansen. Come right time, if Hansen got right ideas, same kinda fallahs come to Hansen tew."

"Now," said Gordon, "I've heard everything; I know how far the revolutionary movement can split itself. Into kindling. If everybody were like you, there'd be as many parties as there are workers."

"Soore," said Hansen, "but dey aint nobody is yoost like me."

They lapsed into silence as the streetcar rattled and wrangled across the Hastings intersection. Then Gordon returned to the attack.

"What do you mean 'summer-time rebel'?"

Hansen swallowed, looked ashamed of his epigram, wet his lips, shut them, opened them. "Ravvalution iss making someting get born, yaw. Iss killing too. Ay tink you run avay from dat part, Paul."

Run away, *my little Thel run off*. You're no different from her. I am. How can Hansen or anyone tell? I could lead men through blood and fire if I had to. Dont boast, you're no man of action. *That pigeon chest of his . . . self-styled petit-bourgeois intellectual.*

"I'm not a lover of killing, if that's what you mean, but I dont think good revolutionaries are."

"Yaw." Hansen drew his silence around him again.

Here I am and here he is. *Here am I, here are you.* A poem of Auden's began to jingle in his mind. *But what does it mean, what are we going to do?* And the lines before?—*I've come a very long way to prove, No land, no water, and no love.*

As the car shuddered to a halt on Powell Street a few blocks from their hotel, Gordon suddenly thought he saw Smith talking with a burly companion in a doorway. But darkness had already fallen and he decided he was mistaken. Smitty was no doubt still stretched out on his mattress in breathless misery. As the car jerked ahead again, Gordon turned to Hansen, who was also staring out the window.

"Why wont you have Smith?" he asked. "He not enough of a killer either?"

Hansen shifted in his seat and looked at him with an odd cold light in his eyes. It was as if the question had startled, even frightened him. "Maybe he iss too much killer. Ay not figgered dat fallah out yet." His tone did not match his eyes; it was almost too laconic. Hansen was concealing something. Had someone told him of the theft from Theda's room?

"Then at least you dont think he's just another tired old Wobbly?"

The eyes masked and turned away. "Maybe no."

"Well what *do* you mean? You think he's not honest with us?"

Hansen had refused to wake Smith that morning of the Relief

Office raid. Was it Hansen or Hughes who had not wanted him?

Ole passed a hand over his thin straw-hair, and seemed to be studying a reply; but when he spoke it was only to say: "Our stop."

As they walked up to the front to leave the car they passed Hughes, and then Merivale, sitting separately. They must have got on at the front, unnoticed, from farther down Fraser Avenue. Neither looked sideways now as Gordon and Ole plodded up the aisle. Hughes, in any case, did not see them for he was in the act of cupping his head in his big veined hands. Merivale turned his to the window. Their silent and deliberate isolation, from each other and from him, multiplied Gordon's sense of defeat and loneliness. The feeling was not lessened when Hansen parted from him at the street corner with nothing beyond a mumbled good-night.

He had an aimless impulse to turn back toward the brighter lights of Hastings Street but he told himself that Smitty was probably in need of companionship, even expecting him.

Thinking about it, as he walked toward the flophouse, Gordon realized that he himself was in equal need of Smitty, the last of his comrades, and that it was only his reluctance to bring him the bad news of the meeting which was making his feet lag. Bill Smith, if he had been there, would surely have defended Paul Green's position at every step, might even have prevented the disintegration that had taken place. For Smitty, whatever his anarchistic fancies, had always been the most eager of the comrades for the growth of the organization. He was an oddity of course—his plans were always the immediate product of an immortal hatred of the Money State. He had been in trouble a week ago for walking up Granville Street and stopping at every news-vendors to spit ceremoniously upon a front-page photograph of J. P. Morgan, caught with a publicity-seeking midget on his knee. And lately he had developed the habit of saluting every policeman with his thumb to his nose. Smitty was an all-year round rebel who should have gladdened Hansen's heart. But Hansen, of course, didn't have a heart.

Fooki's lobby was deserted. Gordon went quickly up to the top floor. Once more Smitty was not in his room.

He wasn't in Gordon's either, nor on the fire-escape platform, where the night's coolness, and the sight, through telegraph poles and wires, of genuine stars in a cloud-ragged sky, seemed at the moment curiously alien and irrelevant.

He started downstairs again, noting on the middle floor that the doors to June's and Lila's rooms were open, a sure sign, at this stage of the evening, that their inhabitants were still competing for green trade at the next streetcorner, or mellowing it in the nearest beer-parlor. And by the sounds coming from behind Theda's thin door it was evident that she was home but not with Smitty, who if he had contrived to find the money, could never have produced the youthful baritone which was at that moment raised with Theda's in beery song.

Gordon dug Fooki out of his kitchen at the back of the ground floor, but Fooki didn't know and didn't care. Smith must have got up out of asthmatic semi-helplessness and gone out. Why? Was it he whom Gordon had seen on Powell Street after all? At this point Fooki remembered that a phone call had come for Gordon half an hour ago. No, he didn't think it was from Smitty. He'd written the number down somewhere. After some rummaging in the old turtleback desk in the lobby Fooki found it. The number was Halloran's.

"Ye had the cops?" Halloran asked at once, loud and anxious, when Gordon, using the phone at Fooki's desk, got through to him.

"Cops! No, why?"

"Well, by the Holy Virgin they been here. Took half me library away. . . . Yah, Red Squad."

"But why suddenly tonight, Mike? They've surely known about your library and the South Vanners for ages."

"You askin me? Looks like they was tipped off we were goin Trotskyist. . . . Well they was very well up on things. They expected to find a meetin, they did. One of em ast me, was that warty-nosed leprachaun McSamus the plainclothes, ast me where was all the boys gone to? . . . I ast him what boys, sure, but I could see 'he'd been wised up to a thing or two. Then they grabbed all the files, and half me books. Even me two-volume Marx, the silly bastards ye can buy it in any bookstore downtown. Said they'd probably be back for me too, after they'd looked them over. Yeah. . . . I told em they'd have to learn to read first. . . . Yah goddam right its serious, that's why I'm phonin ye, there's a stool somewheres, Green, and he's not one of my boyos. They been with me too long for me not to know the smell of their feet. . . . Who? Why one a your group a course, your ex-group I mean."

Gordon's ears ached from the loud righteous voice and the shock of what it was saying. "There's only four of us, I'd swear to their loyalty. Is there any of us you're suspicious of, Halloran, tell me honestly?"

Halloran for the first time hesitated. "Well," he said, "ye can see I dont think it's you or I wouldnt waste me breath phonin yuh. And it dont look like Hughes. The cops was askin specially for him, which is why I phoned as soon's they left. Thought youghta tip him off, nip down to the floathouse, but it's too late now. Better git outa town yerself, Green, while the goin's good." He hung up abruptly.

As Gordon rose from Fooki's desk he was aware that someone was standing quietly in the streetdoor.

It was Smith. He came forward coughing. "Yer back early." He gave a yellow apologetic grin. "What happened to the meetin?"

Gordon checked himself on the verge of pouring out Halloran's news. Three hours ago Smith had sounded as if he were trying to breathe under water, and was too sick to stand. After Gordon had gone, Smith had got up, dressed, and kept a rendezvous with a stranger. If Halloran were right, the informer was either Hansen or Smith. But was all this just nonsense spawned from Halloran's melodramatic suspiciousness? The Red Squad were always raiding somebody; they had to keep in the news. . . . Yet they had asked for Hughes, so far from his known haunts.

"Just about everything happened," Gordon said carefully. "How come you're out of bed, they way you're feeling?"

"Jis gittin a breath a air," Smith said easily. "Feelin some better. Where's—where's the rest the gang?"

"It's all broken up, Smitty. Smashed." Gordon moved toward the dark stairs, wondering if he should try to warn Hughes still. No, he might be trailed on the way, and whatever was waiting for Fred, he would have walked into it by now. Better to keep Smith in sight, pump him. "Come up and I'll tell you, Smitty." Should I pack at once and grab a freight? To where?

Smith hesitated, then followed. "Smashed?" He drew close

behind Gordon on the first landing and lowered his voice. "The cops?"

Gordon waited until he could be sure of his own voice and kept walking up the bare creaking steps. Smitty expected cops. He *is* the stool! No. What had he said that first day? I don't steal and I don't stool . . . *I dont steal*. . . . Smith was already wheezing from the climb. Surely his asthma, at least, is genuine. And if it is?

"I didnt say anything about cops. I mean there was a letter from Toronto today that set us all going our separate ways."

When they entered Gordon's room the sour clinging heat was almost nauseating.

"Mine'll be jist as hot," Smith said, "less try the fire platform."

Gordon paused, then followed him out into the darkness. It was blessedly cooler and there was even a hint of fog in the air. He leant his back against the brick wall of the old hotel and watched Smith take his accustomed place on the rail, hook his toes under the supporting post. His feet looked absurdly conspicuous and pathetic in the new boots he had at last wheedled somehow out of the Pogey. Gordon, postponing any cross-questioning, began to tell the story of the meeting, trying to watch the blurr of the old Wobbly's face silhouetted in the misting starlight. Smith rolled a cigarette from a packet of Bull Durham, and interjected sounds of astonishment and growing anger with a directness that seemed completely honest. Gordon began to feel that he had nothing to fear, not from Smitty at any rate, and gave up the thought of immediate flight.

"Goddam that buckin Swede," Smith gasped, talking around the cigarette alight in the corner of his mouth, and pounding the dim rail beside him, "it's his bloody fault, the old crosscutter, I never seen a sawyer yet was any damned good in a organization, one-man parties all of em. As fer Hughes, well—" he took his butt out and pointed the glowing tip at Gordon, "I've had my suspicions of that guy, Paul, like I told you more'n once, they got pigeons even in the Boy Scouts in this chrisely town. It's the one job the City got a unlimited budget for."

"You dont suspect *Hughes*?" Gordon straightened with amazement.

"I dint. But who else is there for Jesus sake?"

"He's the very one the cops have something on."

"All the more reason he should work a deal with the sonsa-bitches," Smith said with a kind of venomous sadness. "Now I come to think of it, why you suppose they never caught up with him, him walkin round town and even ridin streetcars, you think they dont know about his brother's shack? Nuts!"

Gordon watched the little ruby light of Smith's cigarette talking at him from the darkness. "Then if the police do arrest him, will that prove he's not a stool?"

"No, no," Smith said hastily, "that's another copper's dodge. Pick him up and let him out the nix night and send him out som'eres else to stool. Anyways, who else could it be, if Halloran's on the level? Taint you!"

"How do you know that?"

"Well," said Smith uncomfortably, "it aint." Far off at Point Atkinson the first foghorn of the night began its vast slow mooing. Seafog was on its way in.

"And it isnt you?"

Smith's voice was half truculent, half reproachful. "You been livin practicly on top a me the last two munts, Paul, you oughta found out if I was." The bead of his cigarette was steady in the darkness.

"Yes, I should have."

"O.K., then it's Hughes or Hansen. You think it's that Swede mebbe after all?"

Somewhere below in the alley's black pit a rutting cat wailed as in human agony.

Gordon, beginning to doubt his own intuitions, said despairingly, "I cant believe it's any of us. I think Halloran's just got the wind up, or it's one of his people after all."

"Yeah, sure," said Smith brightly, "no reason why it couldnt be one of their gang jis because that blowhard Mick says it aint. It could be Halloran himself fer that matter, jis as easy as it could be Hughes, and—" Smith's speech suddenly stopped.

The door from the hotel opened and in the fuzzed light cast from the corridor they saw Fred Hughes step down between them onto the platform. His eyes, wide and glowing with uninterpretable emotion, flashed across to Smith, transfixed on the rail, and sideways to Gordon.

"Evenin." Hughes stood tensed, speaking as if grudging the effort of the one word.

"God am I glad to see you, Fred!" Gordon said. "I was afraid for you. The cops raided Halloran's." Hughes' amber stare was on him from a foot's distance. "And they were asking for you." The stare did not change. "Halloran phoned me to go down and warn you but I was afraid I'd be shadowed."

"You did right," Hughes said slowly at last, expressionless, unmoving. "I come up to warn you, Green, somethin was smellin. Now I know what. Just before you got off the car I saw—" he flashed his eyes to Smith—"I saw a flatfoot out the window, for sure, talkin to—" Hughes suddenly swelled his chest and his powerful voice changed with startling suddenness, rose to an explosion of hate—"this sonofabitch of a stool here." His arms shot out.

Smith, who had continued to sit poised on the rail as if afraid to call attention to himself by movement, tried at once to leap sidelong toward the open door. But Hughes' big shoving hands caught him at the chest, heaved him back against the rail. Smith's wind, never very much, was knocked out of him and his knees sagged. But before he could slide to the platform floor, Hughes' body, on the same impetus, came blindly against him. There was a dull crack of the railing.

Gordon, in a paralysis of unbelief at the sudden violence, had merely stood staring, but he lurched forward now, snatching blindly and catching Hughes' belt with enough grip to hold him at the platform's brink. But Smith, with a queer low cry like a man in a throttled nightmare, had disappeared between the gap in the railing. And even as Gordon pressed beside Hughes to look down into the blackness, it sent back to them, with terrible finality, the single ripe sound of a body smacking into the cobbled bottom of the lane's canyon.

Gordon, feeling Hughes leave his side, hearing him bound back now into the hotel, turned then and gave chase. But Hughes was not running away, only rushing wordless, Gordon behind him, down through the unheeding flophouse, through the backdoor, to where, face down and wry-necked, Smitty lay, a blacker patch in the black empty alley.

It had been part of the unreality of that affair that no one seemed to have heard the noises of the balcony, nor the thud of his fall, or hearing perhaps had dismissed them as the sounds of still another drunken ruckus which it was nobody's business to nose into. The two of them were alone with a motionless bundle of old clothes and broken flesh. Hughes, without speaking, thrust a hand under the shapeless figure. A nearer horn at that moment began answering the fitful baying of Point Atkinson, and one corner of Gordon's mind, escaping from numbed awaital of what Hughes would say, was telling him that fog was rolling into the harbor and that he was tasting the first wisps of it on his tongue. Hughes straightened.

"I killed the sonofabitch," he whispered in a voice hoarse with triumph and despair. "I killed the friggin stool. I broke his bloody neck."

Gordon turned, stifling nausea. "I'm going to telephone the police," he said. Hughes seized him then with frightening strength by the arms and Gordon struggled. But Hughes was not trying to hurt him.

"*I'll* phone the cops," he was saying, in a curious almost voiceless shout. Though his eyes flamed they carried meaning; the insanity that had flashed across the landing, if it was that, had gone from them.

"This is my lookout. You get the hell outa here, outa town you get, fast, boy. I'll tell them twas an accident—he was jest talkin and sittin on the rail he was, and it bust."

"They wont believe you," Gordon whispered. "Smitty must have been working for them, all right, selling them information. And anyway, they're out to get you."

"I dont give a goddam. I'm tired of runnin from them. Listen, man, they cant prove anythin else—unless you tell em a different story. Is it *that* yer going to do?" Hughes face burned into his. "Are *you* goin to be a squealer too?"

Gordon stared back, lost in a misery of indecision. "No," he muttered finally, "you didnt intend to do it. And it cant be undone now. I'll say the same. But—I'm not a good liar."

"You wont need to be," Hughes whispered rapidly, urgently.

"Look, man, have ye no friends in this town, on the other side of the Creek say—respectable nobs maybe, some bourgeois will take ye in for a few days without askin questions?"

"Maybe, but—"

"Get up to your room then this instant and pack yer roll and get out to them, son. Dont leave no trace in your room. And if ye cant find a hideout, grab that four o'clock freight before daylight and head east."

"Fooki knows I was upstairs tonight."

"He didnt see us come down. If there's questions, I'll tell em you lit out early, before it happened. Do you owe him money?"

"No. But Fred, if I clear out, they'll be all the more suspicious of me. And beside, then you wont have anyone to back your own story."

"Hell man, so what? You'd only spill the truth of it, as you say. Besides, they know you're a Red and they're jest waitin to pull you in with the rest of us; tis only luck they didnt get us all earlier at Halloran's. They'll figure then you jest made yourself scarce when you heard of the raid, so they will." Hughes gave him an earnest push.

But Gordon resisted. "Fred, they—they might even convict you of murder."

"Listen, perfesser *bach*, you great dumb boy," Hughes said fiercely in a kind of choked Welsh chant, "you got a life ahead yet. Even another name ye've got—I dont know it and I dont want to— and unless you told it to that bastard—did you?" He nodded at the dim shape on the stones, from which, at an unnatural angle, one scuffed boot, incongruously new, protruded in mute irony. Gordon shook his head. "Then another life too you've got. But out of here you must go, now, this minute, and out of politics, man. Yer no goddam good at it at all."

"But I—"

"Ssst—"

They stood tense while at the alley's mouth a figure loomed dimly, in the thickening night-mist, turned in, swayed against a pole. *Looking for trouble? Want to go to jail? . . .* There was the sound of retching.

"A drunk," Hughes muttered, "he wont come no further, but

someone's sure to find us if we keep friggin around here. Listen, man, I'll wait out of sight up the lane till I see the light go on in your room, on and then off. Then I know you're packed and on your way. Then it's me that'll phone the coppers. Hurry, man, hurry, if ever ye did. Ye've got a chance with the fog comin in."

Gordon, having no words, put out his hand but Hughes pushed it impatiently away, put his own hand up to the black mop of his hair, fingering it quickly back over the long red welt in his scalp.

"Frig off, boy," he said, "for Chrisesake."

40

IT WAS JUST AFTER MIDNIGHT, THOUGH IT SEEMED A YEAR LATER, when he stood, pack on back, outside Channing's home. I have not been followed.

The staid suburban street was a faceless cavern of fog, but there was a faint decipherable glow from the professor's livingroom. He tiptoed up the porch steps, peered through the side window, to see if he had company. His luck was holding—a reading lamp haloed Doctor Channing's fuzz-soft rotund skull and made a bright rhomboid of the open book in his lap. The professor, dapper in a military-grey dressing-gown, opened the door and drew him in as casually as if he had been sitting waiting for him to arrive, but his wide wise eyes had darted at once to the blanket roll and back to Gordon's face.

"Come in, son," he said serenely, "come in. Come in and stay the night. Mrs. Channing's gone to bed."

He slipped off the pack in the hall. Bunyan's Christian at the hill. A stupid parallel. Mr. Badman rather.

"When you hear the jam I'm in, you'll probably boot me out immediately."

"No doubt, no doubt," said Channing with enormous asperity, and marched ahead stiff as a little field-marshal into the livingroom. "But the spare bed is made up, and we'll have a little rye while you tell me." He wheeled, thrust his head at Gordon's chin, eyes pugnacious. "A small one, I said. Sit there." He butted against Gordon's chest, shoved, toppled him into the old leather davenport. "And while I'm getting it, here, for god's sake," he plucked from the table the book he had been reading, thrust it, "consider something un-Marxist for a change." Scowling he strutted away into the kitchen.

Gordon began reading automatically, midway in the open page:

In the huge world which roars hard by
Be others happy if they can.
But in my helpless cradle I
Was breathed on by the rural Pan.

Lines Written in Kensington Gardens. Escapism in a London park.
Easier than in Victory Square, or in skidroad alley. One scuffed
boot. . . . The Doc's been doing homework for his Arnold seminar.

The night comes—

A car outside! He stared at the book till the noise died away. That
auto in the canyon the day he last saw Anne. . . . He realized his
eyes had been mechanically deciphering a note in the margin in
Channing's small scholarly hand: "cp Scholar Gypsy." The cozy
academic world, why ever did I leave it? When the devil was sick,
the devil a monk would be. You are penitent only because you're
listening for the next car, police feet on the porch, when you will
lose it for ever. *Force ends in force.* You said it yourself, remember? And many before you. *Life lives on death*, on Thelma, on—

The night comes down upon the grass,
The child sleeps warmly in the bed.

But what dreams may come? Arnold was as sentimental as any
of them. And you?

Calm soul of all things! make it mine
To feel, amid the city's jar,
That there abides a peace of thine,
Man did not make, and cannot mar!

That was *last* century. Man now has learned how to make anything. And mar anything. Glasses clinking in the kitchen; I never
needed a drink more.

Calm, calm me more! nor let me die
Before I have begun to live . . .
The night comes down . . .

Down on that meadow under the Black Tusk, the alpine flowers
so thick everywhere our sleeping bags lay on them, the scent of
lupins and crushed stalks in my nose as I drifted to sleep. But it's

not all that simple, never was. Upon the grass. Anne coming over the grass . . . *She was good to look upon, and seemed a warm-hearted wench.* Another I helped to kill. By now Hughes is in a cell being questioned.

"No doubt," said Channing, reappearing with two great whiskies on a tray, "no doubt, my curly-headed Spartacus, you feel infinitely superior to Arnold. He was frequently dull, and he was never elated about the Class Struggle." He manoeuvred the tray onto the book-piled table, handed Gordon his glass, took his own, sat down puffing. An act—but it is to make me feel better, speak my troubles or not as I wish. I can trust this man, this petit-bourgeois, and him only. *Bot schaw the vice that troubillis thee, And he sall of thy soule have reuth.*

As soon as he began to tell the story of Hughes, Channing visibly ceased acting, listening in blue-eyed gravity. Gordon tried to be circumstantial and brief, but he felt the rye loosening his thoughts— he had eaten little since morning. He let the words flow, wanting Channing to be aware of the possible consequences of sheltering him.

"So, Doc," he said at the end, "you're now harboring an accessory to a murder. Will you phone and turn me in?"

Channing got out of his chair as if offended, walked to the mantel, wordless, and got cigarettes. He began pacing between the far booklined wall and the fireplace, up and down, stopping fitfully to knuckle the downy back of his own skull. Is he going to? Or just trying to think of a polite way to be rid of me? Gleaming slippers.

"To begin with," Channing stopped suddenly in front of him, head back like a general addressing raw troops, "it's quite enough to be involved in the consequences of your acquired Marxist a-morality, Gordon Saunders, without being bedeviled by your congenital tendency to semantic error. You've been a witness, not an accessory, to what was at the most, apparently, an involuntary manslaughter, not a murder. Nor would any jury be likely to convict your friend Hughes even of manslaughter, on the sole evidence of what you've just told me."

"But on his own—?"

Channing pouted, puffed, huffed. "I have a feeling"—he glanced at the mantel clock. "Look here, it's just about time for the one o'clock news on CFRJ. They send out the late police reports." He switched on the radio.

It was the first item. "The body of William Smith," said the clear laconic voice, "unemployed logger, was found shortly after eleven-thirty tonight in the lane behind the two hundred block west on Powell Street, by John Gregson, beat constable. Smith appears to have fallen from the fire-escape platform on the top floor of the hotel in which he was a tenant. No witnesses to the accident are known, but police discovered a freshly broken railing on the platform, immediately above the spot at which the body was found. K. Fooki, proprietor of the hotel, is said to have told police that it was Smith's habit to sit on the railing during the cool of the evening. Police investigation is continuing and an inquest will be held Monday morning . . . Fire broke out late this afternoon in . . ."

Channing, who had been poised, cigarette halfway to his lips on the edge of his chair, jumped up and snapped off the radio.

"As I suspected, son, your friend Hughes didnt stay."

A pulse was pounding in Gordon's ear. "But why, Doc? Did he just lose his nerve, or—"

Channing sat softly down, facing him again. Great compassionate eyes. "Are you sure he didnt persuade you to disappear in order to—" Channing gave a little sigh—"throw suspicion on you?" The sigh was as if he had also said: This is the way the world goes.

"No, Doc. Not Hughes." Channing's too damned worldly-wise. I've failed to make him understand what Hughes was really like. *You still got another life.* The fierce anxious whisper. "He's a lost, violent, irrational man but he's no cunning hypocrite. He's honest, but he's sick. He's wandering around in some kind of a mental blackout."

Channing, as if by great effort resisting saying what he should say, swelled his broad little chest and, exhaling, lowered his head. Quietly then he spoke, but as if despairing of being understood:

"You wont of course agree with me, Gordon, that all this comes of violent means. Hughes believed in them."

"So did the police who clubbed him."

"They were resisting his means."

Gordon got up. *Surely the means. . . .* "Doc, you dont need to say any more. I told you my story tonight but not how I feel about it. Hughes stampeded me back there in that alley. But since, even before the newscast, I've been thinking it out. Hughes was trying to help me, Doc, but he failed, because no one can help me, not now, it's too late. There's a telephone booth up on Fourth. I'm going to get the police from there, so you wont be involved. They can pick me up."

"Wait!" Channing was on his feet too, his eyes rolling in an agony of indecision. "I'll take back what I just said. I dont know, Gordon, for God's sake, no one *knows*. For example, I,—look—" Channing suddenly recaptured for a moment his old bantering manner—"you long miserable Don Quixote, sit down again a minute and listen to me." He pushed Gordon once more onto the old davenport, plumped down beside him. "I'm a socialist, boy, O I know what you're going to say—everybody is these days and what do they do about it? At least I dont conceal my politics, you know that, not any more, but I'm too busy to be a member of anything. I contribute to the CCF campaign funds—O, sure, reformists, mere parliamentarians, poulticing a cancer—"

"You dont need to say all this, Doc! What I'm trying to make you see is that I've lost all my own political faith!"

"You? All of it?" Channing stared at him, tut-tutted. "Well, that's a pity. You could perhaps get along on ninety per cent less, but not a hundred per cent. In any case, damn you, sir, dont interrupt me. I want you to understand that I'm criticizing only your morality. Smith, my dear fellow, was the product of methods of intrigue and double-dealing. He conspired against society until he was offered rewards for conspiring against his fellow-conspirators."

"Doc, pardon me if I remark that this is all very obvious to me too. I've stopped being a Marxist, you see, and I never can be one again. Not even a fellow-traveler. I dont believe any more in the New Atlantis. Maybe it's there, but nobody's yet found a way of getting to it. I've been trying the primitive approach—swimming. And I started a dozen other people splashing and kicking out into the deep sea, why, God knows; perhaps only because I didnt want to drown alone. Well, one of them's gone under already, perhaps more than one and I'm to blame. I killed Smith, as much as anybody did.

And—and you might as well know,—a year ago, by an act of omission, I helped to murder my possible wife and my unborn child."

"What on earth do you mean?"

Confession at last. But I can't find words for what really happened . . . the long dusky curve of her cheeks. "She wanted to divorce her husband and marry me. I wouldnt. She"—she had a new yellow frock—"she had an abortion—the child may have been mine—she died of it."

"My dear boy," Channing said. "Now I begin to see, I begin to see—what a great bloody melodramatic fool you are. You're determined to martyr yourself out of an oldfashioned sense of sin."

No, but I will never speak of her again.

"What's so new-fashioned about your sense of it, Doc? You've just been preaching to me against violent means."

"A purely pragmatic attitude, my child. I—" he stopped at a loss.

"Look, Doc, I agree with you. About means and ends, that is. What I've wanted all along was love, but that was the very thing I stopped giving—except to people who didnt want it. I ran away from marriage and children, because I confused them with bourgeois sterility and proletarian misery. I kidded myself I wanted to do great deeds, be a prophet and pioneer, a destroyer of sin. I thought it would be easy, just like my father who thought he would pick up nuggets on the next river bank. And what did I do instead! I got myself mixed up with a bunch of starry-eyed juvenile delinquents who had repudiated honest childlikeness and who started me out playing blindman's buff and then drifted off, leaving me wearing the bandage. And even when I clawed that bandage off I couldnt see properly. I couldnt see, until tonight, that I was simply gathering around me another bunch of kids, though grown-up kids, bent on pain and power, on the destruction of liberty, and intellectual honesty, or merely preferring the excitement of death to the boredom of life, or choking themselves to death on a surfeit of despotic principles."

Channing was smiling. "You dont believe a damn word of it."

He sighed. "O.K., Doc, maybe I dont. I still believe in social change, too. I still hate exploitation and stupidity, and armament races, and stock market gambling; I want to fight whatever devils breed human poverty, insecurity, war and death. I always will. But I'm a tired radical now, Doc, a Summer Rebel, as the only honest and consistent revolutionary I've ever known called me tonight. All I've been doing was just booing from the sidelines anyway, and now I'm caught doing it. And though I'm still a fool I'm no longer an arrogant one. I'm willing to pay for my folly."

"And your idea of payment is going down now and phoning the police to come and take you for a murder you didnt commit."

"You've forgotten they're after me anyway. If the meeting I told you about at O'Halloran's had lasted another half hour, Hughes and I would both be in jail now. And Smith would be alive."

"Do you honestly think Smith's death is worth atoning for by the negation of your own life?"

"What do you mean negation?"

"Look, I'll tell you that by asking you some questions. First, could the police know your true identity?"

Could they? He had been careful never to betray it, nor to keep evidence of it anywhere in Vancouver, even on his person. Unless they learned from Toronto—steamed open letters on Fooki's rack.

"Almost certainly not."

"But Smith would have described you, as Paul Green, to them?"

"I—I suppose." Would he ever be sure that Smitty had betrayed them?

"So if you give yourself up you will be charged at once with a violation of Section 98?"

"Perhaps. To be honest, I think the police, in dealing with Trotskyists, are torn between wanting to abet them, as disrupters of the official communist movement, and fearing that they may in turn become an even greater threat to civil peace. There's also, of course, the natural police desire to exhibit alertness by exposing any kind of Red."

"Have you considered that, by the same token, they might be willing to remove you from circulation even more effectively by charging you with murder? You roomed next to him. You took your effects out of your room tonight. You may even have been seen leaving. Whereas no one apparently saw Hughes, and he's cleared out. Smith was a police spy; you were the leader of the group he was betraying. There's plenty of motive."

"So what, Doc? I did help to murder him. I created the microscopic organization on which he spied, if he did."

"And how many thousands of other people unwittingly conspired to turn Smith into a radical many years ago, lose him his job in the woods, make him what he was when you met him? Are they to go to jail too? And shall we try for murder the Wisdom and Spirit of the Universe that gave him asthma? Or your lodging-house proprietor for not keeping his railings in repair?"

"You said yourself they couldnt make a murder charge stick, even against Hughes."

"All right, all right, I'm inconsistent, where you are concerned. Do you know why?"

"Why?"

"Because I love you, you damn young fool, because you've brains and education and character and have a chance to use them for the benefit of this ignorant and unhappy world. Because I want you to forget, now, this minute, there ever was a Paul Green. We're going to make ourselves some cold beef sandwiches in the kitchen and then, damn you, you're going up to the spare bedroom and stay there till after the inquest on Monday. Then, pray the Lord, the inquest will find Smith's death accidental, and the police will decide you were simply skipping out to avoid being charged under Section 98, and the heat, as they say in the detective stories, will be off. Right?"

"But Mrs. Channing?"

"Is not in the habit of asking awkward questions of invited guests."

"What about the fact that I've been conspiring to overthrow the Canadian capitalist state? And that you are, at the very least, conspiring with me by concealing me? Doesnt that bother *you*?"

"I, my dear doe-eyed dreamer, am a realist. Also I have a memory. Last time you were here you quoted to me from a poem by young Mr. Stephen Spender. You said you had committed yourself to looking for men born of the sun, so that you might travel a little way with them toward the sun."

"That's a laugh, isnt it?"

"I'm not laughing. I'm thinking you're a little closer to the sun than you were a year ago, but if you go down to jail and public suspicion as a possible murderer, and Paul Green and Gordon Saunders become one—you'll lose not only your academic career, you'll lose all hope and all sight of the sun, whether you stay in a jail or not."

So he had gone, belly-filled and word-exhausted, to the bed Channing prepared for him, and slept all through the morning. And woken to stare mystified at the strange bright wall before his eyes, and the sun glancing from a framed print of Cézanne's Boy in the Red Vest. Then memory returned like a shadow darkening the clean-scented room. After a long while staring at the high white ceiling he got up, looking for his clothes, and planning how to slip out, through a window perhaps, and go down to the police, despite all that had been said the night before, or because of it.

But Channing had come swiftly up, dapper and grave, and without a word handed him the noon paper, folded to an inside page, for neither Hughes nor Smith made the front page with their deaths any more than with their lives.

41

AGITATOR DROWNS IN HARBOUR

Vancouver, August 19 — The body of Fred Hughes, 45, unemployed logger, was found floating in Coal Harbour at an early hour this morning by a night watchman at the Royal Yacht Club.

Later the remains were identified by a relative, Harry Dack, living in a nearby float-house. Police found no signs of violence and believe Hughes may have come to his death by a fall into the harbour during last night's fog, while on his way in the darkness to visit Dack.

Hughes, a well-known local radical, was being sought by police on suspicion of having led the recent unemployed riots.

An inquest will be held Monday.

PEERAGE AWAITS BENNETT WHENEVER HE DESIRES IT, PREDICTS LORD ROTHERMERE

RESTLESSNESS THE REAL PROBLEM SAYS OTTAWA

NRA Plan Only "Loud Timbre" of U.S.A.

Special to the Planet, Aug. 19 —Canada has forty million gallons of liquor ready to be rushed across the American border as soon as the Eighteenth Amendment is repealed, according to . . .

CANNIBALISM & MICE-EATING IN USSR

Four Million Starve In One Year!

CANADA WILL LOP FOUR MILLION ACRES OFF WHEAT-CROP—

Farmers Need Loans But Lack Security

Bank Superintendent Has No Solution

TROTSKY MAY RETURN TO RUSSIA, VATICAN RUMOUR

Reconciliation with Stalin Pending

Toronto, August 18—Two persons were injured and two arrested this afternoon when a large crowd attempted to hold a parade on College Street preparatory to a march on Queen's Park.

Fred Grange, one of the injured, attempted to address the crowd. . . . They are being treated in Toronto General Hospital for cuts about the head. . . . Several other persons are reported to have been slightly injured by running into obstacles as they fled from police. The demonstration was soon dispersed by bodies of motorcycle patrolmen.

U.S. RUSHES BIG FLEET TO HAVANA—	FRANCE SPENDS MILLIONS SECURING GERMAN BORDER
Intervention by Washington Likely	

UNIVERSE MAY BURST IF IT GETS MUCH BIGGER

42

SO HE HAD NOT GONE DOWN TO THE POLICE THAT AFTERNOON, nor, though he had urged it again to Channing, did he attend either inquest. "Accidental Death" each coroner's jury found; in the case of Smith, there was added a wistful small rider hoping the city would in future inspect more carefully the condition of fire-escape landings in hotels and rooming houses.

He had not gone down to that drab clanging town again ever, except the day after the inquests when Channing drove him to the Great Northern Station, Gordon Saunders now, clothed in a half-fitting suit the professor had contrived to have sent up to him ready-made, and bearing a ten dollar bill and a ticket to Utah that Channing had provided.

Turning on the train steps for a last wave at the immaculate and lordly little figure with the white domed head, he had waved good-bye also to Paul Green and to all his ghostly fellowship.

Or so he had hoped.

Certainly good-bye to the watery-eyed ghost of that enigmatic old Judas, Bill Smith, whose misfortune it was that his weary lungs had not failed as fast as his faith, and who must have been glad of his death. Good-bye to Smitty, who had not been born with sagging shoulders and broken yellow teeth, and who walked his streets a long time in patched dungarees and broken shoes before any man could say he was either a thief or a stool.

Good-bye certainly to Fred Hughes, mysterious too, who had already himself said good-bye to his age, given it up, cursed and struck at it, as it had cursed and struck at him and who had perhaps, for all Gordon or the coroner's jury knew, chosen his own moment of departure from it, and who, at any rate, was safely and entirely dead at last, not half-alive in the provincial asylum, with starved flaming eyes and hands passing restlessly over his cracked skull.

Good-bye to honest, deluded Merivale, one of the world's millions fated to be held by Stalinism and broken by it, lanky Peter Merivale, whose name did flash once more before Gordon's eye. It was not on a CLA report nor a coroner's but in the print of a clipping from the *Planet* Channing sent him almost a year later and which reached him in London at the start of that Spartan-poor pedantic solitary and yet happy twelvemonth he spent completing his thesis on the fellowship the blessed Pellatt had at last been able to secure for him. Merivale, Gordon read, had led a thousand unemployed into Vancouver's main post office, sat them down on its floor and held it with them a long fantastic week against the police and all comers, until they were driven out by teargas, and Merivale was beaten and arrested. It already seemed to Gordon, this world of Merivale's, as many years as it was miles away.

And good-bye to Lennard, that revolutionary snob and prissy idealist, who had undoubtedly retired to keep goats in some frugal corner of Vancouver Island, sitting at night with puckered lips and writing letters of doom to the local weekly and dreamily sure now, as always, that he was right and had always been right and would be till his quiet death.

Good-bye to Halloran, who might be anywhere doing anything now, except rotting in a grave—it was impossible to think of him as not being alive and proselytizing—old and apoplectic and Marx-weary, perhaps, but not dead, not Halloran. Somewhere he was roaring exhortations at lesser mortals, even if only as the ferocious chairman of a convention of retail grocers, or the benevolent Irish tyrant at a Great Books Discussion Group.

And good-bye to knobble-cheeked old Hansen, as surely dead as Halloran was alive, dead without ever achieving again the pleasure of working at work he could do, or of toiling at all except at the lonely propagation of his inevitably one-man party. Good-bye to Ole, who might have become a bum, a jail-bird, a canned heat addict, but never, were his ulcers to pierce him through, never an informer.

But the role was not one that ever lacked for actors. Smith played it once, in petty concealment and out of misery, and was rewarded with death. Others were to play it to distinguished audiences and to be clapped as Ulyssian heroes: the new patriots, the McNamees.

Not good-bye to McNamee, whose real name was, or was now, John Langdale.

Good-bye to all the ragged, flea-bitten perpetually defeated legion whose rallying ground was Victory Square, whose bony arms dipped for the daily butts in the morning gutter and were raised in helpless afternoon defiance before the surly clerks of relief offices and the virtuous remote faces of merchant-aldermen—and who were too proud or too doctrinaire to beg dimes from the blue-jowled owners of Buicks, and went hungry and alone to their lousy evening beds. And good-bye to the hopes that he might make their misery serve them, and serve him. For never could he say surely that, either in living among them or in leaving them, he had abated by a day, for them or for him, the long years that were yet to come, before the drab files would dwindle in front of the Pogey and swell outside the Recruiting Office; before glittery-eyed Theda and her colleagues, the red and yellow and black old girls of the Hotel Universe, would up their prices, or graduate into husky-throated keepers of their own establishments; before the deadweight lid of the Thirties lifted at last and revealed the bubbling stew of a war brewing for them all. Good-bye to the millions now living who would surely die.

And to other faces in other towns, farewell, though not to all. To Mrs. Zimchuck who, if she trundled still a barren baby-carriage, wheeled it never again before his bemused and romantic vision; to all the Smeeths and Pilskys and Baumlings pursuing their pedantries God knows where under the common sun; to the grimy caravans of bindlestiffs and rootless kids and psychopaths and Sammy Archibalds jouncing unwanted across a continent; and to those long dead now, the unforgotten MacCraddock and the scarcely remembered Fournier.

But not all apparitions are laid by the sluffing of a name, by the taking of a train or the enduring of the decades. There had been a voice piping unchanged from the past beside him suddenly one day as he clung to a strap in a crowded Toronto streetcar, the month before the war began, when he was on his way down to the station to catch the train back to the prairies after a philological conference.

"Arent you Doctor Saunders?" it said, and of course she knew he was a Ph.D. now because she would not be the one to miss his name in the papers, or any name that ever meant anything to her: honest, earnest Bagshaw, with her blob of a nose bravely supporting the same round spectacles over a face even a little flatter with the years, but scarcely less childlike; Comrade Bagshaw still, he felt at once, even though she was now a Mrs. Somebody or other—"A Minister's Wife," she told him, happily, leaning from her strap across the aisle.

"He's not what some people call a Real Minister,"—she managed to make her capitals heard between the racket of the old Bay Street car, "just a Unitarian. *I* like him though. But tell me about you. It was wonderful to read in the papers that you're publishing a whole book from your thesis and going to a marvellous position in the States—"

"No, my rank's pretty humble but it *is* a rather fabulous university, the one I've always dreamed of getting to. After the bankrupt Saskatchewan college I've sheltered in since I got my doctorate, it'll be pretty good. Though I was lucky to be there even, to get any job in 1938."

"Remember I told you once you had Great Endowments?" She laughed and the car swayed her toward him. "You taught in the States first of all, didnt you? But there's no real risk of your becoming well, Just American, is there, unless—" she gave him an anxious glance—"you dont think about, well, Internationalism any more? Anyway," she gave him, tactfully perhaps, no time to answer, "you have an English Wife now, havent you? I mean English English. Would you mind, I'd like it if you told me her name."

"O sure. It's Diane."

"Diane. That's lovely. She had a bow and arrow, didnt she— I mean the Roman one. Tell me, did you meet her in, where was that place the papers said you studied, the British Museum?"

"Of course. I was leafing through a fourteenth century manuscript and there she was."

She looked sidelong at him with happy reproach. "You always did make fun of me, didnt you, and so you should. And, O yes, the *Star* said you had a baby girl already. What do you call her?"

"Anne."

They were buffeted apart by a dozen exiting passengers. Her face reappeared, glasses flashing at him. "Anne is my name."

"Is it?" he blurted, "I—"

"I guess you just remembered me as—as Bagshaw. Anyway, I'm glad."

"Comrade Bagshaw," he managed. "I'm glad too." He struggled (whether vainly or not he never knew) to prevent his own eyes betraying his confusion, and distracted her with a question as to Roberts' fate.

She was quick to tell him Roberts had long since been purged, jumping a day too late on a change of line, and gone back to being Rabinowitz, and to being supported by his wife and to what pickings were left to him, bereft of Party patronage, among the petty rackets of the Ward. And Wilf, the freckled chairman, was "just a Social Worker" now.

They plopped into two vacated seats. "And you?" she peered at him, "what about your Island, remember? Have you found out how we get to it yet?"

"No," he said. "I cant see where it is any more."

"There must be an Island somewhere," she said. "Not just Bacon's. Anyway—you're still Swimming?"

He shifted in his seat. "Let's say I'm dog-pedaling."

She looked at him with conviction. "Maybe that's all any of us do. But you're not drowning and you—you wont turn back."

"No, I will never turn back and I dont regret whatever swimming I did."

She touched his hand lightly, quickly. "I wish I had time to tell you about—about Unitarians and—and, O so many things but—"

He was framing a dutiful question about her husband but she broke in with a rush: "Kay! You remember Kay?"

He remembered Kay. "Well, she's the only one left. In the C.P. I mean. They say it was Kay that threw Roberts out. She wears Clothes now though, I mean, you know, *girls'* clothes, and gets her hair done. She's a Big Shot these days because she went to Spain and sang songs and things to the Loyalist troops. Like La Pasionaria, you know—O heavens, this is my stop."

She seized his hand, jumped up. "Only I cant imagine *her* being so very—well," the car ground to a halt and she began pushing sideways with surprising ruthlessness toward the exit, "so a-passionate," she flung back, disappearing forever behind two wide disapproving women, clasping parcels. Over their swiveling heads, as the doors shuddered open, came a last gay cry: "Good-bye, keep on dog-pedaling."

And there had been another phantom, grown flatulent and cautious, that he himself had crossed and challenged, only half-believing its identity, as he walked one morning in St. James's Park, in the war's second year, his arm once more back in the sleeve of his khaki tunic, after the smash-up in that training exercise in Sussex, and the last glorious day of his convalescent leave waiting to be spent. A substantial phantom, indeed, two hundred pounds heavy, and cloaked in the best British civilian cloth, though the cut was Toronto, and so too was the kind of surly freshness of the boy-handsome face and the preternatural neatness of the tiny honey-colored moustache; jowled now, a face more ovoid and more earnest, the eyes puffy and, at least at the moment when Gordon hailed him, suspicious. But it was Jack Barstow all right, Sales and Production Manager Barstow now of the Canadian-Imperial Motors, old Phelps' son-in-law J. A. Barstow, who had flown over just yesterday for a liaison job, a spot of conferring with an Ordnance General here and an Under Secretary there. He was on his way in fact now to Whitehall, preferring to walk—the doctor's idea, he had to reduce—to meet Sir Humphrey Soandso, but what about joining him for a drink tomorrow at the Savoy bar, or—? But Gordon, whose three stripes were not enough to brave such a rendezvous even if his leave had stretched to it, preferred to walk young Mr. Barstow's way past the swans and the upending ducks by the weeping willow trees and call up, one by one, the attendant throng this phantom trailed in his unwilling wake.

"Mum? You didnt hear? Poor old mum, she passed away let's see, two years ago I guess it was. Heart. She was awful overweight you know. . . ."

"The Old Man? O hell, yes, he's still full of piss and vinegar. Funny aint it when you think how Mum was always worrying about who was going to keep us when the old bastard drank himself to death. Remember? Yeah, he's spryer than ever, now he's got his pension. Settled down to steady drinking. I dont see much of him, of course. Got a room by himself somewhere. Funniest damned thing, the old bugger, now Mum's dead, is practically turning himself into a Red, I hear. Last time I saw him he was bawling *me* out for 'selling out to the boorgeoisie'; that's a laugh, that language now, ain't it, Gordon? But hell, tell me about yourself. I thought you'd turned Yank on us. Whatcha doing in the Canadian Army?"

Gordon managed a perfunctory sentence or two, told him he had taken leave of absence from his University at the time of Dunkirk, joined the Black Watch in Montreal,—stalling, knowing it was being left to him to ask or not to ask about Thelma, but that it was right, it was the tactful way and Jack, if he had left little of the Jack who had edited the *Spark* and captained the Spartacus Youth League, was still appallingly tactful.

"And Thelma?"

"The Kid? Well sir, Gordie you ought to see her, and those brats of hers. Three of them, the liveliest little hell-raisers you ever did see, two boys and a girl. And big, Thel's going to be big as Mum yet. You ought to look them up when you're back in Toronto— when you're demobbed, I mean," Jack added, as if he had for the moment forgotten that the Canadian Army was not likely to be flying back home with him the following week. He did not suggest that Gordon look him and his Sally up. "She and Hymie would love to see you."

"Hymie!?"

"Say, you didnt know? Hell, she and Sather broke up within a week or less, I guess it was. Just between you and me, kid, it turned out they never were churched or, well, married either, so she came back home to Ma a virgin, and that old watchdog, little old Hymie, finally got her. She could have done better, Gord, we know that, you and me, but still and all he's made her a good husband, it seems, even though he's still just a tailor. Got a shop on Spadina of all places and Thel looks after the business end. Queer eh? I dont see much of them of course, you know how it is. . . .

"Sather went to New York, last I heard. Nobody seems to know what he's doing. Let's see, who else did you know?" Who else indeed who wasn't dead or deadly changed or drearily the same? He couldn't remember a name. "Ah well, lots of water gone under that old bridge since, eh Gordie? Hard to remember what bloody fools we were, isnt it? Romantic as all get out. Still, we had a lot of fun. I was sure for a while you were really going to be president of the first Canadian Soviet or something. But Christ, it was like I used to say remember?—said it'd take a war to get us out of the Depression—and if we won the war we wouldnt need socialism anyway. Not in good old Canada at least. Best place in the world, Gordie, when all's said, eh? And I hope it wont be long before you're back there too."

"Thanks, Jack," he had said, stopping, seeing a chance to break away, "and the same to you." But then the name came suddenly back to him. "Ronnie, Ronnie Mandell, wasnt it? The chap who worked in a slaughterhouse? Whatever happened to him?"

"Ronnie?" Jack took his eyes from a passing brunette and, with a kind of shamefaced casualness, told him.

Ronnie had been recognized one day by Comrade Kay, when she drove past his platoon in a Spanish village, recognized and denounced as one of Trotsky's Marxists, and stood up against a stuccoed wall, and shot by Comrade Kay's Marxists.

"Wouldnt have known what happened to him—I didnt even know he'd beat it off to Spain—if she hadnt boasted about it in the C.P. when she got back, and the story got around. Poor dumb bugger. He wouldnt ever change, Gordie. I guess he was just about the last of the old gang."

Ronnie Mandell, too dumb to change, or too much an artist, after all, to break the unity of his thought and his action. *Our time* —what was it he said that night?—*can make an artist only by the waste of a good revolutionary.* Yet already the rebellions of the Ronnies had passed into a limbo from which only the artist would ever again seek to rescue them.

But those were ghosts which, if they were not exorcized when Gordon Saunders watched, from a Great Northern train window that August day in 1933, the diminishing figure of Professor Roger Channing and the vanishing shadow of Paul Green, were nevertheless spirits willing and some of them eager to be dispersed and forgotten by the drive of the years.

Others, that sun-glinting morning, as the humped bear-shaggy mountains of the North Shore swung out of view, were only reassembling incarnate again at his journey's terminus. And he had gone back to a final year of them; Mr. Saunders had returned intact, a protected hostage, to Dr. Crump, the Man of Sin to the Man of Virtue, the dreamy-faced to the Lincoln-jawed; returned, unforgiven, to the surveillance of Dean Wollonby, to the gay inattention of a new garden of Delphine Youngs crossing delectable legs in far back rows, and to the hungry and forever welcome listening of the solemn bedeviled Eli Swansens sweating in the front seats. Back again, emptied and different, no Tamburlaine of the ultra-left, after all, lonely still, missing Oscar, and even Joan, off already in Hawaii. And also not missing them, grateful and still ashamed of the power which allowed them, even those miles of land and sea away, to protect him for one more year at least. Oscar, whom somehow he was never to see again, but who would always remain for him a sturdy pillar of the sensible and enduring and friendly flesh.

Back to the dry sage-heavy winds sliding down at night from the Wasatch Canyons, down from the alder and the sumac and the home of the whiskey jack and the one ghost in all the scented clefts in these bare elephant-backed hills that could never again be bodied, never again move toward him with long brown arms raised in love, who walked now only in the bright and secret glades of his memory, and in whose eyes, lavender out of the sunlight, he found now neither appeal nor judgment.

Judgment not from her nor from any of the myriad who might in justice be assigned to assess, in the Domesday Book of the Fifties, his soul, his own still searching, bedeviled, inconsistent but inviolate self; judgment from no one until the month, this month, when the cold pistol-finger of Roberts was leveled once more at his head, when the sardonic oratory of Leo Sather rebounded upon him, and when Stephen McNamee, smalltown hoodlum for a betrayed Utopia, was by strangers summoned to fanatic flesh; McNamee, no longer in shiny blue serge, bald now and salaried and Judas-eager; McNamee, the feralteethed who, bearing in his joyful bloodshot eyes the immortal hatred of his kind, had come back from the lost desperate other-world of the Thirties to thrust the swarthy gargoyle of his face into this day, and set the scene for this moment, when

297

a sham-angry and fake-righteous demagogue pounded his flabby fist for Professor Saunder's colleagues to see, and the radio audience to hear, and Gordon sat staring down the long table.

And, staring, Gordon Saunders felt the release at last within him of whatever truth the years had compressed like a coiled spring in his heart. He would speak out now, not because other men, corrupted or merely young, compelled him, or out of any hope that they would understand, but because he too, like those so suavely assembled to damn him, breathed under the necessity of failure and folly and untruth, in the blind common yearning for reason and surety under the ever-dispersing heavens. His eyes, hunting over the belated altar they had set him for the hunting eyes of his confident priests, found in them that doom of error which rendered them equal with him and with all men, and that search for human oneness in the very act of imposing their singularity. For was it not by such ambiguous strivings that he, Gordon Saunders, and his ephemeral Senator, and the thrust witnessing heads of silenced colleagues and poised informers and frightened friends, knew themselves to be a community under their twin destinies of being alive and dying?

I believe in man, he thought, moistening his lips to speak, even in these men, for somewhere in them, as in me, is the power, however denied, to achieve the grandeur of the thinking beast, to hope and to imagine, to adventure into change, to create beauty and to share it, and in self-denial itself to assert the importance of their separate selves and the inconsequence of their mortality.

And now the mortal Senator spread tenderly the scraps of the history he had not made but sought to re-make, because he was its product, as Gordon Saunders was. And Gordon Saunders, *alias* Paul Green, who had not made his history either but had lived it, began now to speak it out, neither in fear nor guilt nor pride, but because it was himself and he was a man alive, staring down the long table.

THE END

THE END

THE NEW CANADIAN LIBRARY

n 1. OVER PRAIRIE TRAILS / Frederick Philip Grove
n 2. SUCH IS MY BELOVED / Morley Callaghan
n 3. LITERARY LAPSES / Stephen Leacock
n 4. AS FOR ME AND MY HOUSE / Sinclair Ross
n 5. THE TIN FLUTE / Gabrielle Roy
n 6. THE CLOCKMAKER / Thomas Chandler Haliburton
n 7. THE LAST BARRIER AND OTHER STORIES / Charles G. D. Roberts
n 8. BAROMETER RISING / Hugh MacLennan
n 9. AT THE TIDE'S TURN AND OTHER STORIES / Thomas H. Raddall
n10. ARCADIAN ADVENTURES WITH THE IDLE RICH / Stephen Leacock
n11. HABITANT POEMS / William Henry Drummond
n12. THIRTY ACRES / Ringuet
n13. EARTH AND HIGH HEAVEN / Gwethalyn Graham
n14. THE MAN FROM GLENGARRY / Ralph Connor
n15. SUNSHINE SKETCHES OF A LITTLE TOWN / Stephen Leacock
n16. THE STEPSURE LETTERS / Thomas McCulloch
n17. MORE JOY IN HEAVEN / Morley Callaghan
n18. WILD GEESE / Martha Ostenso
n19. THE MASTER OF THE MILL / Frederick Philip Grove
n20. THE IMPERIALIST / Sara Jeannette Duncan
n21. DELIGHT / Mazo de la Roche
n22. THE SECOND SCROLL / A. M. Klein
n23. THE MOUNTAIN AND THE VALLEY / Ernest Buckler
n24. THE RICH MAN / Henry Kreisel
n25. WHERE NESTS THE WATER HEN / Gabrielle Roy
n26. THE TOWN BELOW / Roger Lemelin
n27. THE HISTORY OF EMILY MONTAGUE / Frances Brooke
n28. MY DISCOVERY OF ENGLAND / Stephen Leacock
n29. SWAMP ANGEL / Ethel Wilson
n30. EACH MAN'S SON / Hugh MacLennan
n31. ROUGHING IT IN THE BUSH / Susanna Moodie
n32. WHITE NARCISSUS / Raymond Knister
n33. THEY SHALL INHERIT THE EARTH / Morley Callaghan
n34. TURVEY / Earle Birney
n35. NONSENSE NOVELS / Stephen Leacock
n36. GRAIN / R. J. C. Stead
n37. LAST OF THE CURLEWS / Fred Bodsworth
n38. THE NYMPH AND THE LAMP / Thomas H. Raddall
n39. JUDITH HEARNE / Brian Moore
n40. THE CASHIER / Gabrielle Roy
n41. UNDER THE RIBS OF DEATH / John Marlyn
n42. WOODSMEN OF THE WEST / M. Allerdale Grainger
n43. MOONBEAMS FROM THE LARGER LUNACY / Stephen Leacock
n44. SARAH BINKS / Paul Hiebert
n45. SON OF A SMALLER HERO / Mordecai Richler
n46. WINTER STUDIES AND SUMMER RAMBLES / Anna Jameson
n47. REMEMBER ME / Edward Meade
n48. FRENZIED FICTION / Stephen Leacock
n49. FRUITS OF THE EARTH / Frederick Philip Grove
n50. SETTLERS OF THE MARSH / Frederick Philip Grove

n51. THE BACKWOODS OF CANADA / Catharine Parr Traill
n52. MUSIC AT THE CLOSE / Edward McCourt
n53. MY REMARKABLE UNCLE / Stephen Leacock
n54. THE DOUBLE HOOK / Sheila Watson
n55. TIGER DUNLOP'S UPPER CANADA / William Dunlop
n56. STREET OF RICHES / Gabrielle Roy
n57. SHORT CIRCUITS / Stephen Leacock
n58. WACOUSTA / John Richardson
n59. THE STONE ANGEL / Margaret Laurence
n60. FURTHER FOOLISHNESS / Stephen Leacock
n61. MARCHBANKS' ALMANACK / Robertson Davies
n62. THE LAMP AT NOON AND OTHER STORIES / Sinclair Ross
n63. THE HARBOUR MASTER / Theodore Goodridge Roberts
n64. THE CANADIAN SETTLER'S GUIDE / Catharine Parr Traill
n65. THE GOLDEN DOG / William Kirby
n66. THE APPRENTICESHIP OF DUDDY KRAVITZ / Mordecai Richler
n67. BEHIND THE BEYOND / Stephen Leacock
n68. A STRANGE MANUSCRIPT FOUND IN A COPPER CYLINDER /
     James De Mille
n69. LAST LEAVES / Stephen Leacock
n70. THE TOMORROW-TAMER / Margaret Laurence
n71. ODYSSEUS EVER RETURNING / George Woodcock
n72. THE CURÉ OF ST. PHILIPPE / Francis William Grey
n73. THE FAVOURITE GAME / Leonard Cohen
n74. WINNOWED WISDOM / Stephen Leacock
n75. THE SEATS OF THE MIGHTY / Gilbert Parker
n76. A SEARCH FOR AMERICA / Frederick Philip Grove
n77. THE BETRAYAL / Henry Kreisel
n78. MAD SHADOWS / Marie-Claire Blais
n79. THE INCOMPARABLE ATUK / Mordecai Richler
n80. THE LUCK OF GINGER COFFEY / Brian Moore
n81. JOHN SUTHERLAND: ESSAYS, CONTROVERSIES AND POEMS /
     Miriam Waddington
n82. PEACE SHALL DESTROY MANY / Rudy Henry Wiebe
n83. A VOICE FROM THE ATTIC / Robertson Davies
n84. PROCHAIN ÉPISODE / Hubert Aquin
n85. ROGER SUDDEN / Thomas H. Raddall
n86. MIST ON THE RIVER / Hubert Evans
n87. THE FIRE-DWELLERS / Margaret Laurence
n88. THE DESERTER / Douglas LePan
n89. ANTOINETTE DE MIRECOURT / Rosanna Leprohon
n90. ALLEGRO / Felix Leclerc
n91. THE END OF THE WORLD AND OTHER STORIES / Mavis Gallant
n92. IN THE VILLAGE OF VIGER AND OTHER STORIES /
     Duncan Campbell Scott
n93. THE EDIBLE WOMAN / Margaret Atwood
n94. IN SEARCH OF MYSELF / Frederick Philip Grove
n95. FEAST OF STEPHEN / Robertson Davies
n96. A BIRD IN THE HOUSE / Margaret Laurence
n97. THE WOODEN SWORD / Edward McCourt
n98. PRIDE'S FANCY / Thomas Raddall
n99. OX BELLS AND FIREFLIES / Ernest Buckler
n100. ABOVE GROUND / Jack Ludwig
n101. NEW PRIEST IN CONCEPTION BAY / Robert Traill Spence Lowell
n102. THE FLYING YEARS / Frederick Niven
n103. WIND WITHOUT RAIN / Selwyn Dewdney
n104. TETE BLANCHE / Marie-Claire Blais

n105. TAY JOHN / Howard O'Hagan
n106. CANADIANS OF OLD / Charles G. D. Roberts
n107. HEADWATERS OF CANADIAN LITERATURE / Andrew MacMechan
n108. THE BLUE MOUNTAINS OF CHINA / Rudy Wiebe
n109. THE HIDDEN MOUNTAIN / Gabrielle Roy
n110. THE HEART OF THE ANCIENT WOOD / Charles G. D. Roberts
n111. JEST OF GOD / Margaret Laurence
n112. SELF CONDEMNED / Wyndham Lewis
n113. DUST OVER THE CITY / André Langevin
n114. OUR DAILY BREAD / Frederick Philip Grove
n115. THE CANADIAN NOVEL IN THE TWENTIETH CENTURY / edited by
       George Woodcock
n116. THE VIKING HEART / Laura Goodman Salverson
n117. DOWN THE LONG TABLE / Earle Birney
n118. GLENGARRY SCHOOL DAYS / Ralph Connor
n119. THE PLOUFFE FAMILY / Roger Lemelin
n120. WINDFLOWER / Gabrielle Roy

o 2. MASKS OF FICTION: CANADIAN CRITICS ON CANADIAN PROSE /
       edited by A. J. M. Smith
o 3. MASKS OF POETRY: CANADIAN CRITICS ON CANADIAN VERSE /
       edited by A. J. M. Smith

POETS OF CANADA:
o 1. VOL. I: POETS OF THE CONFEDERATION / edited by Malcolm Ross
o 4. VOL. III: POETRY OF MIDCENTURY / edited by Milton Wilson
o 5. VOL. II: POETS BETWEEN THE WARS / edited by Milton Wilson
o 6. THE POEMS OF EARLE BIRNEY /
o 7. VOL. IV: POETS OF CONTEMPORARY CANADA /
       edited by Eli Mandel
o 8. VOL. V: NINETEENTH-CENTURY NARRATIVE POEMS / edited by
       David Sinclair

CANADIAN WRITERS
w 1. MARSHALL MCLUHAN / Dennis Duffy
w 2. E. J. PRATT / Milton Wilson
w 3. MARGARET LAURENCE / Clara Thomas
w 4. FREDERICK PHILIP GROVE / Ronald Sutherland
w 5. LEONARD COHEN / Michael Ondaatje
w 6. MORDECAI RICHLER / George Woodcock
w 7. STEPHEN LEACOCK / Robertson Davis
w 8. HUGH MACLENNAN / Alec Lucas
w 9. EARLE BIRNEY / Richard Robillard
w10. NORTHROP FRYE / Ronald Bates
w11. MALCOLM LOWRY / William H. New
w12. JAMES REANEY / Ross G. Woodman
w13. GEORGE WOODCOCK / Peter Hughes